The Tenerife Alternative

Baskerville Old pt 36.

Cranley Harding

Baskerville Old pt 26.

PART ONE

I DON'T ALLOW MOLES IN MY GARDEN
(Quote: Sir James McKay VC – Head of SIS6)

Introducing Scott Rutherford.

To my dear Pam

Copyright © 2016 Cranley Harding

All rights reserved, including the right to reproduce this book, or portions thereof in any form. No part of this text may be reproduced, transmitted, downloaded, decompiled, reverse engineered, or stored, in any form or introduced into any information storage and retrieval system, in any form or by any means, whether electronic or mechanical without the express written permission of the author.

This is a work of fiction. Names and characters are the product of the author's imagination and any resemblance to actual persons, living or dead, is entirely coincidental.

ISBN: 978-1-326-65569-3

PublishNation
www.publishnation.co.uk

Chapter 1

Limehouse East London 1934

It was 1934 and Britain was still in the grip of the 1931 elected International Coalition party's appeasement policy of pandering to Hitler's rising Third Reich power for fear of another world war. In opposition to this policy was Sir Oswald Mosley who had returned from visiting Benito Mussolini, Italy's fascist dictator, in 1931. He was so taken with Mussolini's brand of fascism that on return to Britain he formed the British Union of Fascists (BUF). This new party was strongly anti-communist and was in favour of the rearmament of Hitler in his fight against communism. However, certain elected members of the BUF hierarchy had branched out with their own agenda. One such meeting was taking place in East London.

The thin wisp of smoke from her black Balkan cigarette, which was housed in a gold holder and held elegantly by a long-sleeved satin evening gloved hand, drifted slowly upwards to join nicotine multi-layered hazes that hung over the crowded hall. She sat at the back of Limehouse Assembly Hall on an uncomfortable wooden seat. She pulled her mink coat tight around her; a reflex action to keep out the damp of the unheated hall. The cold was of little consequence as her concentration was totally transfixed on the speaker at the lectern. His oratory skills reminded her of newsreels she had seen at the cinema of Adolph Hitler, the German dictator. Her name was Lady Dorothy Hooper-Ellis, a trim well-cared-for mid-fiftyish statuesque aristocrat. In her early days, some thirty years previously, she had, as a member of the suffragette movement, flirted with fascism but had never truly embraced its cause while her adored husband Sir Bernard had been alive. Sir Bernard, who had worked in the City as a stockbroker, had had the unfortunate misfortune to find several of his clients' accounts had disappeared to cover his losses through bad investments during the Wall Street meltdown – the Great Depression – or as Sir Bernard had called it, as had Hitler, the

Great Jewish conspiracy. When he had confided in Lady Dorothy of his looming disaster she, being from a landed coal mining dynasty and heiress to her elderly father's vast fortune, had without hesitation agreed to cover his considerable liabilities. Sir Bernard had thanked her kindly, informing her that he did have options but should these fail he would accept her most generous offer. The following day he was dead from an overdose of sleeping tablets. An honourable man, he could not face up to the disgrace of being labelled an embezzler leaving a distraught Lady Dorothy to face the scandal. That was three years ago. Lady Dorothy was convinced he would still be alive if it hadn't been for those damned Jews. The stigma of suicide stuck.

The orator she was listening to so intently was William Joyce. He was in his late twenties, thin and pale but he made up for this with his intense, electrifying, anti-Semitic hectoring to the awed audience. When Joyce brought his lecture to closure the assembly rose as one, including Lady Dorothy. The applause and cheering was deafening. These were the new converts to the Nazi cause. She was now one of them. At the suggestion of a cousin, she had found what she was seeking.

As the delirious crowd slowly ambled from the hall Lady Dorothy made her way against the surge towards the stage. Joyce was packing his speech into an old battered attaché case. As she set foot on the bottom tread of the steps leading to the stage her progress came to an abrupt halt as a black shirt sleeve arm came across her ample bosom. She gave the owner of the arm one of her aristocratic scowls which usually resulted in an apology from the culprit. Not this time – the arm held firm. Joyce, looking up from his packing chore moved towards her and indicated with a flip of his wrist to allow her to continue to meet him.

He stood at the top of the stairs with extended arm to assist her onto the stage. 'Kindly excuse Adrian. He was possibly of the opinion that you are here to throw eggs at me.'

'Certainly not. I have come to offer my support to your cause.'

'Financial donation, then? All donations gratefully received.'

'If needs be. But what I have to offer is……..'

Her answer was interrupted by the assembly hall inner doors bursting open inwards to the now empty seating. Unknown to Joyce, his bodyguard, and Lady Dorothy, was the knowledge that when the enraptured assembly had left the hall they had been attacked by the Jewish community of the area, communists, socialist and anti-fascist movements. A bloody fight had ensued and was still on-going, the skirmish now escalating back into the hall with the aim of harming Joyce. His black shirted lieutenants were putting up a stalwart blockade but were being overrun by the sheer numbers of the opposition. The villainous looking horde, some wielding staves held high were advancing towards the stage. In the distance police whistles pierced the night air.

'This way, William,' shouted his bodyguard, tugging at Joyce's shoulder. 'Out the back door.'

As he turned to join his bodyguard Joyce gently grabbed Lady Dorothy's wrist. 'Come this way with us. They mean harm and I wouldn't like that to come your way.....not before you make your donation,' he chortled.

Exiting the rear of the hall there were no loiterers waiting to ambush them. They set off at a jog with Joyce's bodyguard leading the way. When they reached the main road intersection the bodyguard held a hand up to bring them to a halt. He cautiously looked round the corner then indicated all was clear. However, just as they turned the corner they were caught in the headlights of an oncoming vehicle. Expecting the worst they cowered back into the shadows of a shop doorway. The headlights of a limousine glided silently to a stop outside the doorway.

'It's alright. It's my chauffeur,' exclaimed Lady Dorothy in relief.

'Evening m' Lady. Didn't see you come out the main entrance into the fracas so I thought I would take a twirl round the block,' explained the cultured voice of the chauffeur.

'Very astute of you, Charles. Not to mention impeccable timing.'

Charles removed himself from behind the wheel to open the front passenger door for Lady Dorothy, leaving the others to fend for themselves. When all were settled, he enquired, 'Where to m'Lady?'

She looked around enquiringly. 'Trafalgar Square, please. We will disperse from there,' answered Joyce calmly.

The journey was carried out in silence. When they reached their destination Joyce and the bodyguard alighted. Joyce, realising from the chauffeur's due deference to his mistress's title that he was in the company of nobility, presented himself at the passenger door with an exaggerated bow and said mockingly, 'Thank you ever so kindly, m'Lady. I hope to see you in the near future when we can discuss the matter you raised and……'

Without warning, Lady Dorothy flung open her door forcing Joyce to move smartly backwards. The bodyguard tensed. 'All's well, Adrian,' said Joyce, throwing an arm outward to arrest Adrian's movement towards Lady Dorothy.

She ignored both as she reopened the rear door. 'Inside Mister Joyce, if you please. And you can stay where you are,' she said firmly to a perplexed Adrian. 'I have somebody I would like you to meet Mister Joyce. He is of considerable influence.'

Joyce indicated to Adrian with a hand gesture that he was dismissed for the evening as she closed the door. Adrian could only stand and stare as the Rolls Royce purred off in the direction of Mayfair.

The limousine glided to a silent halt outside a luxury block of apartments. Charles, opening the door for Lady Dorothy offered his arm in support. He left Joyce to fend for himself. As they approached the main doors they were opened by a gold-braided uniformed doorman. Tipping his hat he bid, 'Good evening Lady Dorothy, your cousin has already arrived.'

'Thank you, Tomkins,' replied Lady Dorothy, as the doorman pressed the lift button to the penthouse.

Chapter 2

Gijon, Asturius, Northern Spain, 12th October 1934
With a cloudless blue sky and a welcoming cool breeze blowing to counteract the rising early morning temperature which already had heat hazes shimmering off the old Gijon – Oviedo high road you would have thought the driver would be at peace with the world…but…

José Delgado, crunched the gears of the ancient lorry with a profanity – his task was onerous enough without the wreck playing up. He had recently warned his older brother Jaimé, the leader of the Asturius communist union construction workers, and owner of the maligned vehicle that they needed new transport. The growled riposte, "Won't happen as long as we have this worse than useless Nationalist government in power" was of course the expected response coming from one hell bent on the destruction of capitalism. However, José's immediate problem was that should the van break down as he feared it would at any moment and a passing Guardia Civil patrol show interest then all would be lost.

He had been dispatched by his brother ostensibly to pick up Finnish timber from the port of Gijon but in fact, as well as the timber, he had picked up a cache of rifles and ammunition from Russia. They were hidden in a concealed compartment under the lorry adding to the basic problem that the van was now grossly overloaded. He would have to off-load some of the timber – fortunately he knew where he would get friendly assistance.

The engine was having a bronchial attack as it laboured up inclines and was receiving further linguistic abuse from José whose leg was aching from the constant necessity of double de-clutching every gear change due to the temperamental nature of the ancient gearbox. Thankfully, on breasting one of the inclines he saw the farmhouse. He turned off the road and stopped outside an open barn. Pedro, the farmer, instantly recognised him as Jaimé's brother who had helped him in the farming rebellion several months earlier. José explained his predicament and the farmer was only too delighted to help. With most of its backbreaking load of timber off-loaded the ancient lorry discovered a new lease of life. However, some three kilometres from Oviedo he became aware of a droning noise louder than the recently developed engine rattle. He stopped the engine but the droning grew louder. Then sticking his head out of the window and looking up found the source of the noise – menacing shapes in the sky, aircraft flying in formation. Restarting the engine he stopped on the crest of the next rise; this gave him a good view of Oviedo. He felt his pulse quicken; this could only mean one thing – the expected backlash of the Nationalist Government had started. Unexpectedly there was a brilliant flash and a muffled roar from the part of town housing his brother's yard, where the resistance militia awaited his arrival with the weapons. Other areas of the town were also erupting in smoke and flames. His fury rose – the bastards were indiscriminately bombing the working-class areas. Battle hardened, he wasn't scared of confrontation but his priority had now changed – the weapons had to be now secured for the cause. He had to hide the rifles and he knew where. He turned left into the next minor road, a road he knew well, no more than a farm track that led him down and across the new Oviedo – Gijon road to by-pass Oviedo to the north and take him into the Pecos de Europa foothills.

***

Oviedo, Asturius, Northern Spain 12th October 1934

At the same time as José turned towards the foothills, the still form of a young girl lay on her back amongst the rubble of a razed building the result of the bombing witnessed by José. Seven days prior to her plight a rebellion by the disparate forces of anarchists, socialists and communists had captured the Nationalist Government arms and explosives factory in Oviedo.

Her eyes slowly opened in a face layered in the grime of brick dust, mortar and plaster. The noise was bedlam. When her eyes adjusted to the devastation she became aware that she lay trapped under a door. The thick solid hardwood door had wedged itself at an angle between a shattered wall and the concrete floor. She lay safely cocooned in this life-saving void. Her head throbbed and an acrid smell of burning human flesh assailed her nostrils. She vomited wretchedly. With trembling limbs, she squirmed her way out from under the door, a task not made any easier with a knapsack on her back. Free of the door, she leaned back on what was left of the wall the door had wedged itself against. Her first sighting was that of a dense cloud of dust particles dancing in a shaft of sunlight between a jagged wall leaning at a perilous angle and the pointed shaped profile of a timber roof truss. She raised a hand to the back of her head to locate the throb. The hand found a congealed bloody gash. In the distance she heard explosions, the thruuump of collapsing buildings and fierce outbreaks of sporadic gunfire. She shook her head to free it of debris before making an attempt to gather her wits. She sat there in a numbed state with her mind in turmoil not registering the cause of her predicament and verging on panic when the wall she had first seen leaning at the perilous angle, now behind her, suddenly collapsed with a thunderclap *thruuump*. In fright she flung her arms over her head and as she did the shock of the collapsing wall brought her memory flooding back to her. She had been delivering her papa's forgotten lunch to him at his office when the premises had been bombed. Bombed! Who would want to bomb us? You have to be at war to be bombed, don't you? She shook violently, convinced she was hallucinating.

It had been a sunny morning as she left for work from her parents' home – a typical single-storey whitewashed courtyard building in the main street of a village in the lower slopes of an Alpine-like valley in the Pecos de Europa mountain range. She recalled bidding her mamma farewell at the door. Mamma had flung a hand to her mouth in mock surprise. She postponed her departure whilst her mamma had scurried off to the kitchen to fetch her papa's lunch box. This was a regular occurrence, for he was forever forgetting his lunch. There was no problem as his builder's yard was on her way to work as a nurse at Saint Martha's Charitable Hospital and it might give her a chance to see her fiancé Ramón who was employed as a carpenter by her papa. When she had finished stuffing her papa's lunch into her knapsack, she slung it on her back and eased her slim, lithe, twenty-year old figure onto her cycle and set off for work some thirty minutes distant, firstly through the lush fertile agricultural plains then into the industrial outskirts of Oviedo.

The journey gave her time to reflect on recent happenings in the area. There had been growing tension since May, five months ago, when an industrial strike led by her communist papa had resulted in a bloody struggle with the Guardia Civil. Now, an open revolt, with her papa once again heavily involved, saw the rag-tag bunch of communists, left-wing socialists and anarchists capture the state arms and explosives factories. When she had enquired of her lovable but fanatical communist father what it was all about he had stood up from the meal table and leaned forward with both hands resting on the table edge to start his well-rehearsed oratory. Her mamma, with a sigh, a shake of the head and a sad hurt look at her daughter for inflicting such pain on her took herself off to wash the dishes. Her papa's hectoring began. It would appear that the revolt that had taken place was due to the failure of their, "worse than useless capitalist, Nationalist government in Madrid" to come up with a solution to the Great Depression, other than to further depress the working class of Asturius. The prime cause being the local mine owners cutting wages and laying-off workers due to the dramatic cut in demand for coal. Behind it all was the "greedy Wall Street capitalists of America".....She had nodded her agreement throughout just as she had seen her mamma do on countless occasions whilst her true thoughts drifted to more important things like her forthcoming marriage to her beloved Ramón. She could not imagine a day without him.

Life had returned to normal, or as near possible as the situation allowed, under local libertarian communist rule, albeit, nervously awaiting the expected backlash from the Nationalist forces. These had been her troubled reflections as she crossed the boundary into Oviedo where she headed in the direction of her papa's workplace in an area the local Nationalist controlled press described as a ghetto inhabited by subversives, anarchists and communists. Her papa's workplace was a former stable, the entry being through a neglected stonework archway with bedrooms above, one to each of the two - storey houses either side of the archway. The small bedroom window panes were filthy with several cracked and those that were broken boarded with cardboard or left open to the elements. Behind a filthy tattered sheet being used as a curtain a baby cried. The stench of poverty hung about unmolested.

Contrary to this scene of abject misery were the freshly painted solid wood gates set into the archway bearing the name: JAIMÉ DELGADO CONSTRUCTION. Her papa's business. In one of the gates was a pass door. She was just about to open the door when it was wrenched from her grasp. The ugly scar face of the opener showed surprise at first then hastily lunged past her into the street muttering an apology to the effect that he was dreadfully late for an urgent meeting in town. She thought she recognised him but could not put a name to his face, which with a face like that, surprised her. She would ask her papa. She entered through the pass gate with her cycle, leaving it propped against one of the archway walls and strode into the yard. She came to an abrupt halt – what she witnessed took her breath away. There were twenty plus men of all ages, dressed in navy boiler suits with a red 'kerchief tied around their necks – the uniform of the resistance fighters – cleaning rifles, smoking or lounging about in the early morning sun. She suddenly realised this collection of mish-mash revolutionaries were her papa's militia relief awaiting transport to the captured arms and munitions factory. Of the faces looking towards her there was not a face amongst them she recognised but she did recognise the broad shoulders of one with his back to her – her Ramón. Aware of his compatriots gawping intently at something behind him, Ramón turned. There before him was the girl he deeply and truly loved – his Nina. He opened his arms wide. Nina rushed into them. They kissed lightly to a chorus of cheers. She blushed crimson. She explained her mission to Ramón, holding high the lunch box for all to see as if in excuse for her moment of unbridled passion. She just couldn't help herself – she loved him so. He took her by the hand and led her towards her papa's office in a large single-storey brick-built building housing the office, stores and the carpenters' workshop. He opened the door for her and stepped back to allow her to pass. As she put her hand on the open door to keep it in place she heard a droning noise above. They both looked up only to be blinded by the bright sun; they saw nothing. Without warning Nina received a push in the back and a shrill cry from

Ramôn telling her to do something. She didn't make out what he had cried but it soon became obvious – a warning – as an earth shattering explosion shook the ground and building. As she lurched down the corridor, the result of Ramon's push, ceiling plaster rained down on her head as she met a flying door coming towards her. The door caught the corridor wall edge-on as it was collapsing causing it to spin and strike her on the back of her head. That was the last she remembered. With her memory returned, she struggled to her feet and found her new stockings in tatters, and her shoes lost in the rubble as she looked around at the smouldering carnage. Everywhere – rising clouds of dust, burning timbers and the permeating stench of human flesh. The building had been levelled apart from the odd piece of standing brickwork and a solitary partial door frame standing like ominous gallows. It suddenly dawned on her that the doorframe was part of her Papa's office. Her papa! With a high pitched scream she scrambled barefoot, with no care for herself, over the sharp edged rubble, through the doorframe, to stand where her papa's office had once been. In the now deathly hush that had descended she heard a low moan. She had to peer closely through the swirling dust to establish the location of the moan. Stumbling forward she barely recognised her papa. He lay entombed in bricks with just his face showing. One side of his face was a wrinkled, charred, purple mass with the eye lost in the morass, his once wavy black hair matted in blood. The agony showing on his face was almost too much to bear. Due to his effort of mouthing the moan a spittle of blood was mixed with the grime on his face.

'Papa, papa,' she wailed, sobbing uncontrollably.

'No time, Nina,' he replied weakly, spitting out grime and blood. 'I'm finished....you must leave now....get your mamma and flee...José will take you both to your aunt Maria in Santander.'

'But papa, I must get help....'

'Nina!' The effort of emphasising her name brought on a fit of coughing up blood. With a drooping head he appeared to lose consciousness but sheer willpower forced him to recover. 'There will be no help...I...am...the...enemy...The Nationalists....will seek retribution...on...all...of...us...women...and....children......they... are...evil...men......tell.....José.....this......was....n.... no accident,'

Every word was delivered in a rasping gasp. '....I....was .....targeted...I love you Nina....Tell your mama I love...her..,' His head fell sideways. The one good eye became sightless as it stared skywards.

She dropped to her knees and disregarding the pain from the sharp edged rubble kissed her papa on the forehead, crossed herself and closed his eye. She then, sobbing and near to collapse, turned to where she had last seen Ramón.

Retracing her path back over the unrecognisable rubble-strewn corridor, she stopped many times to remove shards of glass from her lacerated feet and eventually reached what had been the entrance to the office. Looking around her she held a hand over her mouth and gasped in horror – there was an arm lying limp out of a mound of shattered brickwork. Throwing herself down she grabbed the hand. It was wearing a ring – the distinctive gold band she had given to her Ramón on their engagement. He wore it at all times.

'Oh! Please God, not you as well my lovely Ramón. No, no, no.....' she was screaming as she scrabbled at the brick with her bare hands. With fingers, nails broken, and skin bleeding, she finally found his face – handsome no more. She didn't care, she kissed the battered lifeless face with all the tenderness she could muster, crossed herself several times, then collapsed across Ramón in a dead faint. She lay there for how long she didn't know; waking to an eerie silence. Having removed Ramón's ring she clutched it to her heart and once again struggled to her feet. The tears started flowing as her body was wracked with uncontrollable sobs. Uppermost now in her mind was to get home to mamma. She turned towards the yard entrance only to witness the destruction of the bedrooms over the archway and the houses on either side. Of the roofs there was no sign. One of the archway walls was intact, the one that she had propped her bicycle against, held in place by the joists and flooring from the collapsed bedroom above. This formed a passageway between the yard and the street. She prayed her bicycle was still in working order. Ignoring the searing pain in her feet she stumbled over the brick and glass shards towards the newly formed passage. She felt nauseous as she made her way past a still smouldering deep crater where she last saw the militiamen gathered – the smell of burning flesh causing her to retch violently. Recovered, but gasping for air, she picked her way gingerly over the rubble. A lifeless arm pointed skyward amid the stonework of the collapsed archway houses, a baby's cot lay on top of the debris to join the many human body parts scattered around. The haunted wailing of those mutilated but still barely alive drifted melancholy in the air. Nauseated, she finally arrived at the entrance to the passage and saw her miraculously undamaged bicycle still in place. She also encountered a dead male body lying like a rag doll against the wall. She removed his heavy flannel work shirt, tearing it with trembling hands into strips and tied them to her feet. She made her way through the passage to the street and with tears still flowing and in a trance she mounted her bicycle and set off for home oblivious to the devastation around her. When she cleared the town boundary she took refuge behind a wall in a field. Thankful for the rest she removed from her haversack a bottle of water. She drank long and deep whilst fondling Ramôn's ring – water never tasted so good. She wanted desperately to sleep but knew she could not. She must make it to mamma. Suddenly she was aware of a hot sensation at the back of her neck. She tentatively put a hand to the spot to find her wound had reopened. Not to worry mamma knows what to do for she has stitched and patched up many casualties brought home by papa. But no more by papa, she sobbed, the sobbing to be replaced by anger. The anger of revenge was now in her heart. She set off for home – if one still existed.

After two hours of agonising pedalling, walking the cycle uphill and resting her swollen and bleeding feet, Nina finally reached her village. All was eerily quiet – nothing stirred in the road – like the calm before a storm. Her weary eyes recognise in the distance her uncle Freddy's van parked at the kerb outside her mamma's house. A good sign that her mamma was at home. With feet throbbing she pedalled furiously the remaining two hundred metres to the door, dropped the bicycle to the ground and hobbled in the always open door. She heard raised voices from the kitchen.

Her mamma, Isabella, was being adamant. 'I don't care, José, I won't go until I know what's happened to Jaimé and Nina.'

When Nina reached the kitchen door she saw, sitting with his back to her not her uncle Freddy, but her uncle José who was patting one of her mamma's hands across the table in an effort to comfort her for she was in a state of distress, groaning softly and rocking backwards and forwards with a handkerchief held to her mouth. Leaning against the doorframe Nina changed feet and in doing so let out a yelp of pain. Her mamma and Jose caught unawares looked up in shocked surprise.

Isabella wailed, 'Nina, Nina, my child, thanks be to God you're still alive.' She hastily crossed herself and rushed towards Nina, shouting as she did, 'José, get the child a basin of hot water and....' Just then Nina's knees buckled but before she could strike the tiled floor, José moved nimbly to catch her in the cradle of one arm whilst sweeping her legs into the other and took her into her bedroom.

Nina awoke to the familiar surroundings of her bedroom. Had it all been a bad dream she wondered. Obviously not for she noticed a metal wash basin, cotton thread, needles and iodine on the bedside table. Her head throbbed as did her feet. She reached a hand to her head, staring at the broken finger nails she once so carefully manicured. The exploring probe found her head to be bandaged and on throwing back the blanket she discovered her feet to have been similarly dealt with. She became aware of the antiseptic smell of the bedroom as she lay back on the fresh sheets to take stock of her situation. The head pain made thinking tortuous. She was alive, hurting all over, but alive which was more than could be said of her poor papa and her Ramón. Her life, with no Ramón, was finished – of this she was certain. The tears started; she let them flow. She suddenly realised she had not confided in mamma the tragic news about papa and Ramón and instantly felt guilty of putting her own sorrow before her mamma. Quickly she found her fleece lined slippers under the bed and slipped into them. The pain in her feet was still there but in the circumstances tolerable. She dressed in slacks and a heavy knit sweater. A touch of renewed life entered her body as she made her way towards the kitchen. All the Delgado family problems were resolved in the kitchen.

Her mamma was talking. 'And was Freddy accommodating?' Freddy being her brother and one of the largest landowning farmers in Asturius.

'Yes. As usual. He helped me dig a trench in a pig-sty for the rifles just in case the Guardia give the farm a search…..'

'It's not likely they would do that. They think him being a landowner he is one of them,' interrupted Isabella.

'True. But in these troubled times who can say what is going to happen. Jamié's lorry we hid in one of the barns under hay. And Freddy gave me his van to use to take you and Nina to your sister Maria in Santander.'

'Now don't start that again, José. I've already told you. This is my home and I do not intend to let Franco and his African thugs run me out. That's what Jaimé would expect of me.'

A hardened edge crept into José's reply, 'Isabella! Believe me you won't even get that choice. You're Jaimé Delgado's wife; they'll kill you and Nina. For God's sake woman, pack your bags now and go tonight, for tomorrow will be too late. The soldiers are advancing as we speak….'

Nina coughed politely from the doorway to announce her arrival and in a trembling voice croaked, 'Mama, uncle José, I have something to tell you about papa and Ramón.'

José leapt to his feet immediately and lifted Nina bodily to sit her at the table beside her mamma. Her mamma kissing and cuddling her said soothingly, 'My poor, poor, Nina, how you have suffered. Are you sure you are yet strong enough to want to tell us what happened to you?'

'Yes mamma. I must unburden myself.' Nina then recounted the whole horrible episode with her and her mamma stopping every so often to let the tears flow and José interspersing her story with profanities. She finished her encounter with, 'And it was papa's final wish that José take us to Aunt Maria in Santander for safety.'

When she finished a deathly hush descended, everybody wrapped up in their own thoughts about the terrible event. José was first to speak. With a finger wag at Isabella he said angrily, 'There you have it, Isabella, murder. Jaimé, Ramón, women and children, all wantonly murdered by the fascist scum of Madrid. Now will you listen to……'

Isabella held up a hand in acknowledgement of his tirade, 'I understand José, I will go right away. But what of you?'

A smile broke out on his ruddy, unshaven, face. 'I will carry on Jaimé's fight as he would have wanted me to do.'

Isabella nodded her approval and then turned to Nina, 'Go and pack your bag, we are going to your Aunt Maria.'

When Nina had departed the kitchen, José asked of Isabella, 'How are you for pesetas?'

'Our savings are in the floor safe. As you know Jaimé did not trust the fascist bankers. I will get them before I leave.'

'I have here more for you, compliments of Freddy,' said José, withdrawing a large stuffed envelope from his jacket. Isabella, silently protested with a dismissive hand wave. 'Freddy said you would do that, so he told me to tell you if you didn't accept your profit share of the farm, I've to give it to Maria to keep for you.'

With a sigh, Isabella relented and accepted the envelope stuffing it in her handbag. 'You know, José, it's all very well you saying, "you go to your sister Maria", but don't you think we should have at least asked her first?'

'I phoned her before I arrived,' he chuckled. 'She's also got Nina a nursing position at the new hospital.'

'You, you rogue,' she tried to hit him jokingly with her handbag. 'You're a good man, José Delgado, a loss to some poor woman's happiness.'

His friendly face changed to one of anger. (what have I said to upset him thought Isabella) He strode to the door, heard Nina busy in the bedroom and returned to face Isabella and in a whisper said, 'The first wave of bombing I saw was over Jaimé's yard.'

'So?'

'I think it was deliberate.'

'All the bombing was deliberate.'

'Yes. But I think it was a deliberate attempt on Jaimé because he led the attack on the munitions factory. I think he was set-up by somebody.'

'Who?'

'I don't know but I do know that the Mayor, a bastard fascist to the core, was conveniently visiting his sister in Galicia when the atrocity happened...'

Isabella shook her head in way of interrupting, 'That's pure supposition, José.'

'Maybe. But believe me, Isabella, when I find out who the bastard is that is responsible I'll cut his balls off. Now, be packing woman – it's a long way to Santander and I still have rifles to deliver to those poor devils still alive.'

Chapter 3

Headquarters (SIS6) London 19th October 1934
Sir James McKay VC, the tenacious Glaswegian and head of British Secret Intelligence Service, section six, foreign affairs, SIS(6) was proud of his earned knighthood for he thought little of hereditary titles and the aristocracy that clung to them. To him titles, unless earned, suggested a social class entitled to more privileges than the common man – a suggestion that offended his principled socialist roots. He liked to think he had earned his knighthood for service to his country, unlike the Tory imbecile he was meeting at 5-00 pm – Sir Eustace Pennington-Beaumont.

James McKay was the son of a college lecturer and with both his parents being activists in Keir Hardie's Labour party since its inception he had been brought up in the socialist ways and made to appreciate the evils that lay ahead; that of the capitalist establishment. With the advantage of his father's additional caring tuition he had excelled at school. During this period nobody had dared to bully him as was the usual treatment meted out to "swots" for the young James knew how to look after himself in the playground. His fists laying testament to the stupid few that had tried. When he finished school he gained a place at Glasgow University from where he graduated with first class honours in corporate law and languages (French and German). On leaving university he had the choice of legal firms eager to offer him employment. Prior to these offers James had already decided that knowledge gained on how companies operated at boardroom level would help his intended career path – that of altering the atrocious work conditions that existed in the mines and shipyards – so he chose to take one of the offered appointments with a highly respected firm of Glasgow lawyers specialising in corporate law. With his inherent socialist beliefs he gave his spare time free to attend to matters relating to the plight of these injustices much to the annoyance of his employer who acted on behalf of many of these privately owned companies. Even with his employer initially tolerating his brilliant analytical brain being used elsewhere the parting of the ways came when James decided to seek compensation from a prominent shipbuilder for a widow due to her husband's fall from scaffolding. Scaffolding which in James' opinion was not-fit-for-purpose. Backed by Union money he won his plea of negligence against the shipbuilder. This landmark case saw the parting of the ways with his employer and launched his career. Many successful cases were to follow – all unfortunately brought to a halt with the outbreak of war in 1914. Aged thirty one, whilst being disappointed in his idol Keir Hardie's stand on pacifism, he enlisted in the Army. Other than his mother he left behind nobody special amongst his multitude of adoring female admirers. However, many were the boardrooms of the Clydeside shipyards and mine owners that heaved a sigh of relief at the news of his enlistment.

Forfeiting the rights his academic qualifications gave him to be considered for officer placement he entered the war a hard and cynical man. He rose quickly through the ranks from a private to become a sergeant in a special commando unit. His brave heroics were brought to the attention of a certain Lieutenant Colonel Winston Churchill, commander of six battalion Royal Scots Fusiliers. McKay, without consultation, found himself drafted into the Royal Scots with the rank of Captain. The commanding officer, Churchill, was no slouch in the bravery department either. He took McKay with him on several forages into no-man's land neutral zones. These were intelligence scouting missions to locate the position of the enemy machine guns, trenches, strength of battalions and any other pertinent intelligence matter. All these missions were fraught with the danger that McKay now craved. It was on the return from one such mission that he discovered a German soldier about to lob a stick grenade into a trench full of British infantry getting ready to "go over the top" in yet another suicidal mission. Without care for his own safety, he dived onto the German's back bringing him down into the mud. The grenade exploded under the German who bore the brunt of the explosion. The casualty list read: several mud splattered riflemen, one very dead German and, miraculously, McKay, with only a shrapnel wound to the knee. For this valiant effort he was awarded the Victoria Cross. With only this shrapnel wound he survived to the end of the conflict. He knew he was one of the lucky survivors due to the pointless deaths caused by the cavalier attitude and incompetent decisions of the aristocratic officers with men's lives. He cursed the day they were born for in them he recognised the similar arrogant breed that inherited the boardrooms of the Clydeside shipyards. He worried how ironic it was that war had brought full employment to the shipyards and wealth to the owners but in reality how little it had done to stop the poverty of the workers that gave them their ill-deserved riches.

With the war all but over, McKay, now aged thirty six, mused on what life held in store for him. His legal firm had survived the war and was, he knew, in good capable socialist hands still striving for the aims he had set out to achieve but having tasted adventure a return to civilian life did not instantly appeal. However, an unexpected telegram solved his problem. It was from his old commander of the Royal Scots, Winston Churchill, for whom he had the utmost respect and admiration even though he was one of the reviled aristocracy. It would appear that Military Intelligence required extra officers to interrogate captured German officers and military staff accused of war crimes. Armed with his university degree in German he accepted. During his interrogations he recruited as future informants, by the use of blackmail, a certain type of German. At the end of the lengthy war crimes interrogations he was recruited on the recommendation of his head of section Sylvia Sanderson into the Secret Intelligence Service, section six, SIS(6). She had fallen, as many before her, for the rugged good looks of Jimmy McKay.

Due to McKay's shrewd judgement during his interrogation period of the war crimes he was rewarded with one of his informers being placed in the signals and cipher department of the Reichstag in Berlin. An unbelievable piece of good fortune, which went a long way towards his receiving, in late 1933, the appointment as head of SIS(6) to join his knighthood for service to his country. With it being unheard of for the appointment of head of SIS(6) to have gone to anyone who was not a product of Eton, Harrow, or Oxbridge – especially an ardent socialist into the bargain – Sir James McKay,

VC, suspected the hand of Churchill had been at work. When he broached Churchill about the matter he declared he knew nothing of it suggesting that it might well be the doing of that Labour chappie, Ramsay McDonald, the leader of the Coalition government who was appointing everyone into positions above their ability, especially his fellow socialists. The country was going to the dogs. This Sir James took with good humour, knowing it to be Winston's way of not wanting him to know of his involvement in the promotion. However, unbeknownst to Sir James, Churchill had wanted the right man for the job in place, irrespective of his background, for his future re-entry into government.

By this time a new name started making world news – Adolph Hitler. And with communism menacing, fascism threatening, and a civil war in Spain looming – it was interesting times ahead for the new head of the British Secret Intelligence Service – Sir James McKay, VC.

***

Sir James sat at his desk massaging his aching war-wounded knee. He rose with the aid of a walking stick and limped towards a drab pale grey government-issue filing cabinet. Once there he leaned his fifty two year old, six foot, still athletically lean figure on his stick and unlocked the cabinet. He ran his finger along the file tabs until he came to the letter C. He withdrew the Churchill file and returned to his desk – a desk shorn of photographs of loved ones for he had never married telling himself that the perilous nature of the job of an agent, as he had been for many years, did not lend itself to matrimony. If he had been honest with himself he would have admitted the real reason – the woman he had loved he let go for the sake of his career. Her name was Sylvia Sanderson, his head of section during the war crime interrogations with whom he had had, strictly against regulations, a secret affair. The affair came to an end when a vacancy occurred in SIS(6) for an agent. Sylvia, whom he had always assumed to be, like himself, Military Intelligence, was in fact an employee of SIS(6) and as such felt it her duty on account of his natural interrogation ability to put forward his name for the position. She, without informing him, knew this would be a step in the right direction for him. Her recommendation was accepted. He was interviewed by Sir John Holland, the then head of SIS(6) and offered the situation. He accepted and was transferred immediately to London.

Sylvia became Head-of-Station, Berlin. He failed to reply to her letters – they drifted apart. She married a German doctor and settled in Berlin. He, later in life, had felt the sorrow of his failure to reply to her letters – blaming the unsettled lifestyle of the job.

However, some thirteen years later he had by chance met Sylvia on one of his now frequent visits to Berlin only to discover that she was widowed. Julius, her husband, had died from a heart attack. He felt a rekindling of the feelings he had for her all those years ago and offered her a position as receptionist in the Embassy. The situation being primarily to keep an eye on a raw new agent Scott Rutherford that he was sending to the Embassy in the usual euphemistic guise of trade attaché sometime in the forthcoming months when he had completed his training at SIS school. It would be his first mission. Sir James held high future hopes for him. She laughed her infectious laugh and reminded him of the time she once had to do the same for Mr Churchill on a raw young war crimes interrogator sixteen years ago. They both laughed – knowing who she meant. He sighed – she was still a very attractive woman. He invited her to dinner; she invited him home afterwards.

Sir James opened Churchill's file and began to read, immersing himself in the contents for some considerable time. The man fascinated him. He was just about opposed to everything Churchill stood for politically but couldn't help but wonder, having read his latest parliamentary comments, if he and Churchill were the only people to realise the fascist threat of Adolph Hitler was drawing ever closer to reality. He laid the file aside and reached into the bottom drawer to withdraw a bottle of Glenmorangie malt whisky to pour himself a "wee dram" to help ease the pain in his knee which had started to play up again. He knew the reason his knee was giving him gyp – it was the thought of meeting the insufferable Sir Eustace Pennington-Beaumont at the Foreign Office in ten minutes time.

Sir James sighed deeply at the sight of the brass nameplate inscribed Sir E. Pennington-Beaumont, Permanent Under-Secretary of State for Foreign Affairs. Unfortunately, Sir James' department SIS(6) fell under the auspices of the Foreign Office, giving him no choice but to attend the meeting called by Sir Eustace, his token boss. And that rankled with him. He knocked and entered the anteroom to be met by Effy, (Euphemia), Sir Eustace's bubbly secretary. How she remained bubbly was a mystery to Sir James considering the blithering aristocratic idiot for whom she worked.

'Good evening, Sir James, I trust I find you well?'

'All the better for seeing you, my dear Effy.'

'Are you trying to flirt with me, Sir James?' she asked coyly.

'Chance would be a fine thing,' he replied, wishing once again he was twenty years younger. 'Pray tell, Effy, do I find Sir Useless, er, Sir Eustace in his usual unfortunate good health?'

With a drop of her head and a mock stern glare over her glasses she said amiably, 'I'm sure you don't really mean that, Sir James.'

Sir James wilfully replied, 'Yes I do mean that – chance *would* be a fine thing were I twenty years younger.'

She gave a hearty laugh as she hit the intercom button. 'Sir James for you, Sir Eustace.'

A plummy bombastic voice replied, 'Send the chappie in, Effy, there's a good gal.'

Effy rose from her desk to open the communicating door to Sir Eustace's office. Sir James, who usually deplored any form of patronising regarding his infirmity allowed Effy to go ahead without comment, giving him the opportunity to study her pert bottom as it wiggled in a tight skirt on shapely legs towards the door. She held the door open for him. Sitting before Sir James, behind an enormous oak antique desk with elegant carved legs and edge mouldings, sat the obese form of Sir Eustace Pennington-Beaumont under a dense cloud of the finest Havana cigar smoke. To Sir James' way of thinking, Sir Eustace was the most pompous, arrogant buffoon in government high office. But he was also aware that below the façade lay the guile and cunning that he was encountering in his endeavours to extricate SIS(6) from the grasp of Sir Eustace, who viewed Sir James' proposal to remove SIS(6) from the Foreign Office (FO) not as an improvement towards national security but as a loss of power to his fiefdom.

'Tea or coffee, James, old boy?' twittered Sir Eustace, as Sir James settled into a high winged antique chair, one of a pair, to match the ornately carved relief of the desk edging.

'Tea's fine, thank you, Eustace,' replied Sir James, resisting the urge to add what appeared to be the mandatory "old boy".

As Eustace made a production of ordering the tea and cakes it gave Sir James time to reflect on the relationship between SIS(6) and the FO. In his eyes the FO never offered anything original or constructive, were all Tory yes-men, picked your brain and passed off the acquired information to the Foreign Secretary as their own. Unfortunately, protocol demanded he did their bidding – or so they thought.

With the order placed, Sir James enquired, 'You wished to see me, Eustace. What can I do for you?'

'Nothing much, old boy, just thought I'd pick your brains.'

'With pleasure,' lied Sir James, taken aback at Eustace's honesty.

'Rum affair this Spanish how d'you do in Oviedo, eh, what, old boy?'

'Raa – ther, old boy,' mimicked Sir James, electing to minimise conversation knowing it to be the start of the brain picking.

However, Sir Eustace, totally unabashed, continued his quest for Sir James' point of view, 'So what do you make of it all, James?'

The answer had to wait as Effy wheeled in a trolley bearing a solid silver salver and teapot with milk jug, sugar bowl, and a laden cake stand to match. The tea cups and saucers being of finest bone china. They do themselves well, mused Sir James, wondering how Eustace would react should he ever invite him, heaven forbid, to his department for tea out of their chipped enamelled tin mugs compliments of army surplus. Capitalism, fascism, communism, it would always be opulence whatever the "isms" for those in the higher echelons of power.

However, putting his dark thoughts to one side he pulled himself together as Eustace handed him a cup and saucer which he placed on an antique table alongside his chair. He then reached towards the silver cake stand for a scrumptious looking slice of black forest gateau, thinking he might as well get something out of the meeting.

After devouring the slice and liking his fingers he finally returned to the question. 'So what do I make of it, you ask? I'd say it could end up pretty messy,' he answered evasively.

'Messy? You say, messy? Surely it's a mess already. Damned near civil war. Fifteen hundred to two thousand civilians, men, women and children, slain. Bombed and shelled by their own government without warning. Absolute barbarism by the Nationalist government of Madrid,' wailed Sir Eustace.

Sir James did also actually think the act to be barbaric but wanted to see Eustace's reaction when he praised the Spanish government's act. 'Totally agree with you, Eustace. But as you well know it is beyond our remit to interfere. Our masters are opposed to any form of intervention in Europe for fear of another war…..'

'Quite so, old boy. Just about to say that meself,' interrupted Eustace.

'…And,' continued Sir James sharply, annoyed at the interruption, 'The rebels, agitators, call them what you will, acted treasonably when they attacked the Sovereign Government of Spain's munition and arms factories in Oviedo.'

'Couldn't agree more, old boy. Those rebel chappies had it coming to them,' was Sir Eustace's response, totally contradicting his earlier diatribe. No surprise there, thought Sir James, about the master fence-sitter of Whitehall. One minute supporting the rebels; the next Madrid's excesses.

Sir James, allowing himself no more than the twenty minutes his patience could endure in Eustace's company looked surreptitiously at his watch to discover time was up, whereupon he rose from the throne-like chair to take his leave.

Sir Eustace, his eyes blinking owlishly and jowls wobbling at Sir James' sudden intended departure, huffed, 'I say, old boy, you haven't told what you intend to do about Oviedo.'

'Eustace,' snapped Sir James his patience strained, 'I think, had you been listening, you would have heard me indicate that our masters in Whitehall do not wish involvement. However, if you wish to send a "naughty boy" letter to your opposite number in Madrid, I wish you well. Meanwhile, I wish you good evening.'

As he turned towards the door the angry pompous voice of

Eustace made him stop and half turn, leaning on his walking stick. 'I know what this antagonism from you is all about, McKay, it's about your damned diplomatic bag, isn't it? As I've told you repeatedly – in all the years I've been responsible for the bag there has never been a security leak...and that includes the war years. So you can forget your petty nonsense about divorcing your damned SIS from the FO. I won't allow it. What have you to say about that, old boy?' he said triumphantly.

Plenty, thought a furious Sir James.... but now is not the right time. For if he was to linger he knew he would not be responsible for his actions so he about swivelled on his stick, opened the door and once through slammed it shut in frustration. His knee was giving him gyp.

Meanwhile, whilst Sir James and Sir Eustace were bringing their hostile and ill-tempered meeting to a close another meeting was taking place. This meeting was to have an impact on a current agenda Sir James was working on. He had opened a file – The Tenerife Alternative. Code named TENALT.

***

House of Commons tearoom London 19th October 1934
Winston Churchill had requested an informal meeting with Anthony Eden, the Lord Privy Seal. In March the previous year, 1933, the year Hitler declared himself Dictator of Germany, Churchill had made a speech in the House of Commons attacking the 1931 elected National Government (a coalition of Conservative, Labour and Liberal parties) on their appeasement policy towards Hitler. Eden had robustly defended this policy on behalf of the government. His stance was anathema to Churchill who could not believe that any officer who had served in the war, as Eden had, would not oppose Hitler's thuggish rise to power. Eden had taken the opposite view declaring that having experienced war at first hand it was a curse on mankind. However, Churchill had heard recent rumours emanating from Westminster to the effect that Eden had had a change of direction regarding appeasement. It was this rumoured change that Churchill needed to ascertain before proceeding with his newly formulated agenda.

With the House sitting, the tearoom was virtually empty as they sat overlooking the murky waters of the river Thames.

Eden was talking. 'What do you make of this Oviedo rebellion, Winston?'

'I can't help but feel the hand of Herr Hitler hovering over it,' replied the portly figure of Churchill taking a long satisfactory draw on his Havana cigar before continuing, 'Furthermore, I think the carnage in Oviedo might well be the catalyst for a civil war in Spain. A war I would imagine with the aid of Hitler and his chum Mussolini, the Nationalists, under the military leadership of Franco will undoubtedly win hands down.'

'And should that happen France will be surrounded by fascist countries,' mused Eden, stroking his chin.

Churchill nodded his agreement then started his sparring towards his main agenda. 'So, Anthony, what does your leader have to say about it?'

Eden, like a man with the weight of the world on his shoulders, sighed, 'Well, Winston, Baldwin is still continuing to support the ailing Ramsay's (McDonald) anti-war feeling of the electorate.'

Churchill, taking another satisfied draw on his cigar harrumped, 'A blind man could see Hitler's just itching for German domination of Europe – Baldwin's a fool to think otherwise.'

'You certainly made that clear to him in your speech to the House last year, Winston. In fact I would say it more or less ended your chances of a return to government benches whilst Baldwin's in power.'

'Maybe. But it needed saying, Anthony, for we are walking blindly into oblivion, led by one-tuned pied pipers,' replied Churchill who now had to elicit from Eden the man's true feelings on appeasement and not hide behind the feelings he had rhetorically claimed Baldwin to have. So he bullishly enquired, 'And where do you now stand on appeasement?'

'Ah! I thought this might be why you wished to see me, Winston,' answered Eden with a twinkle in his eye.

'In part only, Anthony. But I have to admit your answer will decide as to whether I pursue my main agenda with you.'

'Alright. Let me see if I can help you. Shortly after you and

I had our disagreement on appeasement and I becoming more acutely aware of Hitler's anti-Semitic rants in his oratories, I met Sir James McKay the head of SIS(6).... Do you know of him?'

With McKay being one of the uppermost parts of his main agenda, a fact he did not as yet wish to disclose, Eden's out of the blue enquiry about him came as a surprise. 'Yes indeed, Anthony. Fine chap, McKay, one of the best. We fought together in the war.'

'Well, I asked Mckay what was really happening in Germany. He explained that most of his findings were sub judice, for the Heads of Joint Forces only. He did, however, confirm newspaper reports that the Berlin Jews were leaving the city in their droves following the edict by Hitler for all true Germans to boycott Jewish shops. I could tell where this was leading; to Hitler's Aryan race supremacy. I decided then that Hitler had to be stopped, for it was obvious he had more on his mind than the thwarting of communism.

This reply was welcomed by Churchill for it now permitted him to launch into his main agenda. 'What do you know of this General Franco?'

'Chief of Staff, Nationalist Army, out and out fascist. Friend of Hitler and Mussolini. To all intents a future dictator,' rattled off Eden.

'Thank you. That confirms my own and Admiral Canaris's assessment of Franco.....'

'Admiral Canaris? Head of Germany's Abwehr (Military) Intelligence?' interrupted a shocked Eden, knowing within himself that nothing Churchill knew or did should surprise him.

Churchill, making no effort to explain away his connection to Canaris, continued, 'Yes. The Admiral is of the opinion that Franco, on winning the threatened civil war will join forces with Hitler and allow him passage through Spain to Gibraltar. Gib being a main objective of Adolph.' He let Eden absorb this before continuing to his main point. 'That decision by Franco would make our tenure of Gibraltar tenuous to say the least. Now assuming Canaris to be right about Gib and we have to think the unthinkable – the loss of Gibraltar – I have an alternative plan I would like to discuss.'

He beckoned Eden closer and looking around to make sure there were no eavesdroppers started his narrative.

On completion, Eden remarked, 'Brilliant forward planning, Winston, but I foresee a major difficulty – funding. With you not being a member of government...at present....'

Churchill, expecting this reply, answered, 'Quite correct, Anthony. However, you must also be aware that the relationship between me and the Chancellor of the Exchequer, Mr Chamberlain – *the arch appeaser* – is a little strained to put it mildly. However, with you having Chamberlain's ear, say our mutual friend Sir James McKay of SIS(6) was to apply for the funding through the First Lord of the Admiralty...' He left the sentence unfinished knowing Eden knew exactly what he meant.

Eden rubbed his hand over his chin in deep contemplation. Finally, nodding his understanding, he replied, 'I would say, Winston, that with your being a former First Lord yourself, I imagine that would stand every possibility of success. It might take some time but leave it with me.'

'Excellent, Anthony, excellent. Care for another slice of this delicious carrot cake,' Churchill said exuberantly, pushing the silver cake stand towards Eden, his agenda objective achieved.

Chapter 4

London Chelsea Mews 2nd April1935
With springs protesting, the taxi wended its way tentatively over the uneven granite cobbles of a Chelsea mews to come to a stop under a gas lit lamppost. The passenger door opened and a tall figure of military bearing stepped out into the swirling fog drifting in from the river Thames. He looked towards the front door of the mews cottage, a mere arm's length away; the warm glint of light from a chink in the curtains welcoming him. The invitation to visit had come as a lovely surprise, for his lover had been involved in a new business venture for several weeks.

He rang the doorbell excitedly. The door was opened by a suave gent with sleeked-back black hair, dressed in a maroon velvet jacket with black satin collar and a cravat held in place with a gold brooch tucked into a frilled white shirt, sharply pressed black trousers and black highly polished shoes. The cigarette was held aloof in a gold holder.

He addressed the caller in an aristocratic voice. 'My deah, Adrian, right on time, how lovely to see you again. You look absolutely stunning. So glad you could make it, it's been evah so long, do please come in.'

'That's certainly not of my doing, Guy,' replied Adrian petulantly as he stepped inside. With the door closed, Adrian made an advance towards Guy with the intention of an embrace only to be nimbly side stepped by Guy, who slipped his arm around Adrian's waist and patted his bottom, purring, 'Frisky tonight, aren't we, dahling. But don't worry for the night is yet young. Meanwhile, your hat and coat if you please. I have made us your favourite, a superb chicken coq-au-vin with all the trimmings. For starters we are having the finest Russian caviar which will be served in five minutes. You know where the cocktail cabinet is – help yourself.'

Guy, hung up Adrian's hat and coat and headed for the kitchen, leaving a rather perturbed Adrian to find his way into the dining room to fix himself a large whisky. Not quite the greeting he had expected – he wondered why. Only to find out soon enough, for dinner was served by an anorexic, gorgeously seductive looking Moroccan youth with long eyelashes and scarlet lipstick. The youth was introduced to Adrian as Yousef. Adrian, who couldn't help but notice Guy's eyes glued to Yousef's swaying bottom every time he departed the table, nor the touching lightly of hands after each course, could no longer contain his misery. 'Guy, how could you treat me like this, today of all days?'

'Today?'

'The ninth anniversary of poor Thomas' death in prison.'

'Sorry, old man. Quite forgot about that detestable old paedophile, Holt.'

'After tonight, I don't think you've room to talk regarding that subject.'

Guy replied haughtily, 'Yousef is not a child. He is sixteen years old – and very sexy, don't you think?'

Adrian, who suspected Yousef to be no more than fourteen replied angrily, 'No I certainly don't think. I thought we had something good going until.....now....'

'Surely you're not jealous of Yousef,' interrupted Guy, mockingly.

'Mock if you like, Guy, I no longer care. This incident has quite made up my mind. I'm going to take up an offered post in the Berlin Embassy.'

Suddenly Guy was very attentive. 'The Berlin Embassy, you say. And pray tell, Adrian, who offered you this job?'

'William Joyce, who, as you know, I bodyguard at BUF public meetings.'

'Silly me. Of course, he's one of Mosley's trusted lieutenants in the British Union of Fascists. But how could he possibly offer you a position in the Embassy,' queried Guy, sceptically.

'As you know I joined the BUF at your insistence to infiltrate their hierarchy and ended up his bodyguard. Well, I must have been successful, for I was approached by Joyce after last night's meeting and offered the position but I told him I did not see how a member of the BUF could possibly wield such power. He told me not to worry. I would be contacted by a senior civil servant from the Foreign Office. I told him I would give him my answer once I'd met this person.'

'Who was the senior civil servant?'

'I don't know. No name given. All I can tell you is that it was an, attractive, very aristocratic looking female, who I can't help but feel I have met before, possibly at the Limehouse riot a year ago.'

'And what would be your duties?'

'I understand, as Sergeant-at-Arms, I would have responsibility for security, mail, diplomatic bags, keys, etcetera.'

'You led me to believe you were a lowly courier at the Home Office.'

'I am. But this Embassy offer is promotion. Which I now, especially after tonight's carry-on, intend to accept.'

Guy, who had been making abstract twirling motions with a spoon on the tablecloth, trembled inwardly with excitement when he heard of the promotion, put his spoon down and moved his chair closer to Adrian. He clasped both hands over Adrian's hand on the table and said in a soothing tone, 'Adrian, old chap. I must ask you, nay plead, with all my heart, for you to forgive me – it's this damned new paper, The Red Flag, that I was instrumental in publishing for Moscow, that's been taking up all my time and leaving precious little for you. But I have now completed my task and that's why I invited you this evening – to celebrate. Regarding the situation with Yousef it is simply that I hired him from an agency to help me prepare and serve dinner for you this evening. He means nothing to me. I only acted the way I did on the spur of the moment to make you jealous – to see if you still cared...'

'Oh! Guy, I do care,' interrupted Adrian, 'You did have me worried for I do so love you. I do. Please may I stay over?'

'Of course, I never had any other intention than to ask you,' he lied smoothly.

'And Yousef will be gone by....'

'Just as soon as the dishes are done, dahling. As you must be aware, Adrian, relationships go through rough patches from time to time and when ours does, where do I go to recharge my batteries?'

'Berlin. And it certainly always works for us,' was the coy reply.

'It certainly does. No persecution over there. Civilised people,

Berliners. So what I suggest is that you accept the Berlin offer and I rent an apartment in Berlin and you can set up home there for us. 'How does that sound to you, dahling?'

'Lovely, Guy, but you'll be here in London....'

'Not at the weekends I won't. We publish Fridays.'

'How do I know you will be faithful? I mean after tonight....'

'Or I you... Adrian. However, we are fortunate, for what we have is called trust – trust Adrian. Believe in it!' he lied sanctimoniously. As indeed he had lied throughout since hearing of Adrian's Berlin offer. Lies being his tradecraft he didn't hesitate to tell another, 'Enough of these suspicions. Come, dahling,....' he purred, taking Adrian by the hand, '...Let me show you my new monogrammed sheets.'

Having long ago tired of Adrian he would rather have been leading Yousef upstairs, but unfortunately work took precedence.

***

Margate Kent 4th April 1935

Trevor Lomas was totally relaxed with the world. Seven days leave from the Berlin Embassy, fishing off the coast of Margate, his hometown, was his idea of heaven. He lay back in his rowing boat, waved to a nearby motor launch that had just dropped anchor, and with oars withdrawn from the water, fishing rod dangling over the side and a bottle of brown ale to his lips, he wondered if life could get any better – when suddenly it did. He felt a jerk on the line. He picked up the rod to reel in his catch but there was resistance. It must be a "big 'un" he thought. Another jerk on the line. He reeled-in again, the reeling taking him near the gunwale of the boat. He peered over the gunwale for sight of his catch. Another sudden violent jerk caught him off balance and he tipped over the gunwale. Being a good swimmer he did not foresee a problem provided he had not caught a Great White shark he amusingly thought. As he broke the surface of the water with his fall a dark sinister figure clad in what appeared to be a black one piece rubber suit with a mouthpiece blowing bubbles, face mask, and webbed feet, appeared from under the boat. Trevor was so shocked that he gulped. Not the best underwater reaction for a soon to be drowned man. The nearby motor launch upped anchor.

***
Berlin Embassy 18th April 1935

The uniformed Sergeant-at-Arms bade the attractive silver haired lady, 'Good night, Miss Sanderson,' as she signed herself out of the building. 'Bit foggy out there. Take care crossing the road for your bus.'

She worked in the Embassy in the guise of head receptionist. James' "eyes and ears" as he referred to her. 'Thank you, Adrian, I will.'

It was definitely her intention to "take care" for she had in her possession a key which James had stressed was of the utmost importance to the department – SIS(6) – the diplomatic bag key. This key was usually handed over by the outgoing attaché to the new incumbent. However, she had been asked to care for the key since there was to be a two week delay between the present attaché, Sixsmith, who had left today and the new man, Rutherford, arriving. This situation arose due to James sending Rutherford to a specialist diving course in Italy.

The typing pool gossip was that the new attaché, Scott Rutherford, was a devilish handsome chap. She had once known a handsome chap in Berlin. She had worked with him for three years following the end of the war, interrogating suspected German war criminals. He had been a placement by Winston Churchill in Military Intelligence, a raw but extremely intelligent recruit. She had taught him all she knew about the skill of interrogating techniques, a skill she had perfected with SIS(6) during the war. She also fell in love with him. Unfortunately, the love had never quite been fully reciprocated. She knew his love was there, but needed time to be nurtured. The nurturing was regrettably never to be, for on her unselfish recommendation he was recruited into SIS(6) and that was the last she ever saw of him. She did, however, watch his climb to the pinnacle of the Service – a position, Sir James McKay might not have achieved had he been married. She had lingered in Berlin, eventually marrying a Jewish doctor and became Mrs Goldstein. Life was good until a heart attack took him. With his death and Hitler's anti-Semitic movement gaining momentum she reverted to her maiden name – Sylvia Sanderson.

By good fortune she had met Sir James six months ago in Berlin. He still looked as handsome as ever. They had dined and he had cupped her hands in his and reminisced. She had invited him home. It had been such bliss to find the feelings she had for him still lingered. He offered her the position as receptionist in the Embassy. She had accepted, knowing that with the rise of Hitler he would visit the Embassy regularly. He did. It was heaven being with him again. With this cherished thought she clutched the bag holding the precious key to her bosom as she prepared to step off the pavement at her usual crossing point. She peered into the gloom and deemed it safe to cross. Half way across a swirl of fog descended impairing her vision. From out of the murk she was suddenly aware of two round yellow glows piercing the fog. They were becoming larger. They were she realised, too late, the headlights of a fast moving automobile. She was struck on the hip, and flung high over the bonnet to land legs akimbo in the gutter. As she lay on the cold hard road, stricken, the last vestige of life seeping from her wrecked body her eyes flicked momentarily open. Into her hazed vision floated her handbag lying in the gutter alongside her. The handbag contained the key she must protect for James. With a supreme effort she reached her arm towards the bag. That was the last thing she was ever aware of in life as a heavy black boot smashed down on her delicate wrist followed by a blow to the back of the skull. She felt no pain, only that of failing James. She drifted into the black void that beckoned.

Chapter 5

SIS6 Whitehall London 1st May 1935
    Elizabeth Court, the forty five year old, widowed, extremely attractive personal secretary to Sir James McKay, head of SIS(6) sat at her desk rereading notes left by Sir James whilst awaiting the arrival of the latest recruit to "The Service" – Scott Rutherford. The notes were to help her instruct Rutherford of his maiden duties when he eventually arrived at the Berlin Embassy, for he was running two weeks behind schedule due to a specialist training course in Italy. His duties were ostensibly that of a trade attaché, a negotiator for British companies hoping to do business in Germany. It was, however, a euphemism in Embassies throughout the world for an intelligence agent – a spy. His three month tour of duty was considered safe and non-confrontational for a "first timer", in that it only involved the role of "fetch and carry" of information to and from agents already in place.
    Sir James had stressed to her the importance that she in turn must stress to Rutherford about the key for the diplomatic bag – commonly referred to as the "dip-bag" key. It had been Sir James intention for the Embassy receptionist, a SIS(6) employee Sylvia Sanderson, to hand the key for the SIS(6) "dip-bag" to Rutherford but due to her unfortunate accidental death by a hit-and-run driver this had had to be amended. On Sir James instructions, Sylvia had been replaced three days after her death by agent, Yvonne Rencoule, who would be acting under the same instructions as Sylvia – taking responsibility for handing the "dip-bag" key over to Rutherford.
    Elizabeth recalled that Sir James had been unusually upset on hearing about the death of Sylvia and even more upset when he realised he would miss her funeral due to a prearranged meeting with the Joint-Heads-of-Staff. She knew the reason for his grieving. Sylvia had told her years ago about her past secret liaison with the then, Jimmy McKay, which had come to nothing due to his fear of marriage getting in the way of his ambitious climb up the SIS(6) ladder. And of the ironic and sad fact that Sylvia had set him on the

first rung of that particular ladder.

Regarding Rutherford's general duties – first, he would collect the key for the SIS "dip-bag" from Yvonne. He would then check his drop-point daily for a despatch from Sir James' deep cover agent "Maryhill" by buying a newspaper every morning on his way to the Embassy. This drop-point was a newsagent's shop owned by a German Jew, code name, "Lambhill". Should there be a despatch he would then translate and encrypt the message before sending to London. These London bound despatches were to be locked in the SIS "dip-bag" by Rutherford, and only Rutherford, before the bag was handed to the Sergeant-at-Arms(SAA) for inclusion in the Embassy "dip-bag" for onward transport by courier to the Foreign Office. SIS despatches from London would arrive by "dip-bag" to the Ambassador's secretary by courier for Rutherford to unlock, decipher, translate and forward to "Maryhill" via "Lambhill".

Elizabeth knew this inclusion of the SIS "dip-bag" into the main Embassy bag to be an on-going bone of contention between Sir James and the Foreign Office. Finally, Sir James' third agent code named "Partickhill" posted his messages to the Embassy, marked for the attention of "The Trade Attaché", for similar translation and encryption. She considered these duties mundane for one with such an interesting file, so putting Sir James' notes down on her desk, which she had been ticking off to make sure she had covered everything, she lifted Rutherford's file to refresh her memory. With time to spare she reread: Rutherford was aged thirty two, single, lived with his parents in Portsmouth when not on active service. He had been an outstanding student at the local grammar school resulting in a scholarship to Cambridge University where he gained a BSC (Hons). Spoke three foreign languages fluently: German, French and Spanish with passable Italian and Russian. He had excelled in sports gaining his "blues" for rugby (his preference being football – an ardent Arsenal supporter), and a member of a victorious boat race crew against Oxford. He had also found time to become a Bisley marksman. She was, however, surprised to find that with his active sports background he had a penchant for acting – he had been a member of the Cambridge Dramatic Club. Having met him she could imagine him as the dashing hero. His father was a naval officer and he had been expected to follow in his father's footsteps but elected instead to join the Royal Marines where he swiftly rose to the rank of Captain. His exceptional prowess was brought to the attention of Sir James who took him under his wing and had him transferred to SIS training school where he distinguished himself, with the result that she was about to hand him his first posting – Trade Attaché, Berlin Embassy. What the file didn't tell you, mused Elizabeth, with hand on chin, elbow on desk, and a far-away look was that, having met Rutherford several times with Sir James at SIS training school, he was the most ruggedly handsome man she had ever met. If she was only twenty years younger she thought dreamily, immediately chastising herself for such a wicked thought, considering it a betrayal of her feelings for Sir James. Two years ago Sir James had inherited her on the retirement of his predecessor, Sir John Holland, who had been her chief for fifteen happy years. She had, on Sir John's retirement, been a war widow of some seventeen years standing with no thoughts of anyone else during those empty years until Sir James arrived on the scene. She fell deeply in love with him – a love as yet unfulfilled. But she was working on that.

The six foot, immaculately tailored, Olympian athletic figure of Scott Rutherford strode through the general office towards Elizabeth's inner sanctum. The hubbub of office noise dwindled to nothing as typewriters fell silent and heads turned to follow him. Elizabeth was brought out of her reverie by the sudden silence of the usual background typewriter cacophony from the other side of the door. The silence was broken by a sharp knock on the door. At her beckoning Scott entered and flashed a brilliant white, even-toothed smile, 'Buongiorno, Elizabeth, sei bellissima come sempre.' She felt herself blush, for she knew enough Italian to know he had bid her, "Good morning, Elizabeth, you look as lovely as ever."

Recovering from her schoolgirl blushing fit she put on her strict office persona for dealing with upstart agents. She lectured Rutherford on his duties and the responsibilities expected of him as a representative of His Majesty's Government overseas, handed him his travel warrant for tomorrow's early morning RAF flight from Northholt aerodrome and advised him that from now he would be referred to in communiqués by his code name – "Jordanhill". Finally she withdrew from one of her desk drawers a copy of Charles Dickens' "Tale of Two Cities" and handed it to him with the words, 'Your copy of the cryptic code book. Your first despatch starts from page forty seven. You can expect a despatch from "Maryhill" inside a copy of the morning edition of the Berliner Tageblatt. It will be at your contact tomorrow at 8-00am. And don't make a mess of it, for Sir James is expecting an important reply. I wish you well with, "Operation Glasgow" – "Op-G". It has run successfully for fourteen years without a hitch.' She glowered threateningly at him and for good measure added, 'And don't use the phone to report in. "Dip-bag" or arranged letter drop only. Sir James will only permit phone calls for dire emergencies. They can be tapped.'

'And what is deemed a dire emergency?'

'Any real threat to the realm – he doesn't trust phones.'

Scott had sat listening, thoroughly engrossed throughout, his intelligent eyes taking everything said on board, especially the part about "Operation Glasgow" running without a hitch for fourteen years. He felt this carried the threat of "God help any poor sod that causes it to do otherwise". The only thing that struck him as odd was that agent "Partickhill" had chosen to mail his despatches to the Embassy when he should have known that all mail to Embassies was subject to scrutiny from the Nazis. However, with the operation having run for fourteen successful years he elected to say nothing. So when she finished, he flashed his smile, rose, took her hand over the desk and kissed it, wishing her, 'Arrivederchi, fino a quando non ci incontreremo di nuovo – sei un angelo.' And she knowing it to mean, "Goodbye, until we meet again – you are truly an angel," blushed again. She dreaded what he was going to say to her in German when he finished his tour of duty there.

As he very slowly let go of her hand she pointed to another door. 'Kindly use this door in future. It leads to the main corridor you entered from and offers more privacy. The least number of eyes that see you the better.' And it also offers less of a distraction to my girls she jealously reasoned; immediately chastising herself once again for such a betrayal of her feelings for Sir James. He blew her a kiss as he departed. She suspected he was going to be a real handful.

Chapter 6

British Embassy Willhelmstrasse Berlin 2nd May 1935
Scott Rutherford, had caught the 6-00am RAF Diplomatic flight from Northholt aerodrome, near London, to Berlin's Tempelhof Airport where he was met by a British Embassy chauffeur, who introduced himself as Syd. He was then driven to the Embassy to meet the Ambassador's secretary Beatrice, a sour faced harridan who apologised for the absence of the Ambassador, Sir Eric Phillips who had been summoned to London without warning. *"This made it twice in two weeks due to the antics of that damned little sod, Hitler"* she had in bad temper tut-tutted. She then grudgingly took him to meet Yvonne Rencoule the new receptionist who she knew to have a key for him in her possession. The introductions completed, she discretely withdrew to leave the two intelligence agents alone. On reflection, she thought it better that she had had the job of introducing the agents, for Sir Eric abhorred the thought of them working from his Embassy. He considered them spivs, thugs, and troublemakers, who brought disrepute to the name of "Trade Attaché" and to the good name of his Embassy.

Yvonne, the twenty seven year old product of an English mother and a French father, was an Oxford University graduate, unmarried, and a shapely auburn-haired beauty. She was explaining to Scott in perfect English with just a hint of a French accent, 'I've been told by Sir James to reveal to you that I am a fellow SIS agent. I'm here to replace the receptionist Sylvia Sand…,'

Scott, holding up a hand, whilst melting into her liquid gold eyes, politely interrupted her, 'To save you breath, Yvonne, I was told by Elizabeth why you're here. What I would like to know is, how long have you been here?'

Her intelligent face screwed up in thought before answering, 'Eleven days ago. Three days after Sylvia's tragic accident.'

Scott nodded his understanding. 'And do you have a key for me?'

'Yes. And mail too.' She handed him a small, chubby, well worn, brass cabinet-type key and a plain brown envelope.

Scott took the offered items from her. 'Thank you. And how did you get the key?'

'When Sir James heard of the accident he contacted the Berlin police to find out if a key had been found on Sylvia. They confirmed her bag, with keys, had been found at the scene of the accident. And with your not having arrived at the Embassy, he arranged for internal security – the Sergeant-at-Arms – to uplift the bag and give me the key.'

Scott once again nodded his understanding. 'Now Yvonne, I'm informed we have a third agent in Berlin, "Partickhill", who, unbelievably, delivers his despatches to Sir James by mail. Any idea who he is?'

'No. But you're holding one of his despatches.' Scott looked closely at the plain brown envelope. It was unstamped and handwritten in an almost unintelligible hand, like a chicken with ink on its claws, marked for the attention of "The Trade Attaché". 'It's the first despatch I've received for you since I've been here. It was delivered by the postman direct to my desk who introduced himself as Laszlo – a thoroughly objectionable character.'

Scott, having arrived in Berlin on the flight that one hour later became the noon day diplomatic flight back to London, and now long since departed, realised that with its departure there was no way he could encrypt and forward the despatch Yvonne had given him to London today. With this as a fait accompli, and having not eaten since 4-00am, he asked Yvonne, 'Where can I get lunch?' hoping that she would join him,

'I find the staff restaurant adequate and with the weather fine, you could take your meal into the Embassy gardens. I'm sure you would enjoy that. Unfortunately, I'm busy,' she lied. 'Otherwise, I would have joined you.' She had actually taken an instant liking to him and regretted the lie, but with Sir James warning the agents about getting "too familiar with each other" still ringing in her ears from her last mission in France, where a casual dalliance just about ruined the mission and finished her career, she thought better of the offer.

As Scott turned towards the restaurant with her final words, "otherwise I would have joined you" reverberating in his ears he felt all was not lost for the future, but with Sir James warning about agents getting "too familiar with each other" uppermost in his thoughts from training school, he thought it perhaps for the best that she couldn't join him for lunch – for she certainly was worth "getting too familiar" with.

The restaurant obviously catered for the British palate with steak and kidney pie on offer as the chef's special and to back it up a choice of cottage pie and fish and chips. However, he settled for roast beef sandwiches and electing to take Yvonne's advice headed for the gardens. He found a quiet secluded corner with an empty garden seat. His sandwiches finished he lay back in the seat with his legs fully extended and crossed at the ankles to relax with an after lunch doze in the sunshine. A polite cough a few minutes later brought him awake. His legs were blocking the passage of the gardener and his wheelbarrow. The old, weather gnarled, gent, with an apology offered in German, passed Scott's pulled back feet then set about dead-heading flowers in a bed local to his seat. Scott, who was a keen gardener when at home, rose from his seat to congratulate the old man on a splendid spring display. He informed him, in German, that he was the new trade attaché. They shook hands, the gardener confirming his name as Otto. He had no English, for which he apologised, and was delighted to hold a gardening conversation in German with the fluent Scott. After arguing the merits of sowing sweet pea seeds in the spring or autumn, Otto invited him back to his shed for schnapps to round off his delicious sandwiches. When they arrived at the shed, actually a brick outbuilding built into the high rear wall of the Embassy, Scott noticed an old motor cycle propped against a wall. During the course of the ensuing conversation Scott gathered that Otto was a German Jew; had fought for the Kaiser in the war, and was now in fear of Hitler's persecution of the Jews. Scott told him he was in the right place – the British Embassy. Otto reminded him that that was all well and good but he still had to travel home on his motor cycle. Scott then excused himself and on opening the door noticed a heavy timber gate set in the boundary wall. Otto, noticing him looking at the door said he had permission from the Ambassador to use it as his access. On the days he worked the Marine guard opened the door to allow him entry and bolted it after he departed. Scott nodded his understanding as they shook hands on parting company. Scott promised to come and see him again before briskly striding off towards the main building to translate and encrypt the letter that Yvonne had handed to him. It would catch tomorrow's noon day flight to London.

Once inside the Embassy, he hurried up the marble steps to his office, found his copy of "A Tale of Two Cities" and opened it at page forty seven as per Elizabeth's instruction to enable encryption of "Partickhill's" despatch. It was written in German in the same awful hand as the envelope and warned of an unspecified danger to "Lambhill" whom he decided he would warn later in the day. He then took the opportunity to look around his office. It was actually a suite of rooms located to the front of the building and overlooking Willhelmstrasse. The main room, his office, was spacious with high ornate ceilings as was befitting a former palace. The room was light and airy with long elegant floor to ceiling windows. Leading off was a rest room and a kitchen. The kitchen was fully equipped with cupboards full of emergency tinned rations, cooker and a fridge. The rest room had a divan bed and according to the SIS manual the linen was changed once per week. The manual further informed him this room was for emergencies only. His mind roaming, he wondered if he could classify Yvonne as an emergency. Putting his licentious thoughts aside he discovered that one of the emergencies listed in the manual was that of "fatigued agents". Having been on the go since 4-00am, he felt justified to class himself as fatigued and lay on the bed to read his encryption book. He had never read Dickens', "A Tale of Two Cities". Within half an hour his head slumped and the book slowly sank onto his chest. He fell sound asleep. He woke with a start. It was dark. He fumbled for the bedside light, his watch showed it to be 5-05pm. His intended destination closed at 5-30. With a quick refreshing splash of cold water to his face and a perusal of Berlin on the wall map to locate his drop-point, which fortunately was near at hand, he then dashed downstairs and signed himself out at the SAA's office. He received a smart salute from the duty Royal Marine on the main gate and then walked at a brisk pace to his destination. When he arrived at the newsagents he glanced casually through the window – from a previous viewed photograph he recognised the person behind the counter as "Lambhill". He entered the empty shop and bought the evening paper. At the transaction he said to the proprietor, very self-consciously, expecting to be treated as a mad man, 'The *lambs* are gambolling in the *hills* of Glasgow.'

To his surprise the proprietor, a tall blond male of Scandanavian features, replied seriously, 'Yes. For there are many hills in Glasgow.' Scott, acknowledged this to be the correct reply with a nod of the head. "Lambhill", then said congenially, 'Welcome. My name is Michael.'

'And my name is Jordan Hill,' replied Scott, extending his hand. They shook hands warmly. 'I should warn you, Michael, that one of our other agents has picked up news of a threat against you.'

This information was met with a heavy resigned sigh from Michael. 'Such threats happen every day to us Berlin Jews.... I can tell by the look on your face you are surprised I am one, yes?'

'I have to admit – yes. You look...'

'Aryan.' Michael finished for him. 'That is why I have survived Hitler's many purges. However, many thanks for the warning. I will be on my guard. I will keep a copy of the Berliner Tageblatt aside for you every morning.'

Scott elected not to inform Michael that he was expecting a despatch in tomorrow's Tageblatt as he bid Michael good night before finding a bistro nearby for an evening meal. Meal finished, he walked back to the Embassy and as pre-arranged phoned Syd to take him to his new lodgings, run by a former Embassy staffer now settled in Berlin.

On the way to his lodgings he had Syd drive past Michael's newsagents. It was closed and showed no signs of any of the threatened trouble in "Partickhill's" despatch.

At the same time as Scott was carrying out his drop-point reconnoitre a Fleet Air Arm flying-boat carrying Sir James from Gibraltar was setting down gently on the water of Lee-on-Solent.

Chapter 7

British Embassy Willhemstrasse Berlin 3rdMay 1935
   Scott Rutherford left his lodgings on the banks of the River Spree in the Berlin Fredericshain district and set off for the British Embassy. He was starting his first full operational day with the Secret Intelligence Service. With the early spring morning being dry and clear, he had elected to walk to the Embassy. On the way he would call at his newsagent contact where he would buy a copy of the Berliner Tageblatt newspaper. According to his instructions, before he left London, today was the day he would find slipped between the pages of the Tageblatt a despatch from their Berlin agent, "Mary Hill". He did not know who "Mary Hill" was for his brief was only to pick up or deliver despatches to "Lambhill" or receive and send despatches from "Partickhill" at the Embassy. He reckoned he had a very boring three months of "fetch and carry" ahead of him. Hopefully, his next posting would give him the adventure he craved. However......
   As Scott neared his newsagent contact he witnessed a large crowd gathered around the shop front. He quickened his pace suspecting a happening. He wasn't wrong. Broken glass shards scattered the pavement. The window and door were roughly boarded-up and the stench of charred wood permeated the morning air. The boarded-up window had been daubed in yellow paint – JUDE. He knew this to be "Jew". His senses immediately switched to alert mode. Trying to make himself inconspicuous he moved into the body of the crowd in time to witness two agents of Himmler's newly formed Nazi secret police – the Gestapo – wearing long, black leather belted overcoats (their seemingly trademark), dragging a handcuffed and distraught Michael towards a grey Mercedes saloon car with its back door already held open by another Gestapo officer. It was whilst looking at this Mercedes he spotted another grey Mercedes parked further along the road with two trilby-hatted Gestapo agents in the front seats surveying the assembled throng who were baying, "Jude – Jude" at a now tearful Michael. They were looking for somebody.

How or why, he didn't know but an inner sixth sense alerted him to the fact that that somebody could be him. He averted his gaze quickly as one of the "leather coats" in the front seat stared towards him. Scott slipped away from the crowd and hoping to allay any suspicion he started to look for another newsagent. As he walked he used his shop window surveillance tradecraft. It paid off. Out the corner of his eye he caught the reflection in a window of a shadow – a follower. It was one of the "leather coats". He suddenly realised he had his first decision to make. He could let his shadow catch up with him and disable him by hand, temporarily or permanently, as he had been trained. However, possibly fortunately for his stalker, he spotted a newsagent and bought a newspaper and then found a café, ordered coffee, and started to read his paper. The headline proclaimed: One Hundred And Sixty Jews Flee City. He casually read the paper, endeavouring to give the impression to his follower of nonchalance as though the fire damage to his regular newsagent was a trivial irrelevance. It certainly wasn't trivial – it was a catastrophe. He had been in Berlin less than twenty four hours and it looked like "Operation Glasgow" was blown and with it his future as a SIS agent.

Whilst sipping his coffee, his mind was working overtime: Had Michael talked and the Gestapo found "Mary Hill's" despatch inside the Tageblatt? Or – had it perished in the fire? Or – not even been delivered. Or – it might have nothing to do with the despatch and just been a vindictive anti-Semitic purge by the Gestapo. But how did they know Michael was Jewish? Or – was he totally over reacting? The one thing he did know was that Michael would eventually talk to the Gestapo – training school had taught him that. With the use of torture everybody did or died. No shame. So the least he could now do to lessen the damage done to the operation was to warn "Mary Hill" of the danger. He had to get a message to her as a matter of urgency. But who was she and where did she live? But what if….'

Once outside the café Scott stopped and looked at his watch – it showed 8-15am. This action gave him the opportunity to check the shop windows for his shadow. There was no sign of anybody. He then set off at his usual brisk pace for the Embassy. Being desperate to make amends for the debacle that he felt was his fault but couldn't exactly figure out why – an ember of an idea had formed over his coffee and croissant. Five minutes later he reached the Embassy. A grey Mercedes saloon was parked at the kerb opposite the main gate – in the front seat was "leather coat" and his colleague.

He showed his security pass to the Royal Marine guard who guardedly pointing across the road whispered, 'See you have company, sir.' When Scott enquired how long they had been there he was informed, 'A good ten minutes, sir.' They hadn't followed him – they had known where to go.

He walked briskly through the palatial foyer of the former Palais Strausberg and sprinted up the marble stairs two at a time, his plan finalised. When he entered his office he went straight to the window to view the Mercedes. "Leather coat" wound down his window and gave a mock slashing motion with his forefinger across his throat. He was conveying a message – you've been rumbled – the game's up. Scott, smiled and gave him a wave then the finger. He knew they were taunting him, but the unanswered questions remained. How had they known to look for him at Michael's and why after fourteen years? What had he done wrong? These questions would have to keep until he tried to resolve the problem of "Mary Hill".

Scott made himself lemon tea and sat back in the buttoned leather high wing Victorian chair to mull things over. In his theorising "Partickhill" was the catalyst. He gathered from what Yvonne had told him yesterday that the postman, Laszlo, delivered "Partickhill's" despatch to her direct after signing-in at the SAA. For obvious security reasons he could not believe that Sir James would allow anybody other than his appointed agent to handle his despatch to the "Trade Attaché" – therefore the postman had to be "Partickhill". He needed one final proof and it lay downstairs with Yvonne. But before this he had to report to Sir James of the downfall of "Operation Glasgow". He suspected it would be his first and last report as an SIS agent. He didn't relish the task as he wrote and encrypted the report. However, he decided to leave it unfinished until he had had a word with Laszlo. After locking the unfinished despatch in the safe and finishing his lemon tea he ran downstairs to meet Yvonne.

Yvonne had just arrived at her desk behind the reception counter when the postman, Laszlo, knocked an envelope edge-on to the counter to attract her attention. As she looked up he dropped the envelope onto the surface and in his bad English whined, 'Another special delivery for you my lovely. Two days in a row – he must love you.' She felt her skin crawl at his voice as she picked up the envelope. Ignoring him she returned to her seat. With a sickly throaty chortle he took the hint and departed. She glanced at her watch 9-05am. When she had signed the daily attendance register at the Sergeant-at-Arms desk she had noticed that Scott had been in attendance since 8-30am. Being aware that the despatch Laszlo had handed her had to be translated and encrypted by Scott for handing over to the SAA and his courier before 11-00am for onward passage to London, she thought it best she deliver it to Scott at his office to add to the one he had not been able to send yesterday. This would give her the opportunity of being alone with him. A something she suddenly found herself looking forward to. She rose from her desk, looked towards the staircase and froze. Striding towards her through the foyer in his athletic gait was Scott – and he was beckoning her out from behind the counter. She felt her heart skip a beat as she lifted the counter flap.

They sat in a secluded corner of the foyer. She handed him Laszlo's newly arrived despatch. As much as Scott hated doing it, for he would have loved to lingered with her, he dispensed with the informal niceties and got straight to the point. 'Does Laszlo sign-in to get to see you?'

Something, was on the go – she could sense Scott's adrenalin flowing. 'Yes. He has to sign the visitor's book at the SAA's.'

'*Good*. Just as I thought,' Scott replied, patting her knee and leaving his hand lingering there longer than etiquette permitted.

Yvonne did not object, asking, 'Why did you say – good?'

'Because I think the postman is.... *"Partickhill"*.'

'Never in a million years. Not that creep.'

'It figures. For a start, a postman is brilliant cover. And secondly, why would Sir James risk the use of another person to carry his despatch for him other than his own agent? All I need now is for you to compare the bloody awful writing on the envelope with Laszlo's signature in the visitors' book. Please, Yvonne. It's urgent.'

'You're barmy,' she answered, rising onto her shapely legs and sashaying towards the SAA's desk. Scott let out a lip reverberating sigh at the sight. He rose to meet her two minutes later. They stood face to face, she with a bewitching smile playing at the corners of her full lips, and he, tensed, waiting her answer. 'You're right. They match.'

Scott, tension released, grabbed her by the shoulders and kissed her on both cheeks, and as he whooped, 'Thanks, Yvonne, you've made my day,' swivelled on his heel and moved quickly towards the restaurant.

Yvonne stood, shocked, one hand caressing one of her kissed cheeks whilst, with the other, holding aloft the envelope and crying to his departing back, 'Scott…..what about this despatch. It has to be in the SAA's office by eleven for ….' Scott had disappeared towards main entrance security. Shaking her head in bewilderment, she trudged upstairs to his office with "Partickhill's" despatch to leave it on his desk. Not quite the outcome she had planned.

After stopping by the Marine Guard's security station for a key to the back gate Scott then moved speedily through the near empty restaurant into the Embassy gardens in search of his new acquaintance, Otto. A first glance around the gardens did not show him in attendance. This caused panic, for Otto and his motor cycle were essential to Scott's plan. However, a glance towards the outbuilding Otto referred to as his shed, showed the ancient, but apparently reliable, motor cycle leaning against one wall of the building. That helped ease Scott's rising panic knowing that Otto was at work, for as well as the motor cycle, he required Otto's leather helmet, gloves, jerkin and goggles.

He knocked on the shed door and entered. 'Fine morning again, Otto.'

'It is that, Herr Rutherford. This is indeed a pleasant surprise. Are you here to admit that spring sowing is best for sweet peas?' he replied wilfully.

Scott roared with laughter, and ignored the jibe. 'Otto, I have an emergency,' he lied. 'There is apparently a traffic jam on the road to Tempelhof Airport and I need to get there urgently. May I borrow your motor cycle? For the use, I will fill the tank with petrol.'

That brought a smile to Otto's gnarled features. He had to supply his own fuel and that was rationed, expensive and not always available. 'But of course, Herr Rutherford.'
'And your helmet, jerkin, goggles and gloves?'
'Yes. Please take,' answered Otto pointing to the garments and items hung up on hooks.

Otto handed him the keys to the motorcycle and took his leave to start work. This saved Scott embarrassment for he was shoulder carrying the weapon of his choice – a Walther PPK pistol. He slipped into Otto's jacket. A bit on the tight side but it would do. He then engaged the leather helmet and made good the chin-strap. Finally, he fixed the goggles in place. A look in the mirror satisfied him that even his mother wouldn't recognise him. He opened the back gate with the key gathered from the Marine Guard and pushed the ancient machine through the gate on to its stand and relocked the gate. Remounting the cycle he kick-started the ignition and took off sedately, as Otto would have done. To any Gestapo "watchers" he was trying to give the impression of Otto leaving the premises. He then took a circuitous route to shake off any followers and went looking for Laszlo the postman.

Working back from the postman's mail delivery time to the Embassy of 9-05am, Scott, had a rough idea where he might find him. With Otto claiming that the Great Depression was still in evidence and there being thieves everywhere, he placed and locked his stripped off helmet and goggles in the over wheel pannier then chained the motorcycle to a lamppost. Asking at various reception desks around the town centre which he knew to be Laszlo's postal round, he eventually recognised him coming out of the Berliner Bank thanks to Yvonne's description. He was tall with blond hair and Scandanavian looks akin to Michael's but with cruel looking facial features – the eyes in particular.

Scott approached him as if looking for his mail and enquired, 'Do you know the way to Partickhill?'

Laszlo, at first taken aback, answered, 'Sorry. I'm not from Glasgow.' That answer confirmed Scott's suspicion – he was talking to "Partickhill". 'Not here. Heidi's café is just round the corner. I will meet you there in ten minutes,' continued Laszlo, as he checked his mail at eye level as if looking for a letter. He shook his head to signify no mail.

Scott found the café, ordered coffee and sat in the rear with his back against the wall looking outwards to the pavement. Ten minutes later, as promised, the postman arrived. 'You weren't followed?' queried Scott.

'No. I wasn't. Do you think you are dealing with an idiot?' replied Laszlo, the cruel blue eyes flaring with anger. 'Now what can I do for you, Comrade Trade Attaché?'

Scott elected not to mention that he was dealing with the sort of idiot that would sign the Embassy visitors' book in the same hand as he addressed an envelope to the Trade Attaché, instead replied only to the question of what Laszlo could do for him. 'My contact has been burned down and arrested.'

'I assume you talk of the newsagent in Leipziger Strasse.'

'You know of it happening?'

'Yes. I informed you in my despatch delivered to you this morning, which you obviously have not read.' Scott cursed himself for his failure as he retrospectively visualised Yvonne holding the despatch high and shouting after him as he had fled to find Otto. Coming out of his reverie he heard Laszlo continue, 'It was done by Rohm's storm troopers. I know Hitler had Rohm killed but his brown shirt thugs can still be hired. The Gestapo have no qualms.'

'But why the newsagent?'

'Simple. He was a Jew – as I am my friend. I don't look it, no?'

'Absolutely not. I must admit to being surprised.'

'Your boss, he knows I am a Jew by birth. That one is cunning. He saw this day coming for us Jews.'

'So, the newsagent was fire bombed because he was Jewish – nothing more sinister?'

'I can say no more than – I think so. I will enquire.'

'You don't know where I can find our agent "Mary Hill" that used the newsagent?'

'No. Nor do I want to know. In fact you should not have told me about this Mary Hill.' Bugger, another mistake, reflected Scott. 'As I said before, your boss, he is the cunning one. No one will know who this Mary Hill is but him. Or maybe now, under the circumstances, the Nazis. The newsagent might have talked.' He shrugged off handed. 'Who knows? Now I ask you questions. How you know Laszlo is "Partickhill"?'

Scott explained the hand writing comparison between the envelope and the visitors' book to which Laszlo un-expectantly roared with laughter. 'Laszlo, he have bad handwriting for forty years, so why none of your agents in the Embassy want to know for the previous fourteen years who "Partickhill" is? Maybe the cunning one say to his previous lackeys not to find out real name of Partickhill and forget to tell you.' His attitude then changed as he growled, 'You don't have to be an Einstein to get connection. So for you to find connection as quickly and hope Laszlo tell you who Mary Hill is – she must be very important person, eh, Mister Trade Attaché? I have to go now – take care comrade, these are dangerous times.' He downed his schnapps then stood with both hands on the table edge. 'If you need me you can find me here most mornings at this time.' Scott found himself glancing at his watch, 9-45am. 'Or you can drop me a line in the post,' he chortled. 'Now make sure *you're* not followed comrade.' With that spiteful riposte he departed the café leaving Scott to pay for the drinks.

Scott found himself in a quandary. He had learned nothing regarding "Mary Hill" from Laszlo and had alerted him of another agent. A bad error of judgement. To complete his report to Sir James, he still didn't know if it was sabotage of the network or a Nazi purge on the Jews. And with the 11-00am deadline for the "dip-bag" approaching he mounted the motorcycle and was back at the Embassy by 10-05am. With Laszlo's despatches already telling the story of "Lambhill's" demise, coupled with his own failure to find "Mary Hill", Scott decided to rip-up his unfinished report and instead send a covering memo to Sir James together with his encryption of Laszlo's despatches. With the despatches sent, Scott didn't expect a reply until the RAF diplomatic flight arrived the following morning with the SIS "dip-bag".

This surmise proved wrong. Late afternoon he received a surprise phone call from an anonymous caller. He recognised the voice – Elizabeth. It lasted all of three angry seconds, "Home ASAP." With Elizabeth's use of the forbidden phone this meant her order did not bode well for him.

The next day, he boarded the noon day RAF flight from Tempelhof to London. During the flight he wondered if "Mary Hill" was a tall blonde, Aryan looking female like Michael and Laszlo.

Chapter 8

Office of Sir James McKay Head of (SIS6) London Friday 3rd May 1935
Sir James McKay sat back from his desk and laid aside the file he was working on with a sigh. With his reading spectacles arched across his forehead, he clasped his hands behind his neck, stretched his wounded leg to ease the pain in its knee, and sighed again. He had had an impending thought of doom all day. It wasn't as if he didn't have a choice of doom laden scenarios to choose from.

The scene emerging from Spain was one of chaos. The country was close to anarchy even though the disparate left wing forces of socialism, anarchy and communism had formed a party – The Republican Popular Front. They were pushing for a general election and his agents in place informed him they stood a good chance of winning. Should this happen he could not see the combined forces of the Nationalist Generals, the Catholic Church, the landowners and business leaders allowing that to happen. He felt a civil upheaval was inevitable.

Meanwhile, Hitler had a free rein in Europe – as he took advantage of His Majesty's Coalition Government's dithering appeasement policy. In March, Hitler had extended the size of the Army (Wermach), developed an air force (Luftwaffe) and considerably increased his allowable tonnage of naval vessels (Kreigsmarine) – all in violation of the Treaty of Versailles which had now become an irrelevance in Hitler's eyes.

Nobody in Government realised, or wanted to realise, the significance of Hitler's uncontested hegemony except his old friend Winston Churchill, who, like himself, felt a conflict against Hitler and his fellow fascist, Mussolini, was inevitable. On this assumption of war, Sir James had pin-pointed an overseas strategic defence location that he deemed vulnerable - Gibraltar. The dockyard security had already thwarted sabotage attempts. It was his alternative planning for this eventuality, the unthinkable evacuation of Gibraltar, that was contained in the file he had laid aside. To proceed further he required Churchill's assistance and would therefore get Elizabeth to make an appointment to see him in the near future.

Meditation over, he was in the throes of locking his file in the filing cabinet when his door received a louder than usual knocking and crashed open before he could answer to reveal Elizabeth. His guardian of the outer office was looking flustered and agitated and waving a sheaf of papers. In a voice quivering with panic, she wailed, 'Sir James, I have just deciphered *dreadful, dreadful* news, from the Berlin diplomatic bag.'

'Why, Liz, what's up?' he replied, trying to keep his voice calm for he had an uneasy feeling that this might be something to do with the despatch he was expecting from his principal Berlin agent "Maryhill".

'Look for yourself, Sir James,' she whispered, as with a trembling hand she handed over the papers.

A worried look crossed his face as he read first "Patickhill's" despatches. But his expression was to change to shock on reading Scott's short and to the point memo: *"Partickhill's despatches confirmed. Lambhill arrested by Gestapo. Shop fire-bombed. Operation Glasgow appears blown – Jordanhill".* He drew a deep breath. 'Thank you, Liz. Leave this with me.'

Elizabeth reluctantly withdrew, sobbing, for she had been part of "Operation Glasgow" for all the fourteen years it had been running. She also knew that Sir James was not as calm as he made out to be.

Sir James knew this day might very well come. That didn't make the shock any less. He ran through his list of options. Could it have been an intensified backlash against the Jewish population of Berlin? Possibly. The list was lengthy, but from experience he knew such happenings tended to be security lapses, which he thought in this case more likely. And high on the list was the SIS diplomatic bag which fell under the jurisdiction of the Foreign Office. This had been a thorn in Sir James flesh for some considerable time. He had canvassed the F.O. for a change in Embassy security procedure but to no avail – thanks to Sir Eustace's insistence that there had never been a security lapse. But there was one now – and now would be as good a time as any to endeavour to do something about the situation.

He looked at his watch, 5-15pm. "Sir bloody useless" would have slept off his lunch by now.

Sir James stopped at Elizabeth's desk on his way to Sir Eustace's office. She looked shaken and was still sobbing. Before she could say anything, for he sensed she was about to apologise for her out of character outburst, he said sympathetically, 'Don't worry Liz, you and I will sort this out together.'

This seemed to placate her, for she stopped sobbing and reached for her handkerchief. Eyes dried she replied firmly – 'We will that, Sir James.'

He could understand her anguish, for she had run the operation during his many sojourns overseas with success for all of its fourteen years. Truth be known, he was a little in love with her, but being aware of his own axiom regarding, "agents getting too familiar with each other", felt it would be hypocritical of him to pursue the matter especially in the light of Sylvia's tragic death. With this in mind he held back from going around the desk and putting a protective arm around her. One day perhaps. However, noting that Elizabeth had gathered herself together, he calmly continued, 'Right then Liz, would you be good enough to phone Winston and arrange a meeting for as soon as…..and get Rutherford back from Berlin on tomorrow's noon day flight, please. Meanwhile, I'm off to bend Sir useless's ear.'

Elizabeth looked surprised at that but made no comment for he usually had to be summoned before he would consider meeting the man.

Moving slowly through the myriad of oak panelled hallways, his leg giving him pain and not improving his disposition, Sir James limped into the corridor leading to his destination in time to see Effy, Sir Eustace's secretary, leaving the office. 'Effy, my dear, is Sir useless awake yet from his lunch?'

Euphemia (Effy) flapped her hand at him, 'Shame on you, Sir James. Of course he's awake but in a foul mood.'

'That makes two of us. Good night, Effy.' He entered the now empty outer office and knocked on the communicating door. Without waiting for an answer, he entered. 'Good evening, Eustace.' And with no further preamble growled, 'Time for a word.'

'Do come in, old boy. No need to knock – it's open house. Something bothering you? It's unlike you to come a calling without an invite. Now pray tell, was "Time for a word" a question, like do I have time for a word? Or do you mean that it is time for....'

Sir James, tiring of his childish ways interrupted, 'Time for a word about my diplomatic bag. What exactly is the procedure your end?'

'Nothing has changed since you last enquired – last week,' he answered sarcastically. 'Still doing splendidly the way it is, thank you.'

Sir James did of course know the procedure but he wanted to hear it from Eustace. 'Point taken. But an answer please if you don't mind.'

'Goodness me, James, am I being interrogated?' he queried, pointing at himself.

'Not as yet, Eustace. Just answer the question, please,' he replied with an edge to the voice.

That sharp rejoinder made Eustace realise that something was amiss. He blustered, 'Er, er. When I receive the bags from wherever, I open the seal and peruse the contents as I am permitted so to do. Yours being in that mumbo-jumbo code you use, I don't bother to read....'

'It's in day code so that hostile eyes can make nothing of it. You don't have the code, so what is the point of you receiving my "dip-bag"?'

Sir Eustace ignored his interruption and continued, 'I then distribute the contents to the relevant heads of *my departments*, which just happens to include SIS(6) – *you*,' he replied, staring defiantly at Sir James.

'Do you personally deliver the bag to my department?' asked Sir James innocently, trying and succeeding to upset Eustace.

'Of course not,' huffed Sir Eustace, deeply offended that anyone should think that he would do anything as menial. 'I have one of my minions deliver your pesky bag. And may I remind you, old boy, that I have "dip-bags" coming in from all parts of the Empire with never an incident. So, for the love of me, I cannot see any need for change.'

'Well, I bloody well can – and the sooner the better.'

By this time Eustace had re-gathered his arrogance. He leaned forward with his elbow on his obese stomach and with chin between the "V" of forefinger and thumb, whilst massaging his flabby jowls, to sarcastically answer, 'Rather tough luck, old boy, for until the Foreign Secretary separates your department from the Foreign Office I'm afraid you're just going to have to lump it. And further, if you insist on placing your "Trade Attachés", as you euphemistically call them, in our Embassies I can't see the point of bringing your damned "dip-bag" up again. Now I take it something's afoot with all these tiresome questions – do tell, Eustace,' he taunted.

Sir James, managing to control his rising anger glowered at him, replying, 'There's been a security breach.'

'You surely don't suspect me, old boy.'

'Not per se, Eustace. But I have to inform you that my top agent in Berlin has gone missing. Not an attaché, but a deep cover agent.'

'A tad careless of you, James, if I may say so. But I can assure you it has nothing to do with me, nor my department. Your man has possibly gone on holiday in Prussia – they tell me it's lovely this time of year, don't cha know.'

Sir James glared unbelievingly at the idiot, not believing what he had heard. Impulsively, he felt himself taking hold of his walking stick in a grip that, should he strike out, would wipe the smug smile off the fat oaf's face. With great self-control he resisted the temptation. Instead he snarled, 'No more an answer than I would expect from you.' He rose and without extending any courtesy in way of thanking Sir Eustace for his time, departed shaking with fury. He showed his frustration by taking it out on Eustace's office door.

As he witnessed his office door reverberate on its hinges, Sir Eustace, muttered to himself, 'Damn the man and his impertinence. Typical ignorant Jock bastard. Always the same when you recruit these sort from the ranks.'

Sir James, noticing that Elizabeth was not at her desk when he finally reached his office, let go his pent-up feelings by shouting, 'Does that insensitive, fucking Tory idiot ever do anything right.'

Elizabeth who had been under her desk picking up a fallen paper clip raised her head above the desk and serenely said, 'I really don't know Sir James. Shall I ask him?'

Without a word he strode into his office and slammed the door, cutting off Elizabeth's further chortled, 'Winston will be delighted to meet you for lunch at Chartwell. Date and time to be confirmed. And Rutherford will be here by early afternoon, tomorrow.'

Sir James sat at his desk, still fuming with rage, and massaging his forehead with his finger and thumb in an effort to stave off a headache. He had convinced himself that nobody as pompous an idiot as Sir Eustace could possibly be suspect in the current crisis. His massaging was having little effect. With a sigh he rose and opened his door. 'Apologies Liz for my behaviour, it's just that that bloody man makes me so furious – and gives me a headache; you don't have a headache powder, do you?'

'No need to apologise, I understand from Euphemia he can be quite unbearable,' she replied sympathetically, wanting to stretch out and take his hand for she was hopelessly in love with him. Unfortunately, he had shown no sign of reciprocation. However, with poor Sylvia dead and buried now was the time for change. To hell with his mantra of agents not getting "too familiar".

Sir James interrupted her musings with, 'That messenger chap that delivered my despatch to "Maryhill" in the Berlin Embassy; can you discretely find out what you can about him from SIS(5), please.'

Taking her first firm steps on the road to change she answered with a sigh, 'I remember him well – a Sergeant Carstairs. Lovely chap. Sought my advice about perfume for his wife. It was her birthday. Some fortunate people actually do have a life outside work.'

Sir James looked at her peculiarly. A smile playing around the corner of his mouth. 'Do they indeed. I must try it sometime – a life outside work. Now if you would be good enough Liz to go to the chemist for…'

Sir James watched her still shapely figure sashay to the coat stand. She was right with her unsubtle hint – it was time he got a life.

Chapter 9

Secret Intelligence Service Section (6) London 4th May 1935
Scott Rutherford raised his lithe, six foot, athletically honed frame from the seat of the RAF de Havilland Rapide that had just taxied to a stop on the runway at Northolt airport near London. The flight had given him time to reflect on the Berlin catastrophe he had encountered and the unacceptable result he had achieved in the fruitless task of trying to locate agent "Mary Hill". The outcome of his reflections being that the Berlin posting, which had been his first since promotion from "The Service's" training school, could possibly be his last before being returned to the parade ground at 2nd Marine Commando – Portsmouth. The prospect of giving answers to the gruff, no-nonsense Sir James McKay was one he did not relish. Not that answers mattered now that he had failed and had been humiliatingly recalled by phone to explain his actions.

Scott removed his duffel bag from the overhead rack and slung it over his shoulder and descended the ladder rolled into place by the ground crew. At the foot of the ladder he was met by Elizabeth. They hurried across the tarmac to a waiting chauffeur driven Daimler limousine carrying diplomatic plates. The chauffeur already had the rear doors open. As they settled into the plush leather back seat the limousine drove through a security gate behind the terminal building and by-passed customs.

With the glass screen between chauffeur and passengers secured, Elizabeth broke the awkward silence with a pleasant, 'Flight to your liking, Scott?'

'Yes, thank you, Elizabeth, considering what has happened,' he replied morosely, deciding not to add that the flight had been freezing and he doubted if he would ever get his circulation back.

'There, there, Scott, don't worry. Not your fault. Sir James is delighted with the way you handled the situation,' she said, whilst sympathetically patting his knee. Elizabeth thought him adorable and as well as being a chiselled chin, black wavy-haired, blue-eyed, handsome thirty-two year old with the physique of an Olympian, he was witty, thoughtful and considerate – unlike the usual ex-public school and Oxbridge crowd she was used to dealing with. She also knew his amiable demeanour in no way deterred him from being as tough, ruthless, and determined as they come. And he looked like a younger version of Sir James. That was the clincher for her.

Elizabeth's sympathetic words had done little to ease Scott's miserable mood. He knew she was acting out of character – sympathy towards agents was not her strong suit as he despairingly recalled the immortal words he had sent to Sir James – "Operation Glasgow appears blown". These words alone gave Sir James very little reason to be, as Elizabeth had quoted, "delighted at his handling of the operation". He felt he was being "soft-soaped" for the kill. With that realisation he descended into a sullen silence. Elizabeth was meanwhile reading the Daily Telegraph.

The silence was broken by Elizabeth with sports news gathered from her newspaper that Arsenal was playing at home against Derby County, to which Scott acknowledged with a nod of his head knowing she had found his support of Arsenal from his file. He wondered if she was aware of the significance of today's game: if Arsenal won – they would win the first division championship. But he doubted if she was really interested and dismissed her alleged interest as yet another ploy to put him at ease before his final humiliation at the hands of Sir James.

Shortly afterwards they turned into the gated archway of the Foreign Office quadrangle and made their way to the top floor office of Sir James. When they entered Elizabeth's ante-room office, Scott excused himself to freshen up after his long journey. Finally, fully refreshed, he presented himself before Elizabeth.

How handsome he looks she thought, hoping that Sir James, whom she knew to be still in a foul temper, would go easy on him. She gave him the thumbs-up gesture and then pressed the intercom button, 'Agent Rutherford for you, Sir James.'

'About time too,' growled a Glaswegian accent.

Elizabeth gestured with her head towards the communicating door, 'In you go, Scott. His bark's worse than his bite.'

'I'll need to take your word for that,' he laughed half-heartedly and knocked on the door. There being no welcome, he entered.

Sir James was busy writing. He looked up. No pleasantries – straight to the point. 'Not a pleasant situation. Got any ideas Rutherford?'

'Other than a purge on the Berlin Jews. No, sir.'

'NO! NO! NO! – I mean, what has happened to my agent – *"Maryhill"*. I cannot stress enough the importance "Maryhill" is to us alive,' growled Sir James tetchily. Then realising Scott was still standing, barked, 'Oh, for God's sake man, take a seat.'

Once seated, Scott, fearing Sir James was about to become apoplectic, hesitantly offered, 'All I can say in my defence, sir, was that my first thought after the fire was to warn her of the danger.'

His anger reaching new heights Sir James shouted, 'Her! Who the bloody hell is her?'

'Mary Hill, sir. Mary is a girl's name is it not?'

Sir James leaned back in his chair, fumbled with his walking stick, and stared malevolently at Scott who in panic subconsciously braced himself for an attack. However, Sir James, in a complete mood swing, laid his gold nib du Blanc fountain pen on the desk and guffawed heartily, 'It's not a she – it's a *he* – you dunderheid.'

From a list of weird Scottish vocabulary that Sir James tended to use when agitated Scott recognised "dunderheid". Translated into English he understood it to mean "thick pillock or idiot". He protested, 'But, sir – Mary …'

'Mary-*hill* – Lamb-*hill* – Partick-*hill*. Are all one word. And you are?'

'Jordan-*hill*,' Scott replied tentatively knowing he was being teased.

'And the connection is?' quizzed Sir James, with eyebrows raised.

'They are all hills.' The thought crossing his mind that that was exactly where he was about to be put out to graze.

'Aye. But they're also areas of my home town, Glasgow.'

'Of course – "Operation Glasgow". Stupid me,' replied Scott, as he banged his head with the heel of his hand.

'That's one thing you're not, is stupid, Rutherford, otherwise you would not be sitting where you are. You did the right thing drawing the problem to my attention and not go trying to solve it on your own.'

At those words Scott felt his shoulders sag. If he owned up to his abortive attempt to rescue "Maryhill" that would entail owning up to his failure to seek permission to contact a deep penetration agent – a bad error of judgement – but worse, he had disclosed to Laszlo the existence of a further agent. His mind was in turmoil at the thought of having to expose this folly, especially just when Sir James had calmed down.

Decision time came instantly as Sir James demanded, 'Tell me all. Every last detail. No matter how trivial – I want to hear it.'

Scott, chose to disclose all as he had nothing to lose since he was convinced he was about to be removed from "The Service". He then carefully explained the situation fully – from his finding out that Laszlo was "Partickhill" to his disclosure of the existence of "Mary Hill" to Laszlo. Sir James listened intently, the gold du Blanc nib scribbling notes, nodded occasionally but never interrupted. When Scott finished he waited for the expected explosive outburst. It didn't happen. Instead, Sir James complemented Scott on the use of his initiative, remarking that's what he would have done himself, and finished congratulating him on a clear and concise report.

Sir James then sat with arms folded staring at Scott, deep in thought. After a short time lapse, a lapse that appeared to last an eternity to Scott, Sir James uncrossed his arms and with one hand on chin and forefinger playing with lips said, 'Hmm. Quite a mess to happen on your first mission, eh, Rutherford?' And feeling guilty that he had not foreseen the problem himself added, 'Let's see if we can sort it out together'.

With these encouraging words Scott started his defence, 'Well, Sir James, what I can't understand is how the Gestapo linked me to "Lambhill" – I mean, I hadn't even been in Berlin twenty four hours.'

'That's simple. They know our trade attaché buys his paper from "Lambhill" every morning; has done for years – routine.'

'But I had just arrived and hadn't bought the paper yet.'

Sir James leaned back from his desk and with a resigned sigh said, 'They don't just work nine to five you know, Rutherford. Since the advent of Hitler's Gestapo they follow you every moment of your waking day. *And,* the Embassy is under twenty four hour surveillance – all as you were taught at training school. Did it ever occur to you that by warning "Lambhill" you might have put him in jeopardy?'

Scott who had never given this any thought answered sheepishly, 'No sir, I didn't. How did I put him in danger?'

'By breaking routine. An evening meeting.'

'But I had to. He *was* in danger.'

Sir James sighed and shook his head. 'I regret to inform you Rutherford that amongst the surveillance fraternity there's nothing more suspicious than a break in routine – they don't like it.'

Scott realising his situation had taken a turn for the worst retaliated, 'Sorry, Sir James, but with all due respect, I cannot subscribe to that reasoning. There has to be more to it than that,' he finished emphatically. He then awaited the backlash.

There was none, for whilst Sir James was taken aback at Rutherford's sharp attitude he could, in the circumstances, understand his exasperation. He liked the lad and felt a bit annoyed with himself at his lecturing for he saw in Rutherford the same defiant resilience as his younger self. It had been most unfortunate that an inexperienced agent had been in place at the Embassy when things had started to go amiss. And all told Rutherford had handled the situation to his liking. He had not panicked and what mistakes he had made – meeting and trying to help fellow agents without consent from his control were actions of inexperience and a man of Rutherford's intellect wouldn't make them again. Apart from which he had already made his mind up that the failure of "Operation Glasgow" had had nothing to do with Rutherford. Sir James eased his conscious by telling himself that all he had been trying to convey to Rutherford was the need to be seen sticking to the mundane routines as he had been trained to do. Deviations from the mundane were acceptable, indeed encouraged, provided they were carried out subtly as Rutherford had shown with his admirable subterfuge with the gardener's motor cycle.

So with heel of hands on the desk edge he leaned forward and replied conspiratorially, 'You're quite right Rutherford, there *is* definitely more to it. It's funny it should happen on the day I was expecting a top secret, *and I mean top secret*, reply from "Maryhill".

Then there's that out-of-character taunt aimed at you at the Embassy – the Gestapo agent's throat slash with his finger. That wasn't as foolish as it seemed – that was a clever attempt intended to get an inexperienced agent to take flight and warn your contact, in this case, "Maryhill".' At this juncture Sir James decided to put Rutherford at his ease, 'Fortunately, you out-foxed them with your brilliant motor cycle ploy. Now regarding my thoughts on the guilty party: I don't think it's any of my Berlin agents, they still have too much to lose – tell you about them later. However, unfortunately, I'm convinced we have a mole – *and I don't like moles in my garden.*'

A relieved Scott queried, 'A mole, Sir James?'

'Yes. A spy in our camp. And I think it is either in the Foreign Office or the Berlin Embassy. However, we'll get back to that also for I am about to tell you something that nobody else knows apart from Elizabeth, my predecessor Sir John and Mr Churchill.'

Scott suddenly discovered he had stopped breathing as he awaited the revelation – he was being trusted.

Sir James, with forefinger and thumb gently caressing his chin, sat back in his chair and with a thoughtful look said, 'You know Rutherford it only seems like yesterday. The memory is still vivid. The year was 1921, fourteen long years ago. The war had finished three years previous but we Brits, the French and Americans were still investigating our way through a multitude of lower echelon military staff, military office workers, and civilians linked to the military. We were looking for intelligence leading to prosecutions for war atrocities, art thefts, armament black market dealings, etcetera, etcetera. With none of the personnel being high ranking officers or staffers their files had not been destroyed by the Kaiser's Generals. A bonus to us. I noticed from the files that many were of the Jewish faith. At this time Hitler was beginning to show his true colours – anti-Semitism being one of them. He wanted the future German race to be of Aryan stock. That set me thinking. What if I was to find Jews that could pass for Aryans. I found three candidates, all from Berlin, all tall, blond and well built. Hitler's ideal Aryan, even though he himself failed miserably to fit this description. From further interrogation I discovered my future informers were passing themselves off as gentiles. They were terrified that I would disclose my findings to the Nazis. I then had them by the balls...'

'You mean you were...'

'Yes. Blackmailing them into cooperation. Not particularly proud of the fact because they were, with the exception of one, Laszlo, all decent people, but any advantage you can get in battle you take. I considered it a battle then and I still do – the rise of Hitler and his henchmen. To explain. First there was Dieter, "Maryhill", studious and intense, a first class honours graduate in mathematics from Berlin's Humboldt University. He had worked as a radio operator and cypher clerk with the signals core. Aged twenty six at the time. Tall, blond and Aryan looking. Interviewed and found not guilty. Then there was Michael, "Lambhill". I plucked him out of prison where he had been awaiting execution for desertion. The poor lad was suffering from shell shock, a total neurotic wreck. His father was dead. His mother had a newsagent's shop in central Berlin local to the Embassy. He was aged thirty. Tall blond and Aryan looking. Interviewed and found not guilty. The shop I reckoned was an ideal drop-point due to its proximity to the Embassy. Finally, there was Laszlo, "Partickhill". A despatch rider, volatile, known black marketeer and suspected killer. A Russian by birth. German mother, father Russian Jew. A postman in civilian life. Now as you know, still a postman, but leader of the communist led postal workers' union. Hates fascists and knows that after the Jews the communists are next on Hitler's hit list. Age at time, twenty four. The baby of them. Tall, blond, and Aryan looking. Interviewed. Found guilty of black market armament dealing. Three years hard labour jail sentence. Churchill intervened on my behalf to have him bound over to SIS(6). Be cautious of Laszlo – he is dangerous. Evil in fact. I do not trust him. They were all young men at the time, wondering what the hell the war had been all about, as did I. And all because some ponce aristocrat of German extraction got himself murdered in Sarajevo. Personally if I had my way with aristocrats I would do....'

'What the French did to their aristos – introduce them to Madame Guillotine,' interrupted Scott.

'Er, no. Nothing quite as drastic, Rutherford. I was thinking more a reduction to the ranks of us commoners. That would be worse to them than having their heads removed.'

'Erm, quite so,' replied an embarrassed Scott. 'Tell me, Sir James – will you now still use the hold you have over your agents?'

'Good question, Rutherford. It still definitely applies to Laszlo and "Maryhill" until we find out what's happened to him but is irrelevant to poor Michael now that "Operation Glasgow" is blown. Unfortunately, he will be languishing in the basement at Prinz – Albrech Strasse – the Gestapo H.Q. – a reputedly impregnable fortress. A fact that I have no intention of disproving at present because what is of the utmost relevance is that I find, "Maryhill", real name, Professor Dieter Neuman – alive.' Scott thought, he's going to ask me to go back to Berlin to find him, but Sir James instead asked, 'Do you agree, Rutherford?'

'Yes, sir,' replied Scott, disappointed not to be asked to return to Berlin to find "Maryhill". Sir James was obviously going to use one of his more experienced agents. He was also slightly surprised at Sir James' attitude towards Michael's predicament for it made a lie of the "The Service's" noble sentiment – "We always rescue those colleagues in distress."

'Let's start with what we know. My guess is that the fire was started by Rohm's storm troopers or to be more precise, since Hitler had him shot, the Gestapo's storm troop mercenaries. Nasty man – Rohm. Met him. Raving homosexual and psychopath as were most of his lieutenants. I looked forward to personally putting a bullet in him but Hitler beat me to it.... Now, if it was a purge on the Jews, in this case, Michael, and my information within the pages of the Tageblatt newspaper went up in smoke then Dieter will forward new copy to me. But where will he forward his despatch to now that his drop-point, Michael, "Lambhill", is no longer?'

'Couldn't he use Laszlo. Your idea of using his cover as a postman was a stroke of genius, Sir James.'

Sir James coughed politely in embarrassment. 'Dieter won't. The two agents don't know each other. And, had he, I certainly wouldn't have allowed him to use Laszlo.'

'With it being top secret, and therefore a threat to the realm, won't he be allowed to phone you?'

'He doesn't know who I am other than "G". So he can't phone and he can't now use the "dip-bag", so what do we do, Rutherford?'

'Only thing I can think of is to endeavour to make personal contact,' answered Scott excitedly. 'But somebody has to find him first.'

'Exactly. And that's where you come in. I want you back in Berlin to find him. Is he still at work? If not, what's happened to him? Are we in time to save him? Or was he turned by the Nazis and feeding me misleading information? Many questions to be answered, Rutherford. Are you up for it – finish the job, eh?'

'Indeed yes, Sir James,' replied an ecstatic Scott.

Sir James picked up a file from his desk and handed it to Scott. 'Dieter's file. Address, etcetera, etcetera. Read, memorise and return to Elizabeth. Use the conference room. Liz will bring you tea and sandwiches. He then picked up his fountain pen and with pen poised in air, growled, 'Find him for me, Rutherford – and ....'

'And, Sir James?'

'Just watch your back with Laszlo – as I've said before, he's an evil bastard.' He started writing. Scott took his leave. When the door closed behind Scott, Sir James drew another file towards him, muttering, 'Now to find the bloody mole.' He grimaced as his knee went into spasm. He lent down to his bottom drawer.

Scott, with an ear-to-ear grin in place, turned towards Elizabeth's desk after closing the office door. She was, to his surprise, standing in front of the desk smiling and clutching documents to her bosom.

'You're looking pleased with yourself, Scott.'

'You-would-not-believe it, Elizabeth, from almost being returned to the parade ground I've been asked by Sir James to find "Maryhill",' he replied ecstatically.

'Well, isn't that good news,' she replied, feeling genuinely happy for him. 'Now, you just have time to read your file in the conference room before you catch the Imperial Airways 6-30pm Berlin flight out of Croydon.' She then handed him the airline ticket she had clasped to her bosom.

He suddenly realised that in giving him the airline ticket she had to have known previously the expected outcome of the meeting. So he wagged a finger at her accusingly, 'Elizabeth, you little minx. You knew on the way here that Sir James was going to ask me to find "Maryhill", didn't you?'

She smiled. 'And I know something else you didn't know.'

'And that is?'

The smile disappeared from Elizabeth's face as she said gravely, 'Arsenal were beaten one nil by Derby County.' Scott's ecstatic mood vanished, his head slumped onto his chest. He could not believe what he heard – Arsenal beaten at home. He slowly lifted his head to find Elizabeth, with her smile returned to her face, laughingly proclaim, 'But due to other results going our way, we have won the Championship title,' she finished throwing both arms skywards.

'Elizabeth! I could kiss you.' Don't let me stop you, you gorgeous beast, was Elizabeth's guilty thought as Scott, realising that she also was a "Gunner" supporter, lifted her in the air and twirled her round with the ease of a ballet dancer and on landing, her wish granted, kissed her passionately on both cheeks then headed for the conference room.

As Elizabeth stood looking after Scott, whilst caressing her flushed cheeks, she heard a discrete cough from behind her. She turned to find Sir James standing in his open doorway. 'Looks like you've got yourself a handful there, Elizabeth.' And on his first steps towards her agenda of him getting a life he said, 'There's something I've been meaning to ask you – would you care to join me for dinner at Ferraris tonight?'

She must allow Scott to flirt with her more often, she reasoned, as she accepted the overdue dinner date. She was aware that Sir James had just broken his long standing mantra on agents' behaviour towards each other. Things were indeed looking up.

Sir James, on returning to his office sat down delighted that at last he had finally made a positive move in his tormented love life.

Scott, the file memorised and returned to a very contented looking Elizabeth was chauffeur driven to Croydon airport to catch the Imperial Airways flight to Berlin.

Chapter 10

Berlin Late Saturday 4th May 1935

The thought of a comfortable seat and an in-flight meal delighted Scott Rutherford. It was a great improvement from the cramped conditions his six foot frame usually had to endure on the RAF diplomatic flight to Northolt. At 6-30pm the Imperial Airways flight from Croydon Airport, a de Havilland DH86 bi-plane, thundered down the runway and with its four Gypsy six engines roaring at full power lifted off into the evening sky on a heading due east for Berlin.

Once airborne, Scott opened the London Evening Standard at the sport's page to read happily about Arsenal's championship triumph. The sport's pages devoured, he turned the paper to the front page news and in doing so his elbow accidentally touched the Walther PPK pistol comfortably holstered under his left arm and concealed by the immaculate tailored cut of his Saville Row jacket. Ironic, he mused, that out of the wide selection of hand guns offered to him by the Section's armourer he should have chosen the German manufactured PPK but in his opinion there was no finer weapon. The gloom laden news finished, he laid aside the paper and with the effects of the long tension-filled grilling by Sir James taking their toll he nodded off for what seemed like only moments when a hand gently shook his shoulder.

'Tempelhof Airport, Berlin, in five minutes, sir,' advised the steward.

When the flight came to rest on the tarmac Scott removed from the overhead rack his duffel bag for the second time that day. With the disembarking steps wheeled in to position he descended to be met at the foot by Syd, the Embassy chauffeur. He hoisted the duffel bag onto his shoulder, apologised to Syd for the lateness of the hour, gone eleven, and followed him to the diplomatic plated Rover. Once again, as in London, they by-passed customs and twenty minutes later turned into the Embassy gates, stopping at the gatehouse. The Marine guard, recognised Syd and waved them through. As the

Rover rolled to a stop, Scott slid out and retrieved his duffel bag from the boot. He thanked Syd, and strode towards the Embassy side entrance with the intention of continuing his interrupted sleep upstairs in his office/emergency apartment. Unfortunately, his stomach growled long and loud reminding him he had missed his in-flight meal and had not in fact eaten since Elizabeth had supplied him sandwiches in the conference room in London. Tired and with no intention of preparing supper for himself he turned in time to stop Syd from departing. Syd stopped and rolled the window down, whereupon Scott enquired if he knew of any place still open at this hour where he might get something to eat. Syd replied that he knew of and used a twenty four hour cafeteria near at hand and was about to eat there himself. If Scott liked the idea he could join him. Scott, did like the idea and got back in the car and five minutes later the Rover parked behind a dustbin lorry. As Scott eased himself from the Rover he saw a police car in front of the dustbin lorry and a road sweeper's hand cart on the pavement. These nocturnal vehicle operators, part of the workforce that makes a large city tick whilst others are asleep, were seated at the service counter eating. They greeted Syd with familiar weak wrist waves. Syd, after acknowledging their greetings, joined his fellow late night diners at the bar counter.

Scott took a stool alongside and after ordering felt the need to apologise further. 'Sorry, to be the cause of you eating at an ungodly hour, Syd.'

'Not to worry, sir, I'm used to it as you can tell by my welcome here. What with the hours the Ambassador, Sir Eric, keeps and his various visiting dignitaries an' all, it's a wonder I ever eat or sleep.'

'Doesn't your wife object?'

'Regret to say, sir, the missus passed away three long years ago an' me just retired from the Met's flying squad at the time.'

'I'm sorry to hear that, Syd. Did she enjoy Berlin when...?'

'Mavis, never saw it, sir,' Syd interrupted. 'She died in London. This job came up a year ago and I couldn't wait to get as far from London as I possibly could. An' just in case you're wondering, I'm not just Sir Eric's chauffeur – I'm also his bodyguard. Not that he needs one with an acerbic tongue like his. Have you met him?' Scott shook his head. 'No doubt you will on Monday – I'm picking him up at Tempelhof airport at 11-00am off the diplomatic flight. Smooth as silk. Hard as nails. Has to be, to stand up to Hitler and his gang of thugs.'

Syd had answered one of Scott's unanswered questions: what was a flying squad heavy doing working as a chauffeur? The food arrived. The remaining questions would keep until after he sated his hunger. A silence fell as they munched their way through onion laden German sausage baguettes, complimented with black coffee and schnapps. Finished, Scott wiped the corner of his mouth with a napkin and exclaimed, 'Delicious, Syd. Just what I needed. Now, before we go can I ask you about the workings of the Embassy on Sundays?' Looking at his watch and finding it well gone midnight, he said, 'That is, today.'

Syd informed him that the Embassy had full security at all times but only a skeletal staff of civil servants to handle emergencies and no restaurant facilities. And it was his day off. This he added as he ordered another round of schnapps. Scott further enquired about Otto. At this, Syd gave him a narrow-eyed quizzical look and answered that Otto worked part-time and did not work weekends. This was a set-back to Scott, for he had intended to use Otto's motorcycle for reconnaissance work.

Syd, observing Scott's grimace at this news about Otto, enquired, 'Can I be of help, sir?'

'Not really, Syd. I wanted to borrow Otto's motorcycle – but thanks for the offer.'

'Would that be for a bit of evasive manoeuvring to shake off the Gestapo, sir? They followed us here you know.' Scott wasn't shocked to hear this but was surprised Syd had observed them. Syd, noticing Scott's look, clarified his earlier statement. 'Well used to being followed, sir. The Ambassador, he don't half get upset about it, he do. So if you want me to help – I'm available. Being ex-flying squad, I knows how to handle a motor – an' meself. I'll lose them in jig-time.'

Scott gave this some thought. He knew Sir James would not sanction the use of a civilian, but Syd was not just any civilian. He was a former Metropolitan Police flying squad detective – the crème de la crème of the force – and, being an overseas posting, would have been thoroughly vetted for Embassy duty by SIS(6) and without his help it would be foot slogging and taxis. He made his decision. 'Provided you don't mind giving up your day off – meet me at the side door at eleven o'clock. Oh! And another thing, Syd.'

'Yes, sir?'

'The name is Scott.'

'Yes, sir,' replied Syd, happily whistling, as they left the cafeteria.

***

Berlin Embassy Sunday 5th May 1935

Eight hours later, Scott awoke to a weak spring sun glinting through a chink in the curtains. He ran hot water and soaked luxuriantly in a bath, shaved, dressed, fixed himself toast and coffee and was at the side door at the appointed hour. Syd waited, not with the Rover, but with a gleaming Austin Twelve. The morning pleasantries completed Syd, after a series of skilfully handled manoeuvres through the back streets of Berlin, declared themselves free of any followers. They then completed Scott's reconnaissance by mid-afternoon, whereupon Scott suggested Sunday dinner to Syd who declined with a sly wink, informing Scott he had made other arrangements. This gave Scott the idea of inviting Yvonne for dinner but remembering Sir James' diktat about agents getting "familiar with each other" he gave up on the idea. However, on Syd's recommendation he was dropped at the Berlin Continental Hotel, the lair of British news correspondents, reporters, businessmen, politicians and importantly, according to Syd, a hotbed of gossip. Before Syd departed, Scott enquired if he could cadge a lift in the morning whilst Syd was on his way to pick up the Ambassador at Tempelhof airport. Sensing adventure, he was more than agreeable.

As Scott approached the main entrance the liveried doorman touched the brim of his black velvet top hat then swung open the revolving door and followed Scott through to meet the maître d' who led him to an alcove table. Shortly thereafter he placed his order and with old habits dying hard, ordered Syd's recommended Sunday roast beef dinner. The thought of dining alone did not appeal to him even though the person in the next alcove was dining alone. He supposed the enforced solitude would help concentrate his observance of fellow diners. A second glance at the person in the alcove next to him brought this observance into sharp focus for he was suddenly observing a familiar face – one of the press fraternity. The familiarity stemmed from a recently circulated memo and photograph by his chief Sir James McKay. The memo had advised that the enclosed photograph of Guy Burnett – a well-known homosexual left-wing journalist, late of Trinity College Cambridge, and managing editor of the communist propaganda weekly, The Red Flag – was now the London control for soviet agents. The subject of Sir James' memo was sitting in the next alcove and smiling at Scott every time their eyes met. This eye contact made Scott feel ill at ease, a feeling soon to pass when Burnett called for his bill. With Burnett's departure Scott caught sight of his dinner approaching on a silver salver held high by the waiter as he danced his way through the tables. During Scott's demolition of the succulent cuts of beef, roast potatoes, Yorkshire pudding and fresh vegetables, he turned over in his mind tomorrow's forthcoming action based on his afternoon reconnoitre with Syd. His plan was far from the finished article. There were pitfalls galore but he had quite made his mind up to make the first move and see what the Gestapo's reaction would entail. Not much of a plan he agreed, but someone had to make the first move.

Now well fed and looking forward to tomorrow's challenge he paid his bill and was striding through the foyer when he glanced towards the cocktail bar – he dithered whither to have one for the road but noticing Burnett seated at the bar he decided otherwise. As Scott exited the revolving doors he caught sight of the rear view of a figure heading for the cocktail bar that he thought he recognised but could not instantly place. The incident was still preying on his mind as he hailed a taxi for the Embassy.

Arriving at the Embassy he set about preparing his report for Sir James regarding the sighting of Burnett for tomorrow's dip-bag using Charles Dickens' "Tale of Two Cities" for the encryption. His task completed he poured himself a whisky, transferred himself into a comfortable armchair, and continued his enjoyable reading of Dicken's classic. After a while he switched on the radio. Jack Payne was playing some of that modern music he disliked. His preference was classical. Turning the dial to find a suitable local station playing classical music he received nothing but loud static interference. He gave up after several attempts assuming a valve on the ancient Marconi wireless to be on the way out or the Gestapo making a mess of tapping the lines. He switched off, made a mug of Horlicks, oiled and checked the mechanism of his PPK pistol, ran through his far from perfect hastily-put-together plan, for improvements. None came to him. Restlessly, he peeped out the curtains to find the familiar Gestapo Mercedes sitting opposite, the glow of cigarettes evident inside. He retired for the evening with that gnawing feeling of uncertainty as to who the person was that he noticed in the revolving doors heading for the cocktail bar at the Berlin Continental Hotel.

Chapter 11

Berlin Monday 6th May 1935
   Scott had just finished adjusting his shoulder holster to check that it allowed a smooth draw action when his phone rang. It was reception to inform him that Syd was waiting at the side entrance. Scott exited the side door and as prearranged with Syd slid into the already open rear door of the Rover with his attaché case and lay horizontally along the seat. Syd, from pretending to polish the open door that hid Scott's entry, then closed the door and got behind the wheel, slipped the key into the ignition and pulled the starter. With Syd on official Embassy business, uplifting the Ambassador from Tempelhof airport, there was usually no Gestapo tailing of the Ambassadorial Rover provided Syd was seen to be alone.
   Once cleared by the gatehouse Marine guard who Scott had previously informed of the subterfuge, Syd asked, 'Where am I dropping you, sir?' Scott gave him the address of a well-known importer/exporter in the business sector of Tempelhof airport and in the process made eye contact with Syd in the rear view mirror, who observed, 'See you're tooled up. Expecting trouble are we, sir?'
   Scott, from his prone position looked at his jacket. In sliding horizontally along the seat his jacket had bunched up the buttons causing one lapel to spring outwards to expose the butt of the holstered PPK. 'Just precautionary, Syd. The import/export business can get a little rough at times.'
   'Well, as I've said before, sir, being ex-flying squad I'm no stranger to a bit of the rough stuff.'
   'Thank you for the offer Syd, I'll bear that in mind.'
   They drove in silence for a little before Syd volunteered, 'It's all right to sit up now, sir, we're not being followed.'
   'That's good to know,' replied Scott, stretching his cramped joints.
   When they reached the address Syd enquired, 'Have I to wait for you, sir?'
   'No thank you, Syd. You've the Ambassador to pick up and I

don't know when I'll be back.'

Syd's face showed his disappointment. 'Well, if you need a lift afterwards...'

'I'll contact you if needs be, Syd,' interrupted Scott anxious to be on the move. However, on opening the rear door to let himself out he clapped Syd on the shoulder, thanked him for the lift and with hand cupped to Syd's ear whispered, 'Make sure you have a full tank of petrol on my return.'

Syd's face beamed as he chortled, 'You can consider it done, sir.'

Scott did not reply but gave Syd a conspiratorial wink as the Rover moved off. He stood for a moment on the pavement looking casually around for any sign of a tail that Syd might have missed. Seeing none, he strode towards a small arcade of offices. The import/export company's entry was the first door inside the arcade's foyer. He walked past the entrance and sat at a table outside a café facing the entrance to the arcade. He ordered coffee and brandy, allowed himself ten minutes and being satisfied there was no interest in him paid the bill and exited the arcade's rear entrance. Checking for followers, he walked at a brisk pace following a circuitous route he had reconnoitred the previous day until he arrived at the industrial sector of the airport. A straight road took him past warehousing units leading into a square. On one side of the square sat a mobile coffee stall strategically placed near the employees' gate of the Berlin postal service's new sorting office. He looked at his watch: 10-30am. He ordered coffee, vile and lukewarm, and sat on a low wall to wait. He didn't have long to wait – a mail van drew up alongside other parked mail vans and out stepped Laszlo, the Embassy postman, returned from his morning deliveries. He ambled over to the stall, ordered coffee, and slowly cast his narrow slit-eyes around the milling crowd. They alighted on Scott. He showed no perceptible sign of recognition of Scott other than to nod his head towards the employees entrance of the sorting office and with coffee in hand entered the premises.

Yesterday's reconnaissance had not been in vain thought Scott as he followed Laszlo through a plate glass door set in a floor to ceiling glass wall, part of the glass and concrete modern architectural edifice of the new sorting office. They stopped at a door bearing the signage:

"Union Office".

Laszlo unlocked the door and slumped into a chair behind his desk. He then, with one leg propped on the desk, and chair leaning back at a precarious angle, lit a black Russian cigarette and coughed violently, 'Another piece of lung gone,' he growled, as he spat phlegm into a grubby handkerchief. 'You want a another coffee?' Scott declined, doubting if he would ever touch coffee again after the stall's offering. 'Good choice. The stall owner, Heinreich, he one of my men. Good man – but he make shit coffee,' he laughed. 'Now. Mister Embassy Attaché man, what can I do for you?....After all it was only Friday since we spoke and I have not had time to…..'

Scott held up his open hand towards Laszlo to interrupt him. 'I understand fully, Laszlo. But something has changed over the weekend and my chief suggested I contacted you for help,' he lied, knowing Laszlo to be the last man Sir James would ask for help.

'If I can, comrade,' Laszlo shrugged offhandedly.

'Firstly, however, my chief sends his regards. He hopes you are still devoutly reading Marx.'

Laszlo slapped his desk propped knee, and wheezed, 'The cunning one he knows everything. I like him much.'

'That's good, for he knows what you like too,' Scott replied, opening his attaché case and withdrawing a bottle of Johnnie Walker black label and two hundred black Russian cigarettes and laid them on the desk. They were immediately removed and locked in a desk drawer.

'He has good memory. Now, what can I do for you comrade?'

Scott explained in detail his requirements. Laszlo nodded his understanding throughout until he finally rose from his chair to shake Scott's hand. 'I wish you well with your plan, comrade. But be warned – if this Mary Hill is important the Gestapo swine might very well have surveillance on her. Are you armed, for I feel it could be a trap.'

Scott nodded, opened his jacket to show the holstered PPK pistol and said, 'Trap or no trap it has to be done – my chief wouldn't have it any other way. We look after our operatives,' he stated with no conviction for a guilty feeling was still gnawing at him regarding the failure of any attempt to rescue Michael; Sir James had forbidden any effort lest it compromise his main agent "Maryhill". Scott did not agree with Sir James' decision but appreciated that Michael and his likes, including himself, were but mere pawns in the overall game of espionage.

'I hope the cunning one thinks as highly of me, if the time ever comes…'

'For what you've done for him, how could it be otherwise?' lied Scott yet again.

Laszlo rose from behind the desk. 'Wait while I get you what you need.' He returned twenty minutes later with Scott's requirements.

As Scott departed the sorting office he caught sight of himself in the floor to ceiling glass panel entrance. He was clad in a postman's uniform, with mailbag slung over shoulder to give the impression of just another postman starting his duties. He thought the mailbag heavy. Moving outside, Laszlo already had the rear doors of the van open. Scott un-shouldered the heavy mailbag and threw it into the back alongside two cycles and then slipped into the passenger seat of the van. Ten minutes later they stopped. Scott recognised his surroundings – the alleyway behind Heidi's café, approximately two kilometres from his destination.

Laszlo opened the rear doors of the van and extracted the two post office cycles, pushing one towards Scott he said, 'This is the closest I can take you. From here I start my afternoon round. I warn you again, comrade, watch your back.'

Scott shrugged the warning off but asked something that had been bothering him, 'Why do you do it, Laszlo? You don't have to work, you're the union leader?'

'Who could I trust to deliver the cunning one's mail to the Embassy, other than myself? I am still in his debt. But soon maybe…' he paused, '…tell him Stalin will rise,' he laughed. He then mounted his cycle and shouted over his shoulder, 'Take care, comrade, and….' His front wheel, hitting the kerb, wobbled as he fought for control and won.

'And?'

'And – please to return the cycle to Heidi's in one piece, otherwise Laszlo have to pay post office.' With a final wave over his shoulder he set off on his afternoon round.

Scott was of the opinion that Sir James might just have got it wrong regarding Laszlo.

***

Before Scott placed his mailbag in the cycle's front pannier he inspected the contents to make sure the parcelled brick (to be used as additional weaponry) that he had requested was there. It was. Sitting on top of several old dog-eared phone directories to add bulk to the bag. He pushed off with one foot on a pedal whilst swinging the other over the saddle and started whistling. For some obscure reason, he was of the opinion that all postmen whistled on their rounds. The whistling soon stopped and the puffing began and didn't stop until he stubbornly crested the brow of the hill where he dismounted to take a breather. He made a mental note to devote more time to gym work when this was over. Fortunately, ahead of him the road took a long gentle curve downwards towards his destination. And taking heed of Laszlo's warning about the possibility of Gestapo surveillance he became extra vigilant as he turned off the road into a tree lined cul-de-sac.

For fear of being noticed by any Gestapo surveillance on Professor Neuman's apartment during yesterday's reconnoitre with Syd he had not ventured further than the turn-off for the cul-de-sac. The result being that he now found himself facing a red brick, three-storeyed apartment block at the end of the cul-de-sac set within immaculate manicured lawns. To the side of the block a gravel drive led to the residents' car park and garages. Two of the parking bays were taken with large Mercedes saloons. Nobody appeared to be in them. The locale wreaked of wealth.

Cycling to the main entrance he dismounted in front of a bank of mail boxes and scrutinised the names. Much to his satisfaction was the name he sought on the first floor: D. Neuman, Apartment 3. He had located Professor Dieter Neuman, Sir James' prized informer. Alongside each name was a bell push. He pushed the bell – no answer. He tried three more times – still no answer. His heart skipped a beat as out of the corner of his eye he saw a slight curtain movement in one of the ground floor apartments. Apartment number two – a Frau Kessler. Immediately suspecting Gestapo he undid the top button on his uniform to facilitate ease of access to his PPK.

A weak female voice answered through the intercom, 'Can I help you?'

'Parcel for Professor Neuman.'

The door was buzzed open. He entered an expensively furnished and carpeted foyer. She was peeping around the corner of her door, the security chain obviously in place. The weak voice matched the liver-spotted, scrawny hand holding the door ajar. 'I can save you a trip upstairs, young man. The professor left on Thursday morning with his dog.'

'Will he be back soon?'

'Why do you ask? You're not the usual postman,' she replied with suspicion in her voice.

'Your usual man phoned in sick and if the professor doesn't sign for the parcel he will have to go all the way to the sorting office at Tempelhof to pick it up.'

'That would be a pity. What day is it, young man?'

She's obviously a bit doddery and confused thought Scott but answered kindly as was his way with the elderly, 'Monday, Frau Kessler.'

With finger to lips she gave this some thought before answering, 'If it's Monday he should be back some-time today. He's such a lovely man. When my Po-Po was alive, she was a French poodle too, the same as Dieter's...sorry, where was I? Yes. He used to take Po-Po for a walk. Which was very kind of him because...'

Realising this reminiscing could go on at length and that there were others in the block he would like to question about the professor, he sweetly interrupted, 'I'm sure Frau Kessler the professor was one of the kindest men ever, but I'm running late with my deliveries.'

He had expected her to take the parcel and sign for it then close the door to allow him to go upstairs. Instead he heard the security chain release and she stepped out into the foyer and massaging her chin between forefinger and thumb quavered, 'Silly me. He could of course be at his sister's in Röbel.'

This turn of event brought Scott smartly to attention. 'Röbel? In the Müritz-see?'

'Oh, yes. He goes there often to bird watch. Litzl, that's his sister, is an ornithologist and lives in one of those lovely lakeside houses. I like birds. There are white-tailed eagles and Ospreys up there. Dieter said he would take me there someday soon...'

She prattled on whilst Scott tried to sort out the confusion she had injected into their conversation. Dieter's file did not show him as having a sister. Was she married or was she still a Neuman? This mattered in tracking her down in Röbel. Supposing there was no Neuman listed in the phone book. Coming out of his quandary and now anxious to pursue his findings he graciously cut her prattle short, 'Tell you what, Frau Kessler, you seem a nice honest neighbour. Could I leave the parcel with you for the professor? It would save him a long journey to Tempelhof.'

'That would be very kind of you, young man,' she agreed, stretching out her trembling hands to receive the parcel. 'My, that *is* heavy. I wonder what's in it?'

You certainly don't want to know thought Scott as he handed her the parcelled up brick from his mail bag – his back-up weapon. He bade her good morning.

As he was opening the main door to leave she said, 'And, young man, for your information I don't have dementia – I'm just a little forgetful. I'm entitled to be at ninety.'

'Never thought that for a moment, Frau Kessler,' he lied smoothly. 'By the way – what car does the professor drive?'

'A blue one.... Or is it a green one?' she answered thoughtfully, finger to lips.

Scott laughed, blew her a kiss, mounted his cycle and set off for Heidi's café to return the cycle.

***

As Scott cycled out of the cul-de-sac into the main road one of the Mercedes limousines parked outside the apartment pulled smoothly away from its parking place.

Scott, realising he had an uphill struggle ahead divested himself of the mail bag containing old directories into the nearby bushes and started his climb. To enable him to get maximum power uphill he was out of the saddle, pump-standing on the pedals, and leaning over the handlebars when unexpectedly out of the corner of his eye a large grey limousine cut across his front wheel. He lost control of the handlebars as the front wheel twisted in his hands throwing him against the rear door of the limousine. As he bounced off the door he saw the ground coming up towards him. His Royal Marine parachute training instantly kicked in as he managed to tuck his head into his shoulder blade and roll at the moment of impact. He was shaken, winded, and disorientated as two pairs of hands lifted him bodily and roughly flung him into the backseat well of the Mercedes. He ended up wedged on his back behind the passenger seat and the front edge of the bench back seat with his head against the door and legs trapped along the floor. Suddenly aware of a weight on his legs he looked up – the cause was a brutal Slavic faced, black leather coated thug sitting in the opposite corner with his feet planted firmly on Scott's legs and a Luger pistol pointed steadily at his chest – Gestapo.

Scott tried to scramble upright but had his knuckles rapped with the barrel of "Lugerman's" pistol. He blurted out, 'What the bloody hell do you think you're playing at? I'm the local postman.'

As the driver accelerated from the scene with screeching tyres, "Lugerman", who he now recognised as the Embassy watcher who had given him the slit-throat finger warning, sneered, 'And I'm Santa Claus, Englander. You're not in your Embassy car now. Now hand over your pistol – butt first.'

'Englander! Do I sound English to you? You've got the wrong man,' replied Scott indignantly, in his fluent Berlin accented German as he played for time.

With "Lugerman's" pistol still held steady on Scott's chest he fished from the inside pocket of his leather coat a photograph and laid it on the seat between them. Scott picked the photograph up – it clearly showed him receiving a salute from the Embassy Marine guard. With no further point in continuing the charade Scott, however, elected one last try, 'You do realise I have diplomatic immunity?'

'Not for spying on the Third Reich, you don't, Englander. You think you fool us with all that trade attaché nonsense...?' were the last words "Lugerman" would ever speak as the window above Scott's head erupted in a shower of glass and the back of the driver's head transposed itself onto the inside of the windscreen as a gory mess.

Using this distraction Scott withdrew his PPK and in one smooth action shot "Lugerman". The bullet on its upward trajectory from the Mercedes floor-well entered under his chin and exited through the top of his head punching a hole in the roof. The limousine then came to a juddering halt after hitting a wall. Scott's head was jerked sideways and hit the solid metal inner frame of the passenger seat. He slumped back against the door semi-conscious. A now eerie stillness permeated the scene with only the hiss of escaping steam from the smashed radiator breaking the silence. The door Scott was propped against was wrenched open and for the second time in as many minutes he was manhandled from his wedged position and once again flung bodily into the back of a vehicle, his flailing arms hitting the pedals of a bicycle. He lost consciousness. Before the van fled the scene a figure holding a lit bottle threw it into the open rear door of the Mercedes and ran. As the figure and the van departed the scene the Mercedes erupted in a ball of flame.

The next Scott was aware of was the sensation of water dribbling down his face. Through a misty haze, with a head feeling like a platoon of squaddies had kicked lumps out of it with hob nailed boots he saw a face holding a dripping wet flannel – Laszlo! 'What the hell are you doing here?' he stammered in amazement. 'You're supposed to be at work.'

'And a good day to you as well, comrade,' replied Laszlo sarcastically. 'However, to answer your question comrade – after I left you to do my postal round, I realised that if my suspicions proved correct and the Gestapo were staking out Mary Hill's apartment you were in grave danger. This I could not have on my conscious, so I returned to the sorting office to pick up Hans and Heinreich. We then drove like hell to Mary Hill's apartment in the van just in time to see the Gestapo Mercedes leave the apartments and follow you. The rest you know…'

'Not all. Who did the shooting? It was pretty damned good from a fast moving vehicle.'

'Me, from the passenger seat. I intended to take both of them out with one burst but we hit a bump in the road. Damned German inefficiency. Could have cost me my life,' he growled, 'For when I took aim again, I was in the sights of the back seat Gestapo swine's pistol and all but dead when the top of his head burst open. Good shooting, I thank you Comrade.'

'On the contrary, Laszlo, I have to thank you.'

That reply broke the tension and they both laughed long and loud. 'We good team Mister Attaché Man, eh? Two less Gestapo scum,' enthused Laszlo slapping Scott on the shoulders.

Sir James definitely has Laszlo all wrong reasoned Scott as he asked, 'What now?'

'Hans will drop us off near Templehof and we will cycle to the sorting office.'

'Cycle?' moaned Scott, 'Surely my cycle was a write-off?'

'No. When you went over the handlebars you hit the rear door of the car and the cycle ran into you – soft landing for the cycle. Fortunately, for Laszlo, no damage to post office bicycle,' he smirked.

'*You stopped and picked it up*?' Laszlo nodded. 'Oh, that's all right then – as long as the cycle's O.K – don't you worry about me...,' replied Scott sarcastically, as he rubbed the shoulder he had landed on and had since borne the brunt of his manhandling into the vehicles. He of course realised why the bike had to be recovered – with its front pannier it would have been recognised as belonging to the post office.

Ignoring Scott's moaning Laszlo continued, 'Yes, we will cycle to sorting office all as *your* original plan. Maybe you still a little concussed so I tell you why. We cannot be seen together getting out of this van. The Gestapo have informers everywhere, yes? So, Hans will drop us near the sorting office and then we will cycle separately back to the office as though we have just finished our rounds. You remember plan now?' Scott nodded. The nodding started his headache again.

The van slithered to a halt. The doors were flung open by Heinie who reached in and deposited the cycles on the dirt track and then without a word said returned to the passenger seat as the van drove off at speed. Scott and Laszlo had been dropped on a farm track. Scott could see the new glass dominated sorting office in the distance glinting in the sun. At least he didn't have far to cycle.

As Scott mounted his cycle, he sat with a supportive foot on the ground, looked at Laszlo and said, 'They had a photograph of me – they knew who I was.'

'So what? They're dead and the photograph is ashes, my friend.'

'So – they have a chief, don't they? He'll know of me.'

'Possibly. Possibly not. You'll soon know. If I was you I'd catch the next plane to London.'

'I can't. I still haven't found Mary Hill...but I have a clue given to me by one of the neighbours. There is a sister regularly visited in Röbel. Problem is I don't know if she's married, and if so her married name.'

'I will do this for you comrade. I will contact my opposite number in the Müritz-see sorting office. Please to tell Laszlo the real name of Mary Hill.'

Scott hesitated. But with the clock running he reluctantly, against Sir James' wishes, gave Laszlo the name. He then allowed him a ten minute start and followed. By the time he arrived at the sorting office, Heinreich was back in his caravan serving his "shit coffee". He parked his cycle and headed for Laszlo's office. Laszlo greeted him with the news that his colleague in Müritz-see had come up trumps and he had the information Scott required. He handed Scott a slip of paper – written on it was Professor Dieter Neuman, 89 Lakeside Drive, Röbel, and the telephone number. With refreshing toiletries completed Scott changed back into his attaché suit and bonded together by the deaths of two Gestapo thugs Laszlo and he shook hands and embraced European style.

Scott, using his evasive field craft, very carefully retraced his footsteps to the import/export company in the Templehof shopping mall. Satisfied of there being no followers he hailed a taxi for the Embassy.

***

Berlin Embassy Monday 6th May 1935

As Scott entered the marble coolness of the Embassy foyer he received a beckoning finger from Yvonne. Anxious to keep the momentum of his enquiry going, he was reluctant to procrastinate but nodded agreement to her summons. Apart from which he had a favour to ask of her.

Flicking a wayward strand of hair from her eyes, Yvonne said peevishly, 'Well, hello stranger. I haven't seen you since your rather abrupt departure on Friday. I gather you've been busy. However, whatever it is you've been up to, the Ambassador, according to his secretary Beatrice, is not best pleased with you and she says, quote: "The minute he sets foot in the Embassy he has to report to the Ambassador".' This petulant outburst had been brought about by her feeling aggrieved at his failure to keep in touch with her as his liaison and as SIS protocol demanded.

Scott not wishing to waste time answering shrugged his shoulders and said off-handed, 'Ah! Good. Sir Eric's in. That's fortunate, for I too wish to see him urgently. Meanwhile, would you be good enough to find me a map and guide for the Müritz-see area.'

'Certainly, oh master,' she replied sarcastically. She was surprised at his flippant reply showing lack of concern from the Ambassador's threat but even more surprised at her anger subsiding because of his near presence.

He then turned on his heel and with a short backward wave of the wrist departed with, 'See you later, Yvonne.' Leaving her grinding her teeth at his off-hand manner and frustration at his lack of interest in her which hurt, for he was her kind of man.

Scott, during the taxi journey to the Embassy had formed the outline of a plan for the rescue of the professor, in which the Ambassador played a major role. He took the marble stairs two at a time anxious to meet the man for the first time – Ambassador, Sir Eric Phillips – a man thought highly of by Sir James. The reason for the delayed meeting between the pair since Scott's arrival at the Embassy was due to the fact that Sir Eric had been in London for ten days discussing Hitler's recent antics with Sir Tony Simmonds, the Foreign Secretary.

At the top of the stairs he came to an ornate door. He knocked and entered a palatial ante-room reception area to be confronted with Sir Eric's sour faced harridan and personal secretary, Beatrice, who had greeted him on his arrival at the Embassy and whom, even then, he had taken an instant dislike to. She exclaimed, 'Ah! The much sought after Scarlet Pimpernel – *Mister Rutherford.*' She reached for the intercom on her desk to announce his presence. 'The *late Mister Rutherford* for you, Sir Eric.' She released the switch and said with a tinge of malice, 'Go right in, Rutherford. I hope you have your steel helmet with you.'

Scott, before entering Sir Eric's inner sanctum, and out of sight behind her back, gave Beatrice the finger. With a feeling of satisfaction he knocked on the elegantly carved door and entered. Sir Eric looked up from his writing, put his pen down and rose from his desk. He was tall, eye-to-eye through gold rimmed spectacles with Scott at six foot, a trim neat figure with a full head of black hair going grey at the temples. The pencil slim moustache on his top lip moved to suit the smile breaking out on his face as he moved forward to meet Scott with outstretched hand in readiness for a handshake. They shook hands. The grip was firm.

Sir Eric spoke first, 'Pleased to meet you Mister Rutherford. Please take a pew. I'm Eric Phillips, the Ambassador. Sorry it's taken so long for us to meet but I've been terribly busy with matters relating to that awful twerp Hitler. What a ghastly individual.'

'My pleasure, Sir Eric. I'm Scott Rutherford, your new trade attaché.'

Sir Eric heaved a forlorn sigh before saying, 'Yet another clandestine trade attaché from the Secret Service pedalling his wares from my Embassy. When will I ever be rid of the likes of you?'

Taken aback by Sir Eric's sudden outburst, Scott just smiled dumbstruck and said, 'Sorry about that, Sir Eric.'

'And so you should be, for you have plenty to be sorry about. In fairness I don't suppose I can blame you for the fire-bombing of the Jewish newsagent...or can I? One never knows with your lot.'

'Not guilty. It was the Gestapo using the late Rohm's storm troopers.'

'That's all well and good, but the use of *my* Rover without permission this morning for one of your shenanigans is just not on. Understand Mr Rutherford?'

'Yes Sir. However, I was led to believe I was entitled to use it in my position with SIS(6). Am I wrong on this issue, sir?'

Sir Eric waved him silent. 'Don't be so facetious Rutherford. If I tell you the Rover is for the sole use of the Ambassador then that is the end of the matter. You're not the first SIS agent to abuse the good nature of the Ambassador – ill manners seem to permeate throughout your Service.'

'I must protest, Sir Eric. We are taught to respect the Ambassadorship at all times.' Scott omitted to add Sir James' proviso – provided it is within reasons suitable to SIS(6).

Sir Eric waved him quiet again. With temper rising he spluttered, 'Respect the Ambassador! – what absolute humbug. My secretary informs me that you had the audacity to authorise full tanks of petrol for the gardener's motor cycle and my Rover. You have used up a month's petrol rationing in two outings. Where's the respect in that, I ask?'

The fact that Beatrice was behind these accusations came as no surprise. However, thinking Sir Eric was about to have an apoplectic fit, Scott hastily explained before the Ambassador was overcome, 'Sorry about that Sir. But to explain. Otto's, er, the gardener's motor cycle was used to help me evade surveillance on my departure from the Embassy. This was necessary to assist my on-going investigation. The other item, the full tank of petrol in the Rover, I have yet to discuss with you...'

Sir Eric, interrupting, waved an agitated finger at Scott. 'Discuss with me? You mean you are actually going to discuss something *with me*? And yet another thing, I heard on the radio that a Gestapo car was ambushed and two of their agents murdered and the car set on fire. Not that that upsets me, but it has all the hallmarks of an SIS operation stamped over it which can boomerang on the Embassy – *Me*! And just when I'm trying to keep a tight rein on Hitler.' Scott was by this time beginning to feel sorry for Hitler if all their meetings, with Sir Eric's tantrums, went like this one was going.

'Nothing to do with it, sir,' he lied and carried on, 'The chauffeur only took me to Templehof.'

'I know he took you to Templehof. Beatrice told me. I've had a severe word in his ear and told him to have nothing to do with you in future.'

'Sorry, sir. Wasn't his fault.' I take the blame entirely. Scott noted Beatrice's involvement again. She was due her comeuppance.

'Very commendable of you, Rutherford. That fits in with what

I've been hearing about you,' he said leaning back in his chair with thumbs hooked in to his waistcoat pockets. From this position he looked intensely at Scott with his penetrating blue eyes and in a complete mood swing he calmly announced, 'Now then, young man – I've just returned from the Foreign Office where Sir Tony Simmonds, our boss on high,' he stopped, looked at Scott who nodded recognition of the name and continued '...has instructed me to afford you every assistance I can – no quibbles. This was further backed by your chief, Sir James McKay, who informs me your mission is of the "*utmost importance to the nation*". Sir James I know well and respect, so when he informs me you are the right man for the job what can I say – nothing other than that I have my own reservations about one so reckless. Now assuming you do have a plan, as Sir James assures me you most certainly will have, how may I help?'

A relieved Scott answered, 'Very understanding of you, Sir Eric. I do have a plan and I *do* require your assistance.'

They were locked heads together for a further hour. With Sir Eric finally on board, Scott left the Ambassador's office happier than he had been at any time since he had formulated his plan. Sir Eric suddenly realised he had been co-opted into the Secret Intelligence Service he so despised for invariably bringing his beloved Embassy into disgrace. How Rutherford had persuaded him to be involved remained a mystery. It's a pity Rutherford wasn't a real attaché for he could be doing with a good diplomat on the payroll.

When he departed the Ambassador's office Scott headed downstairs to collect his travel information from Yvonne. This gave him time to try and fathom out the meaning of Sir Eric's "*of the most importance to the nation*", for as far as he was concerned all he was about to do was bring out an agent from behind enemy lines and even that was provided he ever found Professor Neuman. How could the rescue of a cipher clerk be of "*utmost importance to the nation*" he puzzled, biting his bottom lip.

Still puzzling, he arrived at reception where Yvonne handed him a copy of Fodor's guide to northern Germany and queried, 'What's with the interest in Müritz-see?'

'Wouldn't you like to know? I'll tell you when I get back,' he winked as he pocketed the travel guide and with a hasty, cheery wave bid her, 'Auf wiedershen.'

As he hastily departed upstairs she puckered her lips hard against her teeth and stamped her foot angrily at Scott's reply to her question, *"I'll tell you when I get back"*, for she realised with that answer she was not getting an invite to be "on mission". (SIS code for involved). She suspected that Scott's interest in Müritz-see had been linked to last Friday's confirmation of the signature in the visitor's book being that of agent "Partickhill" – Laszlo. At that point she had felt part of the investigation and had expected Scott to further involve her. However, on reflection she knew that she shouldn't have been disappointed for it was common practice in the male dominated Service to treat females as clerical assistants. But her true disappointment came from Scott – she had expected better from him. She hadn't thought of him as a male chauvinist. In temper she kicked her desk at remembering Scott's cheerily waved "Auf wiedershen".

After Scott had fled upstairs to his office, having dropped his bombshell to Yvonne, he was rightfully of the opinion that she must be thinking him a dreadful male chauvinist for excluding her from the rescue operation. He knew from her file that she had, on paper, the necessary qualifications: FAC (Fire Arm Certificate) – PTP (Permission to Terminate) and was highly proficient in unarmed combat. However, he was expecting trouble at Müritz-see and didn't feel comfortable with the thought of female back-up. He presently had a head start on the Gestapo but it was only a question of time before they found out from Professor Neuman's neighbour, Frau Kessler, of his whereabouts. There was a good chance their paths would cross. And truth be told, his conscience couldn't bear the thought of Yvonne being caught and interrogated by the Gestapo – they were a nasty gang of thugs and their interrogation techniques knew no bounds to inflicting pain. He felt comfortable with his decision to ask Syd instead, who being used to the rough and tumble of the flying squad, could look after himself. He would worry about Sir James' prohibition of the use of civilians later. He did not have time to dither.

Finally, reaching his office he poured himself a stiff whisky, lit a cigarette and ordered sandwiches from the restaurant then settled down to read Fodor's travel guide. He read that the area of Müritz-see lay eighty kilometres north of Berlin and was centred on the large eponymous named lake, the largest in Germany the guide claimed. It held abundant fish and was surrounded by forest with many species of birds and wildlife. The photographs in the guide showed the lakeside houses of historic Röbel to be with balconies, jetties and boathouses overlooking the lake. All told a real tourist attraction – ideal he thought, thinking of Yvonne, for a tryst. But unfortunately not this trip. Maybe never the way he had had to behave with her.

When Scott finished reading the guide he walked along the corridor to Sir Eric's office where he picked up a suitcase of the accoutrements he had requested from the Ambassador. Adjourning to his office he set about using his Cambridge Dramatic Club talents. After some time-consuming work, he looked at himself in a full length mirror and was satisfied with what he saw. "Now for the acid test", he murmured to himself as he retraced his steps downstairs to reception. Yvonne was sitting at her desk behind the reception counter. He kept her at distance with a hand movement indicating that she was to stay seated as he laid an envelope on the counter and said in the clipped aristocratic accent of Sir Eric, 'Met that chappie Rutherford in my office minutes ago. He told me he had a despatch for you. And since I was going to the garden I said I would deliver the message.'

'Thank you, Sir Eric,' she answered, thinking it peculiar that Scott would deliver a despatch to her via the Ambassador and equally peculiar that Sir Eric would consider doing such a menial task. However, Yvonne gave no further thought to the matter until she cast her gaze after the Ambassador who was by this time disappearing towards the gardens. She hadn't realised that Sir Eric had such an easy athletic gait for a man of his age.

With "Sir Eric's" newly acquired athletic gait disappearing from view, Yvonne opened and read the despatch from Scott. The contents informed her that he now knew the whereabouts of a Professor Neuman – the agent "Maryhill" (address and telephone number enclosed) who he intended to collect from Röbel in the Müritz-see sometime today. He went on to add that this information was of vital, repeat vital, importance to Sir James whom she was to advise, in her important role of liaison (he had stressed by underlining) if he did not return in time to catch tomorrow's noon day RAF diplomatic flight to London. The contents did not make up fully for her disappointment at not being invited to be "on mission" but partially pacified her as she did understand the need for her to act as liaison between Scott and Sir James in the event of – she could hardly bear to think the words – Scott's demise.

Scott, now satisfied that his subterfuge would work at a distance then strode through the restaurant as the ersatz "Sir Eric" to respectful nods of acknowledgment from the staff and diners into the gardens and on towards the garage to find Syd in the old stables, who he found hard at work polishing the Rover.

Syd, who had noticed "Sir Eric" approach was thinking to himself that the Ambassador's walk didn't quite look the part today, far too athletic, suddenly realised things were not as they first appeared. Taken by surprise he exclaimed, 'Cor blimey, sir, you didn't half give me a turn – I thought you was Sir Eric. Mind you, the way you was walking I thought Sir Eric had taken too many vitamin pills.'

Scott had a good chuckle at Syd's comment, replying, 'Good afternoon, Syd. Will I pass for the Ambassador?'

'At first glance, a dead ringer, sir, provided you don't walk so fast.'

Scott had borrowed Sir Eric's gold framed spectacles, his Homburg hat and Crombie overcoat. The moustache he had made from the hairs of his shaving brush and a strip of canvas and glue. He had dyed his black hair grey at the temples. When you were into amateur dramatics at Cambridge you had to be able to improvise at all times.

'I take it you are available to drive me to Röbel to pick somebody up?'

'Yes, but only as of ten minutes ago after I received a phone call from his nibs. Prior to that Sir Eric had warned me to have nothing to do with you,' he trailed off with a bemused look at Scott.

'Er, yes, quite Syd. A long story. Please don't ask. Meanwhile, apologies for getting you into bother with Sir Eric…'

'Not to worry sir. The Ambassador always has a bit of the hump when he gets back from London,' interrupted Syd. 'But he gets over it quickly.'

'Not with me he didn't,' sighed Scott, the memory of their meeting still vivid in his memory. 'However, before you commit yourself to Röbel I have to warn you that it could turn out nasty – gun nasty.'

Syd's eyes lit up. 'I'm up for that, sir. I'm bored out my tiny. Miss the "Sweeney" something rotten. There's nothing like a piece of action to keep a man alive and on his toes.'

Scott noticed the use of the euphemism "Sweeney" for the Met's flying squad but felt the epitaph "dead and in his grave" more appropriate for the evolving situation than Syd's rhetoric – but replied, 'Good man, Syd. I was hoping you would say that. Now, will you have enough petrol for the round trip?'

'It's approximately eighty kilometres, fifty miles, to Röbel. So yes, I do have enough because I filled the tank as you asked. Scott grimaced as he recalled Sir Eric's views on *that* matter. 'So when do you want us to leave, sir?'

'Whenever you like Syd. I'm ready.' Scott was wearing his soft leather jerkin with holstered PPK automatic under his Crombie overcoat.

'Suits me, sir. We'll leave as soon as I change out of my boiler suit. But just a warning before I do – we can expect to be stopped after this morning's terror attack by the communists that killed two Gestapo shits.'

'By the, *communists*?' queried a surprised Scott. 'Where did you hear that?'

'On Radio Berliner, half hour ago. Now if you'll excuse me, sir, I'll be off and change – then we'll get under way.'

Scott, massaging his jaw, considered the Radio Berliner announcement whilst Syd was changing. They were the mouthpiece of the Nazis. Not like them to give out this sort of adverse information about the Nazi party without there being an ulterior motive. After much deep thought he came up with what he considered a more than likely explanation; that Goebbels the Nazi propaganda minister who had issued the statement blaming the communists for the attack, was hoping that it would crank up the pressure on the British Coalition Government to change its policy from appeasement to that of support for the Nazi party's cause against the rise of world communism. Ironically, what Goebbels didn't know was that he was right about the communists being responsible for the attack because Laszlo, Heinie and Hans *were* all card carrying communists.

Syd arrived from changing. He was now dressed in a resplendent chauffeur's uniform of starched white shirt, black tie, and a smartly tailored wine coloured suit trimmed with black velvet with a gold braided hat to match. Very nice, but a bit posh for a possible shoot-out thought Scott, which reminded him to ask, 'In your capacity as a body guard to Sir Eric, what weapon do you carry?'

Syd opened the driver's door of the Rover, fumbled under the seat and triumphantly waved a Lee Enfield 2 revolver in the air – the type as favoured by officers in the war. 'Here we are, sir. That should stop whoever.'

'Bloody hell, Syd, we're not going elephant hunting,' Scott blurted, marvelling at the size of the revolver.

'Does the job, sir. Of that I can assure you,' replied Syd with conviction.

With those words Scott knew he had chosen wisely. 'I'm sure it does. Now, tell me about these expected road blocks.'

'Well, to start with they will be manned by the Schutzstaffel – the S.S. They're all hand-picked nasty bastards. They make the Gestapo look like Brownies on a Sunday school outing. All roads out of Berlin including secondary and farm tracks will be closed. They will be looking for all vehicles *leaving* Berlin. And on account of the present situation we will, as I've said before, *definitely* be stopped...'

'Surely not our diplomatic plated Rover?' interrupted Scott.

'Absolutely. Me and Sir Eric have been stopped many times. They take pleasure in deliberately stopping us, much to Sir Eric's chagrin. 'He's, as you would expect, fluent in German so he don't half give them a tongue lashing.' This Scott could well believe having been on the receiving end of one.

'What about the boot of the Rover?'

'*The boot*? Never. Sir Eric would not entertain that. There would be another war, god forbid, if they laid a hand on his precious Rover.

He says anyone doing that is laying their hands on British sovereign territory.'

'Good for Sir Eric.'

***

Meanwhile, back at reception during the conversation between Scott and Syd in the garage, Yvonne had been repeatedly mulling over the content of Scott's despatch. With each repeat reading she had become more and more annoyed with Scott's failure to liaise with her, especially after drawing to attention in the despatch her "important role of liaison". Why, she asked herself, hadn't he confronted her face to face about his intention before he had departed? He had made her well aware he was in charge but she had seniority and enough was enough. It was time to challenge him about his male chauvinism. She lifted the counter flap in exasperation and ascended the stairs as quickly as her tight skirt and high heels would allow. She rapped on his door violently. No answer. With a repeated rap and still no answer she withdrew a key from her purse and entered. Checking around she found no signs of Scott other than a messy table top littered with a glue bottle, the remains of a shaving brush, scissors and a piece of canvas. 'What has he been up to this time,' she sighed as she looked out the window just in time to witness the Marine guard salute the Ambassador's Rover. She continued her gaze long enough to witness Sir Eric, as was his custom, wave to the Gestapo surveillance car. She about turned and had just re-locked Scott's door when she bumped into...*Sir Eric!* Shocked she stammered pointing aimlessly at Scott's office door, 'But...but...'

'But what, young lady? You look as though you have seen a ghost.'

Knowing she would appear stupid if she said *"But I've just seen you leave the Embassy, Sir Eric"*, she recovered enough to blurt, 'But...but according to the despatch you gave me, Sir Eric, from Rutherford...' she suddenly trailed off realising she had been duped by Scott and was babbling. She didn't finish, instead deeply embarrassed, she apologised to Sir Eric and hastily headed for the stairs, cursing under her breath at the audacity of Scott confronting her as "Sir Eric" without having the decency of letting her know otherwise.

He would be laughing all the way to Müritz-see at her. Unfortunately, he wasn't the only one. Half way down the stairs she could hear Sir Eric chortling loudly to himself. With his remark about her seeing a ghost he obviously knew of the deception.

With tears welling, she sat in the ladies' toilet until she regained control of her anger. Scott's return tomorrow couldn't come quickly enough. So much for him being her kind of man.

Scott's wishful thinking of a tryst with Yvonne had just become history.

Chapter 12

Muritz-see Monday Evening 6th May 1935.

From the back seat of the Rover, Scott, pleased at his successful subterfuge on Yvonne acknowledged the Marine guard's salute as Syd departed the Embassy and turned right into Willemstrasse. This brought the Rover parallel to a parked Mercedes saloon on the opposite side of the road where as they passed Scott turned and waved to the occupants. Syd had assured him this was how Sir Eric handled his exit when the Gestapo were on surveillance or as Sir Eric was known to put it – "making a bloody nuisance of themselves". As Scott turned back he glanced up at the many windows of the Embassy frontage. He thought he saw a figure at one of them gazing out. He hoped it wasn't Sir Eric or his wife Lady Amelia for he had forbidden them to go anywhere near windows until he returned.

They had been motoring for ten minutes when they encountered their first road block and joined the patiently waiting queue. Syd knew that to try and use their diplomatic plate privilege would draw added attention to themselves, something they did not need, and would be ignored anyway. So after a further twenty minutes of witnessing vehicles being thoroughly checked, including boots being opened, drivers being frisked and documents being handed over for close scrutiny, a Scutzstaffel (SS) officer held his hand out from his side motioning them to stop. He opened the passenger door and leaned in with his knee on the leather seat. In English Syd bade him a good evening which was greeted with a grunt. He looked into the back seat where Scott had his head stuck in "The Times". Scott lowered the paper and stared at the officer noting the silver Totenkopf (skull and bones) badge on his cap before belligerently enquiring in his fluent German, 'I assume you are looking for your communist terrorists – *trooper*. Do I take it next time I meet the Fuhrer, which happens to be next week, I have to report that one of his underlings has the effrontery to suggest that the British Ambassador to Germany is a terrorist?' And as an afterthought added, 'And breached British Sovereign territory by entering my car without permission.' The head as it was quickly being withdrawn was informed, 'And I don't expect a repeat of this on my return. Understand? Otherwise...' The threat was left hanging in the air unfinished. They were immediately waved on. Once clear of the road block, Syd, who had started to snigger as the S.S officer closed the passenger door burst out in uncontrollable laughter. Between heaving shoulder sobs he apologised, 'Sorry about this, sir. But that was an absolutely brilliant take-off of Sir Eric. It was just like listening to the man himself– he would have been proud of you.'

'Why thank *thee*, Sid-*nee*,' replied a delighted Scott, taking a back seat bow like the true thespian of the Cambridge University Dramatic Club he had once been.

With the road relatively free of traffic and no further road checks they made the south end of Lake Müritz-see in less than two hours and took a left fork for their destination. Daylight had gone and a full moon shone overhead as they passed the town sign for Röbel. The main road ran parallel to the lake through the tall trees with badly sign posted roads branching off down towards the lake and these roads, from what they could pick out from the headlights, were little more than farm tracks. They worked their way slowly probing each cut-off for the street name they sought to take them to Lakeside Drive. By this time Scott had divested himself of the Crombie overcoat, spectacles and Homburg and was sitting upfront with Syd. They came across a street name obscured by tall weeds. Syd slid out from behind the wheel and fumbled under the seat for his revolver then walked round to the boot for a torch. In doing so he took the opportunity to change out of his liveried chauffeur's jacket and don an oilskin jacket with large patch pockets into which he stuffed his revolver and ammunition. He kicked flat the weeds to discover it was the road they were looking for and then returned to the car to set it in motion onto an un-surfaced tyre rutted road. In the distance they could see the moon reflecting off the lake's surface. Jolting their way down slowly they eventually came to a T-junction. The sign indicated it to be Lakeside Drive. The house numbers listed right to left. Number 89, their destination, was to the left. They turned onto a tarmacked road and were instantly aware of the dark silhouettes of large "A" frame houses each with a tree lined driveway. At the start of the driveways were mail boxes with the house numbers. They found number 89 and on Scott's instruction Syd drove past and parked in an opening in the trees. He cut the lights and as they were about to leave the car Scott tapped him on the shoulder indicating with finger to lips for silence. Closing the doors quietly they listened to the eerie silence for suspicious movement or sound – nothing but the rustle of branches in the wind and the gentle lapping of the lake on the pebbled shore. Scott signalled for them to proceed. When they reached the mailbox for number 89 they worked their way down the tree lined drive flitting from tree to tree for cover until the house came into view. There was a car parked outside an integral garage. By a shaft of moonlight breaking through the clouds Scott saw the colour of the car – blue. Frau Kessler had said the professor's car was blue or at least she thought it was. Lights were showing to the front and side of the house. Scott slipped the PPK from its holster and whispered for Syd to secrete himself behind a large girthed oak tree near to the front door and await his signal. With his drawn gun ready for action Scott worked his way down the side of the house towards the lake. As he edged himself around the corner of the house he became aware of a balcony overhead at first floor level projecting from the back of the house towards the lake. A stair led from the balcony to a jetty and a boathouse which ran under part of the upper house to join with the rear of the integral garage. A small moored cabin cruiser bobbed gently on the lapping water. He made his way stealthily towards the stairs and started to climb the hardwood treads to the balcony where he heard Wagner playing on the radio. Half way up the stairs a light voice carried to Scott. 'Dieter, supper's ready, darling', followed by Dieter's reply, 'Coming, Litzl darling,' confirming Scott was in the right house. He had found his man. With the grace of a gazelle Scott then took the remaining treads two at a time reaching the balcony in time to see the back of a tall figure enter through sliding doors, the full width of the house, into an interior throwing off flickers of dancing flame from a log fire set in a floor to ceiling stonework fireplace. From the cast flickers he saw the tall figure bend and warm his hands in front of the crackling logs then take a seat facing Scott on one of two sofas placed at right angles either side of the fire. The figure switched on the table lamp on a low marble topped coffee table between the sofas to expose a handsome blond haired Aryan looking male. A jingle of crockery alerted Scott to the entry of a pixie like female with black short hair carrying a tray. She set the tray down and gave Dieter a kiss on the forehead before taking the seat opposite.

Scott stepped through the door with gun in hand just as Dieter's hand, obscured by the sofa that Litzl was sitting on, darted towards something hidden. 'I wouldn't do that, Maryhill, if I were you,' he said menacingly in his fluent Berlin accent.

An alarmed look crossed Dieter's face as he stood with poker in hand. He had been about to stoke the logs in the fire. 'Who are you? What do you want?' he demanded.

'"Lambhill" is in Gestapo custody, Dieter. His shop was firebombed.'

'You lie,' he replied hysterically, showing shock and alarm. Litzl had now moved behind Dieter and was clutching his arm; fear showing on her face.

'I'm afraid it's true. The shop was firebombed by Rohm's thugs at the request of the Gestapo. I repeat – "Lambhill" – is no more.'

Dieter slumped down onto the sofa. 'My God, tell me it's not true,' he moaned aghast, as he washed his hands over his face in grief. Litzl then moved to sit on the arm of the sofa with a comforting arm around him. Comforted he asked, 'Who exactly are you?'

'I am Jordan Hill, an agent of "G"...' replied Scott, with the words he had been instructed by Sir James to use when he met Dieter, '...and I've come to take you to safety. Your cover is blown. The Gestapo have surveillance on your apartment.'

This was met with a gasp of astonishment from Dieter. Holding his hand over his mouth he repeated Scott's words and in perfect English whispered to himself – "G". It has been fourteen years since.....' His thoughts in the past he didn't finish, instead he asked, 'Why are the Gestapo looking for me? I have done nothing out of the ordinary. I took leave due me to do my report for "G", away from snoopers. When I finish it I will deliver it to "Lamb...."' He left it unfinished realising "Lambhill" was no more.

'Did you remove a file from work to do your report for "G"? That would have aroused suspicion.'

'Of course not. I have a photographic memory. No need for files.'

Not wishing to waste time arguing the matter, Scott stated the obvious. 'Well, there must have been a security breach somewhere.'

'Obviously,' agreed Dieter, adding 'It would then appear that we are on the same side. So, why do you still point your weapon at me?'

'My apologies. But take it slowly the next time you stoke a fire,' was Scott's joking riposte, hoping to break the tension permeating the room.

He was successful. Dieter smiled and enquired, 'How did you find me?'

'Your downstairs neighbour, Frau Kessler.'

'Old Marie,' whispered Litzl to Dieter sweetly.

'Look folks, we don't have time for this. If I found you through your neighbour, the Gestapo will too, eventually. We have to leave now…'

Suddenly there was a bark from the direction of the kitchen. 'We-hey. That is Fluff, our French poodle,' Litzl squealed in delightfully French accented English.

'To go where?' asked Dieter, returning them to the main topic.

"I intend to take you to London. We've a noon flight to catch tomorrow. Your sister can deny you were ever here. She can tell those enquiring that she hasn't heard from you recently.'

Dieter and Litzl looked at each other in surprise. Dieter then dropped his bombshell. 'Litzl is not my sister – she's my wife. I don't leave without her,' he said clasping her hand.

'Nor without Fluff,' added Litzl.

A shocked Scott, his brain in turmoil at this calamitous news replied calmly, 'Not a problem, Dieter, just a slight alteration to my plan required.' – "*My plan? What plan? I came here simply to pick up Dieter and now I'm stuck with a wife and a bloody French poodle. Fuck."*

'Don't worry Mr Hill we will follow in my car.'

'You can't – there are roadblocks all around Berlin.'

'Then how will you….'

'Diplomatic immunity,' Scott answered curtly, deliberately looking at his watch in the hope of trying to get them moving.

'But Dieter's a German citizen. He has every right to take his car.'

'German...yes. But also Jewish, and a *wanted man*,' stressed Scott.

Litzl grabbed Dieter's shoulder, 'He knows, Dieter.'

'Yes, my love, he knows. It is a crime to be German and Jewish in Hitler's Germany. But his boss will keep us safe.'

'Sorry folks, we've wasted enough time. We have to go *now*. No time to take anything with you. You'll be recompensed for everything when we get to London.'

'I'm not going without my wedding photos, jewellery and my research notes for my book *and* warm clothing,' Litzl cried adamantly.

'All right, but make it quick.' He turned to Dieter. 'But I've bad news for you, professor – you're travelling in the car boot.'

'And the dog?'

'With Litzl, in the back seat on her lap,' Scott sighed in exasperation.

Whilst Litzl fled along the hall to pick up her bits and pieces from the bedroom Dieter just stood there with a numb look realising that his privileged life as he knew it was over. However, "G" had promised him much when this day arrived. And he trusted him, for he had kept Dieter's Jewish secret from the Nazis for fourteen long years.

Scott put an arm around Dieter to usher him downstairs towards the main door where he intended to summon Syd to collect the Rover when he heard the loud retort of gunfire that he instantly recognised as Syd's revolver. He immediately pulled Dieter to the floor between the sofas, deliberately knocking the lamp off the table plunging the room into darkness. 'Stay down and don't move,' whispered Scott, as he belly crawled towards the moonlit sliding doors. With the moonlight showing no intruders on the balcony he crawled through the door and with PPK in hand headed for the corner of the house. Back to the wall he rose slowly to his feet and edged a cautious look round the corner to observe by a shaft of moonlight glinting through the trees a figure with its back to him at the far front corner of the house. The figure was down on one knee letting loose a burst of automatic fire from a machine pistol. Now worried for Syd's safety, Scott dashed down the stairs with his PPK at the ready, back along the jetty to the lakeside corner of the house. The crouched figure was out of range of his PPK and was concentrating on firing so he took the opportunity to dart from the corner of the house into the trees opposite which followed the line of the house to the main road. Ghost like he worked his way towards the crouched figure. Suddenly there was the roar of Syd's revolver again and the corner of the house above the crouched figure splintered off as the ricocheted bullet whined into the trees over Scott's head indicating, thankfully, that Syd was still alive. Scott took advantage of the diversion to make his presence known. 'Drop the pistol, friend,' he growled. "Friend" had no such intention. As Scott watched "friend's" trigger finger he saw the finger tighten and anticipated his move by flinging himself to the ground just before "friend" turned firing. Fractionally before Scott hit the grass, with "friend's" salvo scything overhead, he let go two rapid shots – the first drilled a hole in "friend's" heart, the second removed his throat. Scott leapt over the body to reach the vacated corner. With back to wall he removed a white handkerchief from his pocket and at arm's-length waved it around the corner. A bullet shredded the handkerchief. Scott in panic shouted, 'Fucking hell Syd – it's me.'

Syd's voice returned, 'Sorry 'bout that sir. All clear this end.'

'Be with you in a sec, Syd. I just need to check the body for identification.' A quick professional frisk found no identity on the body. Picking up "friend's" machine pistol, he inspected it and then slung it over his shoulder by the strap. As he slid around the corner he saw Syd appearing from behind the wide-girthed tree and elbow his way through bushes to join him. He then just about tripped over a near faceless body lying on its back outside the main door with pistol in hand and blood seeping into the gravel drive. Regaining his balance he stooped to check the body for identity and like the other corpse found there was none. He inspected the corpse's pistol and slid it into his jerkin. 'What happened?' he enquired.

Syd explained – 'I was hiding behind the tree like what you told me when a car drew up at the entrance to the drive and stopped. I then saw two figures get out and flit their way down the trees like what we did. When they got level with the front door one of them broke cover with a pistol in his hand and headed for the door. The other continued on as you did. They couldn't be police. They would've come in with sirens blaring. So I figured it was either villains or the Gestapo. So I challenged the bloke heading for the door. His answer was to put a bullet passed my ear. That stopped the other bloke's progress who then took up a position at the corner and let rip at me with a burst of his machine pistol. Lucky I was behind the tree otherwise the burst would have cut me in half. I dived into the bushes as the other guy was taking aim at me. I fired. Hit him full in the face with the result...' Syd pointed at the prostrate faceless figure lying on its back. 'I then scrambled back behind the tree and got off a shot that took out a piece of corner brickwork. Then you finished the job, sir.' As Syd finished they heard a crunch of gears followed by a screech of tyres. 'Sounds like the getaway driver just got away, sir.'

'Time for us to do the same,' replied Scott as he clapped Syd on the shoulder and complimented him, 'Good man, Syd. You did really well. I take back all I said about your revolver. Now, please go and get the car; we have two extra passengers... including a dog.'

'A dog!'

'Yes. A-bloody-dog and a wife. And please hurry for that shooting must have been heard by neighbours and we don't want the local police showing up.' Nor the real Gestapo pondered Scott, knowing the two corpses were not Gestapo by virtue of what he had found out about the weapons. As Syd hurried up the driveway to the road as fast as his fifty five year old legs could carry him Scott replaced the pistol back into the hand of the faceless corpse and the machine pistol beside the other body. He then climbed the stairs from the jetty to the balcony and into the house through the sliding doors. A lamp had been switched on, showing Litzl standing with a small overnight case in one hand and the other holding Dieter's hand. Dieter still had a glazed look on his face.

'Dieter.' The sound of his name awoke him from a far-away place. 'Do you have any valuables you wish to bring before we leave?'

'No. My valuables are my work. But I do have my attaché case with my prepared report for "G",' he replied, leaning over to pick up the case from the sofa. Then nostalgia took over. 'When we got married we rented this house. So peaceful and quiet – allowing Litzl to do her writing. She's an anthropologist, you know.' He pulled her to him with this free arm 'She's writing about the local....'

He was fortunately interrupted by the arrival of Syd carrying Scott's Crombie overcoat over arm and Homburg. They adjourned to the Rover; Litzl with tears in her eyes and constantly fingering her wedding ring. Scott hoped that if stopped at the roadblock, Litzl with her fur coat and hat would pass as "Lady Amelia". However, he trusted that his warning to the S.S officer on the way out of Berlin would allow them an unhindered return journey. They took their allotted places for travel: Scott now returned to his former guise as "Sir Eric" in the back seat with "Lady Amelia" with poodle on lap. Dieter was given a reprieve by Scott. He would sit up front with Syd until Oranienburg, the small town just before the roadblock where he would climb into the Rover boot until they reached the safety of the Embassy. The journey went as planned and turned out uneventful even at the roadblock where with nerves jangling they cruised through. Whether this was due to Scott's previous threat as "Sir Eric" or the fact that the S.S were still concentrating their efforts on outward journeys from Berlin, Scott was never to find out. Not that it mattered. With Litzl crouched in the rear floor-well and Dieter in the boot, both out of view of unfriendly eyes, Syd turned into the safety of the Embassy. As instructed by Syd, out the corner of his mouth, "Sir Eric" waved to the Gestapo surveillance car.

As Syd brought the Rover to a halt at the out-of-sight Embassy side door, Scott realised that phase one of his miss-mash, rehashed, flexible, non-plan had been successful. He looked at his watch – almost midnight. He had twelve hours to complete phase two of the operation. He handed his charges over to Sir Eric and Lady Amelia and retired to bed exhausted.

***

British Embassy Tuesday 7ᵗʰ May 1935

Scott, dressed as a pilot in a brown boiler suit (borrowed from Syd) with collar and tie showing and leather helmet and goggles (borrowed from Otto) in hand, made his way from his Embassy apartment up the wide sweeping marble staircase to the Ambassador's private accommodation on the top floor. He knocked on the heavily ornate oak door and was admitted by Lady Amelia who had taken care of Dieter and Litzl overnight. She showed her delight at meeting him with an air kiss to each cheek before leading him to an open door. At the door she stood aside and with a proud hand gesture presented a distinguished looking gentleman.

'Good God,' exclaimed Scott in amazement, immediately apologising to Lady Amelia for his language. 'What-a-transformation.' The outburst was directed at Dieter who stood before Scott shorn of his long golden locks. He now had a short back and sides, dyed black with tinges of grey at the temples. He wore the familiar gold-rimmed spectacles and sported a thin grey pencil moustache similar to that worn by Scott the previous day. 'Very professional work by whomsoever,' finalised Scott in admiration.

Lady Amelia took a bow. 'Thank you Scott. I too was in amateur dramatics – but at Oxford. When needs must, eh what? Here, I say, your "Sir Eric" moustache hasn't half grown since last night.'

Scott had removed his pencil moustache to replace it with a large bushy type moustache made from the remains of his shaving brush. With him knowing this to be the current fashion statement worn by the RAF pilot of the next phase of action he had decided to adopt the look as part of his deception. 'Chocks away, Lady Amelia,' he joked, giving her a pilot's thumbs up.

The pixie figure of Litzl who was wearing a dress, which had obviously had alterations due to Lady Amelia's large statuesque figure, joined them to adjourn to the dining room for breakfast. During breakfast Lady Amelia whispered to Scott she had taken care of the dog problem. She did not elucidate. But she did so about Yvonne. She told him that Yvonne had been in Beatrice's office early this morning enquiring if there was any news of him. This was said with a "you naughty boy' smile playing on her lips. Scott sighed, knowing he would now have to make the effort to communicate with Yvonne to let her know he was still alive. This was all he needed – a further complication to the already complicated plan he was about to explain.

A casually dressed Sir Eric, who had been signing his mail, then joined the company.

After finishing breakfast Scott called the assembly to order to lay out phase two of his plan. He opened by asking Sir Eric if he had notified the German authorities of his and Lady Amelia's flight to London, as was protocol, and the pilot given his instructions. These requirements had been attended to, Sir Eric confirmed. Scott went on to explain that Syd would drive Dieter and Litzl as "Sir Eric and Lady Amelia" to Tempelhof airport to catch the noon day diplomatic flight to London. Due to the road blocks still being in operation Scott would be in the Rover boot. When they arrived at Tempelhof, Syd would drive as close to the plane as possible, park the Rover with the boot out of sight of the terminal building and the ever-present watchful eyes of the secret police and then escort Dieter and Litzl safely on board – as he usually did with Sir Eric and Lady Amelia. Once they were on board Syd would feign to have forgotten their travel rug, leave the plane and open the Rover boot to retrieve the rug and in doing so would hold it wide in his arms. Scott, masked by the rug would climb out and appear in the similar disguise he had affected to that of the pilot complete with his bushy moustache. He would then be seen to kick-checking the tyres and giving the engines a cursory inspection before climbing on board. Once he was on board Syd would then make sure the ground crew withdrew the access steps immediately. The pilot, Flight Lieutenant Howard, sporting the bushy moustache that Scott had copied, would then give the twin engines of the Gypsy Moth De Havilland Rapide bi-plane full revolutions for take-off. Scott then hoped his next view of Tempelhof would be that of a dot on the ground.

Having outlaid his plan he welcomed any queries. Sir Eric brought up the question of how he and Lady Amelia were supposed to return to Berlin from London whilst still confined to the Embassy. Scott had been expecting this and replied that they were to remain in their apartment incommunicado for these two days. No phone calls to be made or received and never under any circumstances to venture near the windows. In two days-time, late Thursday evening, Syd would meet the incoming 11-00pm Imperial Airways flight from London. They would be on the manifest as passengers but would in fact be secreted in the back seat well of the Rover with a travel rug over them. Later in the dark whilst the passengers were disembarking they would pop up from their hiding place in the back seat and Syd would return them to the Embassy. "And Bob's your uncle – job done," finished Scott.

"How exciting. Such fun," giggled Lady Amelia whilst Sir Eric looked decidedly unhappy about the thought of crouching in the back seat of the Rover for the half hour it took them to arrive at Tempelhof.

Scott, noticing Sir Eric's discomforting look, offered him the alternative of hiding in the Rover's boot. This was met with great merriment and a clapping of hands by Lady Amelia. Sir Eric glowered at Scott wishing he had never agreed to such SIS nonsense. Scott shrugged his shoulders and retorted, "It's not all fun you know, Sir Eric, being a British Secret Service agent." At this Sir Eric relented and laughed heartily, replying that it was indeed a pleasure for both him and Lady Amelia to be of assistance in anything that would put that little sod Hitler's nose out of joint.

Scott then asked if there were any further questions. Syd enquired about the road blocks. Scott reminded him that the ersatz "Sir Eric" had already aired his views yesterday to the S.S about this matter – and if Syd remembered correctly, "Sir Eric" had already threatened to report the matter to Hitler. Syd, with a smile, nodded his head knowingly. Lady Amelia suspected skulduggery whilst Sir Eric looked absolutely bewildered regarding his alleged airing of views to the SS and his future meeting with Hitler. Before Sir Eric could get hold of Scott to explain these comments, Scott hastily closed the meeting informing those involved, Dieter, Litzl and Syd that they were leaving the Embassy at 11-15am prompt. To the cry from Sir Eric of "Come back here Rutherford..." Scott closed the door and beat a hasty retreat from Sir Eric downstairs to Yvonne. From the bottom of the stairs he noticed the scowl on her face. "*Out of the frying pan into the fire*," he muttered as he arrived at reception.

After a cursory study of his apparel – dark brown boiler suit with leather helmet and goggles in his hand and sporting a ridiculous moustache, Yvonne greeted him sarcastically with, 'Well, if it isn't the return of Biggles. Here to liaise are we? And explain to me about, *The important role of liaison.*'

Scott, fully expecting her wrath, retaliated, 'I left you a despatch which explained my movements and what to do in the event of anything going wrong with the operation – that's what... *I call liaison.*'

'Admittedly you did leave a despatch – disguised as Sir Eric. What the hell was that all about? Why not tell me to my face?'

'I was trying out my "Sir Eric" disguise on you. Unfortunately, I didn't have time to discuss my further movements with you. I had to move fast to race the Gestapo to the professor.'

Yvonne was having none of his nonsense. 'And how did the Gestapo find out about your professor?'

Scott let out a deep sigh. 'The Gestapo were waiting for me at Dieter's apartment. It's a long story Yvonne. I'll explain later.'

'That's very good of you,' Yvonne said sarcastically as she continued her verbal assault. 'So, let me get this straight. I heard from Beatrice that Syd drove you to Röbel.' She looked at him for confirmation. Scott said nothing. She took his silence to mean yes. 'To pick up Professor Neuman and when you got there he obviously invited you in for coffee, discuss the weather, then once you had finished you both left for the Embassy – and he's now upstairs drinking schnapps, smoking a cigar and waiting to go to London.'

Scott, playing her at her own game of sarcasm, replied, 'That's truly uncanny, Yvonne. How did you know? Was it your big-mouth friend Beatrice?'

'No. It was Radio Berliner, this morning. They reported an incident in Röbel last night. Robbery, abduction and two brutal murders. Sound familiar to you?'

Still playing her game, he retorted, 'Ah! That would account for the police sirens I heard as I was leaving Röbel with the professor. I wondered what the fuss was about'. He looked at his watch. 'Look, Yvonne, I've got to go now. The noon-day flight to Northolt awaits the professor and me.'

'You! But, you've just arrived,' she exclaimed in surprise, her disappointment showing, 'Yes. I'm babysitting the prof. He's hot property. So, until we meet again... ' With a nonchalant salute he turned from the desk, blew her a kiss and strode off towards the garage taking a short-cut through the restaurant. This was not how he had envisaged their parting. But with Yvonne prolonging their meeting with questions and spiteful obstructions he had no option but to curtail the meeting because once again he was racing against a deadline.

With both elbows leaning on the counter Yvonne watched Scott disappear towards the side entrance. She had achieved nothing. No apology. No true explanation of the professor's rescue. Scott was gone. All she had to remember him by was a blown kiss. And knowing the way "The Service" worked, she might never see him again, her mood changed from the anger she had harboured about his "Sir Eric" subterfuge that had made her look a fool in front of the real Sir Eric into a feeling of melancholy. How she wished she hadn't tried to be smart with him. But unfortunately he was gifted with a natural ability to rile her.

At the side entrance Syd had the Rover boot open awaiting Scott. He climbed in. Syd closed the boot and drove round to the main doors of the Embassy to uplift the bogus "Sir Eric" and "Lady Amelia".

From her position behind the reception counter the misery-ridden Yvonne had a clear view down the foyer to the Sergeant-at-Arms station and beyond to the main doors. She was staring towards the main doors in the hope of Scott materializing before he left for London when suddenly the lift doors to the Ambassador's private apartments opened and "Sir Eric" and "Lady Amelia" stepped out to be met by their chauffeur, Syd. Of Scott and the professor there was no sign. Then it dawned on her. Scott had *not* been dressed as a pilot. Instead he had been dressed for the use of Otto's motorcycle with the professor riding pillion. Idiot! – what must Scott have thought of her calling him "Biggles." She slapped her forehead with the heel of her hand in frustration. Yet another faux pas.

Meanwhile in the boot of the Rover, Scott had developed a crick in his neck while Dieter was luxuriating in the back seat with a Havana cigar presented to him by Sir Eric before departure.

When the diplomatic plated Rover departed the Embassy, Dieter, in his pretence of Sir Eric, tipped his Homburg and waved a cigar held hand at the Gestapo surveillance car as coached by the real Sir Eric. He did not, as was Sir Eric's wont, follow up with an unseen two finger gesture.

The transfer of Dieter, Litzl and Scott from the Rover to aeroplane met with a major set-back at Tempelhof airport. An armed SS trooper was stationed at the foot of the plane's entry steps. Dieter, quick to appreciate the problem angrily retorted, 'Still looking for your communist terrorists trooper? As the British Ambassador, may I remind you that the area around this plane is British sovereign territory and as I am meeting Herr Hitler next week I shall be reporting this incident.' The trooper threw a Nazi salute and turned on his heel. Once inside the plane Syd congratulated Dieter on his quick thinking and said he didn't realise the area around the plane was sovereign territory. Dieter replied that neither did he. Syd roared with laughter as he departed the cabin to open the Rover boot. Before Scott nipped out, Syd told him of Dieter's confrontation.

Sir James had organised that they had the plane to themselves. After receiving further congratulations from Scott, Dieter asked him if his boss walked with the aid of a walking stick and spoke with a peculiar English accent. Scott replied in the affirmative whilst suggesting to Dieter that it would be in his best interest when he met his boss not to mention the accent. For Dieter's further benefit he was informed that the language in question was Glaswegian, a form of English, and as far as his chief was concerned – the national language. Dieter laughed and said that certainly sounded like the same man that had recruited him in 1921.

Scott then asked Dieter something that had been bothering him – how had he delivered his despatch to "Lambhill's" shop? Dieter replied that he hadn't. He explained that whilst out walking his dog he delivered his despatches to a mail box in the foyer of "Lambhill's" apartment which was in an area close to where he lived. This he had arranged with "Lambhill" after his first and only visit to the shop in 1921 because it was easier and less of a security risk. He hadn't told "G" about the change in the procedure and queried as to whether that was wrong. It was, but at this stage in the game, nearly fourteen years on, Scott felt there was no point in making an issue of the matter. Scott then fell silent, analysing the situation. Because Dieter and Michael had never met since 1921his conclusion was that there was no way the Gestapo could have had any reason to link a connection between them. So why had the Gestapo suddenly fire-bombed "Lambhill's" shop and put surveillance on "Maryhill's" apartment. Something didn't add up. He concluded Sir James was right – *there was a mole in his garden.*

The flight arrived in drizzle to be met by Sir James who was at the foot of the disembarking stairs to meet them. Scott immediately noted from the surroundings that they had landed in Biggin Hill aerodrome and not at Northolt as scheduled. Sir James immediately engulfed Dieter and Litzl in a large golf umbrella and whisked them into his SS Jaguar. Scott noticed Elizabeth sitting in the passenger seat as the Jaguar sped away with tyres spinning on the wet runway followed by SIS (5) internal security agents in their Wolsley. This left Scott to fend for himself. Disappointed at no acknowledgement or instruction from Sir James or Elizabeth, Scott trudged in weather that had deteriorated from drizzle to torrential rain into the terminal building to phone for a taxi to take him to his lodgings.

Now soaked through and annoyed at being ignored he squelched into the taxi. The driver noting his sodden flying suit and now bedraggled bushy moustache quipped in his cockney accent, 'Your seaplane sprung a leak then Biggles?' Typical bloody London taxi driver; they all want to be comedians. Max Miller sprung to mind as another rivulet of water ran down his neck, spine, and buttock crevice into his underpants.

Jean, his landlady, herself a former SIS (6) operative, fussed over his damp clothing and ran him a bath. After one of her superb hot stews he rang the office in the off chance that Elizabeth had returned from her travels with Sir James. There being no reply he was transferred to a recorded anonymous voice and asked to leave a message. The following morning the hall phone rang. Jean popped her head round the door to advise Scott that the phone call had been from Liz – he was to attend a meeting with Sir James in his office at 11-00am prompt.

Chapter 13

SIS (6) Whitehall London Wednesday 8th May 1935
The taxi dropped Scott at the Foreign Office. He showed his pass to the commissionaire and proceeded by lift to Sir James' office on the top floor. When he knocked and entered the ante-room reception, Elizabeth launched herself from behind her desk. Throwing her arms in the air she embraced him in a bear hug, almost crushing the large box of Belgian chocolates that he had brought her as a present.

'Scott, my hero – you did it... You saved "Maryhill". I just can't believe it's true,' she lauded, as she kissed him on both cheeks. She then broke the embrace to lightly pinch one of his kissed cheeks between forefinger and thumb and give it a loving wiggle whilst the other hand grabbed the chocolates (her favourites) and laid them on her desk. 'A brilliantly planned operation Scott,' she finished, staring at him lovingly with hands clasped close to her bosom. 'And I can let you into a secret – Sir James thinks the same,' she said as she leaned over the desk to flick the intercom through to announce his arrival.

He knocked on the office door to be greeted with the familiar Glaswegian growl, 'Come in Rutherford.'

As he entered he was aware of Sir James limping round his desk to meet him with extended hand. Sir James pumped Scott's hand as he enthused, 'Congratulations Rutherford – I couldn't have done better myself. Sorry I couldn't linger at Biggin Hill yesterday but I had to whisk Dieter and wife away as quickly as possible – you never know who is watching. However, take a seat and tell me all about your mission and as usual leave nothing out, however trivial.' Scott withdrew from the inside pocket of his immaculately tailored suit several sheets of foolscap and leaned forward to lay them on the desk. 'My full report, Sir James.'

'Excellent. I will read it later. Now commence.'

Scott recapped in detail his meeting dressed as a postman with Dieter's neighbour Frau Kessler and the subsequent discovery of Dieter's country retreat in Röbel, his subsequent rescue from the Gestapo by Laszlo and the gun fight that resulted in the deaths of two of the Gestapo. Then the rescue mission to Röbel that produced a further two deaths of unknown adversaries. And the final escape to London.

Sir James sat silently throughout, listening intently and scribbling the occasional note. When Scott finished he was congratulated again by Sir James. 'Excellent, Rutherford, excellent. A mission well reported and – *executed* – as most seem to be who cross your path, if you'll pardon the pun. However, I must see if I can get you something a bit more adventuresome for your next outing. These Embassy postings can tend to be a bit on the dull side,' he finished with a twinkle in his eye. 'Now, there are a few points I need to clear up. First. To rescue you from the Gestapo outside Dieter's Berlin apartment Laszlo needed to know the address? Did you tell Laszlo?'

'*Absolutely not*, Sir James. But I did latterly wondered about that myself. Unfortunately, I haven't seen him since to ask.'

'But you did disclose Dieter's full name to enable Laszlo to obtain the Röbel address from a colleague in Müritz-see?'

'Afraid so, sir. Time was paramount. I feared the Gestapo would find out Dieter's location in Röbel from Frau Kessler and beat me to him.'

'And, instead of Gestapo at Röbel you reckon you encountered Laszlo and his gang.'

Scott nodded again. 'That is correct. They were carrying no identification. The only clues I have are their weapons. They were Russian Markovs – a hand pistol and a machine pistol – thus making me think that the assailants were not Nazis, for they would never consider the use of inferior Russian machine pistols. The weapons I placed beside the bodies to help direct the Gestapo towards Russian involvement – thus giving me time to get the professor out of the country.'

'Excellent strategy, Rutherford. But I thought you had met Laszlo's gang – Hans and Heinie?

'Yes and no. Hans I never saw – he was always the van driver so it might have been him I terminated at the corner of the house. And if the other assailant – with his face blown off – was Heinie, then recognition was impossible.'

'I understand. Anything else?'

'What happens to Laszlo?'

'I have my own ideas on that. We will discuss that later. Now do you have anything you wish to add?'

'Yes. According to Dieter he has only ever been in "Lambhill's" shop once, and that way back in 1921, so I cannot see how all of a sudden the Nazi's should link them. This causes me to think that it was not a random purge against Jewish people but more a ruse to get me to react to find Dieter, which I unfortunately did'.

'So?'

'So, we have a security leak somewhere.'

'My sentiments exactly, Rutherford. And one I intend to put right. However, I will also come to that later. Pray continue.'

'That despatch I sent about Guy Burnett....'

Sir James interrupted. 'No worries there, Rutherford. I'm informed by H.M customs that Burnett is now a regular visitor to Berlin. Allegedly on his newspaper business and occasionally to meet his Berlin soviet contact. But, his soviet contact informs me the reason he is in Berlin as often as he is now is for casual homosexual liaisons.' Sir James shook his head and indicated his disgust at the thought then continued, 'Are you aware that, unlike Britain, homosexuality is not a crime in Germany and particularly not in Berlin.'

'No, I'm not. But may I be permitted to ask how you know Burnett's soviet agent in Berlin?'

'Quite simple really. He works for me. He is the Embassy postman – Laszlo.'

Sir James watched with interest as Scott's expression changed from one of surprise to that of enlightenment. 'You mean Laszlo's a double agent?

Sir James slowly nodded his head. 'Yes. And that news about Burnett now spending time in Berlin on his homosexual promiscuities is one of the few worthwhile pieces of information I've ever had from him. For all the good he's been throughout the years I might just as well have subscribed to Moscow's *Pravda*. However, I just let him think he is of use to me. But I still don't trust the bastard.'

'So the Burnett business is really just a nothingness…'

Sir James, waving his forefinger from side-to-side, interrupted. 'Men like Burnett never do nothingness. He will be up to tricks – believe me. When you return to Berlin I want you to find out what he's up to. Right, next question, Rutherford.'

'l was under the impression that I was bringing out a blown cipher operator, albeit a head of section, because that's what I understand "The Service" does for its agents – but I keep feeling there is more to it. For example – the sudden swing by Ambassador Sir Eric from antagonism towards me to one of being helpful, in fact, going so far as to suggest that I was on a mission "*of the utmost importance to the nation*".'

A smile played around the corners of Sir James' mouth as he was stroking his chin contemplatively – a quirk he oft did before deciding his next move. His mind made up he said, 'When you signed the Official Secrets Act, Rutherford, I take it you realised the seriousness of the OSA oath?'

'Yes, sir. Every word.'

'To violate the OSA is in certain circumstances punishable by the death penalty.' He stopped and looked at Scott who nodded understanding. 'What I am about to divulge falls into this category. Do you wish me to proceed?'

'Yes, Sir.'

'Good. For what I am about to disclose is "Top Secret" and I think you're entitled to know for all your hard work. I know you won't let me down.'

'Absolutely not, Sir James,' Scott replied gravely.

'Well, as you've rightly assessed, Dieter's role is more than a cipher clerk. He is a brilliant mathematician. That's what most cryptologists are, of course. He was allegedly head of ciphers in the Reichstag but that was only a cover the Nazis used for his real job – and this is where the OSA really comes into force – he was working on the Nazi's advanced Enigma machine. Do you know what an Enigma machine is?'

'lt is an electro mechanical rotor cipher machine. The code was deemed unbreakable until 1932 when Polish mathematicians finally cracked the complexities of the machine,' reeled off Scott.

Taken aback by Scott's knowledge Sir James stuttered, 'Er, er, quite so, Rutherford. However, the Nazis are working on an additional complexities machine that will make the code impossible to break again and Dieter has the necessary valuable information to allow us to break this code when it's operational.'

'But with Dieter missing, the Nazis will suspect he has passed over their secrets to us and....'

'Not necessarily,' interrupted Sir James. 'I say this because, if you remember you did very adroitly leave the bodies behind at Dieter's house with incriminating evidence – Russian manufactured weapons in their possession. That should be enough to incriminate the Kremlin for the time being until we think of something more concrete. I had thought of getting the BBC to broadcast a missing plane from Berlin tragically missing over the English Channel that's why I had us diverted to Biggin Hill. But on reflection that would have been counter-productive – the Nazis would have known he had definitely defected to us. Such are the complexities of the game we play Rutherford'

'Very astute, Sir James. Now may I ask you – where did you get your intelligence regarding Dieter and the Enigma?'

'Certainly. "Maryhill" or Dieter, if you prefer – indicated to me by "dip-bag" three months ago that he was being transferred from his duties at the Reichstag to an undisclosed secret location to work on the new Enigma machine. To hear nothing from Dieter for several weeks was not unusual but when it got to three months I was beginning to fear for him having being compromised and decided to send him a despatch enquiring how his work was progressing on the Enigma. Shortly after – that's when "Op-G" (Operation Glasgow), starting with "Lambhill" being fire bombed, went into meltdown. I'm now absolutely convinced that "Op-G" was a security leak within the "dip-bag" transfer which makes the leak either at the Embassy end or in that idiot Eustace's Foreign Office. Either way, Rutherford, we have a mole. So, let's you and me try to find out who the traitor is from the files,' he finished as he pushed a bundle of grey-blue files stamped "TOP SECRET" across his desk to Scott. 'I'll give you a couple of hours to analyse these. Take yourself off to the conference room and I'll arrange Elizabeth to send in tea and sandwiches – we'll lunch later.'

As Scott passed Liz's desk her intercom buzzed. It was Sir James asking her to step into his office. She rose, picked up her notebook and pencil and set off for dictation. Entering the office she was about to take her usual seat but was stopped by a curt hand motion from Sir James. 'No dictation, Elizabeth. I want you to pay a visit to Sir John at SIS (5) and the MOD. They have files for me which I would appreciate uplifted as soon as possible. Thank you.' On the way past the coat stand she grabbed her out-door coat. Sir John was two blocks away in the Home Office.

With the departure of Elizabeth, Sir James leaned back in the one luxury in his otherwise austerely furnished office – his leather swivel chair. He pinched his eyes before reflecting again on the problem at hand. Since the news of the Berlin disaster he had studied the files of all those with connections to "Op-G" and felt he was missing a vital something. But from what little he had gleaned he did feel the rudiments of a solution forming. However, it depended on the contents of the file he had sent Elizabeth to collect which he hoped, in conjunction with Rutherford's findings, would be the catalyst to solving his problem. With that gratifying thought he opened his new project file – TENALT (The Tenerife Alternative) and busied himself refreshing his memory on the file for his forthcoming meeting with Winston Churchill. Forty minutes later Elizabeth returned with the requested files. Laying aside his Tenerife file he immediately delved into the newly arrived files. As he concentrated on their contents a satisfied smile flitted across his face to accompany the odd nod of understanding. When he finished his reading and note-taking he laid the files on his desk and slapped them closed with an open hand muttering, 'Light at the end of the tunnel at last.' He then reached into the bottom drawer of his desk, withdrew the Glenmorangie malt whisky and poured himself a large celebratory dram, downing it in one swallow. He had no sooner finished his celebration than the intercom buzzed with Elizabeth announcing the arrival of Scott from the conference room. He glanced at his watch 1-45pm. A late working lunch beckoned. He asked Elizabeth to arrange for tea and sandwiches.

Following a knock on Sir James' office door, a confident looking Scott strode in with files under-arm and flashed a wide, white, even-toothed grin. He took the offered seat opposite Sir James and returned the files to the desk top. Sir James with a deep draw on his freshly lit cigar opened the proceedings. 'You look like the cat that got the cream, Rutherford. I assume you've solved the problem.'

Scott finished lighting his cigarette, the exhaled smoke joining the layer of haze over Sir James, before answering, 'Not quite but I've a good idea who it is. Unfortunately, it's based on supposition. No proof.'

'That doesn't matter. Let's hear who you think it is.'

'The Sergeant-at-Arms, Berlin Embassy – Adrian Grenville.'

'Interesting choice. Why?'

'Because I felt it was too much of a coincidence – two Embassy deaths within a short period. First Trevor Lomas the Embassy SAA followed two weeks later by Sylvia Sanderson, the Embassy receptionist. I then asked myself who had the most to gain from their deaths. Answer – Grenville.'

'How so,' Sir James questioned already knowing the answer for he had already gone down this line of reasoning.

'The obvious one first – Lomas. With his demise, Grenville takes over his position in the Embassy. As for poor Miss Sanderson I have to assume it was for the "dip-bag" key she was supposed to hand over to me.'

'How did Grenville obtain the key?'

'He had her bumped off.' Sir James grimaced at the use of this abomination of American slang that was creeping into everyday language. He blamed Hollywood's love of the criminal underworld – Bogart, Cagney et al. 'He made it look like a hit and run accident. It was a foggy night with nobody about. The driver, or an accomplice, stopped, took the key from her bag and had a copy made. When Grenville, as was expected, in his role as SAA picked up her personal effects from the local police he returned the original key to her bag. The original key was then passed over to me whilst he kept the copy.'

Sir James had also worked this out being as he was responsible for Grenville picking up Miss Sanderson's belongings from the

Berlin police. 'How do you know you received the original key?' he queried, genuinely wanting to know the answer.

'It was brass, scratched, well-worn and the patina suggested it to be very old. You can't fake those characteristics at short notice.' Sir James agreed with a nod of his head. 'From the file I wondered how Grenville with his track record of a not specified dishonourable discharge from the Army could acquire a position in the Foreign Office, especially that of a SAA. The file further informed me that he applied for the Berlin position by replying to an advertisement in the Civil Service News. There was no detail of who interviewed him, nor of any vetting, which I understand is our responsibility being overseas ....'

'It most certainly is our responsibility – but we have to know about the appointment before we can do the vetting and that's the responsibility of that blithering idiot, Sir Eustace,' interrupted Sir James indignantly.

Scott, undaunted, continued, 'The peculiar thing is that when Grenville was appointed Berlin SAA, next to Washington our top ambassadorial appointment, he had not progressed beyond the pay grade of courier in the Civil Service since joining the Foreign Office – whenever that was, for his file does not indicate a date. As to who recruited him to the F.O in the first place there is no mention, nor of who vetted him. And that I'm afraid is when I hit the buffers.'

'Shouldn't worry, Rutherford. That's when I hit the buffers, too – until Elizabeth delivered these priceless gems from SIS(5) – the Holt file and Army records,' he said triumphantly as he clapped his open palm firmly on top of the recently acquired files. 'What you've told me so far confirms my own suspicions of Grenville, and like you, I felt that whoever originally recruited him to the F.O might well throw light on the reason he was employed considering his dishonourable discharge. Of course, that in itself could simply mean that he stole the officers' de lux bum paper, were it not for the fact that I now know from his Army files he was dismissed for lewd homosexual acts in the ranks.'

'I did hear that existed, Sir James,' replied Scott.

'Well, there were certainly enough public schoolboy educated officers in the trenches for it to happen. Never saw it myself, too bloody busy fighting the Krauts alongside the rest of our idiotic Generals' cannon fodder.' His cigar finished, he stubbed it out in an upturned tobacco tin lid.

There was a gentle knock on the door. Scott rose to open the door to Elizabeth wheeling in a tea trolley, the centrepiece being a teapot clad in a wool knit tea cosy. Lyons corner house had come up trumps with a fine selection of sandwiches. Elizabeth poured the tea and retired.

'Right where were we?' said Sir James through a mouthful of cheese and pickle. 'Ah, yes. This bastard Grenville. How was it possible for him with his track record to secure a job in the F.O? He obviously had to have had help. So who helped him? Once I had given the matter some considerable thought, I phoned Sir John Husband head of SIS (5) who informed me, after a search in his archives, that a Thomas Holt was responsible for recruitment in 1919 – and the vetting of couriers. Then on reading the file I find that Holt was one of those homosexual individuals and a suspected communist sympathiser.'

'Very interesting, but surely it was early days to link Holt or Grenville with communism? I mean Lenin and the communist revolution had only been going a couple of years and...'

'True,' interrupted Sir James, 'I cannot speak for Holt because he hadn't served in the war – Foreign Office exemption – but there were many disgruntled ex-service men at the end of the war in 1918. They arrived home with bodies both physically and mentally wrecked from a war they knew nobody knew what the bloody hell it was all about. And with no hope, no help and only despair to look forward to, it lent itself to a perfect breeding ground for the growth of unrest and communism. And I would hazard a guess that Grenville along with his perceived injustice of a dishonourable discharge was in this category. However, back to Holt. His file closed in 1926 when he died in prison where he had been languishing for two years after being caught soliciting in the gents' toilet in Hyde Park.

'So how does that get Grenville to Berlin if Holt died in 1926?'

Ignoring the interruption with hand held openly up for quiet, Sir James rattled on, 'What we have so far are facts. But to answer your question Rutherford I have to delve into the realms of speculation as to what chain of events led to Grenville's appointment as SAA Berlin.' He then opened the top drawer of his desk and withdrew a sheaf of his hand written notes. 'Based on what I know about Holt and Grenville I have formed a supposition trail of Grenville's appointment.' He then referred to his notes and looking at Scott said, 'Please feel free to interrupt. My first supposition is that Grenville meets Holt at a communist comrades' meeting in 1919 and they became, er, er…'

'Lovers,' finished Scott on behalf of Sir James whose staunch Presbyterian code of morality could not cope with the thought of such a licentious act.

Sir James shook his head in disgust at the thought and continued, 'Holt then dies in prison in 1926 leaving a footloose Grenville to meet Guy Burnett, possibly in one of the sleazy Soho clubs Burnett is known to frequent…'

'Guy Burnett! That's a long shot, if you don't mind my saying so, sir.'

Sir James, contrary to his invitation for Scott to interrupt, showed signs of irritation at Scott's interruption as he carried on, 'Yes, yes, yes, Rutherford. Please, kindly listen. Burnett is, as you should know from my memo to you, a homosexual and it is therefore not beyond the bounds of reason that before he became editor of the Red Flag he met Grenville at a meeting of the comrades. And, since Grenville's appointment to the Embassy, Burnett is now a frequent visitor to Berlin. More than coincidence I'd say.'

With a hand to his mouth a chastened Scott ruefully recounted, 'Ah! I think you've just solved my mystery man in the Berlin Continental Hotel, the day I encountered Burnett in the next alcove. The back I thought I recognised going into the cocktail bar must have been Grenville's. That would tie-in with your theory about Grenville and Burnett…'

Sir James suddenly sat upright in his seat and with an accusatory finger wag at Scott, he exploded, 'You didn't mention that in your report, Rutherford. You should know by now that every little detail matters, however miniscule. Had I had that piece of information I would have arrived at suspecting Grenville sooner.'

"And had I been given the Holt and Army files I would also have

suspected him sooner", entered Scott's mind, but realising he was in the wrong in failing to disclose all he kept his counsel, instead apologising, 'Sorry, bad mistake, won't happen again'.

Sir James waved away Scott's apology with the back of his hand in way of apology accepted. He referred to his notes once again. 'Burnett then,' he grimaced, 'seduces Grenville and they become....' He paused agonising.

'Lovers,' completed Scott once again to save Sir James further torment.

'Hmmph,' acknowledged Sir James in way of gratitude. 'By this time Moscow wants a spy in the Berlin Embassy but has no way of placing him or her. Burnett is tasked with this placement by Moscow. However, as we know Trevor Lomas, the SAA in Berlin, who was spending leave in Margate, went fishing in his rowing boat. The boat capsized. He drowned. Local police investigate. No witnesses. No suspicious circumstances. A most regrettable accident. And Grenville gets appointed in his place.'

'Do you believe Lomas's death was an accident, Sir James?'

'No. I most certainly don't. It was premeditated murder.'

'I take it you think it was the Soviets.'

'No. The Nazis. Because...' Finding his place again in his notes he carried on, '...Hitler became Chancellor of Germany in 1933 and appointed Göering to form a secret police force – the Gestapo. Göering makes Himmler Gestapo chief of staff and commands him to recruit a spy into our Berlin Embassy.'

'So we now have the Nazis as well as the Reds wanting a spy in our Berlin Embassy. Aren't we popular?'

'Quite so, Rutherford. So as I see it, Himmler contacts William Joyce of the British Union of Fascists (BUF) who he has met on several of Joyce's sojourns to Germany. Joyce informs him he has, as a member of the BUF, Lady Dorothy Hooper-Ellis, cousin of a top Foreign Office mandarin.'

'Would that be the Lady Dorothy whose husband committed suicide in the wake of the Wall Street collapse due to his investing his client's monies without their consent?' Sir James nodded agreement. 'And she blamed his death on the "Jewish Conspiracy"?'

'Indeed, Rutherford. Thus leaving herself wide open for

conscription to Joyce's anti-Semitic wing of the British Union of Fascists, which she did. But the Soviets also had a member in the BUF, Grenville – put there to spy on them by Burnett. Joyce, knowing Grenville was a courier with the Foreign Office, suggested to Lady Dorothy that she contact her cousin in the F.O to recruit Grenville to the Berlin Embassy to replace Lomas.'

'Her cousin being, Sir Eustace?'

'Correct. Sir Eustace's turning out not to be quite the bumbling innocent idiot, I thought. So, as requested, Lady D contacts cousin Eustace who is a BUP sympathizer – but not a member otherwise SIS(5) would know – and he agrees to fix it so that Grenville gets the Berlin appointment. She then duly contacts Grenville herself. Grenville informs Burnett of her approach. Burnett can't believe his good fortune. He spins Grenville some story to get him to accept the offered position.' He stopped to light up another cigar. 'Lady Dorothy notifies Eustace that Grenville has accepted the position. She informs Joyce, and Lomas meets with his "accident". Et voila! Vacancy filled in Berlin Embassy by Grenville one month before you arrive. In Grenville the Nazis believe they have finally got their man in the Embassy little realising he is actually a communist agent.'

'The soviets worked a real flanker on the Nazis with that move.'

'And us Rutherford. And us. Now finally. With Grenville in position at the Embassy and you still in Italy and Sylvia Sanderson still in possession of our diplomatic bag key to hand over to you, he has to act quickly so he contacts Laszlo who is his Berlin control….to do the heinous deed. Murder Sylvia Sanderson and make it look like an accident. Laszlo then arranges for the accident to look like a hit and run and for all I know the bastard may even have killed her himself.'

'But if you didn't trust him why did you keep him…'

'Because if I abandon Laszlo I lose my blackmail control over him with the Nazis and until now I've had no reason to suspect him of treachery. However, I'm a believer in that if you give a fool a long enough rope he will eventually hang himself. And he has. Unfortunately, too late to save poor Sylvia. It could have, should have been avoided because I was already suspicious of Lomas's alleged accident. I should have been on my guard – two accidental

Embassy deaths within two weeks of each other – it can happen, has in the past, but....' he left unfinished as the sentence seamlessly flowed into a short contemplative silence. The quiet gave Scott time to observe the sadness etched into Sir James' face who with a slouch of the shoulders and indrawn breath continued, 'Well, Rutherford, that brings my sad hypothesis up to your arrival at the Embassy. Let's hear what you have to add.'

Scott, using Sir James' favourite debriefing phrases, opened his summary, 'Thank you, Sir James. A very concise and accurate account with nothing apparent, however trivial, left out.' Sir James' eyes narrowed to slits as he suspected Scott of wilful leg-pulling. Scott thinking he may have overplayed his hand quickly referred to his notes, 'My own findings are also based on partial facts and suppositions. I start with Grenville's first day as the SAA at the Embassy. He is shown his duties by Beatrice, Sir Eric's secretary. She informs him one of his principal jobs is to take delivery of the Foreign Office diplomatic bag. The bag arriving daily (except Sunday) by courier from the Royal Air Force diplomatic flight from London. Once in his possession and signed-for, he breaks the seal and extracts two bags. The leather bag embossed in gold leaf and bearing the Royal Crown insignia and seal stamped Foreign Office was to be delivered to her for opening prior to the Ambassador distributing the contents to his relevant section heads. Grenville notes she has the key for this bag which she retains. The other plain unstamped leather bag she informed him is the property of the Trade Attaché and must not be opened by any other than the attaché who holds the key. This means Grenville does not have access to the keys for either bag – especially ours. An unforeseen set-back but one they should have known about. Realising he has a problem, Grenville rushes to Burnett who happens to be in Berlin on one of his now frequent visits. Burnett hastily concocts a plan to seduce Beatrice.'

'Why Beatrice?'

'Because, he now knows she has one set of the keys and knows who possesses ours. And with Grenville and Burnett both being Nancy boys...' Sir James winced at the use of Scott's slang. '...the task of seduction is given to Laszlo since he comes into contact with her often over mail issues at the Embassy. Laszlo indicates it would be his pleasure to give Beatrice.....'

'Yes, thank you Rutherford, no need to explain. I fully understand. For your information the expression used by us to describe your theory is – entrapment.' Scott looked impressed at Sir James knowledge of such matters. 'However, I tend to think you're pushing the boat out too far with your theory. I mean, the woman would have to be either desperate or retarded to have anything to do with Laszlo.'

Scott, with a shoulder shrug and a palms upwards motion explained, 'It happens all the time, Sir James. Sad, lonely, older woman meets younger, good looking, smooth talking....'

'Never met this Beatrice myself but she sounds like she has eyesight problems if she thinks that ruffian Laszlo's good looking.'

'Actually, Sir James, she's a middle-aged spinster and a harridan supreme. She still bears the signs of having been good looking in her prime and in fact still remains, er,....'

'Well preserved, frustrated, and still awaiting Prince Valiant to arrive on his charger,' finished Sir James.

'No better description. She's devoted to Sir Eric and her job – what's known nowadays as a professional career woman. However, having said that, I regret to say I envisage that Laszlo, by bedding her, acquired both of the "dip-bag keys" for Grenville – the FOs and ours.'

'Did she give him the keys or did he obtain them by devious means?'

'I couldn't rightly say, sir. I would imagine the theft of the FO bag key was devious. He would have stolen the key somehow, made a copy and replaced the original from wherever without her knowledge. As to the whereabouts *of our* key he would have used pillow-talk on her. On the assumption that you inform Sir Eric as to who holds our key in case of emergencies...,' he broke off to look at Sir James who nodded his agreement. 'Then I'm sure that in the course of their working day Sir Eric must've mentioned to Beatrice that Sylvia held our key to give to the new attaché. I base this on the fact that when Beatrice met me on my arrival at the Embassy, in the *absence* of Sir Eric, she indicated that Yvonne had *our key* for me.

So if she knew Yvonne had the key for me, it then follows that she knew Sylvia *had it previously*. The inadvertent source of both these disclosures being Sir Eric. I would surmise that it was during these pillow-talk sessions that, either willingly or otherwise, she let slip to Laszlo that Sylvia had the key for the SIS "dip-bag" – *and that,* I'm afraid secured Sylvia's fate.'

An impressed Sir James murmured, 'Well I'll be buggered. I seemed to have jumped the gun about your theory – I do believe it now seems plausible. For I have to admit that in my supposition I had assumed that Grenville always knew Sylvia had the key but on reflection the only people who knew were Sixsmith, your predecessor, who knowing you would be late arriving at the Embassy had given the key to Sylvia prior to his departure. Then after his departure and Sylvia's tragic demise that left only Sir Eric, Liz and me knowing who had the key. So, if you're blaming Sir Eric for source disclosure then you will have to blame me also. Furthermore, I can see nothing wrong in Sir Eric's confiding in Beatrice, for she is after all his personal private secretary, and in his frequent absences she has to be kept abreast of such matters. But for her to be in the position she holds means she has signed the Official Secrets Act and you know what that means, Rutherford – regarding one's mouth?' he finished with chin resting on arched clasped fingers with elbows on desk staring penetratingly at Scott.

Scott knew. Beatrice was in serious trouble. 'Yes sir, I do. But I don't necessarily think for one moment she meant any harm. Laszlo, being the smooth operator he is, could have phrased his questions so that she would have given him answers without her knowing she had disclosed the key's whereabouts. In my opinion she is just another sad, forlorn, lonely, naïve, elderly spinster taken-in by Laszlo's sweet-talk.'

'Personally, I find it hard to believe that Laszlo has the intelligence to use such sophisticated interrogation methods. I would have thought him more the resorting to violence type,' Sir James said unclasping his fingers before sitting upright.

Scott coughed politely. 'Of course there was always the threat of the withdrawal of one's services – if you follow my meaning, Sir James.'

'Indeed I do, Rutherford. As Napoleon allegedly said; "Not tonight Josephine".'

'What will happen to her?'

'Who the bloody hell cares,' retorted Sir James sharply. 'I warned you of the penalties for breach of the OSA. The same applies to her. I will arrange for the Military Police to arrest her.'

'Steady on, sir. We can't go arresting her on my suppositions. We must have proof.'

Sir James, not being used to being told to "steady on", replied angrily, 'I heard you say, *"you thought she meant no harm"*, well let me tell you, Rutherford, I've lost an excellent officer in Sylvia Sanderson – *murdered*. She served her country with distinction during the war. Taught me everything I know about interrogation. And all because of the *"she meant no harm"* careless talk of a bloody frustrated spinster who can't keep her legs closed – Sylvia's dead. That's good enough for me. I want that bloody woman removed from the Embassy immediately.'

'But Sir James she was taken advantage of by a......'

'Enough Rutherford. Subject closed,' Sir James shouted, bringing his fist hard down on the desk. 'Now carry on.'

Aware that Beatrice's comeuppance, which he had to admit he had looked forward to, could now result in the death penalty made Scott feel far from ebullient as he soldiered on, 'I come now to what I consider to be the main downfall of "Operation Glasgow" – *your* sending of *that* despatch to "Maryhill" seeking his progress. Grenville, by this time, with the murder of Sylvia, had his ill-gotten duplicate key to our "dip-bag" which he put to good use by copying the contents and giving them to Laszlo for the Soviets to decipher.'

Sir James, with hand to forehead and headache imminent grumbled, 'Copies the contents! How? Not by hand surely? Even with shorthand the time taken to copy would increase Grenville's risk of exposure.'

Scott, forgetting Sir James still lived in the carbon copy past enlightened him. 'The despatches were copied by the new photocopier in the general office. Possibly during lunch when nobody was about.'

'But what good does copying do? – The despatches are

unbreakable if they don't have our code base, "A Tale of Two Cities", and the relevant page number for the day,' replied Sir James agitatedly.

Sir James was about to find out what good copying does. 'Not unbreakable if you've got an Enigma machine – as I suspect our Soviet friends have,' answered Scott.

This grave news made the niggling headache worse and coupled with a feeling that technology was passing him by caused Sir James to reach into the bottom desk drawer to withdraw the Glenmorangie and pour two stiff measures. He slid a glass to Scott, lit a cigar, leaned back in his chair and from behind a billowing haze of smoke, quizzed, 'I was of the belief that the Germans were the only people to possess the Enigma machine.'

'It was certainly invented by them. An engineer, Arthur Scherbius, around 1920 invented one for commercial use before it was subsequently adapted by the German military. However, the Polish Cipher Bureau broke this Enigma encryption code in 1932 by using reverse engineering which is a form of....'

By way of an interruption Sir James held his hand with palm outwards patting air towards Scott and with his voice showing irritation he growled, 'Yes, yes, yes, Rutherford. What you're trying to tell me is that the Russians realised the potential of the Enigma machine while we were still buggering around with our idiotic "Tale of Two Cities".'

'I believe we were offered the Enigma but deemed it too unwieldy for battle conditions...'

'No comment,' sighed Sir James with a shake of head. 'It was no doubt the decision of some bloody Old Etonian at the MOD who didn't know an enema, never mind an Enigma, from his arse.'

'Er, quite sir. But the point I am trying to make is that the breaking of the code by the Polish cryptologists must be the reason the Nazis are now working on the new advanced unbreakable code model and also why you have an interest in Dieter's knowledge of the new machine.'

'I've already indicated to you Rutherford that I've no further comment to make on the matter,' replied Sir James not wishing to divulge what he knew of HMG's involvements in the ultra-secret establishment at Bletchley Park where they now had Dieter ensconced explaining to their scientists, mathematicians and engineers the technicalities of the new German Enigma. So he hastily changed the subject. 'You were explaining before we digressed that you thought the catalyst for the collapse of "Operation Glasgow" was *my* request to "Maryhill" for an update on the new Enigma.'

'Yes it was. It was desperately unfortunate timing because by the time your despatch reached the Embassy by courier Grenville was in possession of a copy of our "dip-bag" key from Laszlo enabling him to open our "dip-bag" and copy the despatch and then give the copies to Laszlo for deciphering by the Soviet's Enigma machine when he picked up the Embassy mail.'

Sir James nodded his head in agreement. 'It was shortly after this that "Lambhill" was fire-bombed. Do you suppose that was Laszlo's doing?'

'Yes. From the information Grenville stole from our "dip-bag" and passed to Laszlo the Soviets rightly assumed we had an agent working on the new Enigma but fortunately they had no idea who, otherwise Dieter would now be in Moscow, not London. However, as I now surmise, Laszlo anonymously tipped off the Gestapo suggesting to them that British Intelligence had an agent planted in their Enigma programme. Suspecting from surveillance on the Embassy that "Lambhill" was our drop-point, the Gestapo arranged with the late Rohm's mercenary storm troopers to fire-bomb "Lambhill". This had a twofold purpose. First, to take "Lambhill" into custody and torture him for information. Just suspecting him of being Jewish was enough to arrest him and secondly to put the shop under surveillance and see what I did when I found it smouldering. They hoped I would run to "Maryhill" – I didn't.'

'You couldn't, because you didn't know where to go. But you did later.'

'Correct. Because of Laszlo's tip-off to the Gestapo about us having an agent in the Enigma programme they put surveillance on all the scientists working on the Enigma. This, Laszlo craftily knew they would do. And, with me having stupidly probed him to see if he knew where I could find "Maryhill', and him being astute enough to figure out "Maryhill" must be important, he encouraged me, dressed as a postman, to find "Maryhill's" apartment.'

'Ah! So that's how Laszlo knew Dieter's address – he followed you when you cycled there.'

'Yes sir. Told me he was off to do his afternoon deliveries but obviously followed me. Fortunately for me as it transpired.'

'Mmm,' mulled over Sir James. 'Now, pray tell, Rutherford, once you had departed Dieter's apartment why did Laszlo attack the Gestapo and wipe them out? With your kindly assistance of course.'

Ignoring Sir James' sarcasm Scott replied, 'Another twofold answer. First, Laszlo knew that if Dieter was not in residence there was a very good chance that in my disguise as a postman that one of his neighbours would tell me his whereabouts with the outcome that the Gestapo on arresting me would resort to torture for disclosure of Dieter's location. This he could not allow to happen – so he mounted the attack.'

'And secondly?'

'Laszlo did it to ingratiate himself to me to enable him to get "Maryhill's" name and address in Röbel. And, as I have already disclosed to you – because time was of the essence in my race against the Gestapo to Röbel – I released "Maryhill's" name to him and he found the address for me. After that all he had to do was follow me.'

'But why follow? He now had the name and address. He could have got rid of you and taken Dieter for himself.'

'Very true. But he knew I was a British Secret Service agent and stood a better chance of getting Dieter and, as we thought at the time, his sister to leave the house voluntarily.'

'Then gun you and her down outside the house and take him. A clever move until he met up with you and….'

'And Syd.' Before Sir James could ask who Syd was, Scott finished, 'Sir Eric's chauffeur and bodyguard. A handy man with a gun – an ex London flying squad sergeant. He accounted for one of the assailants. I couldn't have managed without him.'

Sir James shook his head and replied grumpily, 'Handy with a gun or not – I don't like civilians involved in our missions, especially civilians that go round shooting people, villains or otherwise –

understand Rutherford?'

Scott didn't apologise. He felt that Sir James should at least have conveyed his thanks for a job well done to Syd, but he finished, 'And those Sir James are my findings. Very little proof but with the both of us coming to the same conclusions as to the guilty party I don't think we can be wrong.'

'Thinking and proving are two entirely different matters. I feel we might have to resort to *other means*, Rutherford. What say you?'

'I certainly wouldn't like to think Grenville or Laszlo got off with the murders of Sylvia and Lomas…'

'They *weren't guilty* of Lomas's murder – that was down to that obese piece of shit Eustace. He wilfully employed Grenville in the full knowledge that Joyce had Lomas killed.'

'I think we will find it quite hard to find evidence against them, sir. Everything so far is circumstantial or supposition. No hard proof.'

'Believe me I will find a way – for Sylvia's sake,' thundered Sir James.

Scott gave Sir James' *"resort to other means"*, some thought before replying, 'What about me confronting Grenville, Laszlo, and Eustace individually with our guilty findings about them and asking them *politely*, for confessions…..'

Sir James crossed his arms and leaned back in his chair and made lengthy eye contact with Scott. They both knew what by *"other means"* meant. Sir James also knew what Scott meant by *"politely"*. Finally, with a deep sigh he said, 'But not Eustace – he's mine. I want to have the satisfaction of seeing the traitorous swine hang. Regarding the others one can only but try. But Rutherford….'

'Yes, Sir James?'

'Please remember confessions are always best if the confessor is still alive – I point this out because people seem to have a tendency to drop dead around you. You do understand the Oxford dictionary meaning of the word *alive* Rutherford?'

'Yes, Sir James,' replied Scott with a grin twitching on his lips.

'Well, make bloody sure you bring Grenville back alive for the hangman. And tell that chap Syd, who incidentally did a splendid job for you in Röbel and who you will no doubt make use of again – tell him no shootings, either.'

'I notice you didn't include Laszlo in your instruction.'

'To do so, Rutherford, would be but to kidnap a German national. And we can't have that. So I leave that solution to your own initiative.'

'I could always phone the Gestapo and tell them Laszlo was responsible for the shoot-out at Röbel and that he snatched Professor Neuman with the result that the professor is now in Moscow.'

'*What-an-excellent-idea* Rutherford – do that.' It's just a pity Laszlo will still be alive to tell them otherwise....of course if he were to meet with an accident. Sorry, Rutherford, just wishful thinking. What say you?'

'Wishes can come true, sir.'

'Good. I'm glad that's settled. Now off you go and arrange to pick up your travel voucher from Liz for tomorrow's flight to Berlin on your way out.'

'Yes sir,' replied an elated Scott rising from his chair to leave. He had just been given the nod in Sir James' roundabout fashion to avenge the deaths of Sylvia and Lomas. This he assumed was what Sir James' meant when he had earlier in their conversation indicated he had ideas for Laszlo.

Scott heard the barked voice behind him as he opened the office door, 'And remember Rutherford – keep Grenville alive please. That way I've got that traitorous bastard Eustace half way to the gallows.'

Scott, half in, half out, leaned back round the door edge into the office to give Sir James the "message received" thumbs-up. Closing the door he turned towards Elizabeth and was in time to witness her surreptitiously slipping one of the Belgian chocolates into her mouth. With a guilty look she tried hurriedly to replace the lid on the box and failed allowing Scott to see the contents: a solitary remaining chocolate. When Liz handed him his travel voucher he pulled her from her seat and waltzed her joyfully round the desk then kissed her on both cheeks before bounding into the corridor gleefully holding her last milk chocolate truffle. As he departed into the corridor she dreamily held a hand to her kissed cheek, the other searching unsuccessfully for the last truffle.

Scott, as he unwrapped Liz's last truffle whilst sitting in the taxi realised as he slipped his travel voucher into the inside pocket his immaculate tailored jacket that Liz had yet again known that Sir James was going to send him to Berlin the following day. The two of them played their cards very close to their chests.

Chapter 14

Croydon Airport Wednesday 8th May 1935
Scott boarded the Wednesday evening flight to Berlin from Croydon dressed in his business attaché attire, carrying an overnight case. Arriving some four and a bit hours later at Berlin's Templehof airport and with no Embassy Rover to pick him up he proceeded to custom control, submitted his passport in the name of William Willis with a photograph showing him sporting a pencil thin moustache and horn rimmed spectacles. Reason for visit – Business. Hotel – Berlin Continental. Passport – stamped. It being a long day he hailed a taxi to the Continental and bed.

***

Berlin Continental Hotel Thursday 9th May 1935
After an early breakfast he made two phone calls. One to an unlisted number. The recipient being a sullen Yvonne who still hadn't forgiven him for his last alleged misdemeanours – duping her with his impersonation of Sir Eric and failing to inform her of his intended mission to Röbel. The second call was to Syd. Sharp at 7-30am a black, ancient and battered Auto Union pulled up outside the hotel.

Scott opened the passenger door and slid alongside Syd. 'Morning Syd. Nice to see you again.'

'An' me you, sir. Here's a present from Yvonne,' he replied handing Scott a cardboard box. Scott opened the box to find his favoured pistol – a Walther PPK with silencer. 'Mechanism checked and oiled by me earlier.'

'Thanks for the present Syd. I take it you're carrying?'

Syd patted the patch pocket of his waxed jacket. From the size of the bulge Scott did not need to be told it was Syd's giant Lee Enfield service revolver. 'Ready for action, sir. Yvonne tells me you have the address of SAA Grenville's apartment.'

With Scott confirming the address Syd moved off with an apologetic crunch of gears from his battered Auto Union. 'Sorry sir. Had to use me own car. Beatrice is keeping a tight rein on the petrol vouchers after our last soiree.' But not for much longer thought Scott as he envisaged her being escorted from the Embassy by military police. 'Which reminds me, sir, how did it all finish?'

'Apologies, Syd, but I'm afraid I'm not allowed to say – classified.'

Syd tapped his nose with his forefinger. 'Sorry sir. Fully understand.'

'However, I can tell you my chief was absolutely delighted with your contribution and suggested I retain you for this mission.'

To Scott's delight a large, proud, gap-toothed grin spread over Syd's face as he concentrated on the road. Twenty minutes later they arrived at the address. It was a drab, grey stone building – conversion from commercial premises into apartments on the north bank of the River Spree. They parked outside and used the pass gate in one of the two original large timber doors to enter into a cobbled quadrangle with housing on all four sides. Access to Grenville's first floor apartment was via an ancient stone spiral staircase with a rusting iron handrail. According to the numbers at the top of the stair they turned left. Grenville's apartment was located in the far corner overlooking the river with the door entry exposed to the cobbled yard from below. Scott rang the doorbell. There was no answer but loud music was coming from inside. He rang again – still no answer. Scott nodded to Syd and moved his body to shield Syd who withdrew from his pocket a penknife and a length of stout gauge wire. Ten seconds later they entered a dark hall. They tip-toed on the plush carpeting to the first door and with weapons drawn swung it open with their backs to the hall wall either side of the door. The room, the dining room, leading into the lounge through French doors and overlooking the river was empty. The next two doors opposite revealed a kitchen and bathroom – also empty. Faced with the final two doors, presumably bedrooms, they chose the one at the end of the hall that Scott had worked out would overlook the river and should be the master bedroom. The loud music was coming from there. They followed the same door opening procedure. Guns at the ready they entered cautiously with eyes scanning the vast room for the slightest movement. There would be no need for the guns, nor would there be any forthcoming movement from the occupants. The silk pyjama clad bodies of Sergeant-at-Arms Grenville and Guy Burnett lay between the silk sheets in a pool of blood, the sides of their heads a gory mess. A service revolver lying on the floor appeared to have dropped from Grenville's hand which dangled over the side of the bed. Scott looked at Syd and made a circular gesture with his hand above his head then turned off the wireless. It had been turned up full volume to disguise the noise of gunfire. They left the flat.

As they were scurrying across the cobbled quadrangle a door opened and an elderly lady approached them. 'Are you the police?'

Indicating Syd to go on ahead, Scott answered her in his fluent Berlin accented German, 'Yes, madam. Why do you ask?'

'It was me that phoned you about the man that fled down the stairs ten minutes ago. He looked villainous and as though he was up to no good.'

'Description please, madam,' asked Scott curtly.

'A very tall, blond, long haired, unshaven, nasty looking ruffian. A criminal if I ever saw one...'

'Thank you madam, you have been very helpful. I will send one of my officers to interview you later,' replied Scott, now anxious to leave before the police arrived.

By the time Scott reached the car Syd had the engine running. He jumped in as it started to move and when they reached the top of the street and turned on to the main road they encountered a police car with bell clanging passing them on the opposite side of the road. In the rear view mirror Syd reported it turning into the street they had just exited. On the return journey into the city Syd retraced their route giving Scott time to come to the conclusion that it had not been a suicide pact – it had been from the description of the old lady, the work of Laszlo. The problem now being that Sir James would never believe he had not been responsible for the death of Grenville.

Syd, who had so far remained silent during the journey, mulling over how he had missed Grenville being homosexual, broke his silence, 'Cor blimey, sir. Fancy Grenville being a pansy, especially him being a Sergeant - at - Arms 'an all. I've always found them to be usually real tough guys. Whatever next?' he finished with a big sigh.

Syd waited in the car whilst Scott dealt with the next task. He walked down a dark service alleyway between shops and restaurants until he reached the road intersection. Heidi's café was on the corner of the alleyway. He looked at his watch 9-50am. He had only waited five minutes when he spied from the shadows of the alley a figure in postal uniform advancing towards him. He waited until the figure dismounted outside the café then showed his face around the corner of the alley and whispered Laszlo's name. Laszlo turned and headed towards the corner of the building only to encounter the dull gun metal of a silencer aimed steadily between his eyes. The silencer waved him enter the alley. He said nothing, his eyes darting about for means of escape. The silencer did not waver as it bid him sit on a metal refuse bin.

'Why the pistol, comrade?'

'End of the line, Laszlo…..'

'But why, mister attaché man? There is no need – I am your friend.'

'Friends do not try to kill each other…..friend.'

'I don't know what you're taking about.'

'Röbel. Müritz-see. Your gang tried to kill me and take Professor Neuman.'

Scott watched Laszlo's eyes narrow to slits. The PPK did not waver as Laszlo protested his innocence. 'Not me comrade. How could you say such a thing. You seem to forget it was me and *my gang*, as you call my work colleagues, Heinie and Hans, who saved you from the Gestapo when they rammed you off your cycle.'

'That was only to keep me from possibly disclosing to the Gestapo the whereabouts of the professor's location – which I foolishly gave to you.'

Laszlo, pointing at his chest growled, 'It was I that gave you his address.'

'Only after I told you it was in Röbel.'

'But if I had meant you harm I would not have given you the correct address, I would have kept it for myself.'

'Good try Laszlo. But you gave me the address knowing I could convince the professor to leave amicably. With you there, there would have been resistance – so you set up the attack for Heinie and Hans to take me when I left the house with the professor. What you didn't realise was I had somebody posted as a sentry. When the going got tough I noticed you didn't hang around.'

A silence ensued as Laszlo mulled this over. He finally broke it. 'Look, you've got this all wrong – the traitor is not me but your Sergeant Grenville. I have just done the "cunning one" a favour by shooting Grenville......'

'And his homosexual partner, Burnett,' interrupted Scott, letting Laszlo know he knew that both were dead.

Ignoring the interruption Laszlo carried on, '....he was passing secrets to the Nazis....'

'No Laszlo. He was passing them to you. And you being jealous of his affair with Burnett – your fellow homosexual contact..,' interrupted Scott, hoping to goad him about his sexual preference. '..killed them both.'

He succeeded. A furious Laszlo violently pointing at his chest with one hand as the other slid into his mail bag roared, 'Me! I would rather die than you think me an arse bandit......'

Scott who had seen Laszlo's hand slide in to the mail bag snapped, 'Wish granted Laszlo,' as his silenced PPK spat twice and Laslo's face exploded. 'That's for Sylvia and the others – you evil bastard.'

As Laszlo's body slid slowly down the refuse bin the mail bag slipped from his shoulder and the contents cascaded onto the dirty broken asphalt exposing a Russian Markov pistol dangling by the trigger guard from Laszlo's lifeless finger.

'The Embassy's mail is going to be a little late this morning,' muttered Scott quietly to himself as he stepped over the slumped body and retraced his steps down the alleyway to Syd.

A taxi from the hotel enabled Scott to catch the early afternoon Lufthansa flight back to London.

***

SIS(6) Headquarters London Friday 10th May 1935

Sir James commiserated with Timothy the lift operator, a one-arm casualty of the war and a Tottenham Hotspurs supporter like himself at Arsenal's winning of the league, as the cage made its laboriously slow journey through the many storeys of the building to his top floor lair overlooking the Houses of Parliament and the river Thames. On its eventual arrival Timothy deftly manoeuvred the awkward latticed steel grille doors open to allow Sir James to hobble to his office where he bid Elizabeth a grumbled good morning and enquired in a bad tempered tone if Rutherford was on the premises. She informed him Scott had phoned to announce that he was writing up his report and would be in presently. Sir James mumbled something indistinctly, entered his office and slammed the door. Now what could be his problem this morning – was it the realisation that his team Tottenham had been relegated (being an Arsenal fan she was secretly delighted) or could it be that he had heard the early morning BBC Home Service news bulletin about the suicide pact deaths of a Berlin Embassy employee and the editor of the Red Flag newspaper. These dilemmas Elizabeth was pondering as her phone rang. It was Sir Eric, the Berlin Ambassador. She connected him with Sir James. This did not bode well for Scott.

Sir James had in fact heard the news of the alleged Berlin suicides on the car wireless. He was furious at Rutherford. Another death. No. Correction. Two deaths. He was beginning to wonder if he had employed a psychopath. At this rate Rutherford would end up the patron saint of undertakers. His knee started to play-up. He reached into his bottom drawer for the Glenmorangie and was about to withdraw the bottle when the intercom buzzed. It was Elizabeth to announce the arrival of Scott. "Bugger", he muttered as he slipped the bottle back into the drawer.

Scott, forewarned of Sir James' disposition by Elizabeth, knocked timidly on the door and entered to a gruff, "Come in Rutherford."

On entry Scott's "good morning, sir," was not acknowledged but cut short by Sir James waving him to take a seat. Leaning back in his chair with arms crossed Sir James' voice was calm. Scott knew this to be a bad sign; the calm before the storm. The mood was then set by the curt Glaswegian growl, 'How did you get on in Berlin – Rutherford?'

'Hectic, Sir James, as my report will show,' he replied as he withdrew from an inside pocket of his immaculately tailored Saville Row suit a sheaf of neatly hand written papers.

Sir James grabbed custody of the papers and angrily spread them fan-shaped over his desk. He gave them a cursory glance. 'Now tell me about this hectic day of yours. Was it successful?'

'To a degree, sir.'

'And do you have Grenville in custody or did you save the taxpayer the cost of a trial?'

Scott, having been warned by Elizabeth that Sir James' bad mood was due to the fact that he knew of Grenville's untimely death was acutely aware where this grilling was heading, so he decided to finish it quickly by answering, 'The taxpayer was saved money – twice.'

Sarcastically Sir James queried, 'Twice indeed? My that's very cost effective of you, Rutherford.' Then the expected eruption took place as an apoplectic Sir James bawled, 'Have you taken leave of your bloody senses, Rutherford? Not one, but two sodding fucking deaths for me to explain to my Joint-Heads-of-Forces. Just when I've got them on my side to agree changes regarding security to our "dip-bag". Not to mention the death of my principal witness – that bastard Grenville. You...you ...dunderheid.'

Scott, now knowing this to be a weird Glaswegian insult took pleasure in correcting Sir James. He said innocently, as he pointed at his report still lying on the desk, 'With all due respect Sir James you will find when you *eventually* get round to reading my report that it was Laszlo that topped Grenville and Burnett.'

Sir James, grimacing at Scott's use of the slang term "topped", stopped short in his tirade as with forefinger raised he exclaimed, 'Ah!' The finger dropped. 'You had best explain then, Rutherford – I do apologise for my outburst. But that does not excuse your gross impertinence.'

'Sorry Sir James. No impertinence meant,' he lied, but with point made he then very hastily started the narrative of his and Syd's Berlin encounter.

Sir James, now with temper under control, listened intently and on hearing the association of Burnett's name with Grenville's nodded his head with satisfaction. This confirmed his earlier theory, contrary to Rutherford's earlier scepticism, about Grenville and Burnett knowing each other. 'Thank you, Rutherford, for your usual concise and thorough report but you do understand that impersonating a Berlin police officer is an offence,' he amiably chuckled.

The tension between them now lightened, Scott queried, 'What I can't understand, sir, is why Laszlo terminated Grenville when he was still of use to the Soviets at the Embassy. Burnett I do understand – he was in the wrong place at the wrong time and therefore convenient for Laszlo's devious brain to make it look like a suicide pact.'

'I don't agree about Burnett.'

'Why? He was important. He was soviet control for their agents in the UK and editor of...'

Sir James held his hand up for silence. 'To explain, you have to understand the Soviet psyche. The Soviets had failed to get Dieter. The mission was, therefore, a failure. The Soviets do not tolerate failure so they instructed Laszlo to get rid of Grenville *and* Burnett. Burnett was responsible for recruiting Grenville and would have been considered by Moscow as being instrumental in the failure of the diplomatic bag key fiasco. If you recall they thought Grenville as the SAA was to be in charge of the FO bag keys. That failure resulted in the death of Sylvia and the compromising of that infernal Beatrice woman. Both these incidents Moscow knew were possible security breaches which we would eventually pick-up on – as we have – rather belatedly. Therefore, end of Burnett. He was replaceable. Plenty more where he came from. Your old alma mater Cambridge University for one. A hot bed of subversives. So, Laszlo, on receiving his instructions from Moscow, could not believe his good fortune finding Burnett and Grenville "in flagrante delicto". Two birds killed with one stone. And I would imagine had you not terminated Laszlo – they would have.'

'Surely that doesn't answer the fact that Grenville could still have been of use to the Soviets at the Embassy.'

'Not really. They knew that their failure to kidnap Dieter at Röbel would alert us to a security breach and force us to change our "dip-bag" procedure which, as I've already told you, I am now in the process of concluding with the approval of the Minister and my bosses – the Joint-Heads-of-Staff for us to receive our dip-bag direct from the courier. Moscow were aware that once we had implemented the change then Grenville became surplus to their requirements.'

'But Grenville could still have been of use regarding the Foreign Office's diplomatic bag if not ours,' persisted Scott.

'The Soviets would never have got any secrets from the F.O bag other than the cost of paper clips or toilet paper for the Embassy – and they knew that. The real secret stuff between Hitler and Sir Eric takes place at Sir Eric's regular meetings in London with the Minister. No. Their main objective was our diplomatic bag. Laszlo's failure meant the end.'

'What will they do now about Laszlo?'

'Rejoice. You saved them from having to arrange his demise. Which reminds me – did you tip-off the Gestapo that Laszlo was responsible for Moscow kidnapping Dieter?'

'Yes. Got put through to a bloke called Himmler.'

'Excellent. You got their top man. I now assume that with Laszlo dead, the Russian made weapons from Röbel in their possession, and the eventual identification of Heinie and Hans proving a further soviet connection that Himmler will believe that Moscow did kidnap Dieter.'

Scott, not wishing to let go the subject of Laszlo said, 'Surely the Gestapo will think the circumstances of Laszlo's death strange?'

'Laszlo had failed......'

'But if he failed you don't expect the Gestapo to believe that the Soviets kidnapped Dieter...'

'Please let me finish, Rutherford. As I was saying – Laszlo had failed because he had left two bodies behind at Röbel which the Gestapo, as I have said, will eventually identify as Hans and Heinie, known communist associates of Laszlo. And the Gestapo knowing the Russian psyche on failure will assume the Kremlin terminated Laszlo for leaving identifiable bodies behind.'

'Yes. But conversely what will the Soviets think of Laszlo's death?'

'They, hopefully, will assume that once the Gestapo had put names to the Röbel bodies and associated them with Laszlo that they tried to arrest him. Laszlo resisted. There was a shoot-out and Laszlo came off worst. So all told, the death of Laszlo has turned out for the good. About the only good thing he ever did in his miserable life. As they say Rutherford – it's an ill wind that blows blah, blah....,' enthused Sir James.

After a pause to let Sir James' hypothetical summary sink-in, Scott finalised, 'Well, that just about clears up "Operation Glasgow".'

'Except for Sir bloody useless. That bastard has so many deaths on his hands to account for I can't wait to interrogate him. But that's my problem.'

'Problem, sir?'

'Proof, Rutherford, proof. I found none. Grenville alive was my last hope.'

'You don't mean that Eustace will walk free.'

'Not if I can help it but.... it's not looking good,' and with a shrug Sir James finished, 'Off you go, Rutherford. I'll see you on Monday to discuss your new assignment. And thank you for your help in solving this one. You did well, my boy.'

The "my boy" in lieu of the usual Rutherford did not escape Scott's notice as he, in turn, thanked Sir James for his invaluable help and guidance throughout the mission. He then rose from his chair deep in thought about the grave injustice that would be caused should Eustace escape punishment, and then departed Sir James' office mind awhirl.

Closing Sir James' door he turned to face Elizabeth who exclaimed with a beaming smile, 'You didn't get your head bitten off then, Scott!'

'Not quite Liz, but damn nearly.'

'Never mind. I can tell you without breaching the OSA that he thinks the world of you. He sees you as a younger version of himself. That aside, you must be proud of your first solo mission being such a success.'

'Not a total success Liz. For with Grenville dead Sir James has no proof of Eustace's wrongdoing – and unless he is brought to account for Lomas's and Sylvia's deaths then we have failed.'

'If you didn't terminate Grenville – who did?'

'Ah! I'll leave Sir James to tell you over dinner at Ferrari's tonight.'

Elizabeth looked at him in stark amazement. She stuttered, 'D..d..did…did Sir James, tell you that?….N..n..no he wouldn't,' she

145

trailed off disbelieving that Sir James would break a confidence.

Scott laughed out loud. 'His desk diary was open and I read it upside down. All part of my trade craft that he taught me.'

'Oh, you really are the limit Scott Rutherford,' she shot back at him and in frustration threw her notebook at him as he sat on the corner of her desk.

Moving smartly to catch the waywardly aimed notebook, he offered advice, 'If I was you I would cancel Ferraris and invite him to your apartment for a sexy candlelit dinner and......'

'And?'

'You never know your luck – Wahey! And...'

Elizabeth continued humouring him, 'And?'

'Don't mention the Spurs being relegated. And...' Elizabeth said nothing. She just looked quizzically at him. 'For God's sake tell him you love him. One of you has to make a move soon before senility sets into both of you.'

She stood, stretched out both arms and took hold of his hands and looked at him lovingly – her, gallant, young Sir James – the son she never had – kissed him lightly on both cheeks and wished him success with his new assignment wherever that might be, for Sir James had not as yet disclosed the theatre of operation to her.

Scott in return hugged her close. Elizabeth, then with an arm round his waist walked him to the door doing her best to supress tears. Scott with a nostalgic lump developing in his throat departed with a wink and a blown kiss.

Meanwhile inside Elizabeth's office Sir James had pulled his door closed quietly behind him and was leaning on his stick with both hands staring at the shapely figure of Elizabeth, who was staring at the back of the corridor door that Scott had exited. He was thinking what a fine looking woman she was, when suddenly sensing his presence she abruptly swivelled on a well-turned ankle to face him as she wiped a tear from an eye.

Embarrassed at having caught her off guard he mumbled, 'Sorry Liz. I didn't mean to intrude in your private, er....farewell. I shouldn't worry he will be back on Monday.'

At that she reverted to her old caring self, 'Now where are you off to, Jimmy?' she replied, cheerfully using his out-of-office-hours name.

Sir James, taken slightly aback at the use of his Christian name answered, 'To fire a salvo right up that traitorous bastard Eustace's arse.'

'Oh well, that should be nice for him,' Elizabeth replied absentmindedly, her mind concentrating on tonight's dinner menu. 'Now, when you get back – chances are I won't be here. I'm leaving early to prepare us a nice evening meal....'

'But we're booked into Ferraris at eight....'

'We *were* booked in. Change of plan. We are dining at my place tonight. I'm preparing your favourite – an Aberdeen Angus steak done in a Glenmorangie sauce – so don't be late. And don't drink too much at Mr Churchill's this afternoon so as to ruin your appetite. And if you're going to Mr Churchill's straight from Sir Eustace's make sure you take your top coat and hat with you – it's very cold out.' Elizabeth then turned and headed for the ladies' toilet.

A flabbergasted Sir James just stood with mouth agape – struck dumb. He had just been dictated to like a married man and liked it. But he wouldn't be struck dumb or dictated to at his next port of call.

He made the tiresome journey along the labyrinth of corridors to Sir Eustace's office during which he promised himself to keep his temper with the fat Tory oaf. When he arrived at his destination he did not announce himself with a knock instead he barged straight into the ante-room office.

Effy was thumping the keys on her typewriter. She looked up, 'I didn't realise you had an appointment, Sir James.'

'I don't,' he replied, as he moved past her and threw open Eustace's door without prior warning. Once in he slammed it shut.

'What in the name of blue blazes do you think you are doing, McKay?' demanded an aghast Eustace. 'Don't you Jocks have any bloody manners whatsoever?'

'Frightfully sorry, *old boy*, left them in the trenches fighting Jerry whilst you were in charge of the first paperclip division,' Sir James sarcastically answered whilst pulling up a chair to sit directly in front of Eustace.

Sir Eustace, regaining his bluster mocked, 'I suppose you're here to tell me you found your Berlin agent chappie. On his hols like I said he was, eh what!'

Sir James, as he had promised himself, resisted the urge to strike the pompous balloon with his walking stick, 'No I'm here to ask you about a *chappie*,' he mimicked, '...called Grenville.'

'Who? Never heard of any such.'

'The Sergeant-at-Arms – Berlin Embassy.'

'As I said, never heard of the blighter.'

Sir James tried out one of his uncorroborated suppositions that he had used on Rutherford. 'Well I am surprised you don't know of him considering you recruited him at the suggestion of your cousin Lady Dorothy Hooper-Ellis who asked you on behalf of William Joyce of the British Union of Fascists.'

'What utter tosh McKay....,' he barked, then paused, as deep in thought he massaged his double chin before suddenly blurting, 'Wait, just a sec. I remember him now. He applied to a "situations vacant" ad in the in-house "Whitehall Today" magazine. I interviewed him. Ideal candidate. Just lost his wife. Needed a change from London. And he spoke German.' Sir James could tell from the body language and countless previous interrogations of others that Eustace was telling lies. He was also aware that Eustace knew that he would check the magazine's "situations vacant" column so it was bound to be a bona fide advert. 'And with regards to your allegations about my cousin and this fellow Joyce – you must have taken leave of your senses.'

'She's a member of the BUF,' Sir James said in a flat matter of fact voice.

'As far as I'm aware that's not illegal. Being a man in your position you should know that. So, what's all the fuss about this Grenville chappie anyhow?'

'Grenville was a spy. Not for the Nazis as your cousin Lady Dorothy and Joyce assumed, but for the Soviets....' Sir James witnessed the slight flicker of surprise cross Eustace's face as he embarked on his second uncorroborated theory, '....Grenville had led Lady Dorothy to believe he was an ardent BUF fascist but he was in fact a Soviet agent placed in the BUF by a certain Guy Burnett. You know Burnett of course, a fellow old Etonian and managing editor of the communist Red Flag rag.'

Sir Eustace leaned back in his seat, arched his hands with steepled fingers over his obese stomach and spluttered, 'What absolute rubbish, never heard the like. You been at the Glenmorangie again, McKay?'

Sir James, sensing that he had rattled Eustace with his disclosure of Grenville being a Soviet agent, pressed on, 'You, my traitorous friend, are responsible for the deaths of two Foreign Office employees – Sylvia Sanderson and Trevor Lomas.'

'Who the hell are they?'

'Lomas was Grenville's predecessor in the Embassy. Found drowned.....'

Eustace interrupted, 'Yes, yes, I remember now. Tragic accident whilst on holiday. I sent one of my chaps to his funeral in Margate. The police found no suspicious circumstances.'

Ignoring the interruption Sir James carried on, '...Murdered, so that Grenville could get Lomas's job.' Sir James knew Laszlo was actually responsible for Sylvia's death but proceeded along the lines that it had been Eustace. 'Then you arranged for the demise of Sylvia Sanderson, the soon-to-retire receptionist....'

'It was a hit-and-run accident for God's sake, McKay. I was here in London when it happened,' wailed Eustace.

'Ah! Nice to see you've got your memory back – you've suddenly remembered who Sylvia Sanderson was and how she was killed. Correction – murdered. Murdered – for the key to my department's "dip-bag." He then pointed an accusatory finger at Eustace, 'Maybe you didn't actually do *the deeds* but you as good as murdered them.'

'Look here McKay – I know nothing of this balderdash. Murders indeed. That's the trouble with you secret service types you see double dealing and mysterious deaths at every turn where none exist. Where's your proof?'

'My proof is a confession from Grenville of your involvement in their deaths gained by my man Rutherford,' Sir James lied, playing the ace card of his subterfuge.

A twisted grin caused Eustace's jowls to quiver, 'Good try, old boy. Unfortunately for you I've just received a phone call from our boss, Sir Toby Simmonds (The Foreign Office Minister) to advise me that he has received a phone call from Sir Eric in Berlin informing him that one of his employees, Grenville, is dead as is this other fellow Burnett you mentioned. Apparently their deaths were made to look like suicide but the police think otherwise. They, the Berlin police, have a witness who claims she can recognise three possible assailants including two who impersonated police officers, one of whom she spoke to. I'm sure in the light of what you've just disclosed, old boy, the Berlin police would be delighted to hear from your chappie, Rutherford, as to how he obtained this alleged confession. I get the feeling you've been hoist by your own petard – old boy.'

Sir James cursed under his breath. He realised his hoped for confession from Sir Eustace was now impossible due to his ace card, the lie about Rutherford obtaining Grenville's confession, being trumped unwittingly by Sir Eric's revealing phone call to Sir Toby. That fact now forced him to go on the defensive for he knew Eustace's next move would be an anonymous tip-off via Joyce at the BUF to the Berlin police that Rutherford, the Embassy attaché, was involved and a major diplomatic incident would ensue – one that would cause embarrassment to HMG – not to mention his own department. He would just have to take this one on the chin and bide his time. Eustace would slip up – they always did. So he replied, 'Looks like I've been misled, Eustace.'

'Glad you've seen reason at last, McKay. An apology wouldn't go amiss followed by a promise of no more of this nonsense about me being a traitor.'

'Very well, Eustace. I agree,' said Sir James, whilst thinking, *he's getting no bloody apology from me – the traitorous bastard.*

'Now that we've agreed my innocence, I bring to your attention that this Grenville chappie should have been vetted by your department before being employed by me. How very remiss of you McKay to allow somebody like that to be appointed to a position of trust.'

'He would have been vetted had we been informed that you intended to employ him.'

'Tch, tch, I'm sure I remember sending you a memo to that

effect, McKay. I'm afraid your secretary must have mislaid it. Now if you'll excuse me, old boy, I've *more important* matters to deal with so I'll bid you good day.'

He could have pointed out to Eustace that it was a violation of the OSA to employ anybody without prior clearance from SIS(5) or (6) but knew Eustace would use his memo lie to cover his deception, so he bid him a grudging good afternoon.

In the corridor he looked at his watch, still in good time for lunch with Winston at Chartwell, and departed Eustace's office furious at the circumstances, namely Sir Eric's ill-timed phone call that had allowed Eustace to outmanoeuvre him. However, on reflection he should have realised Sir Toby Simmonds would contact Eustace. It had all been in the timing, yet again – fuck.

Rutherford and he would need to get together on Monday and work their way through the files again. He was sure they had missed something regarding Eustace. He wondered if Rutherford was giving the matter any further thought.

Chapter 15

Winston Churchill Chartwell Friday 10th May 1935
Sir James, wearing his topcoat and trilby to keep out the recently arrived cold weather, exited the portals of the Foreign Office to be met by the duty chauffeur, Stanley, holding the rear door of the Rolls-Royce open.

'Parky for May, Sir James.'

'It is that, Stanley,' replied Sir James as his knee gave a twinge as always in the cold weather.

'Mister Churchill at Chartwell, I believe, sir.'

'Aye, the man himself, Stanley,' he acknowledged as he slid along the leather upholstered luxury of the rear seat towards *The Times* newspaper.

As the Rolls-Royce purred silently forward he picked up *The Times* and started the crossword. At the first awkward clue he turned to the front page news and after a relatively short read which made him feel depressed at the state of the world in general he returned it folded to the seat for the return journey. He then turned his thoughts to today's objective – the garnering of advice from Churchill regarding his latest embryonic idea which he had been working on prior to the Berlin debacle of "Operation Glasgow" – "Op-G". Churchill's knowledge of "Op-G" stemmed from 1921 when McKay had approached him with the project. With Churchill's backing they had put it forward to the then head of SIS(6) Sir John Holland for approval – which was granted. This had been the start of James McKay's upward climb of the SIS(6) ladder.

Fourteen long years ago mused Sir James sadly as he looked out the window at the grey sleet-carrying clouds scurrying over the fields and hedgerows of Kent which signified a nearing of Chartwell, home to his friend and mentor Winston Churchill. A friendship that defied all logic – Churchill the archetypal conservative and Sir James the militant socialist – but for all these differences the friendship endured. Sir James was aware that Churchill had been out of office since the general election of 1929 but still remained well connected, still privy to privileged information from elements within HMG and senior civil servants. Being out of office had not stopped him from making an outspoken speech in parliament against the National Coalition Government – led by the ailing Ramsay McDonald – on their appeasement policy. It was this speech that decided Sir James to finalise his plan and seek Churchill's opinion as he had for "Operation Glasgow" all those years ago.

As the limousine turned off the main road and glided its way along the tree-lined asphalted driveway towards a creeper-hung, pink brick building with stepped gables, a portly gentleman drawing pleasurably on a Havana cigar stood up from his seat in the sun lounge overlooking the Weald of Kent to witness the stately parade of the Rolls-Royce. He had just finished reminiscing about the approaching limousine's passenger, Jimmy McKay, a gruff, no-nonsense, intelligent, hard as nails Glasgow socialist with an enormous chip on his shoulder regarding the aristocracy. He had recalled their first meeting, 1916, in the trenches with the 6th Battalion Royal Scots and their forays into enemy occupied territory. Those were the adrenalin filled days. Then after the war his subsequent intelligence sector mentoring of McKay – a watching brief on his progress up the intelligence ladder – and finally a little help against the prejudices of "the-old-school-tie brigade" to McKay becoming head of SIS(6). It had all been worth the effort for there was no finer man he would put his trust in than Jimmy McKay. He waited eagerly to hear about McKay's new unspecified project – for he too had a project that required McKay's valued counsel.

Churchill's portly figure arrived at the main door only to find it already held open by his butler and bodyguard Larkin. 'Thank you, Larkin. Quite safe. It's an old friend, Sir James McKay.' Larkin nodded his head in understanding, his smartly tailored dinner jacket not quite hiding the bulge of an under-arm firearm.

When the resplendent Silver Ghost marque complete with Foreign Office pennants fluttering briskly in the bitter cold wind drew to a halt the chauffeur opened the rear door for Sir James. As he slid out from the warm interior and leaned on his walking stick he grimaced in pain as his knee went into spasm from the biting cold. Gritting his teeth he arrived at the open door, divested himself of coat and trilby into the outstretched arms of Larkin, thanked him and turned to Churchill with hand ready for greeting.

'Saw the face contortion as you got out the car, Jimmy. Still taking your medicine for the knee?' enquired Churchill as they warmly shook hands.

'But of course, Winston.'

'Good. For it just happens I have a bottle of Glenmorangie for such an emergency.'

Sir James followed Churchill into the sun lounge. As he lowered himself into a sumptuous down filled cushion of a cane chair Churchill poured two large measures of Glenmorangie malt whisky. He then took a similar seat opposite Sir James and offered him a Havana cigar from a silver cigar box on the large glass topped coffee table between them. The two men sat there with looks of contentment on their faces as with legs crossed over knees they puffed and sipped two of life's luxuries. Churchill was intrigued to discover that even the most ardent of socialists enjoyed reviled aristocrat tastes.

Churchill broke the comfortable silence. 'Clemmie sends her humblest apologies. She had to attend an important meeting in London – Harrods,' he chortled. 'However, she did get chef to lay-on a Scottish salmon lunch. Then down to business. How does that suit?'

'Excellent,' replied Sir James stubbing his cigar out in a cut crystal ashtray, thinking it a better offer than sandwiches from a Lyons Corner House and stubbing out cheap cigars in tin lids.

During the excellent fresh salmon lunch washed down with a bottle of Chablis from the cellar and Drambuie liqueurs, followed by another round of Havana cigars, Churchill insisted that he be informed about the Berlin affair. Sir James obliged.

When Sir James completed his account of the episode Churchill asked, 'And what of the villain Laszlo who disposed of Grenville and Burnett?'

'Pushing up the daisies.'

'Your man Rutherford?'

'Yes. Pity it hadn't been Eustace Pennington - Beaumont.'

'Oh! That sounds tasty. Please to continue.' Sir James explained his quandary regarding Eustace. 'Never trusted the man. When I get back in government he will be a casualty, believe me Jimmy. That of course doesn't solve your immediate problem. So, what do you have in mind – Rutherford?'

Sir James replied with tongue-in-cheek, '*Really*, Winston. How could you suggest such a thing…..contrary to what you may think about Rutherford, he's not an assassin. In being gifted with knowing right from wrong he has to make delicate moral decisions for the good of the realm.'

Churchill laughed deeply at Sir James feigned protest before changing the subject. 'Now please tell me about this new project of yours.'

'Well Winston, having read the Hansard transcript of your Commons speech regarding the government's appeasement policy I couldn't agree more with you. Hitler does intend to make a fool out of the Coalition Government.'

'Mmm,' mused Churchill from behind a lingering waft of cigar smoke. Brushing it away with his hand he remarked, 'Thank god somebody agrees with me for we appear to be thin on the ground….. So?'

'It is common knowledge that a civil war is brewing in Spain. The Oviedo situation is just the start. As I see it, Hitler will bide his time doing what he's doing now – supplying the Nationalists with arms and aircraft…'

'The Nationalists being General Franco and his fellow fascist generals representing the Monarchy, the Catholic church and landowners.'

'That is correct, Winston. Regarding Franco representing the Monarchy and church I think time will show him to be representing himself…'

'And become a dictator like his chums Hitler and Mussolini,' interrupted Churchill.

'Correct again. However, it is pretty much a foregone conclusion that with Hitler's aid the Nationalists will win. This achieved Hitler will strike a deal with Franco, or even use force, to allow him access through Spain to our strategic key acquisition in the Mediterranean – Gibraltar.' At the mention of Gibraltar, Churchill laid down his cigar and studied Sir James attentively as Sir James continued, 'Now what would you say if I were to suggest an alternative to Gib....'

'Tenerife,' blurted a shocked Churchill at hearing aired the same idea that he was about to discuss with McKay. 'Have you been talking to the Admiralty?'

'No,' answered a taken aback Sir James. 'Why?'

'Because I have put forward a similar plan to the Admiralty through Anthony Eden for funding approval.'

'Well I'll be buggered,' replied a dumbfounded Sir James.

A grinning Churchill said, 'A coincidence indeed, Jimmy. So let's hear what you've got.'

'First off it's what I've not got. I don't have an agent on Tenerife. We have no representation whatsoever.'

'Do you have one in mind?'

'Yes. The one that brought Professor Neuman out from Berlin – Scott Rutherford. But I need a cover for him.'

'Now funnily enough, Jimmy, this is where I can be helpful. In my plan I intend to use an American cousin on my mother's side of the family and to whom I don't readily admit to being related. He's in the travel business and has recently set-up in opposition to Thomas Cook in the Canary Islands which, as you know, Tenerife is the largest. You might well have seen his rather vulgar advertisement in the travel section of *The Times*. It caused an avalanche of "Disgusted. Tonbridge Wells" letters to the editor. Better still I have a copy to hand in my file.' Churchill left the room and returned with a file and withdrew a newspaper cutting which he slid across the glass top to Sir James.

Sir James read: CAN TRAVEL? THEN LET CANTRAVEL TRAVEL YOU. Followed by advertising copy. 'I think it's rather catchy actually, Winston. I assume CANTRAVEL stands for Canary Travel?'

'Mmm. Quite so. Typical American Madison Avenue advertising rubbish. He claims to have a clientele of aristocracy, socialites, film stars and directors, industrialists and bankers, etcetera. He has motorised luxury yachts leaving Tilbury Docks to travel to Santa Cruz the capital of Tenerife where they are met with omnibuses in his livery, a *ghastly* yellow and orange, and bussed to

Puerto de la Cruz, a fledgling holiday resort where, somewhere in the mountains, he bought a derelict farm, a finca and turned it into a luxury complex. Bars, five star restaurants, dancing, cabaret with international artistes, horse riding, swimming pools etcetera, etcetra. Not quite San Tropez but getting there. Ideal cover for an agent wouldn't you say?'

'Indeed.'

'And he's looking for a diving instructor – so I thought about approaching the Admiralty. Does your man Rutherford dive perchance?'

'Of course – he's a former Royal Marine. In fact, he is not long back from a course in oxygen re-breathers with the Italian Navy in Spezia.'

'Oxygen re-breathers?' queried Churchill.

'Think of a frogman. Oxygen cylinders on your back for breathing but instead of exhaling your spent oxygen you recycle it through a filter. This allows you to stay underwater umpteen times longer for the same cubic capacity of oxygen.'

'Clever stuff, I must say. I would say cousin Eugene has acquired a diver, and we now have cover for your man Rutherford.'

'But we still need a conduit. A means of communication with our agent, but the choice is limited. There are no direct commercial flights from London. The operation being unaccountable we can't use the RAF...'

'And, in the present diplomatic climate I doubt if the Spanish Government would give landing permission for fear of upsetting Adolf,' clarified Churchill.

'...And the telephone would be a security nightmare – can you imagine the number of re-routes it would take. By ship is the obvious solution but it would take for ever,' lamented Sir James.

'Look, Jimmy. Can we dot the I's and cross the T's later, something will turn up. If all else fails we can use Eugene's yachts. If we do, do you have someone in mind to act as courier?'

'Yes. A very competent young lady. She's presently in Berlin and she has worked with Rutherford. If we were to use Cantravel's yacht she could act as a stewardess or whatever you call them.'

'Excellent idea. Being American, he of course doesn't have

stewardesses, he has facilitators. Man's a blaggard. I hate dealing with him. He's a typical American, views everything in dollar signs. Only thing going for him is having been educated at Oxford. However, when needs must, Jimmy....'

Sir James was interrupted with an urgent knock on the sun lounge door. On Churchill's bidding Larkin entered to advise Churchill that it was Sir Reginald Tyrell, Admiral of the Fleet, on the secure line in the study. Churchill jumped up eagerly and disappeared to return five minutes later to announce jovially that his meeting with Anthony Eden some seven months earlier had come up trumps in that he had received funding for his – now "their" – project from the Admiralty's "emergency war chest" subject to a full plan being submitted by SIS(6) for their approval. They let out a triumphant whoop together. Celebratory whiskies were poured.

With the crossword completed a deep-in-thought Sir James, having mentally finalised "Operation TENALT", suddenly found Stanley opening the door to let him alight outside Elizabeth's apartment block in Fulham.

***

Late Evening Outside the Foreign Office Friday 10th May 1935

The weather was particularly bad for this time of year as the almost horizontal rain laced with sleet drove into the windscreen of a Lagonda sports tourer parked in the shadows between two dimly lit ornate cast iron lampposts in King Charles Street. The wipers were struggling to cope with the ever accumulating sleet as the figure behind the steering wheel occasionally wiped the misted inside of the windscreen with the edge of a chamois leather glove as he watched with never faltering eyes the wrought iron gates to the entrance of the Foreign Office. A slight opening movement of the gates alerted the watcher to stub out his cigarette in the dashboard ashtray and take up a driving position in readiness. The sleek graceful lines of a silver Bentley Vanden Plas limousine slid through the gates, the driver the sole occupant. The person in the Lagonda confirmed the Bentley's licence plate with a nod then waited until the Bentley turned into Parliament Street before slipping the Lagonda into first gear and tickling the accelerator of the four and a half litre engine into life.

The chances of being observed in such atrocious conditions were remote but even so the Lagonda kept a discreet distance behind the Bentley as it crossed Westminster Bridge heading for the A3 London to Portsmouth main road. Following the quarry as far as Wimbledon the driver of the Lagonda now knew for certain the Bentley's destination and overtook at the first opportunity. Several miles later just through the market town of Guildford, with the weather conditions having not improved any, the Lagonda slithered to a halt on the treacherous road surface of a layby. A cigarette was lit as the wait started. The cigarette had just been extinguished as a Bentley, the number plate hardly distinguishable in the murk and spray, passed at speed. The driver recognised the number plate and slipped the Lagonda into gear, floored the accelerator and the great beast of an engine leapt into life with the rear tyres spinning on the compacted sleet as it hurtled in pursuit.

Sir Eustace was driving his Bentley Vanden Plas flat out on the A3 London to Portsmouth main road on his way to the family estate in Liphook for the weekend. He was meeting his cousin Lady Dorothy and her chum William Joyce and several other prominent business and political supporters of the British Union of Fascists. It was a dark night, his powerful headlights reflecting the sleet-driven rain back on to a windscreen that, with wipers barely coping, made for extremely difficult driving conditions. His speed from the three and a half litre engine was excessive for the conditions but it exhilarated him – taking his mind off that infernal socialist Glaswegian upstart McKay who had had the audacity to call him a traitor. Him – a staunch supporter of the new ultra-right wing of fascism – the only party that could save a nation in decline from the destructive ravages of socialism and communism and Jews. If innocents like Lomas and Sanderson had to die to promote the cause – so be it. Suddenly, his dark wanderings were abruptly jarred as he became aware of two yellowish glows of headlights closing in behind him at speed as he was approaching a notoriously dangerous sweeping curve in the road near Hindhead. As he applied the brakes he saw out the corner of his eye in the rear view mirror a brilliant flash, similar he thought to that given off by a gun muzzle. A ridiculous thought, of course – more than likely on a night like this a flash of lightning. Without warning the Bentley went into a side skid on the treacherous road surface. Damn! What a night for a puncture. Before he had time to correct the slide the car hit the kerb and the steering wheel was wrenched from his grip and his obese body swung out of its seat as his feet came off the pedals. He had lost control. The Bentley, still at speed crashed through a low stone wall and took off to land on its radiator and somersaulted onto its roof on the acute rock-strewn banking, breaking out in flames as it came to rest violently against a tree. His body was trapped with no way of escape as the flames engulfed the Bentley.

High above the stricken vehicle a Lagonda sports tourer whipped past at speed. As it did an arm withdrew a Walther PPK pistol from the open window.

***

Elizabeth's Apartment Saturday Morning 12th May 1935

Elizabeth sat at the breakfast table dreamily watching the greying, mature, handsome man opposite her reading *The Times*. She was glad she had cancelled their dinner date at Ferraris, on Scott's advice, and substituted instead a candlelight dinner at her apartment. She had also taken the liberty of changing the menu from Aberdeen Angus steak to her speciality, a hot spiced Bombay Madras curry. Her late husband had always declared it put lead in his pencil. To her delight she had discovered last night that it had the same effect on Sir James. He stretched for his coffee cup took a sip then folded the newspaper, laid it flat with headlines up, and slid it across the table to Elizabeth. The banner headline read: TOP FOREIGN OFFICE DIPLOMAT IN HORROR ACCIDENT. Elizabeth anxiously read of the tragic death of Sir Eustace Pennington-Beaumont. She gathered that the police had concluded from the skid marks on the compacted sleet main road that a puncture at excessive speed had caused the death of the well-respected and loved civil servant.

After reading the article Elizabeth declared, 'Bit of a coincidence don't you think Jimmy with you interrogating him yesterday, things not going to your liking and this happening...' pointing at *The Times* headline.

A laconic smile set on Sir James lips as with forefinger pointed heavenwards and hand on heart he solemnly attested, 'I prefer to think of it as divine providence, Liz.'

'Mmm,' she sighed. 'I wonder.' She wondered if the "divine providence" he referred to was the same one that had advised her to invite Sir James to her apartment for a sexy candlelit dinner instead of dining at Ferraris. She rose from the table, straightened her dressing gown, and belatedly laughed at his attempt at pious fervour.

'I recognise that intonation, Liz. What's not to your liking?'

'Well,' she paused bending over to pick up the breakfast plates for washing, 'Of your five suspects, Eustace, Grenville, Burnett, Joyce and Lady Dorothy – three have met with untimely deaths.'

'Elizabeth!' barked Sir James firmly, 'I don't, contrary to what you seem to think, run an assassination bureau. It was not in my best interests to have Grenville terminated. I wanted him brought in for interrogation – his death was downright inconvenient; it played right into Eustace's hands. Had Rutherford got to him first we would've had the whole story – enough to hang Eustace.'

'But Laszlo shot Grenville and Laszlo is your man….'

'Laszlo is not *my* man – you know as well as I do, he's a Soviet agent. Now does that satisfy you?'

'Not quite. What have you planned for the other two? – Joyce and Lady Dorothy.'

'Stick pins into wax effigies of them,' replied Sir James exasperatedly. 'If you must know I've handed my findings on them over to Sir John at SIS(5). Being an internal matter, it's their problem now.'

'In that case shouldn't Eustace have been five's responsibility?' She persisted.

'Liz! I cannot be held responsible for every blasted road accident in the country,' he growled as he uplifted the newspaper to start the crossword – signifying discussion over – only to discover it was already completed. Damn the woman, he couldn't put up with that; you don't do another's crossword. Things would have to change.

As Liz walked towards the kitchen sink with the dirty dishes she was of the same opinion regarding change. During dinner with hands held over the table he had thanked her for drawing to his attention the need to have a life outside of work. He had conceded that since meeting her on taking up his position as head of SIS(6) that she was the only person that had come close to his expectations. He had desperately wanted to do something about this but due to his mantra of agents not getting "too familiar with each other" he felt it would have been hypocritical to pursue and there were also the lengthy periods of work overseas for a wife to contend with. He appeared to have had amnesia regarding his affair with Sylvia but she thought it best not to remind him. What a waste of their life. However, it was these anomalies that she intended to change in his life because she knew that under the tough, gruff exterior lay a caring and lovable man – hers. To start the change, perhaps a few more of her special Bombay enhancing curries she giggled to herself as she turned on the hot water tap.

***

SIS(6) London Monday 13th May 1935
'Pleasant weekend Rutherford?'
'Yes thank you Sir James. Went to visit my parents in Portsmouth.'
'By train?
'No. Took the Lagonda for a spin.'
'You do surprise me. According to the police the A3 was icily treacherous when the accident happened.'
'Accident, sir?'
'The tragic and fatal accident of Sir Eustace at Hindhead.'
'Ah yes. My parents informed me when I arrived in Pompey there had been a fatality. They were worried about me, knowing I was using the A3 in such appalling conditions.'
'You didn't see the accident then?'
'No sir. It must have happened after I passed Hindhead otherwise there would have been a diversion. A truly tragic accident.'
'Indeed, Rutherford, indeed. Truly tragic. What a sad loss to the nation.'
They looked understandingly at each other. Scott broke the silence. 'Will you be attending the funeral?'

'I regret to say Rutherford that on that particular day I have an appointment with my dentist for root canal treatment.'

'How *very unfortunate,* Sir James.'

Sir James coughed, 'Mmm, quite. As you say, unfortunate, but these things do happen unexpectedly. However, Rutherford, I have your next assignment. It is a fairly mundane reconnaissance job which I'm sure you will liven up with the odd body or two,' he chortled. 'It is in Tenerife. Code name TENALT – Operation Tenerife.'

Sir James then explained his intended modus operandi.

PART TWO

MAGEC'S REVENGE
(Magec: The Gaunché God of Light and Sun)

Chapter 16

Santander Northern Spain Early October 1935
As she waited at the bus stop for her homeward bound service the gaunt and fatigued figure of a despondent Nina Delgado shivered as she felt the chill of the biting cold evening wind blowing in off the Bay of Biscay. She turned the collar of her coat up against the icy blast.

Nina had been living in Santander with her mother Isabella since that never to be forgotten day – Oviedo, the 12th October 1934 – the day she had lost her papa and her beloved fiancé Ramón; the day her beautiful life as she knew it came to an abrupt halt. Her mama's sister, her Aunt Maria, had obtained her a position in Santander's newly built Valdecilla hospital where she herself was a nursing sister. Unfortunately the only position available for Nina had been in the casualty department. Her present feeling of despondency hadn't been brought on by her failure to cope with the unfortunate victims – for there could have been no worse trauma than that which she had experienced in Oviedo – no it was the waste of life that invariably came with each admission. This she had experienced less than an hour ago at the end of her shift when a young Ramón lookalike died on the operating table; victim of a hit-and-run driver. Yet another pointless death. *"Did it all only stop with your own mortality."* Much to her horror she realised that this latest reminiscence had been spoken out aloud and with most of the queue being out-patients at the hospital they were scowling in her direction – having no wish to debate the question of mortality. Mercifully the bus arrived to save her further embarrassment.

She took her seat and wiped the condensation off the window with her sleeve to allow her a view of Santander's fine architectural buildings, parks, squares and plazas all splendidly lit up at night. She thought it pretty – but it wasn't home. How she longed to be home. During the journey her mind wandered to her mama. The ever loving bond between them had become strained since leaving Oviedo to live with Aunt Maria. Nina was aware that it was her own attitude that had caused the schism but try as she might she couldn't bring herself to repair the broken bond. Her mama, a devoutly religious Catholic, was in despair of Nina fearing her daughter had lost faith in God. Nina had wrestled with the problem, desperately wanting to believe that the god she had been taught to believe in was caring and forgiving but could not accept this belief – for how could he callously allow such dreadful deaths to happen to those innocents such as her beautiful Ramón. What had he done to deserve such a fate – blown to pieces aged twenty two. This had been the catalyst that had convinced her that there was no such thing as a caring God only an uncaring creator and death. Her new found dogma when expressed had sent her mama into despair, offering up prayers for the guidance of her daughter whilst crossing herself repeatedly and fondling her rosary beads frantically.

Alighting from the bus Nina still had a ten minute walk ahead of her to the front door of the direct-to-the-pavement, single storey, whitewashed, double-fronted terraced house where she and her mama now lodged with her mama's widowed sister Maria. As she turned into her street she shielded her eyes with one hand from the fiercely driven horizontal sleet whilst with the other she clutched her coat collar close to her throat. Through the slit fingers of her protecting hand she could just make out the shadowy outline of a vehicle parked outside her aunt's house which was unusual, for in this part of town vehicles were rarely seen except for hearses or ambulances. Ambulances! Her heart skipped a beat. Mama had not been keeping well this morning when she had left for work – they had rowed as usual over her lack of faith. As she neared the van a sense of relief overcame her as she realised it was not an ambulance but a mud splattered van which she vaguely recognised. The sleet was melting on its bonnet. It had obviously recently arrived.

With trembling fingers she opened the door to hear a highly agitated voice which she instantly recognised. They all had their backs to her and the speaker was pleading, 'José needs your help urgently Isabella.'

An answering voice, her Aunt Maria's, replied aggressively, 'I don't care Freddy. Isabella's been through enough. Get one of your own to do it and leave her alone for God's sake.'

Freddy was her mama's and her Aunt Maria's brother. The farmer from the foothill's of the Pecos de Europa mountain range begged, 'I can't Maria. We are being watched every move by the Guardia Civil.'

'There you go then. If you're all being watched by the *Civilies* then so will you be. You will no doubt have brought them to this very door you dumb oaf.' As Maria finished her rant a blast of icy cold wind wrenched the front door she was holding ajar from her grasp and whipped it closed behind her with a loud bang. Three alarmed faces turned towards Nina expecting her to be the Guardia. Realising it was not who they thought Maria wailed, 'Nina! What are you doing girl? You almost gave us a heart attack.'

'Phewh!' was all Freddy could muster as he wiped his freely perspiring forehead with the back of his hand.

'Surely it's me that should be asking you what you lot are up to,' retaliated Nina.

'It's your Uncle José – he's been shot.'

'Again?'

'Yes – *again*, young lady,' answered her mama tartly. 'Only this time it could be fatal.'

Nina hung her head shamefully at her mama's rebuke. She had not meant offence towards her uncle. 'Can't he be taken to hospital in Oviedo? I know from working there that Doctor Rodriguiez is usually sympathetic to ….'

The three siblings looked at each other before her mama interrupted Nina by putting a comforting arm around her shoulder and leading her to the settee. They sat down together. 'There's been a shoot-out between José's men and the Guardia – two police dead. It's a very bad situation.'

'A very, very, bad situation,' repeated Freddy.

Nina suddenly found herself not breathing and exhaled a moan, 'And?'

'And Freddy wants me to return to Oviedo to take care of José but Maria doesn't….'

'Well mama – what are we wasting time for. You know papa would have wanted you to help Uncle José and it's not as if it's the first bullet you've ever been asked to remove, is it?'

Isabella broke into tears as she sobbingly replied, 'You're just like your papa.' She flung her arms around Nina and held her close to her bosom as she whispered, 'I'm so proud of you.'

Maria joined them on the settee. Freddy put on his driving gloves.

***

The journey to Oviedo was uneventful due in part to Freddy's knowledge of the back roads leading them into the familiar landscape of his farmlands on the outskirts of Sama de Langreo in a snow peaked mountain valley at the foot of the Pecos de Europa range. When they arrived at Freddy's farmhouse they parked the van and changed into heavy woollens, sheepskin coats, fur lined boots and woollen hats and gloves. Suitably prepared for the trek ahead they set out on foot into the mountains.

After what appeared to be an eternity of ankle-breaking rock-strewn paths they finally reached the tree line whereupon on entry darkness engulfed them. Freddy led them like a sure-footed mountain goat through this darkness in a zig-zag pattern between the snow laden trees until he encountered by torchlight a large round boulder partly hidden by bushes. He bid them wait whilst he brushed aside the bush and slid his hand behind the boulder to locate a rope which he pulled to release a timber wedge. The boulder rolled sideways in a vegetation concealed compacted earth track to reveal a cave opening which they quickly entered before the boulder rolled back under its own weight and gravity to reseal the opening. He slid the timber wedge back in place.

Nina looked quizzically at her mama who interpreted the look. 'Don't be fooled Nina. Your Uncle Freddy may be useless at many things…' At this remark Freddy scowled at his eldest sister. '… but organisation isn't one of them – thankfully. He'll have everything we require. All neat and clean – won't you Freddy dear?'

Freddy's owl-like face lit up as he said proudly, 'I have indeed Isabella.'

'You've been here before mama?'

'Many times. And by many different routes.'

They travelled by torchlight through a labyrinth of interconnecting caves – some requiring them to double up for passage others soaring majestically in height with fresh water lakes and rivers running through them. After twenty minutes Freddy diverted down a crevice in the rocks and came upon a curtained entrance. Freddy pulled aside this curtain to enter a lit cave fitted out as a hospital ward. Nina was aware of a generator humming quietly in the background. There were several beds. On two of them lay heavily sedated resistance fighters still in their dark blue boiler suits – militiamen. At the end of the cave there was another curtained-off area. They entered. José was awake. He did his best to acknowledge them. He was gaunt – colour grey. The usual sparkling eyes sunk and dull. He was breathing in short rasping gasps.

Being a former hospital matron in Gijon Isabella immediately took charge. 'Who bandaged him Freddy? The local butcher?' Freddy flinched at the criticism being only too aware that Isabella was referring to him. José tried a smile at his sister-in-law's acerbic tongue but gave up in pain as she lifted a scalpel and shook her head in disgust. 'Nina, boiling water please. This looks like it's been used to chop treacle,' she said holding the scalpel at arm's length between her finger and thumb. 'And while you're at it Nina, please sterilise these,' she added handing over a selection of surgical instruments. With Nina not knowing where to carry out her chore Freddy tapped her on the shoulder signalling her to follow him. As they turned to go Isabella growled, 'And don't let Freddy anywhere near them. I take back what I said about his organisational ability.'

Freddy in way of an apology whispered to Nina, 'All the tools – no tradesmen. All the local doctors and clinics are under surveillance.'

'You did the right thing Freddy.' He brightened. His two oldest sisters had always bullied him. He thought it nice to know that one of them had produced an understanding daughter.

***

A week later after the extraction of the bullet, José still under heavy morphine sedation, sat up in bed and smiled. Isabella wept tears of joy – Nina laughed in glee. Together they had pulled him back from the brink.

Freddy, who had worked the farm during the day, when he heard the good news about José, crossed himself and declared his sister a saint. He knew the Catholic Church would not agree with this assessment for being supporters of the Nationalists and the Monarchy they were his avowed enemy.

Two weeks later José took his first steps towards recovery. Sitting on the edge of the bed he was delighted at the visit of Nina. 'Is your mama coming?'

'Possibly later. She's exhausted.'

'That's understandable. I owe my life to you both. How can I ever repay you?'

'Learn to live in peace.'

'That's the one thing I can't promise you, Nina.'

'Why not? Why all this unnecessary bloodletting?'

'Because of the two thousand men, women and children slaughtered by the Nationalist forces in Oviedo – including your father and fiancé. Surely you haven't forgotten?'

'No. And I never will forget. But these killings can't go on.'

'It will as long as Canizares and I have breath in our bodies.'

'Canizares?'

'With your papa's death, him and I now run the resistance.'

'I thought you were papa's number two.' Canizares distantly rang a bell with her but she couldn't put a face to the name. 'I never heard papa mention him as a leader.'

'You wouldn't – they hated each other. Your papa, my dear brother, professed to be a communist but in reality he was more a hard left wing socialist – an idealist. However, on the other hand Canizares is a hard line communist who requires no justification for killing. Jaimé had a hard job keeping him under control. *And* he was jealous of your father.

'Jealous? In what way?'

'Because of Jaimés' leadership of the men and business. Filipe Canizares was a small-time builder compared with your papa but when Jaimé was murdered he miraculously secured all your papa's contracts to rebuild the razed and dilapidated areas of town.'

'So in death papa lost not only his life but the leadership of his beloved resistance fighters.' José nodded agreement. 'Please describe this Canizares to me uncle José.'

'He's squat and ugly.'

'A brilliant description uncle. Apart from Ramón that describes most of the men I've ever met. Present company excepted of course.'

'Glad you added that,' retorted José preening himself. 'Oh! And by the way Canizares has a large scar over his right eye.' Nina drew a deep inward breath; she finally had a name to the face she had seen leave her papa's yard on that fateful day in October exactly one year ago. 'To tell you the truth, Nina, I have suspected for some time that somebody informed the Nationalists that we were gathering in Jaimé's yard on that barbaric day. The bombing was too precise – it started at your papa's yard. He was a marked man. I initially suspected Canizares for he had all to gain from Jaimé's death – the leadership of the men and the Ayuntamiento (local council) contracts. So I confronted him. He informed me he had been arrested by the *Civilies* on the morning of the bombing for a drunken brawl with one of their officers the previous evening. I checked this and found it to be true. He retaliated by accusing me. Asking why I hadn't been in the yard at the time of the bombing – I replied that I would have been, had it not been for the old boneshaker of a truck I'd been driving not being able to carry the load Jaimé had sent me for and having to stop at Pedro's farm on the way back to off-load half the timber.'

'How did he react to that?'

'More or less implied I'd made it up, so now I watch him like a hawk and he me. Pedro told me later that Canizares had contacted him to ask about the off-loading of the timber. However, to Canizares credit he was on the raid the night I got this,' he said patting his wound dressing. 'He got shot in the leg – in fact his stitches come out tonight.'

Nina now realised without any doubt that it had been Canizares she had encountered leaving the gate of her papa's yard on *that* day. He had not been arrested and jailed that morning – he was the traitor. She said nothing to José for she did not wish to upset his recovery. Canizares was due to have his stiches taken out at Freddy's farmhouse by her mama this evening. She suggested to her mama over their evening meal that she have a night off and go visit José in the cave; he had been asking after her and she would remove Canizare's stiches. Her mama thanked her. Freddy gave her a peculiar look.

The door rattled. Nina looked at the mantelpiece clock – eight o'clock exactly. Uncle Freddy put his book down and rose from his chair to answer the door. This done he took his leave into the kitchen. Canizares entered the room, the scar tissue above his eye stood out as a smooth white line set against the ugly weather beaten features. Nina looked intently for any sign of recognition of her from him. There was none. 'Come take a seat and roll up your trouser leg,' she said calmly to put him at ease. He sat. His small, dark, evil eyes never leaving her face as she lifted a pair of long surgical scissors. 'Don't you recognise me, Filipe?' she enquired.

'No,' he replied curtly followed by a growled, 'I'm a busy man señorita, just do your job.'

'That's funny Filipe I remember you well.' He glowered at her. 'Jaimé Delgado's builder's yard 8-30am on the twelfth of October 1934 when I bumped into you as you were leaving rather hastily through the gates. The day you claimed you were in jail. I must have changed a lot for you not to recognise me Filipe.'

He shook his head. 'Never saw you in my life before. You must be mistaking me for somebody else. At the time you speak of I was in custody at the Guardia's headquarters. Not that it matters now where I was you nosey bitch....,' he snarled as he pulled open his jacket and withdrew a knife from his waistband. Before he could attack Nina there was a cough from behind Canizares and the click of the double barrels of a shotgun locking. He swung towards the click. That was the last conscious movement he ever made as a pair of surgical scissors pierced his lungs. With a high pitched whine he collapsed face down. Nina straddled his back stabbing him repeatedly in a frenzy of blows, screaming, 'That's for papa and that's for Ramôn and that's for all the others you murderous....'

Trembling she felt a pair of hands gently easing her off Canizares as she dropped the blood dripping scissors on the tiled floor and the kindly voice of Uncle Freddy whispering in her ear, 'There, there, my lovely Nina it's all over now.'

Still trembling violently, she was given to bouts of anguished sobbing muttering the name of Ramôn over and over again. She had lost him exactly twelve months to the day – today being the 12th October 1935.

Canizares' body was stripped and unceremoniously dumped naked in an off the beaten track deep barranco for the night-life of the Pecos de Europa to feed off.

***

It's amazing what a razor sharp knife held at the throat can do to a hostage other than leave a pool of urine or the stench of a bowel movement . This was the situation Canizare's obese wife found herself in as she disclosed all to José. It appeared from her confession that the Nationalist supporting mayor of Oviedo had tired of Jaimé's constant construction strikes bringing to a halt the mayor's ambitious attempts to modernise certain areas of the town. So when the rebellion at the munitions and arms factory broke out he saw his opportunity to be rid of the problem and Jaimé Delgado once and for all. The Nationalist supporting mayor, having been previously warned of the intended air strike against the rebels, approached Canizares with a proposition. All Canizares had to do to secure Jaime's local authority works was to inform him where Jaimé would be at 8-30am on the twelfth of October. Canizares knew immediately, for he himself would be at a meeting of the resistance militia called for in Jaimé's yard at 8-00am on that particular date. He had arrived in the yard to make sure Jaimé was in place then made his phone call to the mayor. He was arrested when he arrived home by the Guardia Civil – an alibi arranged between the Guardia and the mayor. With Jaimé's location confirmed all it took was a phone call by the mayor to the Spanish Air Force base in Bilbao advising of the whereabouts of the resistance leader for the massacre to start.

The reason for the mayor's and Canizare's downfall had been nothing more than jealousy and ambition. Canizares had been envious of Jaimé's Local Authority contracts whilst the mayor's ambition to become Governor of the region of Asturius was being thwarted by Jaimé's continual strikes.

Shortly after Canizare's wife's revelations the mayor had

unfortunately met with a most unusual accident that made his worry of strikes seem an irrelevance – a chandelier had fallen from the town hall ceiling and killed him whilst being cleaned. Ironically the Guardia Civil were looking for Canizares to help them with their enquiries, for as main contractor he was responsible for maintenance at the town hall. They were of the opinion that he had fled the country. Canizares' obese wife had received her husband's tongue by post. Her silence was for ever sealed.

José arranged for Nina to go to his brother Xavi in Tenerife hoping this would aid her recuperation.

Seven days later her Uncle Xavi met Nina off the boat in Santa Cruz.

Eight days later Nina was serving aboard Xavi's boat, "The Sea Dolphin," hopefully on her first steps towards recuperation.

Ten days later she fatefully met her beloved Ramón.

Chapter 17

Late October 1935

Three months after his Berlin escapade Scott Rutherford completed his two week training at Cantravel's luxury headquarters near Virginia Water in the London stockbroker belt during which he learned the rudiments of how to cow-tow to aristocracy and socialites and butter up captains of industry and their wives and flatter the egos of thespians and film stars. After two weeks of mind numbing boredom he achieved his certificate of excellence and was welcomed into the Cantravel faith and given his posting – Puerto de la Cruz on the island Tenerife. This location was courtesy of Eugene Crozier, American owner of Cantravel and Winston Churchill's second cousin. Eugene had grabbed the dangled carrot by cousin Winston – the opportunity to have in his employ an Italian Navy trained re-breather diver – one of only a select few in the world. Eugene, being of entrepreneurial spirit immediately saw this as an opportunity to open a new venture in his already lucrative tourist business. He had agreed to his cousin's demands and been fed only what he was required to know of the ultra-secret operation. The fact that the re-breather diver was a British Secret Service agent did not faze him, for he was well acquainted with the devious reputation of his cousin.

Scott had already been made aware of Puerto de la Cruz as his destination during a secret rendezvous with Sir James and Churchill prior to his training at Cantravel. At this meeting "Operation TENALT" (standing for Tenerife Alternative) was explained to him in detail. They informed him that the premise of the fall of Gibraltar was based on the fact that Hitler had already given succour to the Spanish Nationalist Government in their putting down of the anarchist, socialist and communist rebellions of 1934. It was therefore not beyond reasonable doubt that with further aid to the Nationalists, come the inevitable civil war, that Hitler would expect reward. The problem that worried Sir James and Churchill was Hitler being given passage through Spain to Gibraltar. Should Hitler's forces overrun Gibraltar he would then control access to the

Mediterranean and his U-boats (submarines) would wreak havoc with the merchant fleets on route to Britain. An alternative scenario had to be found. The answer lay in Tenerife which Churchill proposed they take by force if "Operation TENALT" failed. Scott, on hearing this, inwardly wished them more success than Admiral Horatio Nelson's two failed attempts to conquer the island in 1797 – during one of which he lost an arm.

***

It had taken seven months for the Admiralty to agree funding from their "war chest" and a further two months since Sir James' and Churchill's submitted plan to successfully convince the Admiralty of its viability. And with the British National Coalition Government still clinging rigidly to their appeasement plan for Germany and to the hope that Hitler would honour the Treaty of Versailles – HMG were nor advised of "Operation TENALT". This then meant the operation became covert, meaning funding became tight and was depending solely on the Admiralty "war chest" and the benevolence of Eugene Crozier – an Oxford educated American.

Ostensibly, as the plan stood Scott was to be Cantravel's oxygen re-breather diving instructor. However, his true vocation would be to source suitable coastal inlets or the underwater lava caves that were known to exist along the north face of the island – according to the National Geographic magazine – for submarine bases.

Scott was given the name "Drago" by Sir James, who he had met during the war and who was, apparently, the leader of a non-aggressive movement on the island known as the "Free Canaries Movement" (FCM). There was no further intelligence available.

***

Eugene Crozier the owner of Cantravel had also been busy. Through skilful Madison Avenue advertising in all the socialite magazines on both sides of the Atlantic his agency had come up with suitable hype regarding the re-breather scenario to satisfy the curiosity of the British aristocracy and the oil rich American tycoons. The advance bookings for his "re-breather experience" showed that the underwater experience of viewing "the wonders of the undersea" was a must have extra for his clients. However, Eugene realised it was all very well his Madison Avenue executives promoting "the wonders of the undersea" but where were the wonders located around the island to be found? To compensate for this flaw of his over-zealous advertising executives he had found a local diver named Pepé through the owner of the "Sea Dolphin" which was a fifty passenger, double-deck cruise boat moored in Los Gigantes. Eugene hired this boat annually from the owner and skipper, a tough weather beaten, unshaven, cigar chewing local rejoicing in the name of Xavi. Pepé just happened to be his nephew.

***

The bow of the ocean going yacht Eugene Crozier One (Affectionately known as Genie one) sliced effortlessly through the becalmed Atlantic Ocean on a south west course out of Casablanca bound for the port of Santa Cruz de Tenerife. In the distance the island was bathed in an orange glow from the high overhead mid-day sun turning the snow-clad peak of Mount Teide into an orange halo. Witnessing this magnificence from the bridge of the yacht was Scott Rutherford bound for his new assignment. With calm seas and the weather balmy he had had a pleasant seven day cruise from Tilbury docks, London, stopping over at Madeira and Casablanca. Sir James had informed him that Yvonne who he had last worked with in Berlin was to be his courier between London and Tenerife. He had been delighted to hear of this arrangement provided, of course, that she had got over her fit of pique with him. However, he had not been delighted to hear that there had been no improvement in the fifteen day turnaround of information – known to SIS(6) agents as the conduit. Seven days either way and a day for bunkering and provisions. He would have to work on this anomaly.

Scott had never been to Tenerife, nor to any of the six other islands forming the Canary Island archipelago and knew nothing of them other than what he had researched from travel guides which had informed him it was a volcanic eruption rising out of the sea with its central core being Mount Teide rising to over twelve thousand feet above sea level. It lay some one hundred and eighty six miles off the coast of West Africa and fifteen hundred plus nautical miles from London. And since the late 1890's a tourist attraction for those Victorians seeking all the year round sunshine as afforded by the favourable Trade Winds of the archipelago. He knew also that it had a wide diversity of landscapes from the lush green valleys of the north to the semi-arid deserts of the south. The north coastline, where he was to be quartered with Cantravel on the outskirts of Puerto de la Cruz, was typically rugged, lush, and steep whilst to the south lay volcanic ash beaches. With the archipelago being an overseas semi-autonomous territory of Spain the spoken language was Spanish. This was of no worry to Scott as he was as fluent in Spanish (spoken with a Madrid accent) as he was with German, French with get-by Italian and Russian.

As the "Genie One" entered the Santa Cruz harbour walls to a cacophony of shouted instructions to the engine room from the bridge Scott thanked the captain who had been instructed, and had, afforded him ever courtesy. He then slung his duffel bag over his shoulder to join the disembarking queue. His personal diving gear was in the hold to be off-loaded into a waiting Cantravel van which he spied waiting at the quayside. He allowed the loud, mayhem antics of the excited guests (Eugene insisted that his clients/holidaymakers/vacationers be referred to as guests) to go ahead of him to the orange and yellow liveried coachwork of the Cantravel open coaches awaiting them.

His final step off the gangway took him towards the waiting Cantravel van where he pulled open the passenger door and took a step back in surprise – the driver was Yvonne. He stared at her long shapely sun tanned legs on the pedals before he raised his eyes to her face. She was leaning on the steering wheel, her head turned towards him with her seductive smile firmly in place. He felt a pleasant shudder run down his spine.

'Hi Scott – nice to see you again,' she greeted him.

Scott, happy that there was no sign of any residual pettiness from Berlin replied, 'Nice to see you, too. You're looking well sun-tanned and healthy.' *And looking gorgeously beddable flitted through his mind.*

'Merci Scott,' she purred, her French ancestry coming to the fore. 'Look, let's get your diving gear in the van and get on our way – then I'll bring you up to speed,' she replied in a business-like tone as she swung her long legs nimbly out of the driver's seat to go and meet the stevedores at the rear of the van as they prepared to load Scott's crate into the van.

This chore completed they moved off and had travelled less than a hundred metres when Scott suddenly shouted – 'Stop!'

Yvonne brought the van to a jarring halt. 'What's the matter?' she said in panic as her well-practiced hand slid inside her blazer to withdraw a concealed pistol.

Scott put an arm across her chest to stop the withdrawal. 'Sorry Yvonne. Back up a bit please.' She did. 'Stop.' The reverse enabled a view between the gables of dockside warehouses. 'Look a seaplane. What a beauty.'

'Yes. It's the Lufthansa mail plane.'

'Interesting,' mused Scott, deep in thought. 'Sorry about that. Drive on.'

Once through port customs, where Scott showed his passport in the name of Jordan Hill, they settled into the traffic flow – a mixture of cars, lorries, vans and horse drawn wagons. Yvonne then explained, 'I left Cantravel headquarters in Virginia Water the day before you arrived for your induction course...'

'Did you get a certificate? I did. I'm the head diving instructor,' said Scott in mock bravado as he blew on his knuckles and rubbed them in his chest.

'Yes. And I'm now a head group facilitator,' she laughed. 'However, when I left Cantravel I came straight here. So I've been here two weeks – Voila! La tan. The weather's been heavenly. However, you're not here for a weather report. Did Sir James advise you that I am now land based and not yacht.'

'Yes, he did. But my understanding is that you will still be taking despatches back to London as required. In effect working as my courier.'

Her reply staggered him. 'Yes. In fact I am taking a despatch back to London tomorrow.'

'Why? And from whom?'

Her smile disappeared. The tone of voice hardened. 'From me. I have information that Sir James must be made aware of urgently. Not unless you, as mission control, wish to return by tomorrow's yacht to tell Sir James.'

'Tell him what?'

'That the Nazis have beaten us to it. They have set up a diving school in Puerto de la Cruz.'

Scott's mind raced. How much had Sir James told her about the operation. 'How much do you know?' he asked sharply.

'How much do I know about what? Your mission or the Nazis?'

'Both.'

'Sir James called me to London before I left for Tenerife and briefed me fully about "Operation TENALT".'

Scott, shocked at this news stared at her silently as she concentrated on the road, his mind awhirl. Sir James had obviously made her – in SIS(6) jargon – "Active-in-the-field" as he had witnessed no more than five minutes ago when she had made the attempt to draw her firearm. Recovering, he quizzed, 'And how do you know of the Nazi diving team?'

Yvonne did not instantly reply. She was concentrating on her gear changing as the van laboured up the hill to La Laguna the former capital of the island and a university town since the sixteenth century. Once through La Laguna the road levelled out as they passed Los Rodeos – the island airport. A bi-plane looking like something from the Bleriot era of flying sat at the entrance.

With the road now level she then turned to Scott and answered his query about the Nazi diving team. 'As I have already said, I've been here two weeks. I didn't know what to expect. All Sir James instructed me to do was familiarise myself with the area and keep my eyes and ears open till you arrived. However, workwise, being head group facilitator, one of my group on a trip into Puerto de la Cruz took herself off to watch a swimming gala at the open air municipal pool on the seafront and reported back that she had seen German men in rubber suits…'

'How did she notice these men? Were they part of the gala?'

'No. She was sitting on the back row, heard a chug-chug noise, looked over the low back wall and saw them alighting from a motor boat amongst the rocks.'

'And what made her think they were German?'

'She's a German Jewess and of course recognised the language. She and her surgeon husband fled Berlin last year to settle in New York. I asked from which direction it approached. She said – from down the coast. That would be from the Los Gigantes direction. So I decided to investigate. Cantravel have a "see the whales and dolphins" boat, the "Sea Dolphin", hired daily to pick up their guests at Puerto's harbour. It travels up from Los Gigantes every morning..'

'Why is it not moored in Puerto harbour?'

'Because the Puerto de la Cruz harbour is way too small for a boat that size. So I then organised with my group, a trip on the "Sea Dolphin". I took my binoculars and map and just beyond Garrachico at Punta Gaunché I observed a diving team close to the cliffs. They were dressed in wet suits, masks, flippers and oxygen cylinders strapped to their backs. Your type of frogman equipment.'

'Where's Garrichico and Punta Gaunché?'

'I'll show you on a map when we get to base. Since that trip I've used my position as head group facilitator to take groups on board the "Sea Dolphin" for the last four days and they are still diving. Don't you think that suspicious?'

'I do indeed. But how do you know it's the same team as your guest saw?'

'Yesterday I secreted myself in the rocks at the open air swimming pool and waited until they got back – they *were* speaking German.'

Knowing Yvonne was fluent in German, he asked, 'Did you pick up anything useful from what they were saying?'

'They were too far away to make out the conversation. But I did pick up the words – explosives and underwater.'

'What set-up do they have?'

'A shop fronting the road with a high barbed wire wall yard to the rear. The yard having a sliding door leading to a small inlet to the sea. This is why I feel I need to contact Sir James.'

'I agree. He most certainly needs to know about this right away. This is terrific news, Yvonne,' he praised, clapping her shoulder. An action that just about put them off the road. 'When will you be back?'

'Fourteen days at the earliest including bunkering and provisions – and that is provided Sir James makes a decision right away to allow me to catch the next day yacht back to Tenerife. Otherwise....'

'Fourteen days at the earliest! What sort of bloody conduit is that? Sir James said he was going to look into this matter,' he moaned in despair. 'Bloody hell! The Nazis could have invaded Gibraltar *and* Tenerife in that time.....in fact the whole archipelago.'

Yvonne shrugged her shoulders and said, 'Well you should know. You've just disembarked the "Genie". How long did it take you to get here?'

'Seven days.'

'There you are. You don't have to be a mathematical genius to work it out. Times two is?'

Scott, with a shake of head ignored her sarcasm and instead replied, 'What's wrong with using Gibraltar as a listening post?'

'Because we can't use the phone, morse, or crystal set to communicate – that would cause the listeners, even if the message was encrypted, to investigate the source. I shouldn't have to tell you that.'

'We passed an airfield at Los Rodeos....'

'You can forget the RAF. Even if Sir James granted permission the Spanish Government wouldn't allow a foreign nation to land aeroplanes in their territory without agreement between the governments. And ours doesn't even know we exist. Apart from which Gibraltar doesn't have an airstrip – so it would have to be a seaplane.'

'I was thinking private charter.'

Yvonne laughed. 'Not a chance. First off, where would you find a commercial chartered seaplane? Secondly, there's no spare funding available if you did find a charter. And finally, Sir James would not sanction a privateer due to the security risk involved. Look Scott, as it is, it happens to be a safe and secure conduit. It *was* fifteen days – but Mr Crozier now has the yachts bunkered and provisioned overnight.'

'Good for Mr Crozier. At least *he's* trying. Pity he couldn't cut out the Madeira and Casablanca stops. There's just got to be a better way.'

Her affable effort to quell his rant having failed, she snapped, 'Listen Scott – this is as you have said – a *top secret* mission. The only secure way is personal contact.'

'Agreed, Yvonne. But surely Sir James must be aware of the Lufthansa seaplane we saw in the docks?'

'As you well know we have no intel on the island, so he won't know about the Lufthansa seaplane until I tell him.' With Yvonne's patience being now sorely tried with Scott's prevarications she said through clenched teeth, 'And, the plane, *as-I've-already-told-you,* has all the necessary Spanish Government permissions to land. And, apart from the Admiralty, HMG does not even know of our existence. Need I say more? However, I suppose I could always ask the nice German pilot if he would be good enough to divert to London and drop me off on his way back to Berlin.'

Scott laughed off her sarcasm. 'Ha, ha. Very funny. The point *I'm making* is – that it flies from Germany to here. *And our* Imperial Airways now flies direct to America. *And*, Amy Johnson has flown to Australia!'

'And the point *I'm making*, and have *already* made, is that all aircraft require permission to land from the Spanish Government which would then mean involving HMG. End of argument.'

Scott shrugged his shoulders but doggedly continued, 'Well why don't you inform Sir James when you get to London that it might well be in Mr Crozier's interest to invest in a seaplane for use in inter-island tourism in the archipelago. Could be a winner for Cantravel.'

Exasperated, Yvonne shook her head at Scott's failure to comprehend the financial implications and said with a deep sigh, 'OK Scott – I will mention it to Sir James when I see him but don't hold your breath.' Scott nodded his agreement, stretched his legs out and with his ankles crossed he yawned. She was pleasantly surprised that her sarcasm, which she once again regretted, had not drawn Scott's ire.

The remainder of the journey passed with easy, comfortable small talk. Yvonne confiding about the guests and the nefarious goings-on between them. The midnight furtive meanderings of figures flitting between bungalows. She claimed to have seen a famous film actress, in the wee small hours of the morning, enter the chalet of an Earl but would not be drawn on names. Meanwhile Scott tried to prise out information about her love life in the interval since he had last seen her. There was nothing forthcoming from her there either. Suddenly, she broke a lull in the conversation by telling him not to worry about her being foisted upon him for she knew, after Berlin, he was not happy about a female "in the field". He protested his innocence that she should think such of him. Why! Hadn't he already congratulated her on a job well done regarding the German divers? She looked at him sceptically advising him that she had a PTT (permitted to terminate) grading. This Scott knew but did not pass comment other than nod and ask whether she had ever made use of the grading. She confirmed she had on many occasions and witnessed a look of relief cross Scott's face.

Scott had moaned again about the fourteen day conduit. She had hoped that might have something to do with him about missing her company but doubted that because of her truculent attitude towards him in Berlin which she had been determined not to repeat but unfortunately already had. She would have to learn not to rise to his irritating jibes.

Scott was meanwhile thinking back to the unfulfilled Berlin Embassy tryst he had proposed with her. Albeit, due to other events happening, he had never actually got round to mentioning it to her. However, here in Tenerife, he intended to reverse that Berlin misfortune. He would just have to accept that the French side of her nature was responsible for her sarcasm.

They started the downward journey along the high coast road from Tacaronte when suddenly the small town of Puerto de la Cruz sprung into view nestling far below on the shoreline of the Atlantic. Just before the Jardines de Botanico Yvonne turned left off the main road into a single volcanic ash road leading steeply upwards into the mountains. At the end of this road they encountered a massive archway akin to the entrance to American ranches that Scott had seen in Westerns at the cinema. The archway bore in raised timber lettering the name: THE CANTRAVEL COUNTRY CLUB. However, instead of a gun-slinging Gene Autry or Tom Mix they were waved down by a security gateman wearing a uniform of orange blazer, yellow trousers, shirt and shoes. An orange tie hung loose at the neck of the shirt.

'That guy colour blind?' queried Scott out the corner of his mouth.

'Sh!' whispered Yvonne giving him a kick on the shin. 'That's the Cantravel colours. I shouldn't mock if I were you – you will be issued with yours by the store man,' she chuckled gleefully giving him a playful punch on the arm.

The gateman logged the entry and saluted Yvonne with a toothy smile, 'Buenos dias señora Yvonne. 'Av a nice day.'

'You've got a fan there.'

'Roberto. He's a real sweetie.' She then set the van in motion.

'Incidentally how come *you're* not wearing the team colours?'

She was dressed in a crisp white low cut blouse showing off her ample cleavage under a well-cut navy blazer hiding her Beretta pistol. The blazer bore the Cantravel logo of a palm tree on a beach on the breast pocket. Her ensemble was completed with white shorts and gym shoes. 'Because, I'm a boss,' she replied smiling and pointing to her lapel which had an enamelled badge proclaiming her to be "Head Group Facilitator".

Scott mockingly saluted her, 'Lead on Ma'am.'

With the barrier lifted they entered the complex through a long avenue of pines and log cabins set into the face of the cliff in steps giving panoramic views of Puerto and the rugged north coastline. The fresh smell of pine and the exhilarating feeling of fresh mountain air drifted through the open windows.

'What are those rock buildings?' queried Scott.

'They're the administration, reception area, squash courts, gym, and swimming pool. Dance hall, cinema, bars and restaurants, etcetera, etcetera,' reeled off Yvonne. 'It has to be seen to be believed. But wait till you see the outdoor pool. It's Olympic standard and is something to behold, built into an overhang of rock projecting from the cliff face it gives the impression when you're standing on the top platform of the diving board that you are about to dive into the far off Atlantic. Not for those of a nervous disposition.'

'Can't wait to give it a go.'

'I knew you would say that, Tarzan,' she said giggling.

They then entered a cutting in the pines with a notice board nailed jauntily to a tree at an angle announcing: Staff Only. There were no log cabins or bungalows here just local yellow pumice block chalets with red terra cotta pan tile roofs. Basic buildings, but still attractive architecture.

Yvonne drew up outside a spacious corner site containing one of the basic chalets. However, this particular one had a newly built double garage. Parked in front of the garage was a van in Cantravel livery bearing the logo "Diving Unit" and towing a four-wheel trailer. Mounted on the trailer was a powerful twin-screw motor-boat.

'Your new abode,' said Yvonne with an open arm gesture towards the chalet. 'The garage is your storeroom. Two of your team, once you train them, uplift the motor boat and take it down to the harbour at Puerto with two guests. That's the drill. I've arranged a meeting for you at 8-00am for tomorrow in the staff restaurant with Hank the swimming instructor and Pepé the local diver. I suggest you use the rest of the day introducing and acquainting yourself with the layout. There's a map of the island on top of the breakfast bar – you will find Punta Gaunché on the north west coast. Now here's your keys and welcome to Tenerife.'

With the unfulfilled Berlin tryst uppermost in his mind and sensing she was about to leave he asked, 'Aren't you going to show me around the inside then perhaps we can adjourn to the cocktail bar?'

'Sorry Scott,' she yawned, looking at her watch. 'I really would love to but today was a change-over day. New guests in – old out this evening. And I'm in charge this evening of attending to the old guests being driven to Santa Cruz docks, berthed, wined and dined and breakfasted in the morning prior to their departure at 8-00am. I've been on the go since 5-00am. I will be glad to get back to London for a rest. So I must bid you adios. See you in fourteen days.'

As she prepared to leave, Scott, feeling aggrieved that her work was getting in the way of bedding her there and then, groaned, 'It sounds to me as if you're in full time employment with Cantravel.'

'Some of us can multi-task you know,' she replied tartly

forgetting the promise she had made to herself regarding sarcasm. '*And*, after all I did manage to find out about the German divers whilst still doing my Cantravel work...' Scott conceded her sarcasm with a nod of head. '*And* – for your information when I get back from London my new cover is that of your Diving Unit's receptionist. This should give me more flexibility.' With that she stood on her tip-toes and kissed him lightly on the cheek – then turned towards her van. As she opened the door and turned to face him she pleaded, 'And please Scott – do not get involved in any shenanigans until I return with instructions from Sir James.' As she slid behind the steering wheel she knew she had wasted her breath. Scott did not do – not getting involved. However, they had parted reasonably amicably for a change.

Scott turned towards the garage dragging his timber crate with duffel bag on top to the door. Yvonne had tagged the keys. He found the garage key then unlocked the door and looked around. The oxygen cylinders he had requested were in place in racks as were wet and dry suits and the various paraphernalia associated with diving – masks, flippers, goggles, etcetera and the latest array of Rotary underwater watches. However, pride of place went to a gleaming Harley Davidson Flathead VL motorcycle, as used by American State troopers, sitting on its stand. He had requested a Triumph 650c.c parallel twin but Eugene being American had obviously overruled him with an excellent alternative. He found a jemmy and prised opened his crate and hung up his Pirelli one-piece diving suits along with the others on a rack and removed a suitcase containing his personal effects. This chore complete he slung his duffel bag over his shoulder, grabbed the suitcase and headed for his chalet.

Scott discovered that the exterior of the outside of the Spartan chalet belied the well-appointed interior, designed along the lines of an upmarket American motel – an open plan fitted kitchen off the lounge with a separate bedroom and bathroom. The lounge window was wide and floor to ceiling in height. The lounge was separated from the kitchen by a breakfast bar with stools. The floor was tiled. The tasteful pale pastel walls were fan-rippled plastered and hung with contemporary prints. To one wall of the bedroom were fitted wardrobes either side of a king-size bed. (The sight of this brought to mind his recent encounter with Yvonne and thoughts of yet another wasted opportunity gone a begging.) In front of the lounge window sat a large low chrome and glass coffee table with a white leather sofa and chair to match. The bath had a shower facility. He at first wondered about a cast iron stove with the flue vented through roof and logs piled to the side until it dawned on him that at the altitude he was at it could possibly get cold at night. Everything – to his satisfaction. He set his suitcase on the bed and proceeded to put away his effects. From the duffel bag he extracted his favoured Walther PPK, tucked it into the back of his trouser waist band, hid his spare ammunition in the robe, then slipped into his black Moroccan leather jerkin, locked the door and with hunger driving him he set off for the staff restaurant where he received some very admiring glances. None more so than from a "group facilitator" named Sandie who in her Texas drawl asked if she could join him. The meal finished they adjourned to the bar. On the way back to their respective chalets they passed Scott's. He invited her in for a nightcap.

The following day – day one of Yvonne's departure to London.
Scott awoke with a start. The alarm clock showed 6-00am. He was sure he had set it for 7-00am. He sat upright drawing his knees up towards his chin – the sheet clung to his knees, covering his nakedness. Suddenly the waft of coffee assailed his nostrils as a Texas drawl jarred the silence. 'Sorry 'bout the time change, honey, ah had to reset the alarm. Unfortunately, I've got an early start this mornin'. Gotta be at the "The Geenie" in Santa Cruz to pick up the guest list before it sails, an' I've still gotta go an' put on ma face an' change into ma uniform. But, I've got coffee made. Stay there an' I'll bring ya a cup.' She bent down in her bra and panties and kissed him good morning. He felt a growing sensation develop in his groin.
By the time Scott had rubbed the sleep from his eyes Sandie had returned with the coffee. 'Why do you have to pick up the guest list?' he enquired, slipping a hand out of bed to grab her.
She expertly evaded his clutching hand and grasped it by the wrist. 'So's admin can see nobody's jumped ship for the return sailing on their watch,' she chortled as still wrestling with his wrist with one hand she handed him the coffee with the other. As he

grasped the cup handle she added, 'Yeah, ever since that English girl Yvonne with the sexy French accent became head group facilitator, admin's become a stickler for the rules.' The shock of hearing Yvonne's description made him fumble the cup. The cup then bounced off his knees and slid down the valley formed between his knees by the sheet. The coffee soaked into the sheet and scalded his foot causing him to leap naked out of bed – hopping about on one leg massaging his foot while the horrible realisation sunk-in that Sandie knew Yvonne. Of course she would.

He was still hopping about on one leg as she fastened her skirt and buttoned her blouse. Her dressing chore complete she chortled, 'Saw ya getting in the van at Santa Cruz with Yvonne yesterday when "The Genie" docked. It looked like you two knew each other. So do you want me to say goodbye to her from you? – Or do ya think it's best I say nothin'?' She smiled at him wilfully, let it linger, then winked before turning for the door. When she reached the door she stopped and stared at him trying to cover-up his wobbling manhood and chuckled, 'Lordy, Lordy. Well ah never. I've heard about the English stiff upper lip but that…' she pointed, '…. sure as hell gets ma vote.' She left giggling. They'd had fun.

After treating the scald and being thankful that it was only his foot he kept the 8-00am appointment with Hank the head swimming instructor – an American and an ex US marine. Also there was Pepé, the local diver, who was acquainted with dive sites of interest around the island. They breakfasted together whilst Scott explained the closed circuit re-breather technique. He enlightened them that the idea wasn't in fact new, that it had been around for some considerable time and was adapted from the British Davis submarine escape apparatus. The Italian Navy, under licence, had refined the apparatus and were now the acknowledged experts. Basically the re-breather method of closed circuit breathing was as the name suggested – rebreathing the diver's exhaled air, carbon dioxide, through a loop-line back to the oxygen cylinders. The exhaled air being poisonous required to be filtered – scrubbed clean being the technical term – through a soda-lime scrubber in the breather loop. The oxygen supply was from a tank strapped to the back of a one piece Pirelli rubber suit incorporating a head hood. The supply fed a breather mouthpiece strapped to the face. The nose was clipped. It was the mastering of the mouthpiece that was paramount to the success of the dive operation. The question of how long they could stay underwater was asked by Pepé and answered that it depended on the life of the scrubber. The three-litre steel oxygen cylinder was good for seven hours depending on the diver's exertions but the scrubber no more than three hours. Hank asked about the maximum depth of dive. He was answered by Scott that without fear of decompression (the bends) approximately twenty feet. Six metres for Pepé's benefit. This depth suited Pepé's depth for interesting dives. The technicalities over, Scott asked Pepé if he knew of any quiet cove they could use for practice. Pepé knew of a perfect inlet off the beaten track just up the coast. Prior to the meeting Scott had loaded the diving unit van with all the required diving gear paraphernalia. When they finished breakfast they set-off leaving Lex one of Hank's assistants to take care of the guest's swimming needs. Driving slowly through a banana plantation they arrived at the secluded volcanic ash beach cove. The diving lessons commenced and within three days both Hank and Pepé had mastered the re-breather technique and were anxious to put their practice into use.

Four days later - five days after Yvonne's departure to London
They got the opportunity on the fifth day of Yvonne's departure. The operation started at 7-00am. Hank, Lex and one of their assistants Chuck, arrived at Scott's chalet, picked up the van, trailer and motor boat. They then uplifted the two guests at reception for the morning session and drove down to Puerto harbour to meet Pepé. When they arrived, the trailer with Hank, Pepé and the two guests changed into their re-breathers in the custom made changing room in the van and climbed into the motor boat and then were winched down a concrete slipway into the sea by Lex and Chuck. Once the motor boat floated free of the trailer Lex and Chuck winched the trailer back to shore and hitched it to the van, drove to waste ground and unhitching the trailer and left it there for later uplift. Lex and Chuck then returned by van to Cantravel to take the morning swimming lessons. The procedure was repeated after lunch. Scott who had followed the van to the harbour on the Harley Davidson sat

astride watching the operation. He deemed it a success. The Cantravel re-breather Diving Unit was up and running, giving Scott the freedom of movement he sought. After a further three days supervision he decided Hank and Pepé could successfully go it alone and resolved to put into action the following day a plan that had been forming during this training period.

Chapter 18

The following day – nine days after Yvonne's departure to London.
To put his idea into reality Scott awoke at sunrise, made lemon tea and toast with honey, mounted the Harley and by 7-30am was sunning himself on the rocks between the municipal swimming pool in Puerto de la Cruz and the sea. The Harley he had parked in a quiet side street. Previously he had checked the front of the premises housing the diving school. It was a typical whitewashed Canarian single-storey building with the usual terracotta red pan tile roof. From the front the building was attached to its neighbour on one side whilst on the other, between it and the municipal swimming pool, was a narrow overgrown path leading to the sea. The main road door of the diving school was closed and a sun bleached hand written notice in the window announced a diving school to be opening soon. The faded state of the notice in the window suggested to Scott that it had been there for some time. He walked up the narrow weed and rubbish strewn path and discovered to the rear of the premises, as Yvonne had reported, a high wall. It was protected with shards of broken glass imbedded in mortar to the wall head. It was further protected by barbed wire strung between metal posts. This wall formed an enclosed compound. Set in the sea-facing wall was a steel sliding door with a new concrete slipway leading to an inlet and the sea. He secreted himself on the rocks out of sight of the door. Twenty minutes later, having just got himself comfortable on the rocks, he heard a screech of metal on metal coming from the opening of the sliding door on its rusty runners.

There were four of them dressed in black rubber diving suits man-handling a four wheel, pneumatic rubber tyre, low-slung, metal cradle accommodating a large twin propeller cabin cruiser. There was much cursing – in German – as they tugged and pushed the cradle along the concrete slipway which eventually sloped gently seaward. When the cradle gained momentum on the slight downslope, a steel hawser between the cradle and a winch, secured in concrete in the compound, became taut. In a well-practiced drill, three of the four divers retreated to the winch to control entry of the cradle into the sea whilst the remaining diver clambered aboard the cruiser. Then the same floating of boat off cradle technique, as used by Scott's diving team, was adopted. The moment it floated it roared into life. The three ashore divers recovered the cradle and stored it in the compound and returned to the speed boat with sack barrows loaded with timber boxes. The cabin cruiser now under power idled slowly towards a flat stretch of rocks acting as a jetty and of the three remaining crew, two loaded the boxes aboard whilst the other returned the barrows to the compound and secured the gate. He thought he heard the growl of a dog in the distance. The car tyre fenders hanging from the cruiser's side were lifted on aboard and it then roared towards the open Atlantic and turned south leaving a well churned wake behind. He gave the vessel time to disappear from view before creeping from his hiding place to inspect the launch area. He found the slipway to be newly laid concrete. A look along the slipway seawards revealed access to the sea via a natural inlet channel between the rocks. Scott reckoned that somebody, in finding this gem, had done their Teutonic homework thoroughly. He checked the steel gate – a heavy duty padlock denied entry. The compound wall was over eight feet high. The block work looked rough enough to allow him to scale it and snip the barbed wire on top but with it being daylight he considered it not worth the risk. However, there was a tree with gnarled twisted intertwined trunks located at the junction of the wall where it met the sloping pan tiled roof of the office – which if climbed would afford a good view inside the compound. Looking around he could find nobody in evidence so he took the opportunity and climbed the tree. The gnarled trunks offered easy access into the upper branches. Once hidden in the foliage he edged along a branch projecting over the wall at the roof junction. He felt the branch give under his weight and stopped. From this position he could see the far wall. There was nothing there except weeds sprouting through the volcanic ash at ground level. In the middle of the compound the cradle was parked in front of the winch which was bolted to the continuation of the slipway. He tentatively edged closer to the wall until he heard the branch give a warning crack before it started to snap. A few feet away lay the corner of the pan tile roof where it intersected with the wall head. He leapt cat like just before the branch snapped. Clearing the barbed wire by fractions of an inch he landed with hands and feet squarely on the roof. He felt the tiles crack but hold. Below him he could now see the back of the wall he had leapt over. Stored against the wall were irregular shapes hidden under tarpaulins. These needed investigating. Scott slid down the roof until he came to the eaves where he sat with his legs dangling over the gutter. The top of the tarpaulin was four feet below, showing a flat rectangle. With hands flat on the roof he slid on his rear off the roof until his feet touched the solid feel of the rectangular tarpaulin. He then dropped to his knees and crawled to the edge. The ground lay six feet below. Lying on his stomach he swung his legs over the edge and lowered himself to the ground. Once there he flung back the corner of the tarpaulin and instantly recognised the universal warning sign stencilled on a timber box – one of the box type he had witnessed being loaded onto the cabin cruiser. Whilst at ground level he decided to try the back door of the office. It was as he made his move towards the door he heard the deep resonating throated growl. He looked towards the growl and his heart went into overdrive; a Dobermann Pinscher with posture set for attack. Out the corner of his eye he noticed how he had missed the beast – its kennel had been hidden by the cradle and the winch. It wasn't really a life or death problem as he reached inside his jerkin and withdrew from its holster his PPK pistol. He did not have time to fit the silencer so there was the problem of the shot being heard. However, the main problem was that if he killed the animal they would know somebody had been in the yard. He eyed the distance the Dobermann had to travel to him and the distance he had to travel to the packing cases. He re-holstered the PPK. It was *now* a life or death situation. He turned and ran and as he did he heard the manic scrambling very close behind of the powerful paws trying to get a grip in the loose volcanic ash ground. Three feet from the six foot high stack of crates he launched himself landing palms flat on the crate edge to allow him to gain extra height. The instant his palms landed he made use of his momentum and with biceps screaming heaved his upper body skywards twisting it inwards towards the wall as he lifted his legs just in time to evade the salivating limb-gnawing jaws of the mastiff. As his swinging legs reached above his elbows he flung himself inwards towards the wall and safety. On landing he bounced off the crate top into the wall, winding himself in the process. When he eventually got his breath back he sat with his back against the wall and toyed with the idea of kicking the Dobermann in the face the next time the evil snarling face came into view as it continued its vicious assault. However, he thought better of it, for with the amount of adrenalin coursing through him he could easily have removed its head. He waited, with slow deep breaths, until his heartbeat returned to normal then climbed back onto the roof. From a higher overhanging branch above the one he had snapped, he leapt up and secured hand holds then worked himself hand over hand from the branch into the tree. Reaching ground level he looked at his Rotary underwater watch – only 9-00am – plenty of time to catch the "Sea Dolphin" cruise from Puerto harbour. He retraced his steps down the narrow passage until he came to the main road. He peered around the corner in case there was any activity at the front of the building. There was none. But there was an unmarked black Peugeot van parked at the diving school door. He mentally noted the licence plate number then strode across the road to the parked Harley.

As he drove towards the harbour he was wondering why the German diving team needed dynamite.

***

Scott parked the Harley in the harbour car park and removed powerful binoculars and a map from the over-wheel pannier then retired to the café to order coffee and brandy and use the gents' toilet to freshen up. He left enough pesetas on the table to pay for the drinks and tip and walked briskly to the "Sea Dolphin" hoping Sandie would not be on duty, for he had much to do and did not need any distractions. Unfortunately, she was at the foot of the gangplank encircled by bustling guests shouting questions. Taking advantage of her situation he slipped behind her. She saw him, waved, winked and pouted her lips in a kiss. He acknowledged with a wave back as he boarded. Bugger.

He had previously gathered from Sandie that the majority of the guests spent their time on the top deck sunbathing. Those that didn't tended to be the elderly who spent the time reading their papers, magazines or books whilst indulging in tea and toasted crumpets in the lower deck restaurant. This suited Scott who strode through the restaurant with the intention of secreting himself under the bridge amongst the anchor chains and winches assured that no guests, nor Sandie, would use this dangerous forward area. He opened the door exiting the restaurant advising: "Crew Only". Once opened, he came face to face with a grizzled, weather beaten, unshaven face, chewing an unlit cigar stump.

Grizzled face, pointing at the door sign, growled, 'You no understand the English? I go to all the troubles to change the signs and still you no understand.'

'Sorry señor, I wanted a good view of the cliffs without being pestered...'

'Pestered? I no understand this pestered.'

'Annoyed. Interrupted,' suggested Scott.

'Si. I understand.' Grizzled face suddenly noticed Scott's tin plate badge. 'Ah! You from Cantravel. My nephew he work for them too. He is diver. His nombre is Pepé. You know him?'

'Yes. A good lad. I'm his boss.'

'You his jefe? No bothers then. You come up to my bridge. You no be *pestered* and I learn more good English from you.'

'Certainly, Captain...?'

'Xavi. Your nombre? ¡Perdon! Your name please?'

'I'm Jordan – Jordan Hill.' They shook hands.

The bridge comprised a wheelhouse where Xavi with unlit cigar stub still being chewed barked orders to the engine room as the "Sea Dolphin" pulled away from the quayside. On either side of the wheelhouse were flying platforms with guard rails used for docking purposes by the captain. One platform linked the bridge with the deck below via a companion ladder. This was the ladder Scott and Xavi had climbed to the wheelhouse. The other platform had a door giving access into the upper sun deck and was locked. Scott chose this platform since it was facing land and refused entry to the wheelhouse to the guests *and* Sandie. Excellent for his intended Xavi handed him a stool and propped his wheelhouse door open to allow communication with Scott. 'Hi Jordan Hill – you no need map. I tell you everything you wanta know. I know this coast like the backs of my hand.'

Scott, who had been studying the map given to him by Yvonne, folded it and tucked it into an inside pocket replied, 'Will you tell me when we get to Garachico?'

'You know story of Garachico, Jordan Hill?' Scott shook his head. 'Very bad. Garachico was the most important town in all of Tenerife – it was chief town – what you say in English?'

'Capital.'

'Si. Muy Bueno. Very good. Another new word I learn. But it had bad disaster. The volcanic landslide of 1645 killed over a hundred peoples. Then if that no bad enough came the big eruption of 1706. The lava rivers flowed over the cliff and – poof,' he flung his hands up in the air together, 'it swallowed the harbour and town. That the end of Garachico as a commercial port. Today it very nice town for tourists. Your Mr Thomas Cook, he like it very much – muchos tourists. Nice squares, cobbled streets, wooden balconies and the Castile de San Miguel.'

'You seem to know a lot of the history of the island,' complemented Scott, having been totally absorbed by what he heard.

'Before I hire my boat to Cantravel I used to do the speaking to peoples when we sailing to see the whales and dolphins.' He paused and looked quizzically at Scott. 'Speaking to peoples – that no proper English, Jordan Hill?'

'No. Try running commentary.'

'I like that Jordan Hill – *running commentary*. It sound good too. You good teacher. Anywhere else you want to know?'

'How about Punta Guanché?'

'It the furthest point west of the island. You know the story of Punta Guanché?' Scott shook his head again. 'The Guanché, our island forefathers, like many ancients before them held the sun sacred. Legend has it that as the sun set over the horizon the last rays of daylight struck Punta Gaunché and were captured in the cave of Magec, the Gaunché god of light and sun, and not released until the following morning. Magec declared that should there be any attempt to desecrate his cave the world would be thrown into darkness.'

'Cave? Is there a cave?'

'Rumours say so. Many divers have tried and failed, including Pepé. Unfortunately, they can no hold their breath long enough to find entrance to cave.'

'Maybe just as well otherwise we would all have been plunged into darkness,' replied Scott, with tongue in-cheek.

'Do not mock, Jordan Hill,' replied Xavi in a grave tone as he concentrated on his course. 'For I am of Gaunché blood.'

Ten minutes later Xavi, pointing, informed him that Punta Gaunché was coming into view. Scott trained his binoculars on the sheer-faced dark monolith projection towering some fifteen hundred feet high. The binoculars picked up movement close in at the base of the cliffs. As he adjusted the binoculars he witnessed the cabin cruiser he had seen leaving Puerto with the German divers on board. A diver in a wet suit was climbing aboard from a ladder hung over the side. There was no sign of the crated dynamite on deck. However, one of the other divers was operating something from a housing on the deck which he did not recognise. Scott slowly lowered his binoculars – deep in thought. He looked over at Xavi who was staring straight ahead, steering with one hand and crossing himself with the other whilst muttering something about "Forgive them Magec for they know no better". He looked at Scott and shook his head sadly as they rounded the light house at Punta Teno heading on a course set further out into the Atlantic Ocean informing Scott he was now heading for the dolphins and whales.

With the morning temperature at a seasonal 72° Fahrenheit (22°C) and the sun-deck awash with human flesh turning lobster red from the high overhead sun, the shout of "Dolphins sighted" brought the sunbathers to the rails with their cameras and cine cameras to witness the antics of the dolphins at play. Thirty minutes later the cry of "Whales" brought a similar stampede of holiday revellers to the rails to see the small minke variety. Not quite the giant bluff jawed sperm whale the size of the "Sea Dolphin" and weighing in at fifty tonnes that Scott had expected. However, Scott's disappointment was not contagious – for it did not dampen the enthusiasm of the lady guests who, fortified by free champagne cocktails between sightings, were screeching with delight. Xavi then set course inland and cruised along the coast past the small villages of Las Americas and Los

Cristianos with its new port until he came upon an inlet east of Las Galletas and dropped anchor. Time for lunch and sea swimming.

This was also the return point of the cruise and gave Scott the opportunity to discuss with Xavi a matter that that he had been mulling over since watching the German divers at Punta Gaunché. He started, 'Magec's cave, Xavi...'

'Si,' he replied, crossing himself.

'Why did we not see the cave? If it was to catch the last rays of daylight before it delved into the cave it would have needed to be above sea level.... and it isn't.'

'Jordan Hill, my amigo,' answered Xavi, leaning out the wheelhouse and sympathetically clapping him on the shoulder, 'Let me tell you a story. My ancestors have been on this island since befores two hundred years B.C and ruled until *the dreaded Spanish* conquered us in 1494. They – *the Spanish* – recorded that a volcanic eruption at Boca Conrejo on the Santiago North West rift had taken place in 1492.'

Scott not following Xavi's line of reasoning other than his obvious dislike of the Spanish conquerors by spitting overboard every time at the mention of their name, prompted, 'And?'

Xavi wagged his forefinger at Scott. 'And – Jordan Hill – on an island born from volcanic eruptions you are not going to tell me that during the period of my ancestors arriving and *the Spanish* conquerors recording the eruption of 1492 – that's a one thousand six hundred and ninety two year period – that only one eruption ever took place?'

Scott suddenly realised where Xavi was going with his reasoning. 'What you're saying is that the Santiago rift has always been unstable and that lava from an eruption flowed over the cliff above Magec's cave and could have covered it ....*at-any-time* during this period,' he finished lamely. Xavi nodded his agreement and crossed himself. 'Thank you Xavi for a concise history lesson. I too have learned something.'

Xavi's face beamed at Scott's praise. '*What is concise?*'

'Brief. Compact. Short and to the point.'

'Gracias, Jordan Hill. I learn another four new words. Soon I become English scholar, eh?' With that he departed to the platform on the other side of the wheelhouse to supervise the lifting of the anchor.

During the return journey Scott spent time thinking about the German activity at Punta Gaunché. Their base at Puerto had a settled look evident from the sun bleached poster in the window advertising their future opening. This suggested they had been on the island for some time – but how long? Were they searching for the same thing as himself – suitable submarine bases – but why so many divers? His brief from Sir James had only specified suitable inlets easy to defend. Had they found something suitable? If so what should he do about it? He could acquire their dynamite and blow-up whatever it was…..but that would more than likely cause a diplomatic incident and the last war had started for less. He could of course wait instructions from Sir James. But he knew that whatever it was they were up to required investigating *now*. He kept thinking about Yvonne's overheard words uttered by the Germans – dynamite and underwater.

Before the "Sea Dolphin" reached Punt Gaunché Scott asked Xavi how long the divers had been in the area? Xavi had replied six weeks. Had he seen them diving elsewhere? No. But he could only speak for the stretch of coast between Puerto and Las Galletas. Scott nodded his understanding, indicating the end of questioning. Xavi turned back to his steering wheel frowning and wondering why Jordan Hill had asked such questions of him. What and who was this man Jordan Hill?

As they passed Punta Gaunché Scott once again used his binoculars. He picked out a diver in a brass helmeted diving suit with umbilical airline running to the housing he had previously seen on deck. This housing he now realised contained a compressor for air supply to the brass helmeted diver which suggested that they were obviously diving to depths in excess of the re-breather safety limit of twenty feet. The diver was being assisted out of his suit by two divers wearing re-breathers while the other attended the compressor. He noticed that the diver's belt holding his buoyancy weights was empty. Very interesting thought Scott as he lowered his binoculars and looked at his watch – it read 4-30pm. He recalled Yvonne mentioning that she had seen the Germans return to their base in Puerto at around 5-00pm. A plan was forming but would keep until tomorrow.

After thanking Xavi for an enjoyable and entertaining history lesson he set about a problem that he had put to the back of his mind – the avoidance of Sandie. He need not have worried for when he came to disembark he found her surrounded by an assortment of males wishing to whisk her off to the harbour café for pre-prandials. He sneaked past the throng and found a local fisherman sitting on a capstan disentangling his nets. He enquired in his fluent Spanish if he had missed the arrival of the Cantravel diving boat. The weather beaten fisherman pointed seawards where the diving team boat was just coming into view round the San Telmo headland. Scott after offering the fisherman a cigarette took up a position on another capstan to await the arrival of the diving team. A glance back at the "Sea Dolphin" showed a flustered Sandie and her colleagues trying to round up tipsy stragglers for the bus back to the Country Club. She would be kept busy for some time.

Five minutes later Lex and Chuck arrived in the van and hooked up the trailer from the waste ground then drove to the slipway to position the trailer ready to accept the boat. This always drew a crowd which served Scott's purpose – it acted as a diversion between himself and Sandie. Twenty minutes later he found himself helping Hank, Lex and Chuck winch the boat onto the trailer after which he took Hank aside and suggested that he stood in for Hank at tomorrow's dive, using as an excuse the need to assess Pepé's progress with the guests. Hank immediately agreed. Lex had told him that the film star Jean Harlow had taken to using the Olympic pool every morning at 10-00am and her he had to see, he told Scott with a two-handed gesture indicating her hour glass figure.

Scott mounted the Harley and set off for Santa Cruz to dine and familiarise himself with the dock area.

Chapter 19

The following day – ten days after Yvonne's departure to London
As agreed with Hank the previous day, Scott was in his diving gear on a small secluded beach with Pepé and two Cantravel guests. The guests turned out to be highly proficient scuba divers allowing them to adapt quickly to the re-breather technique. This pleasant surprise presented Scott with time to pursue the real reason he wanted to be alone with Pepé, who he knew from initial training spoke excellent English. He could of course have communicated in Spanish but he still had not made Xavi or Pepé aware that he spoke fluent Spanish – and intended to keep it that way. Scott probed Pepé's background and discovered that he was one of those fortunate people whose hobby – diving – was also his job. His work came from hotels and the influx of new tour operators. He was twenty four years of age and of similar build to Scott, lithe, sinewy, muscular but with swarthy Spanish good looks. He was single and lived at home with his parents. His mother was Xavi's wife's sister.

Scott then set about his true agenda. 'I had a pleasant cruise on the "Sea Dolphin" yesterday. The skipper informs me he is your uncle.'

The white even teeth broke into a broad smile. 'Ah, you've met Uncle Xavier – Xavi. Quite a character.'

'I'll say. He informs me his family's ancestors are the Gaunché.'

'That's something I've never been able to understand. My father told me Xavi was born in Spain – Oviedo. His brother José who used to visit us before the mainland troubles there also comes from Oviedo. So…' he finished with a shoulder shrug and hands open.

'That *is* peculiar. Especially as I got the impression that he dislikes the Spanish.'

'He possibly does. He sees them all as Monarchist fascists whilst he's a Republican – a Gaunché Republican of course,' he quipped. 'If you want to know anything about the Gaunché he's your man.'

'I found that out also. He told me the legend of Magec's cave and….'

'….About the sun setting in a cave and not allowing the daylight to escape,' interrupted Pepé.

'That's the one. He says you tried to find the cave.'

'Yes. Me and my friend Paco tried possibly six or seven years ago. Back then I could hold my breath underwater for two and a bit minutes. That proved not to be long enough to find the cave entrance. Later when I had scuba gear I had girlfriends and found the cave had lost its excitement.' He shrugged. 'C'est la vie.'

'How far did you get in your explorations?'

'The projecting face of Punta Gaunché is facing true west and rises vertical, is smooth and flat and approximately twelve metres wide. We picked the centre of the face to dive. I went first. Paco was in charge of the safety rope from our rowing boat fitted with an ancient outboard motor. The currents are tricky at the Punta. This was the first time we had tried and we did not know if there were hidden rocks underwater. This stopped me from diving in to gain extra distance with breath held so I had to ease myself down the face of the cliff. Not possessing an underwater watch I had to count the seconds as I went. I reckon I slid four to four and a half metres before my foot lost the wall and slid inwards. I had found the top of the cave, or so I thought. A back-flip turned me inwards towards the cave and going with the current I felt my way along the roof. It was smooth from centuries of erosion and pitch black. I travelled say another four metres into what I presumed to be the cave but was unable to find a break in the smooth surface. By this time my mental clock had reached sixty seconds – confirmed by a tug on my safety line. Paco was also counting. I made a full body about-turn and found myself fighting against a very strong current. I tugged the rope and got the hell out before my lungs burst. I just made it. Paco, undaunted, had a go as well. He too failed. We decided it wasn't a cave but an underground river running in a rock fissure. I mean if it had been a cave it would have been above sea level, wouldn't it?'

'That's what I said to Xavi.'

'And he told you that an eruption above could have taken place and lava cascaded over the precipice to cover the cave entrance.'

'Yes.'

Pepé looked questioningly at Scott. 'Why do you ask about the cave?'

Scott had expected this question and had his answer prepared. 'Xavi aroused my interest in the Gaunché – that's all.'

Scott was trying to manipulate the conversation around to Pepé helping him with a dive at Punta Gaunché and didn't really need him asking questions when unexpectedly an excited Pepé gushed, 'You and me could try to find the cave now we have the re-breathers.'

'That's a good idea, Pepé. We must give it a go sometime in the near future,' replied Scott calmly, not wishing to appear anxious.

A disappointed look crossed Pepé's face. Scott elected not to elaborate. He did not wish the matter pursued for the present. The awkward situation was resolved by the appearance of two rubber suited bodies breaking the surface of the calm inlet and padding in their flippers towards Scott and Pepé who were sitting on a rock smoking. Scott stubbed out his cigarette. Having achieved what he set out to achieve he declared the session closed and they returned their guests back to base in time for lunch.

***

Later in the afternoon Scott departed for Puerto and the German diving school. From his hiding place amongst the rocks Scott heard the powerful throb of the twin propped motor boat change to idle as it manoeuvred its way down the inlet. Two of the crew jumped from the gunwale of the boat onto the rock jetty and made their way to the back gate, unlocked it and slid it back on its runners then fed out the cradle to recover the boat from the water.

As the boat was winched through the gate into the compound one of the two remaining outside, a short, older and squat figure with cropped white hair and a Kaiser moustache, barked instructions to the other, 'Kurt, you're remembering the unused dynamite has to be removed back to Perez and Schuster's warehouse tonight and that includes the empty boxes.'

'But Commander Müeller – why? Most of the boxes are now empty,' protested Kurt.

Müeller turned on him, 'Because my orders from that Gestapo bastard Kruger are to remove all traces of us being here and that includes the unused boxes.'

'But the van won't carry them in one go,' persisted Kurt.
'Tough *fucking* luck. Just do it – even if it takes you all night. That's an order.'
'But Commander we leave tomorrow for home...and much needed shore leave. What about the dog and the boat?'
'Kurt! You are trying my patience. I hate the beast. Kill it for all I care. Regards the boat – that's being taken care of by Kruger. That's the end of the matter. Understand?'
'Yes Sir,' saluted Kurt taking one step behind the Commander and giving him the finger.
They entered the compound and the door was slid shut and locked.
As Scott broke from his concealment and made his way to the alleyway between the compound and the municipal swimming pool he heard the unforgettable growl of the Dobermann and remembering the salivating jaws quickened his pace.
Sitting astride the Harley in a street opposite the alleged German diving school Scott witnessed the loading of the van by three tall Aryan-looking individuals dressed in military-style coveralls with the fourth Commander Müeller still barking orders. Nearly an hour later, with the springs of the Peugeot van showing signs of distress, Scott kick-started the Harley into life to follow the van as it slowly moved away from the pavement. He let it disappear in the distance along the coast road heading north before slipping the bike into gear. He knew from the overheard conversation between Müeller and Kurt that their destination was to be Perez and Schuster. It made sense for it to be a Santa Cruz warehouse in the dock area. He figured that the speed the van was travelling, due to the heavy load, meant he had time to stop for a snack at a roadside café on the outskirts of La Laguna, so he overtook. Sitting next to a window in the café he kept an observant eye open for them. Thirty minutes later they passed the café. He paid his bill and followed. When he was satisfied they were heading for the dock area he overtook and parked up between the gables of two warehouses on the main road leading into the docks. It was now dark. Five minutes later the van entered the road with its headlights on and passed him. He slowly eased the Harley into the main road and was in time to observe the van take a left turn into a

street two blocks down. He followed. By the light from a lamppost he was in time to see them getting out of the van and enter a building bearing the signage Perez and Schuster Importers. It was a corner building, the frontage being parallel to the main road, but with the main entrance in the street they had turned into. He drove past the warehouse entrance and turned off into an alley a block further on. In the alley there were industrial sized refuse bins which he used to conceal the Harley. His task complete he walked back towards Perez and Schuster whistling as he strolled looking like a man happily finished work. As he approached the main entrance of the importers he stopped to light a cigarette. The van was gone – he assumed to pick up any remaining crates in Puerto. The light of the same lamppost that had allowed him to see the Germans enter the building also gave him the opportunity to survey the building for possible security weaknesses. The boundary was hard against the adjoining warehouse. Both buildings were two-storey and shared a continuous roof – part of a four-in-a-block back-to-back development giving total security to the inner conterminous walls. There were no ground-floor windows; instead only continuous clerestory glazing at the first floor level. It was fair to assume the main daylight to the warehouse came from roof lights. Also there were no rainwater pipes on display that would lend themselves to climbing and the only openings at ground floor level were the doors. The main vehicular entrance was made of stout timber double doors, ten foot (three metres) high with an applied sheet metal skin showing no locks to the outside. This suggested to Scott that both were bolted top and bottom from the inside and further secured with a drop-bar. To open this type of door you required a pass door and sure enough as he moved further along the street towards the corner he noticed the pass door cut out of the sheet metal in one of the main doors. It had two mortise locks and a bolted-through hasp and staple provision for a padlock. The fact that it was not padlocked was, Scott reckoned, due to the Peugeot van being expected back. He strolled to the corner to inspect the main road frontage. Except for the doors it was as the main entrance elevation. The pass door was the weakness. As he retraced his footsteps towards the pass door he removed his lock picks from his jerkin pocket. His immediate problems was the light being given off from the lamppost and with it being a warehouse an alarm system, even though there was none in evidence from the outside. After a quick analysis of the problem he realised the problem would still exist whatever or whenever. So with a slow look around and finding nobody lurking in the shadows he strode towards the pass door with picks at the ready. He was a couple of steps from the door when he heard voices from the other side. Instantly his survival instinct kicked-in telling him to about turn, start to whistle and head for the corner of the building and disappear from sight. When he did the about turn on his heel, he made out in the gloom on the other side of the road an open vehicle entrance gate in high pointed steel railings. Through the gaps in the railings he registered stacked oil barrels. In a change of mind he sprinted across the road and threw himself headlong in a trained paratrooper roll into the entrance and landed with a further side roll behind and between two barrels. This gave him a view of the pass door across the road which was already opening.

The street light showed a tall figure with blond hair protruding from a forage cap perched nonchalantly on the back of his head step over the threshold. His Hamburg accented voice carried in the still night air, 'That shit-face Mueller's a right pain in the arse,' he moaned over his shoulder to the two others following as he removed a cigarette packet from the top pocket of his coverall and offered it around. They all lit-up.

'Put that cigarette out immediately, Volmer. No smoking in here you fucking idiot. Don't you realise there's dynamite in those boxes,' Volmer mimicked, to sniggers from his colleagues.

The last one to join the group commented, 'The commander's entitled to be a pain – after all he's working with that bloody stuff daily.'

'And what do we do? We fetch and carry the stuff for him. Does that not count as dangerous, too?' retaliated Volmer.

'We don't drill and place the charges, prime and detonate them underwater – he does. One slip and he's a goner.'

'The sooner the fucking better,' finalised Volmer with venom.

'What's Mueller doing down there anyway, Kurt?'

'All I know is that he's getting rid of underwater rock

projections for the engineers, Leo.'

'What for?' persisted Leo. Kurt shrugged his shoulders in way of an answer.

Volmer continued his moan, 'Shit-face says we're the Führer's chosen ones. More like his hand-picked fucking idiots. We've been here six weeks and we haven't had a day off. Work, work, fucking work. And tomorrow we're heading back to base at Keil.'

'You're all mouth, Volmer. Right let's go and finish our packing before old shit-face blows his top. We want no hiccups between now and when we leave,' replied Kurt, who appeared to be the ranking officer.

As they turned to enter the warehouse there was a loud reverberating clang and echo from across the road. A Luger pistol instantly appeared in Kurt's hand from inside his coveralls. The others likewise as they turned crouched and fanned out in a well drilled semi-circle towards the echo and Scott's hiding place.

By the street lighting glinting off their attentive faces Scott recognised the three Aryan types as the divers from Puerto de la Cruz. He also noticed their badges on the short upward turned lapels of their coveralls – Kriegsmarine Kommandos. Hard men. Trained killers.

His paratrooper roll when he landed on the compacted volcanic ash entranceway had created a small dust cloud to linger and permeate his nostrils causing an irritation. This irritation had grown into the need to sneeze. He had tried desperately to suppress a sneeze but failed. The outcome being that when he did sneeze his left leg involuntarily shot out kicking one of the empty barrels against the other causing a thunderous racket in the stillness of the night. He had immediately regained his composure ; the PPK appearing in his hand seamlessly. Scott looked between the barrels to witness the one referred to as Kurt bearing down on him with his Luger aimed between the barrels. Scott fitted the silencer to the PPK knowing it was a fight to the death. These men would never believe he was the night watchman.

He rolled between the next two barrels, sighted the PPK between Kurt's eyes and was about to squeeze the trigger when a large calloused hand engulfed his and lowered the pistol. As it did a voice whispered in his ear, 'No shooting Jordan Hill, please. We do it our way.'

The familiar voice made him hesitate but his training as a fighting unit took over. He drew back his free left arm to aim a blow in the direction of the voice in his ear. This too was caught in a powerful grip and another familiar voice whispered, 'We mean you no harm. Please do as my uncle wishes.'

Scott lowered both hands and as he did he was aware of shadows rising from behind the other barrels. Suddenly all around him there were *Whurping* sounds in the air. He saw Kurt momentarily hesitate at the sound as did the others. Kurt's error. A brick from a slingshot rendered him instantly unconscious. His compatriots met with similar fates. The shadows gagged and tied the unconscious Kommandos. Now realising who he was dealing with Scott relaxed. 'I thought the slingshot was the South American way – or is that the bolas.'

'Maybe the Gaunché migrated to South America, eh, Jordan Hill,' chortled Xavi. 'Now señor. What are you doing here?'

'I could ask you the same thing, Xavi.'

'Does the name Drago mean anything to you?'

Scott drew a deep breath. 'You're the leader of "The Free Canaries" resistance movement that I was told to contact.' Xavi nodded, smiling. 'Funny, I was going to ask you if you knew how I could contact him.'

Xavi took a bow. 'Well, you have, señor. No time to discuss this now. There is another one in the warehouse and we need him out of the way to raid his weapons.'

'Weapons?'

'All will be explained. Now please, we have to move before the *Civilies* – the Guardia Civil – do their rounds of the dock warehouses because I intend to reverse our van into their warehouse.'

'Leave this to me, Xavi. I speak German. Help me strip this one out of his coverall,' Scott said referring to the immobile Volmer. He donned the stripped coverall, applied the forage cap and strode across the road to the warehouse.

As Scott cautiously entered the open door of the warehouse an angry voice boomed out from the dark interior, 'That you Kurt?'

'Yes, Commander,' replied Scott in German coughing as he did to hide any accent problem.

'How long does it take you lot to smoke a cigarette. And by the sound of that cough it's not doing your health any good.'

'Sorry sir,' wheezed Scott.

As the shadowy figure of Commander Müeller turned on its heel Scott swiftly and silently closed the gap between them and crashed the butt of his pistol down on the silhouetted skull. Scot checked Müeller's eyes. He wouldn't make breakfast. Using a torch he stealthily scouted the premises for further occupation. There was none. He did, however, find upstairs a dormitory with eight double-deck bunks of which the four lowest tiers showed signs of recent habitation. Next door there was a glass panelled office overlooking the floor below. The door was ajar. He entered. There was a drawing pinned to a cork board on the wall that caught his eye. The drawing carried the title Punta Gaunché. Scott gave the drawing a cursory glance and decided it was of intrinsic interest to him but he first had to give Xavi the all clear to enter the premises. He retraced his steps downstairs and with his eyes now accustomed to the dark noticed timber crates piled high between the pass-door corridor and the loading bay that Xavi would reverse his van into. He opened the pass-door and gave a low whistle – seconds later Xavi and others bundled through the door. Xavi and Pepé slid between the timber crates to open the double doors to allow entry for their van but were pulled up short. The Peugeot van the Germans had arrived in was parked hard against the double doors. Scott did an about-turn to search Müeller for keys. Plenty of keys but no van key. The others were tied-up and unconscious across the road. To check them for keys was but to waste valuable time. The Peugeot doors were fortunately not locked. The double doors were unbolted then opened and the Peugeot freewheeled into the road and parked. Xavi's van was reversed into the loading bay. Whilst this was happening Scott took himself upstairs into the office. He studied the drawing and decided not to remove it from the wall – to do so would alert the Commander that something other than a robbery had taken place. Not that Müeller was in any fit condition to pass comment. However, there must be others involved. Müeller had to be taking orders from somebody – more than likely a local Gestapo cell. Possibly this Kruger he had heard mentioned. He gathered a pencil and paper from the office desk and copied the relevant details. He stuffed the copied papers inside his jerkin and joined Xavi downstairs.

They had jemmied open the crates. To Scott's amazement the crates, all labelled "Agricultural Machinery" and stamped with the necessary Spanish Government seals of entry, contained Schmeisser MP28 machine pistols and ammunition. Four of the machine pistols were already slung around the necks of Xavi and his gang.

Xavi, noticing the arrival of Scott moved to shake his hand. 'Gracias amigo – you go now. I do not want you involved with the Guardia if they show.'

'What do you want with MP28's? I thought "The Free Canaries" *movement was a peaceful movement.*'

'*Were*,' Xavi emphasised with a throaty laugh. 'We just getting armed for the coming civil war.'

'You think?'

'I know.'

'The crates were marked "Agricultural Machinery"…'

Xavi cut him short. 'No time to explain Jordan Hill. The *Civilies* may come any time. You go now. You come and see me manyana on the "Sea Dolphin" – yes?' With that he ushered Scott towards the pass door.

Scott exited the doorway, nodded to the look-out in the Peugeot van and slid into the night shadows towards the Harley. As he entered the alleyway where he had concealed the Harley he was sure he saw a shadow from an overhead security light attached to a wall disappear around the far corner of the alley. He rushed to the corner. Nobody was in sight. He retraced his footsteps to the Harley. An inspection showed no apparent signs of interference. He mounted and departed. The shadow worried away at him.

Chapter 20

The following day – eleven days after Yvonne's departure to London.
The following morning before Scott's meeting with Xavi he prepared a drawing based on the notes and sketches copied from the drawing that had been pinned to the wall in Commander Müeller's office. From his notes he established the drawing issue date to be August 1934 and from the office of Hitler's architect Albert Speer.

The original drawing contained such detailed information that Scott realised a hard-hat diver (deep sea) of the type he had witnessed at Punta Gaunché with the Puerto based German diving team must have been used to gather the information. He also figured that surveyors with theodolites and dumpy levels must have been engaged in the internal work – for what he had in front of him now were the astonishing details of an underwater cave. There had obviously been a previous survey of the cave that had gone unobserved by Xavi.

Scott had also copied the relevant points of interest from the geologist report that had been pinned to the board. The report noted that the cave entrance had at one time been above sea level prior to a volcanic eruption in the Santiago rift above the fissure resulting in a lava river overflowing the precipice of Punta Gaunché. The cooling lava had stopped four metres below sea level thereby hiding the cave entrance. A core sample taken from the lava suggested it was fifteen hundred years old and samples from the cave walls to be from the Miocene period (eight million years) – the founding period of the Teno massif in which the fissure is situated.

Scott sat back to admire his handiwork. It showed in cross section an elongated triangle – the fissure – being twelve metres wide at its base tapering to zero at thirty metres above sea level. The base was thirty metres below sea level. However, it was the longitudinal section that had revealed the cave's secret to Scott. The outer Atlantic face was near to vertical rising to five hundred metres above sea level and stopped four metres below sea level leaving a gap of twenty six metres to the fissure base (the cave floor). Entry into the fissure was through this gap. The gap being a twelve metre long sea-filled inlet before it opened out into the enormous cave. This confirmed Scott's theory that he'd had when he first saw the original drawing – that of its suitability for use as a submarine base were it not for the jagged needles of rock projecting from the fissure floor at the cave mouth. However, somebody (possibly Commander Müeller?) had used a red coloured pencil and crossed them out with the word kaput.

Remembering the stored dynamite at the compound in Puerto and the Kreigsmarine Kommando Kurt's talk of Commander Müeller having to prime and detonate, "*the stuff*" it all suddenly clicked into place – they had blasted away the needles! He needed visual proof.

Looking at his watch he realised he would have to get a move on otherwise he would miss the "Sea Dolphin" departure.

***

As Scott boarded the "Sea Dolphin", Sandie, the attractive bubbly blonde of their previous – "*why don't we get to know each other better, honey*" – acquaintance beckoned him over. 'Hiya, Jordy,' she drawled in her Texas twang, 'Got some hot gossip for you buddy – Satchmo is the star guest at the night club.'

'Satchmo?'

'Ya know, silly – Louis Armstrong the trumpet player. He's just arrived off a cruise ship that docked this morning. Mr Crozier's booked him for tonight. Isn't that fantastic? He's doing a sort of one night stand – ya know what a one night stand is, dontcha Jordy,' she added teasingly, with a hint of a smile playing around her lips. 'So, how'd ya like to join me for dinner tonight and we'll take in the show?'

Scott whose preference in music would have been the London Philharmonic thought "why not?" – and figuring he was due some relaxation – found himself answering, 'That sounds great. I've heard him on the wireless and would love to actually see him perform,' he fibbed.

'O.K then, that's it settled. Meet ya in the cocktail bar at 7-30pm before ya disappear again to where evah ya go.' She blew him a kiss and joined her milling charges.

A blast from the boat's horn signified departure and sent Scott scurrying up to the bridge to take up the position he had occupied previously.

Xavi, after performing his captain duties, clearing harbour and setting course for the open Atlantic turned to Scott, 'Buenos dia, Jordan Hill. How are you today after last night's escapade?'

'Very well. All went well after I left you?

'Si. Before we departed we removed the fascist swine from across the road, untied them and left them in the Perez and Schuster warehouse. Moved their van into the warehouse and locked-up.'

'Good move, Xavi. That saved the police from getting involved. And the good Commander Müeller most certainly won't report the theft to them. Too many questions to be answered if he does.'

Xavi nodded his head in acknowledgement then stated gravely, 'I know you are a British intelligence agent Jordan Hill. This I know when you tell me you want to contact Drago. But what are you really up to I ask myself. Would you care to answer – no lies please?'

'We, British Intelligence, heard there was German activity on the island and I was sent to investigate,' he lied.

Xavi looked long at Scott, his brows furrowed deep in thought as he picked his words carefully. 'I like you Jordan Hill. You were of muchos assistance to me last night…' He paused. '…but I will not help your country do to us what your great Lord Nelson tried and failed to do to us one hundred and fifty years ago – conquer us.'

'What ever gave you that idea?'

'I think you know only too well Jordan Hill. The civil war in Spain is imminent. The Nationalists with Hitler and Mussolini's help should win.'

'So?'

'Hitler will want reward for his help – passage through Spain to Gibraltar. But your Winston Churchill is no estupido. He will have an alternative to any loss of Gibraltar – Tenerife. What you think Jordan Hill?'

What he thought was that Xavi was nobody's fool but instead answered, 'Your theory is good, Xavi. I must inform Mr Churchill if I ever meet him. He might want to put it to use.'

Xavi roared with laughter. 'You good liar Jordan Hill. But you know what I say is true. So tell me, what are the Germans up to?'

'I don't know. However, with the Germans now out of the way I will know for sure when I have dived at Punta Gaunché.'

'How you know the Germans are out of the way?'

'The guys we incapacitated last night were the Punta Gaunché diving team. But apart from that they are returning to Germany today.'

'I hope their ship has a hospital.' Scott raised his eyebrows as to why. Xavi solved his problem, 'One has a broken jaw, one a broken nose and one severe concussion – maybe brain trouble. Slingshots do muchos damage. Oh! And the one you hit on the head will be lucky if he regain conscious by Christmas,' he laughed as he crossed himself.

'Good. Now, Xavi, or should I say Drago, what were *you* doing there last night?'

He shrugged his shoulders and flung his hands outwards as he answered, 'We have many eyes in the docks. We know Señor Perez met with an accident eight weeks ago – his car it decided to take a swim in the Atlantic. Schuster is German – but he, too, has disappeared – ill health, apparently. But since his ailment we know that from importing household goods – cookers, fridges, furniture etcetera – they are shipping in, "agricultural machinery". Suspicious, yes?' Scott nodded. 'As we found out – weapons. Now my turn Jordan Hill? Why you there?'

'From a tip-off by a colleague I knew where they were operating from in Puerto de la Cruz. So, yesterday I followed them to Perez and Schuster's warehouse to try and find out what they were up to. Then you and your merry men stepped in....you know the rest. And having found the machine pistols we know there's skulduggery afoot.' He made no mention of discovering the drawing showing the intended use of the cave.

'What is this – "skulduggery"?'

'They are up to no good.'

'Skulduggery. I like skulduggery. Now amigo. For the dive tomorrow you have everything you need?'

'Not quite. First I need Pépé. Then an oxygen-supplied deep diving suit and compressor. You know the one – brass screw helmet with air lines attached to the compressor.'

'Si. I know the one. Pépé and his friend Paco will have for you. What time you want them to pick you up in the morning?'

'8-00am at the harbour. Incidentally, say I was to find Magec's cave – what about the curse?'

Xavi roared with laughter, 'You don't believe all that bullshit do you, Jordan Hill? That's only for the tourists.'

Scott looked at Xavi and joined him in the laughter.

***

Docking of the "Sea Dolphin" completed Scott headed for a quick workout and shower in the gymnasium after which he retired to his chalet and dressed in a pale blue short-sleeved linen shirt, lightweight beige jacket with beige sharply pressed trousers and tan tasselled slip-on shoes for the short walk to the restaurant. His PPK, which he would have felt naked without, concealed in a patch pocket of his jacket. When he reached the restaurant he made for the cocktail bar only to discover that Sandie had arrived before him. She was not alone. Sitting alongside her on a bar stool was a very attractive brunette. Sandie immediately slipped down from her stool and placed herself between her companion and Scott.

She was pulling a face, which he imagined to be a grimace, as she grabbed him close to kiss him on both cheeks. As she did she whispered, 'Sorry.' He couldn't imagine what for as she turned towards her companion with an out held hand, 'I'd like to introduce you to ma very good friend, Professor Charlene Rogers or Charley as she likes to be known.' Charley wiggled off her stool holding her tight skirt from riding up and showing more of her shapely leg than was already exposed. She held her hand out as Sandie introduced Scott, 'An' this is ma friend Jordan. He's our head of diving.'

'Pleased to meet you, Jordan,' she said, in a pleasant mid-Atlantic accent.

'My pleasure entirely, Charley. Can I get you ladies a drink?'

'No, we're fine,' chirped Sandie holding high a Martini.

The hovering bar tender enquired what he would care to drink and was informed a large straight Glenfiddich malt whisky. As the whisky arrived an immaculately clad maître d' arrived to announce in a French accent that their table was ready.

"*Their table*", puzzled Scott. This was confirmed as Charley joined them. He gave Sandie a narrow-eyed glower behind Charley's back as they were being led to "*their table*". She just lamely smiled and shrugged her shoulders. The dining area was raised and near the stage. Premier seats. Scott and his now two guests would have an excellent view of the cabaret.

Once they were seated Charley spoke first. 'I trust you don't mind my joining you, Jordan?'

'Certainly not Charley,' he lied smoothly. 'Delighted in fact.' This final declaration brought a pleasant smile to Charley's face and a scowl to Sandie's.

'I'm glad you feel like that for I do hate playing gooseberry between two lovebirds.' Scott stared hard at Sandie. What had she told Charley? But Sandie just rolled her eyes and giggled. Charley oblivious to the silent warfare being waged, carried on, 'In case you were wondering how I came to be here – I was in Santa Cruz this morning picking up our mail at the main Post Office with a colleague when I overheard Cantravel vacationers...'

'Guests,' corrected Sandie.

'Apologies. *Guests*. They were all discussing looking forward to seeing Louis Armstrong here tonight. Well, I just had to see him. I often call in to see Sandie unannounced and I knew she being a cabaret facilitator would have tickets. So here I am.'

'You're more than welcome, Charley. Isn't she Sandie?' he answered through gritted teeth.

'Sure is, honey,' she replied, smirking at Scott's hidden annoyance.

The meal was excellent as you would expect from Cantravel's five star chef. Scott, unexpectedly, enjoyed the relaxed atmosphere and the small talk of the ladies' whilst dining, sipping wine and waiting for the cabaret to start.

During the small talk Scott enquired of Charley about her professorship. 'I majored at Harvard in geology and have the tenure of the Geology Department there.'

'So what brings you to Tenerife?'

'I'm part of the National Geographic team analysing the

possibility of a future eruption on Mount Teide at the Chinyero cone area.'

'Is this likely?' Scott asked, with a pretend worried look.

'There have been indications of late that this might well be the case. That's why the Cabildo (Local Government) invited us to investigate.'

'How very interesting.......'

'And frightening. Am I safe in my bed?' interrupted Sandie.

'Depends who's in it, Sandie,' chided Charley, winking at Scott and smirking at her friend. 'Now as you were saying Jordan....'

'Er, yes....Interestingly enough I read in an article recently that some fifteen hundred years ago there was an eruption in the Santiago rift and a lava river cascaded over the cliff at Punta Gaunché and hid the cave of Magec, King of the Gaunché, resulting in everlasting darkness being thrust upon the island should anybody violate the cave.'

Charley sighed. 'I cannot speak of the Gaunché folklore, but for you to have read about the finding of the "Great Fissure" you must have read Professor Edwin von Nida's paper published in 1927 in the National Geographic Magazine (NGM) – not exactly the sort of thing you find in a cocktail bar....is it Jordan?'

Caught out, Scott confessed, 'Now that you mention it Charley, I heard it from the skipper of the "Sea Dolphin"....he claims to be...'

'Descended from the Gaunché. I've been on the "Sea Dolphin" and heard all his tourist bullshit,' interrupted Charley. 'However, with your obvious interest in science you must come up to our camp in the rift near the small town of Santiago del Tiede. You're welcome anytime.'

'I would love that, Charley,' replied Scott, much to Sandie's annoyance.

Suddenly the lights dimmed and the wail of a trumpet blasted out the first notes of the "Saint Louis Blues" as the purple velvet curtains drew back to a hushed and crowded auditorium of devotees to reveal the great Louis Armstrong backed by the resident Cantravel orchestra. Even with Scott's preference for classical music he could not stop his foot tapping to the beat of Armstrong's swinging rhythm and was pleasantly surprised that Armstrong in his gruff syncopated growl could sing as well as play trumpet. The finale rendering of "When the Saints Come Marching in" brought the audience and diners to their feet of which he was one – to the extent of joining in the cry for an encore. By the end of the concert he had become an advocate of jazz.

'A thoroughly enjoyable evening, ladies,' conceded Scott as they rose from the table, and with Sandie excusing herself to go to the ladies' toilet this gave Scott the opportunity of speaking alone to Charley with a view to ridding her from the rest of the evening. 'Can I organise a lift for you back to Santiago del Tiede?'

'Thanks for your consideration Jordan but I'm staying overnight with Sandie. But thanks again for a lovely evening, you were fun,' she said, and drew him close as they shook hands to kiss him fully on the lips. As they parted she whispered, 'Remember Jordan, that's an open invitation to visit. Make it soon.' She moved to follow Sandie into the ladies' toilet but stopped and turned to face Scott. 'By the way, Jordan, I just remembered something. Our Richter scale has been picking up violent readings akin to explosions from around the Punta Gauché area. So just watch yourself if you're diving there – it could be Magec trying to escape from his cave,' she chuckled and finger waved him goodbye.

Ah, well that's the evening well and truly buggered Scott was thinking as he made his way to the exit whilst cursing Sandie's stupidity. He had just set foot outside the restaurant when an arm linked into his arm. 'Sandie,' he exclaimed, pressing the arm close to him with his elbow. 'How did you manage to ditch Charley?' This was said without looking at her as he, patting her hand, forgave her stupidity.

'Quite easily really,' replied a familiar voice but not that of Sandie.

The answer shook him rigid as he turned towards the voice. '*Yvonne! How-the-hell-did-you-get-here?* I wasn't expecting you for another three days.'

'Obviously not. Did you enjoy your evening entertainment with Charley and the Texas tease bag?

Did he detect a hint of jealousy. Did he really care? He was feeling totally perplexed by the turn of the evening events, so he retorted angrily, 'Look Yvonne you have me at a complete disadvantage. Kindly explain your early arrival and keep it relevant to mission. I don't want to hear your personal grudges.'

'As you wish Scott, even though a "good evening, Yvonne, nice to see you again" wouldn't have gone amiss.' With Scott glowering bad-temperedly at her she became aware that a situation had arisen that once again she wished had not. 'I passed my findings regarding the German divers in Puerto to Sir James. He was extremely interested. He asked what you were doing about them. I told him I had asked you to do nothing until he heard from you. He said that was the correct procedure and that you were to monitor the situation until he decides what course to take. She looked penetratingly at him. His glower had changed to one of innocence. She sensed that something other than monitoring had taken place. 'I also informed Sir James of your displeasure at the conduit. He agreed but asked me to remind you that there were severe budget constraints to the operation. However, Sir James told me that Mr Crozier like all good multi-millionaires now has his own flying-boat and that it was moored in the Thames whilst he visited his European Headquarters in Virginia Water. Sir James then phoned Mr Churchill. Mr Crozier then phoned Sir James. The outcome was that Mr Crozier who was due to leave for Tenerife the following day arranged to give me a lift. He was due in Tenerife for his monthly visit. He invited me to have dinner with him and hear Louis Armstrong who he had booked at personal expense for tonight... and, Sir James said to inform you that Mr Crozier might just have something to disclose to you later into his visit.'

'Sounds interesting. Do you know what it's about?' Yvonne shook her head. Scott carried on, 'How long did the flight take?'

'Including refuelling and a rest break in the Azores – thirty hours....'

'Now you're talking. That's more like it,' he interrupted, 'So do I take it that this flight is the start of our new conduit?' he enthused.

Yvonne shook her head again. 'Sorry Scott – it's a one off...'

'Buggeration. Why?'

'Because the flying-boat is going to be used at Mr Crozier's other complex in the Caribbean.' Before Scott could air his views on the matter she hurried on, 'But what I can tell you is that Mr Crozier is returning to London three days from now and I've been instructed by Sir James for you to hand any despatches you may have for him over to Mr Crozier.'

'Not possible, Yvonne. The information I now have is *"Top Secret"* and I mean *"Top Secret"*. For Sir James' eyes only. So, since you are mission vetted by Sir James I better tell you what I've been up to in your absence.' Scott retold the whole story. As trained, she listened attentively without interruption.

When he finished she shook her head in disbelief. 'By jove you've been a busy beaver. Well, so much for Sir James wanting you to only monitor the situation. I don't think he or Mr Churchill are going to be pleased at your findings when they discover they've been usurped by Hitler. Maybe they'll even abort the mission?'

'Not if I come up with something – like a workable plan.'

'And do you have one?'

'Possibly. But first, tomorrow morning, I leave with Pepé to investigate the cave to find out if my plan is viable. After which I'll write my despatch. Now, you said Crozier leaves three days hence?' Yvonne nodded her head. He paused and looked intently into the honey-gold eyes, 'Well, you can join him on the flight to London and deliver my despatch personally to Sir James.'

'But...'

'No buts, Yvonne. I'm the agent in charge – you're the courier. This is *Top Secret* intelligence. I don't want strangers involved.'

'But Mr Crozier's not a stranger, he's part of "Operation Tenalt" – a cousin of Mr Churchill and we're using his Cantravel facilities. He'll think we don't trust him.'

'Yvonne! I don't care if he's the King's cousin – he's a foreign national and will not have signed the Official Secrets Act and that disqualifies him as a person suitable to carry HM official secrets – understand?'

'But Sir James told me to give your despatch to Mr Crozier...' she replied stubbornly.

'Not – *this despatch*. If you'd been listening, I made constant reference to it being – *top secret*. Now if you won't personally deliver the despatch – I will. And I don't think Sir James would care

222

for that, do you?'

With the gravity of the situation dawning on her she nodded her head in acknowledgement. 'I understand – *sir,*' she finished sarcastically.

'Good. I'll walk you to your chalet,' he said amiably hoping for a coffee in way of a peace offering.

This was not to be as she retaliated tetchily, 'Believe it or not Scott, I can see myself home.' She then brushed past him.

As she passed, a pleasant lingering fragrance wafted to his nostrils causing him to lay a sympathetic hand on her shoulder, 'Don't worry, Yvonne, I'll speak to Crozier and explain the situation regarding the despatch and the OSA. All will be well.' She knocked his hand from her shoulder and stormed off.

With a deep sigh of regret Scott set-off for his chalet alone. Alone was not how he had intended the evening to work out but it was for the best he assured himself looking at his watch and finding it to be 2-00am. He had an early start this morning.

With murderous intent in her heart and trembling fingers Yvonne turned the key in the lock of her chalet and flung herself face down on the bed thumping the mattress in frustration and hollering in rage, 'That pig-headed, chauvinist-pig has done it again – and all I was doing was trying to protect him from that Texas nymphomaniac - Sandie.'

Alone and fully clothed she fell sound asleep. Not quite how she too had intended the evening to work out.

Chapter 21

The following day
Within a half hour of awaking to the trill of the alarm clock Scott was showered, dressed and on his way to Puerto harbour. The morning was as usual clear and balmy and even at 7-30 the heat haze was dancing off the tarmac of the main coast road. He opened up the throttle fully on the Harley and let the mighty 650c.c engine rip. With the wind whipping into to his goggled face and sail-bagging his leather jerkin as he topped a hundred mph on the straight, it gave him enough of an adrenalin boost to try and forget last evening's disasters with Sandie and Yvonne.

Five minutes later he roared into the harbour car park and adjourned for breakfast on the café patio overlooking the harbour. Twenty minutes later Pepé's van entered the harbour and parked alongside a fishing boat. He finished his coffee, paid and strode over to the harbour. He stopped at the already open rear van doors and helped Pepé to load their diving gear aboard. The task complete Pepé introduced him to his friend Paco and Paco's Uncle Tony in the wheelhouse. Scott was delighted to find out during the introductions that Tony was an experienced deep sea underwater salvage diver. This was an added bonus.

The trawler was old but in pristine condition and owned by Tony – a weather-beaten, cigar-chomping, old sea-dog out of the Xavi mould. It had recently been converted to suit his marine salvage – a business he ran from the newly completed harbour at Los Cristianos. Scott cast his trained eye around and found what he was looking for – the deck mounted air compressor. A check on the compressor, diving suit, air lines and sundries convinced him that he could not have wished for a better standard of equipment than that supplied by Tony who enquired why he needed a deep dive suit. Due to the fact that he had not disclosed to Xavi or Pepé his findings about the cave, Scott had expected this question. His answer was that he had seen one of the German divers at Punta Gaunché wearing a deep dive suit and reasoned there must be a need for it at depth unknown to him.

This answer seemed to satisfy Tony and twenty minutes later they reached Punta Gaunché and dropped anchor close in to the vertical cliff face. Tony then lowered a lead weighted shot line overboard. The line, knotted at one metre intervals, settled on the bottom at near enough thirty metres (one hundred feet). He enquired Scott's bottom time – the time he intended to investigate below. Scott reckoned after descent he would need thirty minutes. Based on this time and the use of pure oxygen Tony worked out from his diving charts the number of ascent stops to eliminate decompression sickness (the bends). The charts indicated three minute stops every five metres – an ascent time of eighteen minutes. When all the airlines and oxygen valves had been checked and rechecked Scott prepared to dive. He donned the rubberised fabric suit and Tony screwed the brass helmet in place on the shoulder plate. Scott then, by nature of the cumbersome diving suit with its attached air and safety lines and belt of buoyancy weights, required the assistance of Paco and Tony to lower himself into the Atlantic via an iron ladder fixed to the trawler's side. Pepé, on Scott's thumb-up signal, did a back flip off the gunwale to join him in the water. They descended together until Pepé reached his depth of four and a half metres on the shot line and with a hand signal indicated that he was turning inwards to the cliff face, knowing that he should find the ceiling of the fissure entrance at this level from his previous dive of several years ago. Scott then concentrated on his dive-depth of thirty metres. The depth was recorded on the shot line at one metre intervals. In a slow descent he reached the twenty eight metre mark on the shot line then seconds later his weighted boots touched hard bottom. He took a step and stumbled. His powerful torch showed strewn and fractured rock where there should have been jagged rock projections rising two to three metres according to the drawing. On the drawing the entrance had been shown to be twelve metres long before it became the start of the cave. Reckoning he was lucky if he took three paces to a metre due to his weighted boots and the strewn-blasted rocks lying around, he paced out forty potential ankle breaking paces to cover the twelve metre entry into the cave which he found on arrival to be clear of the projecting obstructions shown on the drawing. This confirmed Scott's theory that the dynamite removal of these projections by

Müeller at the fissure entrance now offered enough headroom to allow the passage of a submarine into the cave. Thirty metres above him from where he now stood would be the cave – and Pepé. Satisfied, he retraced his path back through the dangerous sharp blasted rock segments taking care not to snag his dragging airline. This proved to be an onerous task and he was thankful to find his shot line and give it two tugs to alert Tony that he was beginning his ascent. He stopped at the agreed decompression stops and three minutes after his final stop and the dropping of his final buoyancy weight, he broke the surface of the water and was assisted out the water by two pairs of willing hands. As he looked through the porthole window in his helmet the first person he saw was Pepé giving him the thumbs up with a large grin on his face whilst doing some sort of Spanish jig. The helmet was unscrewed by Paco while Tony attended to the airline. After the equipment was cleaned and stored they adjourned to the wheelhouse where Tony had prepared welcoming hot glasses of the local Ron Miel honey and rum which Scott had to reluctantly turn down. It would take him a further twelve hours to rid himself of the after effects of his dive and alcohol in the blood stream was strictly forbidden. The atmosphere in the wheelhouse was one of bonhomie. Pepé was beside himself with delight – he had at last found the mysterious Magec's cave. To much jocularity Pepé said he was going to tell Xavi that he had shaken hands with Magec who had asked him to tell Xavi to stop all the bullshit he was telling people about him and the cave. Once the hilarity had subsided Pepé described the inside of the cave. He said that for a cave that was supposed to store the setting rays of the sun for release the following morning that it was extremely dark. But by the light from his powerful torch he had ascertained that there was a ledge one metre above the high tide water mark and two and a half metres wide running along one wall for as far as the eye could see and the ceiling of the cave was so high it disappeared out the range of his torch. Paco and Tony were in awe of this description – to Scott it confirmed the detail on the drawing. When it became Scott's turn to describe his findings he told them that at thirty metres he had found the floor of the entrance to the fissure and discovered it to be full of sharp projecting rocks. He made no mention of the demolished needles guarding the cave entrance. So, when Pepé asked what the dynamite had been used for Scott shrugged his shoulders in a non-committal gesture and informed them that his torch had not been powerful enough to make out detail at that depth in the pitch dark and with him concerned that his airline would snag underfoot in the dark on the sharp rocks he had about turned. He would dive again at a later date.

Pepé accepted this reasoning but Scott knew Xavi wouldn't. It was all now a question of timing – and secrecy. They set sail for Puerto harbour with Scott now sure in his own mind what the Nazis had been up to. He was beginning to feel tired from the effects of his dive.

***

Later in the day, fully recovered, Scott sat on the soft leather sofa writing his despatch to Sir James on a coffee table placed in front of the floor to ceiling picture window. From his chalet's location on a bend it allowed him a commanding view up the tree lined avenue to the avenue's access roundabout. Hearing a deep throated growl of a motor cycle engine he looked up from his writing to observe a motor cycle negotiating the roundabout. He laid down his fountain pen and rose to look out the window. The bike he recognised instantly as a Norton super twin 500cc. The rider, with suit jacket flying wide open, he didn't recognise. The rider was wearing a leather pilot's padded helmet and goggles and was revving like mad as he brought the Norton to a tyre shredding halt in the driveway. A tall distinguished-looking figure in his early sixties dismounted and in one fluid motion located the bike on its stand, dusted himself down, retired to the rear wheel and placed his helmet and goggles in the pannier. He then buttoned his jacket, smoothed his ruffled silver hair and strode elegantly towards Scott's chalet in his immaculate tailored Brooks Brothers, lightweight, tropical tan-coloured suit, black shirt open at the neck and highly polished black loafers. An American by all accounts. Scott didn't have to guess who – Eugene Crozier, entrepreneur and owner of Cantravel.

There was a knock on the door. Scott shouted, 'It's open,' as he strode from the window to welcome his visitor who had already entered and was moving towards him with extended hand for shaking.

'Mr Rutherford, I presume,' he exuded in a Stanley meets Livingstone pseudo-English tone. They shook hands firmly as he confirmed in his real voice, a mid-Atlantic accent with just a hint of time served Oxford University education, 'I'm Eugene Crozier.'

'Pleased to meet you, sir.'

'We can dispense with your English formalities – the name's Gene. That O.K with you Scott or should I call you Jordan?'

'Scott's fine with me. Can I get you a whisky?'

'You certainly can and I'll leave the measure up to you – straight up, no rocks. That's ice to you.'

Scott returned from the kitchen to find Eugene sitting at the table with cigar lit. Scott handed the large whisky into the ready waiting outstretched hand. Eugene thanked him, took a sip and rolled it around his palate before declaring, 'Glenfiddich – twelve year old.'

'You certainly know your whisky.'

'Should do. I've spent a lifetime drinking the stuff. Started at Oxford University over forty years ago,' he guffawed. 'Here, have a cigar.' Scott obliged, accepting a large Corona from the offered cigar case and lit up. Crozier from behind a dense swirl of cigar smoke continued, 'I saw you admiring the Norton. I had one when I was at Oxford. It's good, very good but not in the same class as my Harley Davidson you're driving.'

'Want to swop?' enquired Scott.

'No point. I'm leaving tomorrow morning first light.'

'You're leaving tomorrow? I was informed you were departing the following day.'

'Change of plan. I found the person I was looking for quicker than I thought possible. In fact I have just left him to come and see you. Now Scott, I am led to believe you are unhappy with the fourteen day conduit turn round…'

'Not exactly enamoured, Gene.'

'Can't blame you – nor would I. Unfortunately, my flying-boat was purchased for use in the Caribbean islands starting next week. This visit is strictly a one-off. To explain – I was due my quarterly trip to Tenerife so I took the opportunity to test-fly the Sikorsky flying-boat with my co-pilot….'

'You're a pilot?'

'Yes. I'm coming to that. It just so happened cousin Winnie required a charming young lady, Yvonne, to be flown here so I was glad to be of service. You know her of course...' Scott nodded, sighed, and was about to inform Eugene that he required her to be taken back with him to London when he was upstaged by Eugene. 'Now listen, Scott, this will be of immense interest to you. As I promised Sir James, the person I just left holds the key to a three day conduit depending on connections with RAF Gibraltar. His name is, Marcus "Maverick" Bentyck. Ever heard of the Bentyks?'

Scott being thrilled to hear the new turn round time of the conduit asked Gene to repeat the name. When Eugene did, Scott jokingly replied, 'Only Bentyk baked beans.'

'That's the people. Billionaires many times over and he's the heir apparent. We served together in the war, in the Confederate Volunteer Corps as fighter pilots. All Yanks of British lineage. He was a hero. An ace. He had twenty seven kills including Baron Ludwig von Eisberg the Krauts ace pilot. He was once shot down and fought his way back to base with a plane stolen from a German airfield. Mind you he was damned near shot down again when he tried to land it in England,' he hooted, slapping his knee. Then he continued in a serious tone, 'Umpteen medals for bravery, blah, blah. The all American boy. Totally unaffected by riches or fame. One of the nicest guys you could meet. *However,* back to you. At the last meeting I had with Winston, the one I had to tell him I could not help you out with my flying-boat, I suddenly remembered something. The last time Marcus had been shot down he was nursed to health by an Anglo Spanish nurse whom he subsequently married after the war against his parents' wishes. They moved to Tenerife where her parents lived. I found him this morning in a large villa on the outskirts of La Laguna,' he broke off and leaned back on the sofa lost in a cloud of cigar smoke. Scott who had been following every word intently still didn't see where the story was going. This must have shown in his face for having brushed aside the lingering smoke fug Eugène carried on, 'The punch line is, Scott – that he has two aeroplanes – a Sopwith Camel biplane he flew in the war and a Bleriot 290. Both are out at Los Rodeos airfield. To supplement his meagre allowance from his father of a zillion bucks a month – I joke, it's more – it's actually five cents on every can of beans sold worldwide – he carries inter-island mail, does general deliveries and takes Cabildo dignitaries to the other islands, etcetera, etcetera. So, as I said before, I paid him a visit before I came to see you...'

'And?' Scott asked excitedly, finding himself intrigued by Marcus.

'And he's agreed to help. He will fly you to Gibraltar.'

'Can he be trusted?'

'Oh, yes. He can be trusted. After all it was on the Brits side he fought in the war – not Jerries,' laughed Eugene. 'In fact I owe my life to him.'

'Pray tell.'

Eugene heaved a sigh of nostalgia and started, 'Nineteen years ago, 1916, just shortly after Marcus had captured a misfiring German Fokker Eindeker over the English Channel and forced it to return to our base, we got orders to scramble; an incoming Jerry raiding party. When Marcus's plane had previously landed it broke an undercarriage strut and was further found to be riddled with bullet holes and deemed not airworthy. There were no spare planes except one that had been badly shot up, repaired, but not test flown. Marcus was then without a plane for the dog-fight that he so relished. The Fokker he had captured was now in the hands of the intelligence boffins for this was the machine that had conquered the design problem of shooting through the propeller without smashing it, and yourself, to pieces. Against all advice about using the repaired but untested machine he decided to fly the blasted thing. As he pointed out the name of the squadron contained the word *volunteers*. So we took off – with Marcus in the untested plane.

It was a bright morning and we were heading into the rising sun. As Marcus's wing man I could see he was in trouble; his untested machine was not responding to the rudder. The Sopwith Camel he was flying was a brilliant fighter aircraft, manoeuvrability exceptional. It could turn on its length – but full concentration of rudder trim was required at all times. From his actions he was not in control – his plane was not airworthy as he had been warned. I signalled him to return to base. Not Marcus. For ever the hero.

Upwards and onwards. Jerry came screaming at us out of the sun – Messerschmitt 109's. Marcus had drilled into us that in these circumstances not to engage but to gain altitude. The man on top always had the advantage. I immediately put my Sopwith into a vertical climb near to stalling point and on flattening out was aware of a 109 under me. I then brought it round in a tight roll to end up on the 109's tail. I let loose with the cannons and the wings of the 109 tattered. He went into a downward spiral. I followed him down. Lucky I did for I saw Marcus in trouble. He had not been able to gain altitude because of his faulty controls and there were two 109's bearing down on him. I didn't think I had time to catch up with them before they downed him. I had forgotten of course the master aviator that Marcus was – he still had a trick or two up his sleeve. One of which I had seen him use before and hadn't dared to use myself. He cut his engine, stalled and fell instantly like a stone. One Messerschmitt overshot him the other confused by his manoeuvre turned towards me and took a lethal dose of bullets to his underbelly from my guns. Out the corner of my eye I saw Marcus's Sopwith, now in a vertical nose dive, with engine trying desperately to catch as he endeavoured to pull out of the dive before he hit the sea. From my position above I estimated there was not enough distance between him and the sea to pull the Sopwith out of its dive. He had overplayed his hand this time. This piece of pure theatre gave me the chance to catch the other Messerschmitt. We engaged in a duel which was relatively short lived. The 109 pilot must have seen me coming for he banked sharply and with the use of full throttle got behind and above me. I would then have been in his sights. I tried to take evasive action but he hugged my tail. I awaited the burst of cannon into my cockpit when suddenly below me I saw Marcus rising vertically from out of the sea. I was between Marcus and the unsuspecting 109 pilot. I veered sharply out of the way allowing Marcus a clear view of the 109's underbelly. He hit it with a violent burst of cannon as he shot upwards and out of my view. I escorted him back to base. To this day I still don't know how he managed to pull out of that dive. When I asked him at the time he just grinned that smug grin of his, shrugged his shoulders, and said, "I must've hit the right thermals, ole buddy." So if you trust me you can trust

Marcus. Believe me. I assume this meets your approval?'

Scott nodded his agreement, now itching to meet the indomitable "Maverick" Marcus Bentyk.

'Excellent. Now here's Sir James' new arrangements. The young lady I flew over, Yvonne, is coming with me to Gibraltar to act as your courier – her new posting. Sir James is in Gibraltar right now as we speak – bit of sabotage bother in the dockyard apparently. When Yvonne arrives she will hand your despatch to Sir James. Future despatches to be handed to Marcus for delivery to Yvonne for onward passage to Sir James in London.' Eugene noticed Scott looking puzzled. 'Is there a problem?'

'Yes. With sabotage in the dockyard it is obviously being watched by unfriendly eyes and that means any commercial flights, that is Marcus, into the Admiralty zone will be suspicious to them – whoever "them" are.'

'Ah! I should have explained. Marcus has for many years picked up his spare parts from Gib. So that shouldn't be a problem.'

'Good. Now tell me how does Yvonne get in touch with Marcus?'

'BBC World news shipping forecast. The newscaster will say something like "A low in area Biscay... sorry, "I will *say"* that again. A high in area Biscay...'

'What if the newscaster makes a real mistake?'

'That is covered too. He will say... sorry, "I will *repeat"* that.'

'This means Marcus has to be listening at 6-00am every morning.'

'5-55am to be precise. Of the four times available to him he chose that one. It allows him at this time of year to make the return journey from Gib as far as Casablanca in daylight. From Casablanca to Tenerife he says he can do with his eyes closed.'

'What about me contacting Gibraltar?'

'Anytime. Get Marcus to get up and go.'

'Well, you seem to have covered all contingencies...'

'Not quite, Scott. Sir James asked me to ask you how you liked reading Dickens,' "Tale of Two Cities"?'

Intrigued, Scott replied, 'Very much. Why?'

'Because he tells me you've to start reading this,' he said, producing from his pocket a copy of Dickens' "Christmas Carol". Your new code book. Happy reading – Jordanhill. I'm told you've to start at page ten – today.' With that he rose and shook hands across the table. 'Please tell Yvonne of the changes to her itinerary and that I'll pick her up at 7-15am tomorrow. And please make sure you get your report to her before I take off at 8-00am.' They shook hands.

The door closed and Scott felt the sudden emptiness of Eugene's absence in the room as he sat mulling over his words. He couldn't believe he had been worried about Eugene not signing the Official Secrets Act for it was obvious he knew more about the Operation TENALT than he did. However, he had his new three/four day conduit and he hadn't had to ask Eugene to take Yvonne to London. That had already been taken care of with her posting to Gibraltar. All good. However, he sighed, fate seemed to be against them ever getting together. He then set about rewriting his despatch from his new code book.

The following morning Scott saw off the giant Sikorsky flying-boat from its berth in Santa Cruz. He shook hands again with Eugene who as he bent to enter the cabin said, 'Pleasure to have met you Scott. I hope we meet again soon. Next time I'll take you up in this beauty.'

'Pleasure's mine, Gene. I would look forward to sitting behind the stick once again.'

'Nobody told me you flew.'

'Fleet Air Arm trained, sir,' responded Scott with a snapped salute.

Eugene saluted in return and disappeared into the cabin. Scott then turned to Yvonne who had been waiting patiently behind him to board and handed her his despatch for Sir James. She accepted it in sullen silence and a disparaging look before she too entered the cabin without any attempt at a farewell. He could only assume that her reluctance to communicate had something to do with finding her new itinerary scribbled on an empty cigarette packet stuck under her door whilst she had been on duty yesterday.

Meanwhile, as he watched the Sikorsky flying-boat disappear over the horizon – many miles to the north east over Bavaria......

Chapter 22

Berchtesgaden – Bavaria November 1935
The Heinkel He70 broke through low cloud over Berchtesgaden. The pilot made the necessary control corrections to enable him to line the aircraft up with the landing strip at The Berghof – Adolph Hitler's lofty home in the Bavarian Alps. In the cabin of the converted mail plane sat the solitary passenger – the uniformed figure of General Wilhelm Canaris chief of the German military intelligence – the Abwher – wrapped in an Army great-coat to try to keep warm in the unheated fuselage. He had been summoned by Hitler. He had been given – date, time, location, flight – come alone. No indication as to why. Hitler's way.

The flight from Berlin gave Canaris time to reflect on his relationship with the Führer. He was not a member of Hitler's Nationalist Socialist German Workers Party, (Nazis) – nor had he shown support at any time for Hitler who the previous year had appointed himself Dictator of Germany. However, he did recognise the threat of world communism and was prepared to follow Hitler's anti-communist lead for the time being until he and his fellow Generals rid themselves of Hitler.

Canaris had a fine aerial view of The Berghof as the descent began. The house was the property of Adolf Hitler, purchased in 1933 from the proceeds of "Mein Kampf" – a book that was in the opinion of Canaris the drivel of a self-indulgent maniac. The house had grown since his last visit a year ago. The landing strip was new as was the barracks for the Waffen Schutzstaffel (SS) troops – Hitler's personal bodyguards.

As the Luftwaffe pilot brought the Heinkel through the snow clad mountain peaks to a smooth landing, a Mercedes staff car immediately drew up alongside and steps were rolled to the fuselage exit by SS troops. The Mercede's SS driver jumped out and as Canaris approached he opened a passenger door and gave the straight right arm Nazi salute accompanied by a "Heil Hitler". Canaris gave a flip of the wrist acknowledgement; he had no time for the Nazi salute. The Mercedes then sped off and deposited Canaris at the main entrance to The Berghof.

Hitler was waiting to greet him, wearing a fur coat, scarf, Bavarian soft hat and gloves. He was stamping his fur lined boots and body clapping himself with his arms for warmth. No salute – just a handshake. 'Have you had a pleasant flight, Wilhelm?'

'Very pleasant, Mein Führer.'

'Adolf, if you please Wilhelm. We are alone.' With the bestowed use of Christian names permissible, and no Bormann, Heydrich, Göring or Himmler, Hitler's ever present thuggish lieutenants in attendance, it suggested to Canaris a classified meeting between only himself and Hitler was about to take place – which was a relief for it could just as easily have been a firing squad. 'I see you are wearing your military top coat, Wilhelm. A wise precaution for it is my intention that we sit on my new sun terrace and take in the view whilst we talk.'

It's all very well for you dressed like an Eskimo to suggest sitting outside but due to the bloody plane having no heating I'm frozen to the marrow and a large brandy wouldn't go amiss – even though you don't imbibe – were Canaris's deliberations on an outside meeting. However, from experience he knew that deliberations in Hitler's presence were best kept to oneself, so he grovelled, 'That sounds a marvellous idea, Adolf.'

The sun terrace boasted a majestic panoramic view of the snow-capped Alps of Hitler's native Austria and once seated opposite each other at a large slatted wooden bench protected by a bullet proof glass screen Hitler's paranoia came to the fore. 'We are free to talk out here. We can't be overheard. Now, Wilhelm, I understand you are fluent in Spanish.'

'Si señor,' replied a wilful Canaris.

'I trust that is not your total vocabulary, Wilhelm, for I have a little something special for you to do for me involving one of Spain's overseas territories – Tenerife,' retorted Hitler. 'Tell me Wilhelm, have you ever encountered a General Franco in your travels?'

'No. But I know he was responsible, as commander of the African Army in Morocco, for putting down the Republican rebellion in Oviedo in a rather barbaric fashion.'

'And quite right too. But, please bear in mind that Oviedo was only successful thanks to my help with the bombing. Remember that for future reference – for it has a bearing on what I want you to do for me. I want you, with all secrecy, to carry a message to Franco at his HQ in Morocco. When you meet him, Wilhelm, be on your guard for he is a dangerous man and carries the army generals of Spain with him. Come the inevitable civil war, I expect him to be the man to lead the Nationalists.' Hitler held up his hand to stop any questions from Canaris. 'Franco's heard that should Britain lose control of Gibraltar that Churchill intends to invade Tenerife...'

'Heard from whom?'

A smile crossed Hitler's lips. 'I might just have *inadvertently* mentioned it in Franco's company. And as I was saying – to counteract this rumour Franco is currently building fortifications in way of gun emplacements along the south coast of Tenerife.' With hands on the table edge he pushed himself upright and crossed his arms, the smile now one of self-satisfied smugness.

You devious bastard thought Canaris, but playing along with Hitler's intended subterfuge he snorted, 'Pah! How can that be? Churchill's not even in government.'

'True. But let Franco continue to think Churchill will invade Tenerife. It helps my cause.'

'What cause.....?'

Hitler held his hand up once again to stop Canaris. 'Patience Wilhelm – all will be revealed. What do you know of Gibraltar?'

'It is a British overseas protectorate. A key strategic location for access to and from the Mediterranean.'

Hitler nodded his approval. 'Let us, Wilhelm, assume the Spanish civil war has taken place and the Nationalists have won as they surely will with Mussolini's and my continued support. I would then expect Franco to allow me unhindered passage through Spain to Gibraltar. My problem is that Spain might declare neutrality and......'

'But Adolf! Any attack on Gibraltar will start a war between us and Britain and France and we are not war ready.....'

'Yes. Yes. Yes.' Shouted Hitler in an angry rising voice as he rose from the table and started to thump it with his gloved fist. 'We may not be as *yet* ready but we will once I regain my industrial heartlands that have been stolen from us by that innocuous, "Treaty of Versailles". Then in one of his infamous mood swings he slowly and calmly sat down giving Canaris time to think of the lands confiscated from Germany after the war. Any of these lands retaken would most certainly result in war. Hitler, having composed himself restarted his rhetoric in a conciliatory tone as if he had read Canaris's mind. 'This prime minister of the British, Baldwin, is scared of war. He is an appeaser. So do not worry, Wilhelm, I will take advantage of his appeasement and regain the Rhineland without a blow being struck. However, we seemed to have digressed somewhat, so back to the main agenda. I have an alternative to Gibraltar without the use of force.' Thank god for that thought Canaris as the master orator continued, 'With the recent seismic tremors that Mount Teide is giving off once again we could, in the interest of international concern and cooperation, offer to send our scientists and geologists to help…'

'Where did you get that information about Teide?'

'From the National Geographic magazine,' was Hitler's unexpected reply. 'The Americans do have their uses.'

'How does the National Geographic know?'

'They have a sponsored team of scientists on the mountain monitoring the tremors,' he rattily replied. He was not used to constant interruptions but grudgingly had to concede that that was the way of a good intelligence officer. And he knew Canaris was exceptional. That was why he had picked him against the wishes of Himmler and Göring who were convinced Canaris was in league with the plotters. The Army Generals' that would have an end to him. 'It's getting chilly now, Wilhelm, so let's move quickly along. With Franco busy building his coastal fortifications against his imaginary invasion by Britain there is much movement of building materials and machinery into the port of Santa Cruz. We have been using these movements for the last few weeks to cover the shipping of our own materials and machinery into the port…'

'What for?' interrupted a shocked Canaris, inwardly furious that as an overseas operation it fell under the jurisdiction of his Department.

Hitler held his hand out to stop any further interruption from Canaris. 'We have known for some time that there are underwater caves in the coastal waters around certain islands in the Canary archipelago….and before you ask Wilhelm – yes, we also got this information from the National Geographic. An article by a Professor von Nida insisted that there was, whilst he had never seen it himself, enough evidence to prove a Great Fissure – an enormous underwater cave in Tenerife – existed. He just couldn't find the entrance. So I used the recent tourist boom in Tenerife to conceal our investigation into the cave by setting up a pseudo diving school in the holiday resort of Puerto de la Cruz. The divers were Kriegsmarine Kommandos – trained in the use of dynamite. They have just recently located the cave and prepared it ready for my purpose….'

'Which is what?'

'Patience, Wilhelm. The cave is on the north west face of the island at Punta Gaunché near Garichico.'

'Isn't Garichico the town that in seventeen hundred and something was buried by lava from an eruption by Mount Teide?'

'Indeed. You are well read, Wilhelm.'

Risking a tongue in cheek reply, Canaris lied, 'National Geographic.'

Failing to follow Canaris' attempt at humour, Hitler snapped, 'In that case you will have read that the north face of Teide is considered unstable. The last eruption of 1909 was in El Chinyero, when it sent lava flows towards the villagers of Santiago del Teide. This is the area the National Geographic scientists have their base camp and I need them out of the way to allow us freedom of movement so that our engineers can locate the Great Fissure below.'

'For what pupose?'

Hitler, showing signs of annoyance at being interrupted yet again rose to his feet and adopted his rallying speech pose, thumped the table and in his oratory voice declared, ' For the purpose of the –- *Third Reich*. The engineers will sink a shaft down to meet the now prepared cave…'

'Prepared for what?' queried Canaris, expecting the wrath of Hitler to descend upon him for the interruption.

Instead Hitler's voice rose an octave as he triumphed,

'Prepared...,' he hesitated for effect. '... for......' An aghast look crossed the flabbergasted Canaris' face as he was made witness to what he considered the ranting of a deranged idiot. Hitler, taking the look to be one of wonderment, continued, 'Yes, Wilhelm. My back-up plan should I fail to convince Spain to allow me eventual passage to Gibraltar.' He then sat down with arms folded daring Canaris to challenge him about Germany's readiness for war.

Canaris, his mind now awhirl at what he had heard – a virtual proclamation of war – needed time to think, so he blustered, 'A truly magnificent achievement Adolf. But what of the American scientists on the mountain?'

'I need them off the island, so I have given instructions to our agent in the Tenerife Cabildo, their local government, to discredit the American scientists. He will inform the local paper that he has found out the scientists intend to publish in the National Presses of Europe their findings that Mount Teide could erupt again at any time. This will be disastrous for the island's fledgling tourist trade. I think even you Wilhelm would have been proud of that plot.'

Knowing that they still had not come to Hitler's main agenda and now being anxious to leave The Berghof, Canaris grovelingly said, 'Indeed Adolph. You seem to have thought of everything, Mein Führer. So how may I help?' The words uttered turned his stomach as he listened to them.

'Excellent, Wilhelm. I am glad you agree with me for I can now reveal to you the full extent of my plan. He then put his hand under the table and withdrew an Army ordinance map and laid it out on the table. Pointing at a spot on the map he said, 'This is Punta Gaunché. As you can see from its location at five hundred metres above the cave it commands an ideal view of the north and south faces of the island. An ideal location for a large howitzer gun,' he proclaimed, stabbing his forefinger at Punta Gaunché. Canaris sensed they were finally coming to the main agenda. 'So when you visit Franco, Wilhelm, I want you to suggest our willingness to supply scientists to monitor the mountain to replace those about to be expelled in disgrace. Then – and most important of all – I want you to convince Franco to allow us to build the gun emplacement above the cave – for *our* future use of course. Not that you will disclose this matter.

But you will disclose – *All at no cost to the Spanish government!*"

'I should imagine at that price he will be only too delighted to accept.'

'He's no fool, Wilhelm. He knows I will want to be repaid in other ways. But his obsession to build his fortifications against Churchill's imaginary invasion will demand he accepts my offer and worry about the cost at a later date.'

'And what if he declines?'

'Remind him that come his civil war, a war that he craves, that myself and Mussolini might just withdraw our aid that his country currently enjoys and concentrate our efforts against the red menace of communism.'

Canaris, having to admit grudgingly to the cunning of Hitler's plan, nodded his head slowly and enquired, 'Why me? Why not our Foreign Minister – von Ribbentrop?'

'Simply Wilhelm – you are a skilled negotiator and interrogator *and* of the utmost importance, you speak fluent Spanish. When I or von Ribbentrop communicate with Franco it is through an interpreter – because the ignorant little man has no German.' Canaris did well not to laugh at the irony of that statement. 'And I want no interpreters or hangers-on as witnesses to your meeting.'

'What if he insists on an aide?'

'When Ribbentorp fixes up your meeting he will tell Franco to be alone otherwise no meeting. Personally I can't abide the upstart. He sees himself as a future dictator. He even struts like Mussolini. Both of their actions irritate me.'

Canaris, not sure if Hitler's last remark was an attempt at humour allowed his much practised non-committal smile to cross his face.

The chosen smile was obviously the right one for as Hitler rose from the table he moved towards Canaris and threw an arm around his shoulders, 'Come, Wilhelm, I have been a bad host. I will get cook to fix us lunch and you a large Johnnie Walker black label which I believe is your preference.'

At times you could almost be lulled into believing that this madman was human thought Canaris as he entered the welcoming heat of The Berghof.

On the return flight it gave Canaris time to collect his thoughts.

He knew the Generals were opposed to war with Britain and France irrespective of whether Germany was war ready or not. They agreed that should there be another conflict it must be directed at communism – Stalin's Russia. From what he had learned from Hitler – his reckless intention to take back the Rhineland – showed total disregard for the "Treaty of Versailles". And as regards that piece of covert outrageous nonsense in Tenerife – that was just pure provocation against Britain. The dreams of a megalomaniac. Either of these campaigns would surely lead Britain to scrap her appeasement policy and to renewed hostilities against Germany. This must not be allowed to happen, for war with Britain and France would distract from the Generals' aim of a proposed alliance with them. However, until the overthrow of Hitler by the Generals he had little choice but to agree to Hitler's wishes. On the other hand he had been invited to a function at the British Embassy in Berlin where he happened to know that Churchill would be attending…

Canaris made himself as comfortable as possible in the unheated cabin and endeavoured to work out his stratagem for his meeting with Franco. He did not particularly look forward to this meeting but it would give him an insight into the man. He might even be able to convince him of the futility of another war in Europe. It even entered his mind that he might surreptitiously mention Hitler's covert work on Tenerife. After reflecting on this notion he decided nothing would be gained. Franco would acquiesce to get his big gun and Hitler would further tighten his blackmailing grip. He also appreciated that that would lead to his own demise and with him still having much thwarting of Hitler to be achieved for the betterment of the German people he abandoned his idea. He would seek a word with Churchill at the forthcoming British Embassy function.

Canaris nodded off and woke up at Berlin Tempelhof frozen to the core. His chauffeur handed him his Luger pistol that had been removed by the Waffen SS when searched before his outward journey to The Berghof. Pity thought Canaris. Never would his pistol have been used more wisely for the benefit of mankind on that sad and delusional madman.

Chapter 23

Professor Charley Rogers November 1935
With Eugene's flying-boat a speck in the cloudless sky Scott threaded the Harley expertly in and out the bustling town traffic of Santa Cruz onwards to Santiago del Tiede to visit Charley at her research station. The start of his journey after climbing the hill out of Santa Cruz took him through the familiar territory of the university town of La Laguna and on to Puerto de la Cruz. However, Pepé had warned him that from Puerto onwards the road leading to Santiago had to be handled with caution. In some places it was little more than single track with hidden S bends, very little straights and severe drops into rock strewn valleys. He had also warned him to look out for goats for there were more goats being herded on the roads than vehicles. This he found out the hard way, as at speed on one of the few straight lengths of road he had encountered he careened into a shallow left hand bend with his left knee millimetres from the ground only to encounter before him a herd of goats. In one seamless action he put the bike into a sideways skid. It lost traction on the compacted volcanic rock surface and slid towards the road edge and a drop of several hundred feet into a ravine. With the Harley's rear wheel spinning close to the precipice, Scott with his left leg braced and acting as a pivot, slewed the machine through 180° to end up straight across the front line of goats. The goats gave him a cursory glance and with the bells round their necks jangling carried on nibbling the grass at the side of the road. The shepherd acknowledged their right of way with a nod of his crook against his forehead. Scott sat there until the goats cleared thinking how fortunate he had been to possess the expertise to avert a disaster to which his aching forearms and left leg bore testament. Lesson learned the remainder of the journey was carried out at a sedate speed to suit the road conditions.

The small town of Santiago del Teide lay at the intersections of roads leading into the village of Masca and the steep descending road to Puerto Santiago on the Atlantic coast. He stopped and asked the way to the National Geographic research establishment. His directions led him higher up the mountain on what was little more than a dirt track to a large chain-link fence with a vehicle gate and a sign confirming it to be the research centre. Sitting astride the Harley he could see four static caravans, a single storey local lava block building and an open shed housing a tracked machine and two American Ford station wagons. There was a bell. He dismounted and with the ground being uneven for the bike's stand, he leaned it against a sturdy fence post then rang the bell. A bespectacled young man in a white laboratory coat appeared from the lava block building. Scott introduced himself and asked to speak to Professor Rogers. He was informed in an American accent that she was out "in the field" taking samples. He didn't know when she would be back but if he cared to follow the path he was on for a kilometre he would come across her. He was warned to observe the hazard sign posts. To stop at the second post and blow his horn to attract attention. Scott thanked him and after zig-zagging his way along and up he stopped at the first post in an overtaking/turning layby and propped the Harley on its stand. With helmet and goggles removed and tucked underarm and hands on hip he looked around him. The view was breath taking, the Atlantic sparkled clear in the distance and with a slight balmy morning breeze blowing, the air fresh and pure he felt invigorated and looked forward to renewing his acquaintance with Charley. However, at the second post the atmosphere changed dramatically to one of a throat-clinging, sulphuric pall. He placed a handkerchief over his nostrils and mouth and blasted the horn twice with the heel of his hand and hastily retraced his steps to the layby he had vacated. Five minutes later a tracked vehicle similar to the one he had seen at base camp drove into the layby. A gas masked apparition clad in an ash stained white protective suit with clinging hood and long sleeved rubber gloves holding a vacuum flask opened the driver's door and stood on the vehicle's track then jumped to the ground.

Removing the gas mask she pulled back the hood and shook her lustrous brunette hair free. 'Hi Jordan. I didn't expect to see you again after last night. For that I surely apologise.'

'C'est la vie, Charley,' answered Scott, with a shrug of shoulders.

'I suppose it was especially when you didn't go – without.'

He looked at her quizzically as she drew her hair back into a pony tail and secured it with an elastic band, whilst a devilish smile flitted across her attractive volcanic ash smudged face. 'Without? Without what?'

She didn't answer, instead laughingly replied, 'Let's park ourselves and have some of this good ole freshly ground American coffee. It helps to get the taste of hell out of the mouth,' she finished, as she poured two cups of steaming hot, aroma-wafting coffee, into the flask's metal cups. Chin on drawn-up knees she parked herself on the ground looking seaward towards the, glistening, rolling whitecaps of the Atlantic.

Scott joined her alongside. 'So what are you actually doing up here?'

Charley pointed with thumb over her shoulder, 'Back there, *in hell*, is the Chinyero cinder cone area, the result of the last eruption in 1909. It is showing signs of seismic activity again and that's why we're here – something weird is happening inside...'

'Is it about to erupt?'

'To say yes would be scaremongering but with the activity we're experiencing from the present open fissure spewing out yellow sulphurous gases at high pressure – it is usually indicative of magma rising into the edifice.'

'Sounds dangerous to me.'

'It usually is a precursor to an eruption. But, and I repeat but, that is not always the case and that is why it requires constant monitoring. But I'm sure it won't erupt until after we finish our coffee.'

'I've read that Teide has a history of eruptions.'

'It does indeed, but it is of interest to note that of the recorded historical eruptions of 1704 and the very well documented one of 1707 – the one that engulfed Garachico – and then the one of 1798 known as Teide's Nostrils, that there has not been one single fatality.'

'Well, I'll be damned,' voiced Scott, 'I thought the Garachico one killed hundreds.'

'No. None. Though the tourist guides would have you believe

otherwise. They don't actually say "killed" they use the word "engulfed" and leave it to your imagination.'

'What about this one – the 1909 Chinyero?'

'A lava flow from a side fissure similar to the one we are at present investigating. Fortunately, the discharged lava cooled before it reached Santiago. No casualties either.'

'Sounds similar to the one two thousand years ago that overflowed the cliff and entombed Magec in his cave,' said Scott, mischievously.

'Yes, if you believe such rubbish as extolled by the skipper of the "Sea Dolphin" plus his hundreds killed at Garachico rubbish. Unfortunately, without access into Professor von Nida's alleged Great Fissure we have no way of knowing if it exists or even in fact if there was a cave above water level. He is a highly respected scientist and I have no doubt it exists but it is not relevant to our investigations. However, Jordan, *I was serious* about explosions being picked up on our Richter scale. They are definitely man-made and come from the Great Fissure area at Punta Gaunché.'

'You don't know the exact location?'

'No. Why?' she enquired suspiciously.

'Er, mm. I was just interested in Gaunché folklore – that's all.'

'That's all – my ass. There's something fishy going on…'

'What made you say that?'

'First a guy from the tourist department of the Cabildo, name Alonso, asks if we know anything about the Great Fissure and its location…'

'What did you tell him?' interrupted Scott.

'I told him we knew only what we had read in the National Geographic – von Nida's paper. How he knew about the Fissure I have no idea. As far as I know I don't think the Geographic do a Spanish edition. Then you ask the location. What's going on Jordan?'

Scott shrugged his shoulders and replied as innocently as possible, 'I've really no idea, Charley. Coincidence, perhaps?'

'Yeah! And pigs might fly. Let's leave it at that,' she replied, unconvinced but knowing she would not get the truth. 'There's more to life than asking stupid questions. So what brought you up here?'

'The Harley.'

She thumped his shoulder. 'Trust me to ask a dumb question.'

'I'm here to invite you out for lunch,' laughed Scott.

'After what I did yesterday; you must have a very forgiving nature.'

'That's me, Char – *lee.*'

She looked at him coyly before answering, 'I really do like you Jordan. You're my kind of guy. So let me tell you what actually happened last night. After we broke up at the table and we had our little tête á tête. You know the one? Where you tried to get shot of me so you could have your evil way with Sandie.' She stared at Scott. He just laughed. 'Well, I went to the ladies' toilet to find Sandie. Knowing her nympho tendencies she obviously had you in her sights for a roll in the hay; then I showed to mess things up between you. So I suggested to her that she got her ass in gear after you and that I was old enough to look after myself. Sandie then gave me the keys to her place and rushed from the toilet after you. When I reached the exit doors on the way to her chalet she was standing there looking dejected and miserable. She pointed down the road. There you were, arm in arm with a long legged, shapely brunette. So as you say, "C'est la vie", which I thought was French for, "That's life" but now realise it must mean, "always have a bit in reserve".

Scott stood dumbfounded. He stammered, 'Er. Er. It's not as it seems Charley, she's a work colleague. She had just arrived from London and came looking for me to pass along instructions from Cantravel's HQ – honest.'

'Honest indeed? Now there's a thing,' said Charley as she rose to her feet with the aid of Scott's offered arm. Once upright she said, 'That lunch offer still on, Romeo?'

'Absolutely.'

'Good. I'll drop of my samples into Wally, that's our lab technician, have a shower and off we go.'

Scott followed Charley to base where she disappeared into the laboratory with her samples. He noticed one of the station wagons was missing from the open shed. Ten minutes later she appeared from the laboratory and signalled him to follow her. She informed him that the missing station wagon was being used by Professor

Davis, the leader of the team, who had been summoned by the Cabildo's tourist minister to Santa Cruz. Professor Hogan who was in the laboratory with Wally did not know the whys or wherefores but it sounded urgent, she was informing him as they entered her caravan. It was then that he noticed a motor bike on its stand around the side of her caravan. She confirmed that was how she got to last night's concert.

Once inside she adjourned to the bathroom and return moments later to stand opposite him naked. 'Care to join me for a shower?'

'Sure. It saves water and that's essential for the ecology of the island.'

'You learn fast,' she whispered in his ear as she unbuckled his trouser belt.

An hour later they set off with Charley in her biker's gear on the Harley's pillion for Santa Cruz. They were aware that a seismic eruption, its reading well off the Richter scale, had taken place.

After lunch at a down-at-heel looking dockside fish restaurant, which proved to be anything but, they booked into the Grand Plaza Hotel, Santa Cruz's finest, for one night only then spent the afternoon doing the rounds of the museums and galleries. After a severe dose of culture interspersed with the odd café stop they opted to dine in the hotel. Then to round off a memorable day they went bar hopping, ending up in a jazz club and finally in the wee small hours of the morning collapsed into bed exhausted. Unfortunately, Charley had a meeting with her colleagues at 8-30am at her base. He dropped her off and headed back to his chalet for much needed rest. She was some girl.

***

Scott had managed to drag his exhausted body into the kitchen by 10-00am. He was standing waiting with the honey for the toaster to pop out its two slices of bread whilst enjoying pleasant memories of the early hour romp he had this morning with Charley when he was woken from his reverie by the phone. He lifted the receiver to hear a female American voice in a state of panic hollering down the line, 'Jordan, have you seen yesterday's edition of El Día?'

'No Charley. I spent most of yesterday with you and if you recall reading wasn't high on the list of priorities. So what's wrong?'

'This is what's goddamn wrong. Listen to this for a headline : SCIENTISTS WARN OF MOUNT TEIDE ERUPTION.'
'So?' he yawned.
'What do you mean by so? – It's a goddamn disaster – we're getting deported from the goddamn island.'
Scott rubbed the sleep from his eyes. 'Why are you getting deported?'
'Because the headline is goddamn bad for tourism.'
'Why were your colleagues daft enough to inform the paper?'
'They didn't. They didn't even mention it to the Cabildo. It turned out that the summons to Professor Davis yesterday morning was to account for the headline. The inference being that we were responsible. His denials were not accepted and he was told we're being replaced by a *reliable* team of German scientists. We've been shafted.'
'Mmm, Germans,' mused Scott, finger pinching his lips as he contemplated this news. 'That's interesting. *Very* interesting.'
'What do you mean? Mmm, Germans – that's interesting. What about me, goddamn it?'
'Look ,Charley, I'm going to be busy the best part of today but I'll come up and see you this evening.'
'*Oh-no-you-won't*. This evening's too late. We're being deported and that means I won't be able to see you honey before I leave.'
'Why not?' Scott replied in a rising panic.
'Because, right now there are about twenty of those olive green clad creeps – the Guardia Civil – rounding up my colleagues. We've to leave on an American merchant man – at noon!'
'*At noon*! That's only....'
'Sorry Jordan, one of the creeps is heading my way....don't you dare....I'm an American citizen....you can't .....' Then the phone went dead.
Scott put the phone back on the cradle and sat down on a breakfast barstool to spread the honey on his now cold toast. He cursed himself for not asking who her Professor Davis had spoken with at the Cabildo. He lit a cigarette and contemplated the Cabildo's sudden irrational decision to deport the National Geographic team.

The fact that they had a German team on instant stand-by sounded highly suspicious.

It could only mean one thing – phase two of the Nazi operation at Punta Gaunché was in motion.

Chapter 24

Marcus Bentyk the Third
Scott had been caught in a cleft stick regarding Charley. He had wanted desperately to help her and her colleagues but could not risk exposing himself to the Guardia Civil, for as far as they were concerned, all he was was a diving instructor in the employ of Cantravel. And that's how he wanted it to stay. It was a pity because he really liked Charley. She was one great *ous* lady – glamor*ous*, humor*ous* and extremely amor*ous*.

Guilt-ridden he set off for Los Rodeos airfield to meet "Maverick" Bentyk. The entrance to the airfield was announced by the hand painted wording "Los Rodeos" on two oil drums either side of the entrance driveway. Twenty metres or so along the drive he encountered the ancient bi-plane that he had noticed previously from the road and thought of as a testament to the Bleriot period of flying turned out in fact to be a replica of Bleriot's history making plane. A life size bronze of Bleriot stood alongside the plane and a commemorative plaque mounted on a lava rock pedestal bore the story of one of the most historic events in aviation – the crossing of the English Channel in 1909. He dismounted and read the plaque. When he had finished reading he wondered what the tenuous connection was between Bleriot and Tenerife for he knew for certain that Bleriot was French. He would enquire of Marcus.

Scott remounted and rode upwards through a natural cutting in the rock. Cresting the slight incline he sat astride the Harley to view the layout of the airfield. Expecting a crushed and compacted volcanic ash runway he was surprised to observe it to be tarmacked. He drove on until he encountered a single-storey block work building with a two-storey tower at the end – the terminal and control tower he assumed. To the side of this were a few zinc corrugated clad industrial hanger buildings each carrying the name of the business overhead. He drove along until he came to the end unit: Bentyk Aviation. There was a Buick limousine parked outside. Dismounting, he did as the notice on the door announced – he rang the bell and entered. There was nobody in the office but as he looked down the length of the hanger to the open sliding doors at the other end he made out an aeroplane with its nose jutting into the hanger. As he walked the length of the hanger towards the plane, avoiding oily pools from derelict engines and engine parts, he noticed a Sopwith Camel bi-plane lurking in the shadows. A few paces further on he stopped at a bi-plane he did not recognise other than to note it had wheels – and floats! There was a figure dressed in overalls atop a ladder, with legs only visible as it leant into a noisy running engine compartment. The ladder was held by a stocky built man with white close cropped hair who on seeing Scott made him aware of the slowly revolving propeller then over the noise of the engine pointed back towards the office and signalled with the use of his fingers – five minutes. Scott sat in the untidy office on a hard seat and picked up an Aviation Monthly to read from a stack thrown on the floor. Five minutes later the muscular ladder holder limped into the office and shook hands with Scott. He then took a seat behind a battered desk and kicked a cylinder head aside to allow him to put his good leg up on the desk.

His weather-beaten face crinkled into a warm smile, 'Howdy, pardner. You must be the Jordan guy Gene told me to expect – I'm Marcus.' The accent was pure Texan. They shook hands firmly.

'Yes, I'm Jordan. Pleased to meet a real war hero,' replied Scott taking an instant liking to Marcus.

'Aw, shucks. Gene told you about that did he? – It's so long ago I forgot all about it.'

'But once an aviator, always an aviator, eh Marcus? I stopped to read the Bleriot plaque. What's the connection?'

'Yeah, I had it commissioned for the great man. I used to work for him in Paris as part of the 1909 test team that put together the Bleriot for the English Channel attempt.'

'You were?'

'Yeah. That's one of his planes we're servicing. A Bleriot 290 sesquiplane. A sea-plane that can take off from a runway and land on water or vice-versa. Handy for this part of the world. There was only ever one of them built in '31. Unfortunately, due to it being underpowered the French Government cancelled an order for four without compensation. This put Bleriot out of business. I offered to help him financially but he said he had had enough so I ended up buying the 290 from the administrator and put in new Rolls Royce engines. It now goes like greased goose shit.'

'How did you, an American, end up working for Bleriot?'

'I had graduated in aeronautical engineering from MIT – the Massachusetts Institute of Technology. Agin ma parents' wishes I got a job with the Wright brothers as a test pilot. Suicide pilot would have been a more apt job description. Nothin' was guaranteed to stay up in the air in those days,' he laughed. 'However, Bleriot was looking for engineers and being young and wanting to see the world I applied and got the job. Speaking the French lingo and working for the Wrights helped.'

'You were in Paris at the outbreak of war?'

'Yeah. Wanted to stay on but ma and pa insisted that I return to learn the bean business. I ask you Jordan – goddamn beans. What's there to learn about beans? So I returned home. Tried my hardest to take to a life of beans – couldn't. So after much pleading pa allowed me to form the Confederate Volunteer Air Core to help the Brits. After all, the Bentyks go back to Tudor times and beyond. Ma squadron were all Texas volunteers of British stock.'

'Eugene's from Texas?'

'Yeah. Don't sound it, do he? He had a fancy education at Oxford. He ended up my wing man in the Volunteers and a good buddy. I was real happy to see him again yesterday when he asked me to help you. I said I would and I will. He told me I was to deliver sensitive despatches to Gibraltar.'

'That's about it, Marcus. I thank you for your assistance.'

'Think nothin' of it. Amazin' to think we're still at war with the Krauts…'

'We're not really, Marcus – it's the Nazis – Hitler.'

'Proving to be a right pain in the ass – aint he?'

'Indeed.' Scot then changed the subject. 'Did Eugene tell you he's bought a flying-boat?'

'Yeah – a Sikorsky. Thirty two seats, twelve hundred mile range. O.K for what he wants it for – island hopping in the Caribbean. I told him aeroplanes were the way forward. He agreed, for he knows it's only a question of time before we develop engines large enough to carry the increased weight of fuel required to cover longer distances. Boeing is working on this at present.'

'Very interesting Marcus. You know I saw him off in it this morning?'

'Gees, I wish it had been me. I would love to have seen the brute – the plane that is – not Eugene,' he chortled.

'I see you've still got your Sopwith Camel.'

'Yeah. Ole Soppy the second. The first one is lying in a field in Belgium where I got shot down an' got this…' he patted his leg '… an' got a wife,' he chortled. 'Millicent. English mother, Canarian father. She nursed me back to health and the rest they say is history. That's our son Louis out there with his head stuck in the engine. Good boy and an excellent flyer.'

'The Sopwith looks in great condition.'

'Not bad for a twenty year old crate. Still take it out occasionally for a spin. Unfortunate there's no Krauts to shoot down.'

'You mean it's still armed?'

'Sure as hell is. Twenty five mil cannons in the machine gun. Spares in the hanger but no bombs left,' he hooted.

'Bombs!'

'Yeah. We used to lob them out by hand – not at each other of course – into the enemy trenches as bullets from the trenches ripped through the airframe. Those were the days,' he said, with a far-away reminiscing look in his eyes. Coming back into reality he continued, 'You appreciate the sesquiplane can't make the flight to Gibraltar without refuelling in Casablanca.'

'Christ Marcus, I never gave that a thought. That's a real problem. How will you make sure the despatch remains safe while you refuel?'

Marcus opened the drawer to the office desk and withdrew a pearl handled Colt 45 revolver. 'Simple. I just blow away any bastard that comes a lookin' for trouble.'

Scott shook his head. 'That's my boy, Marcus. Just knew you'd have a simple solution. Well, it's time for me to hit the trail. It's been a real pleasure meeting you and I look forward to working with you.' As they shook hands Scott confided in him, 'The name is actually,

Scott.'

'But you're not a Scot. We had a few Scots as ground crew in the Volunteers – great guys – and you don't talk like them – *ye ken*?'

'My mother's a Scot – from Perth. And the family story goes that she was feeling homesick when I was born in England. Thus Scott.'

'That bein' the case I'm just glad my ma wasn't homesick when I was born...'

Scott, fearing the worst felt obliged to ask, 'Why? Where were you born?'

'In *Alice* – Texas – the home of Bentyk baked beans.'

Roaring with laughter Marcus saw Scott to the door. When he saw the Harley and realised it was Scott's he insisted on a drive, informing Scott he hadn't driven one since he was last Stateside. He jumped into the saddle in a wide straddle leap over the rear wheel and with full throttle let the clutch engage and took off to a spray of volcanic ash. Scott watched him disappear into the distance, side slide the bike in one fluid movement to have it facing back towards Scott then opened the throttle full and came to a slithering stop amidst a volcanic ash cloud alongside Scott.

'Gees, that was real fun, Scotty. I must get mine sent over an we'll race. See ya buddy,' he drawled as he snapped a quick short salute to Scott and disappeared through the door into the hanger.

Scott mounted the bike and drove sedately down the drive. He saluted Louis Bleriot – mentor of Marcus Bentyk the third.

***

After his meeting with a fellow kindred spirit in Marcus, Scott decided to lunch in Santa Cruz the capital of Tenerife. Amidst the fine Spanish colonial architecture in the town centre he chose a café with a kerbside parking space for the Harley. He placed his helmet and goggles on the vacant seat alongside him and picked up a copy of El Día that somebody had left behind then ordered a shredded beef sandwich and with the temperature hitting near 25°C, an ice-cold beer. Applying his sunglasses he picked up the paper and using his fluency in Spanish started to read. It was then that a shadow blocked out the pleasant ray of sunshine in which he was basking. Scott, blinking, looked up to encounter the reflection of himself in a pair of sunglasses worn by a male of similar age and physique but with long blond hair peeking from under the brim of a straw trilby hat worn at a jaunty angle.

The stranger enquired in perfect but accented English, 'I assume, sir, that these belong to you.' He was pointing to the helmet and goggles. 'Thus making you the owner of that exquisite piece of engineering – the Harley Davidson.'

'Perdón Señor, I speak very leetle English – I am Español – Spanish,' replied Scott in faltering English as he pointed to the copy of El Día he held in his hand as way of proof of his nationality. For with the stranger's blond hair and Germanic speech intonation he had been instantly put on his guard. It appeared to work for the stranger apologised and departed.

'I've a feeling we will meet again, my friend,' murmured Scott as he visualised the departing back of the stranger in a leather belted coat. The coat being the trademark of the Gestapo was bad news for Scott. Had it been the very conspicuous Harley the Gestapo had seen near the Perez and Schuster warehouse that had aroused their interest? Could he have been the fleeting shadow he had seen near the Harley? Care was now of paramount importance.

***

As soon as he arrived back at base he exchanged the Harley for Eugène's Norton – an equally powerful a machine but less ostentatious. The exchange completed he took the Norton out for an exacting road trial, which, as expected, with it belonging to Eugene met with Scott's approval.

Back in his chalet Scott lit his Piccadilly cigarette, poured a large Glenfiddich malt whisky from a decanter on the coffee table and was comfortably seated in the sofa giving further thought to Charley and her NGM colleagues' plight. He started with the newspaper headline. The paper had obviously been fed false information that had been published in good faith. For this to happen the source must have been considered reliable. But who had fed them this information? He couldn't believe it was the collective members of the Cabildo but he figured it did have to be someone of influence within. He pondered that for a moment and came up with what he hoped would be an answer. He lifted the phone and dialled Cantravel's public relations manager who was also responsible for placing adverts for staff in the paper and would most certainly have contacts within the paper. The manager replied that, "Yes, he knew the editor of El Día and he was at present trying to ascertain who fed El Día the misleading headline because some of Cantravel's guests had already made enquiries about their safety. The headline had caused major problems and he was currently working on damage limitation publicity. He would phone back when he had a name." Next on his list was the reason why the National Geographic team had been deported. After mulling it over at length he decided the reason had been more likely to be their location above ground rather than anything they had discovered below ground in and around the Santiago rift area. For with them off the island the sparsely populated area above the fissure (cave) would be free of persons with inquisitive natures who could recognise any unusual happenings and query them – such as Charley.

But why the German replacements? Scott was not aware of any alliance between the semi-autonomous Cabildo and Hitler's Germany. Of course, there was a very good chance the Cabildo knew nothing of the decision to deport the NGM scientists – it could be a powerful Nazi sympathiser within that was responsible. And with the covert U-boat base unknown to the Cabildo or the Spanish Government it seemed to Scott more than likely that there was a Nazi sympathiser within the Cabildo ranks. He felt the presence of Hitler near at hand.

The phone rang. Cantravel's public relations manager informed him that El Día had received their information from the Cabildo's Tourism Minister – a Señor Fernando Alonso. This rang a bell. Hadn't Charley mentioned that the NGM's Professor Davis had gone to see an Alonso at the Cabildo? Further discreet enquiries from his source revealed that no other members of the Cabildo knew at the time of publication about the deportation. Scott had found Hitler's Cabildo mole and he had a good idea how to handle Señor Fernando Alonso's demise.

Satisfied he had solved the deportation of Charley he gave thought to his next move. A meeting with Xavi would be required to discover if there had been any further developments elsewhere. However, this would have to keep until tomorrow morning due to his stomach suggesting a visit to the resort's restaurant was in order.

***

Scott, showered and dressed in casual clothes, was about to open the door when the bell rang. He opened the door to come almost face to face give or take six inches with the petite figure of Sandie looking stunningly beautiful as the late evening sun reflected off her long blonde hair.

'Hi Jordy,' she drawled with both arms held at an angle across her face in pretence of warding off blows. ''Spect you're still mad at me about the other night. But Charley just showed up unannounced and…..and anyway you ended up all right with that Yvonne, didn't cha?'

'All forgotten Sandie. No harm done. Water under the bridge. Now if you'll excuse me I'm off for dinner.'

'Sorry Jordy, I didn't come here to drag the whole unfortunate incident up again. Ah actually come to tell ya that Xavi wants to see you about a something tomorrow morning…'

'Good,' interrupted Scott abruptly, closing the door behind him. 'I'm off to the restaurant.'

'Alone?'

'Yes, *alone*,' he said emphatically.

'I haven't eaten yet maself. How's about me joining you?'

Suddenly Scott couldn't understand why he was being off hand with Sandie. After all it wasn't her fault that the evening with Charley had turned out a disaster between them – apart from which she was looking sexily appealing. 'Tell you what Sandie, have you ever ridden pillion?'

'Ridden bulls, mustangs an' men but never a pillion.'

Scott went over to the Norton's pannier and withdrew helmets and goggles. The spare being Charley's that she had left in the Harley when Scott had dropped her off after their Santa Cruz dalliance. Unfortunately, Charley would no longer be in need of them.

Sandie grabbed the helmet and used one of the overtaking mirrors to rearrange her hair. 'Where we going, Jordy?' she asked, as she slipped on her goggles.

'Down to Puerto,' he replied, jumping into the saddle.

'Woooowee,' hollered Sandie, hugging him tightly around the waist.

Next morning

Scott awoke to the aroma of coffee and the sweet Texas drawl of Sandie. 'There you go Jordy, a nice cuppa coffee – that'll help clear away any cobwebs.' Being aware of what had happened the last time she handed him a coffee in bed he indicated delivery of it to the bedside table. She laughed at the memory of him hopping about naked on one leg whilst trying to hide his wobbling manhood. Still giggling, she trilled, 'Thanks, Jordy for a lovely time but I gotta go an' get changed into ma uniform, put on a face and round up our guests. I'll see you on board the "Sea Dolphin" later.' She kissed her forefinger and applied it to his lips then still giggling she slipped out the door.

Scott looked at the bedside clock 7-00am. He had had three hours sleep and with him now having no intention of catching the sailing of the "Sea Dolphin" at its usual departure time of 10-00am he turned over on his side to catch up on much needed sleep. He would meet Xavi when the "Sea Dolphin" returned to Puerto later in the day. That way there would be no unwelcome intrusions for there was much to discuss.

Chapter 25

November 1935

After a thorough workout in the gymnasium Scott finally rid his body of the previous evening's excesses of alcohol that he had enjoyed with Sandie. His usual well-honed physique which had of late been neglected, was feeling all the better for the two-hour torture inflicted on him by a masochistic ex US Marine Corps physical training instructor.

Later in the day, with all his body joints howling in agony, he was deliberating as to whether all physical training instructors were born with the same sadistic streak as he sat in the patio of the harbour café watching the "Sea Dolphin" disgorge its lobster-red, well-under-the-influence guests. Once Sandie and her colleagues had shepherded their rowdy charges into the waiting open-top omnibuses, he rose from the table leaving enough pesetas to pay for the coffee and brandy. He then proceeded to the car park and rode the Norton to the foot of the gangplank.

Xavi noticed him from the bridge and waved him and the Norton aboard. After the usual pleasantries Xavi said in his broken English, 'Sandie, she tell me you were coming this morning but you no show. She seemed very, very disappointed when I sail without you. Me, I don't mind, I know I see you later. But she very upset. I think she like you,' he winked knowingly.

'Er, mm, yes – I had a slight change of plan.'

Xavi hooted, rolling the ever present cigar from one side of his mouth to the other, 'She too much for you to handle, Jordan Hill, eh?' Before an embarrassed Scott had time to answer, Xavi summoned him into the wheelhouse. 'Come. I have much to tell you. We can do the talks as I take the "Dolphin" back to Los Gigantes.

He then shouted his orders from the bridge and with the anchor lifted and the tethering ropes free of the capstans they were underway. Once clear of the harbour and into the open waters of the Atlantic with a course set for Los Gigantes Xavi bent down and pulled from an ice bucket two bottles of beer. He snapped their tops off on the edge of the wheelhouse's metal framed window and handed one to Scott. By the looks of the window frame many bottles had been opened over the years.

'!Salud!' hailed Xavi raising the bottle to his lips and downing the contents in one swallow. Burping he continued, 'Now to business Jordan Hill – my men in the docks at Santa Cruz tell me of muchos increase in freight from German vessels in the last few weeks....'

'Oh. Off-loading what?' interrupted an interested Scott.

'Mostly building materials. Cement, timber, bricks, etcetera, etcetera. Oh! And prefabricated timber buildings. All more than is required for the island's building needs which have virtually ground to a halt due to the unstable political situation.' He paused for effect, rolled his cigar and growled, 'And men that don't come back to their ship when it sails!'

Scott, lighting a cigarette, gave this some thought before replying, 'Where do they go?'

Xavi shrugged his shoulders, 'We don't know.'

Scott nodded. 'OK then – who delivers the materials?'

'Local haulage contractors. Some of them my men.'

'By *my* men – you mean the "Free Canaries Movement"?'

'Si. Jordan Hill.'

'And did you ask where they delivered the timber buildings and materials?'

'Si. Somewhere near Punta Gaunché.'

'Somewhere?'

'Si. The Guardia Civil have road blocks at Buena Vista Norte. The drivers have to drop their loads there in a field and about turn.'

Scott appeared to digress but had actually found the opportunity he had been waiting for to avenge Charley and her NGM colleagues. 'Mmm. Risky business building in that area when according to El Día there could be an eruption at any time – don't you think?'

Xavi furrowed his brow. 'Ah! Jordan Hill I was going to speak to you about that – is there any truth in that headline because it could affect my business if nobody come to Tenerife anymore.'

With Xavi falling for his ruse Scott continued, 'No. My sources reliably tell me it is not true – it was a malicious rumour circulated to El Día by....'

'By who, Jordan Hill,' snapped Xavi angrily.

'By a Señor Frederico Alonso. Do you know him?'

'Oh, yes I know the gangster peeg. He big-shot Tourism Minister. Everyone say he next island President. He big bully. The members of the Cabildo are muchos terrified of him. I don't get my boat license to trade unless I give him – what you say for hidden dinero?'

'A back-hander.'

'Si. Back-hander, I like. But why he do this?'

'A bit complicated to explain, but basically to get the Americans scientists fired for alleged scaremongering that would hurt the tourist industry and have Nazi scientists replace them on the mountain.'

'But why? What he gain?'

'Because, my amigo, the swine is a Nazi sympathiser. They are his paymasters. He treacherously does as he's bid for muchos, muchos, dinero.'

Letting go of the steering wheel Xavi imitated a throttling action with his large calloused hands and snarled, 'The Nazi peeg. He go too far this time. For this I kill him with my own hands.'

Knowing this would be Xavi's reaction Scott shrugged, hoping to convey his indifference to the threat, whilst inwardly being delighted that his attempt at auto-suggestion had had the desired effect. He figured the odds on Señor Alonso surviving in this world had just shortened.

Xavi, with hands returned to the wheel, sighed, 'Jordan Hill, it is all getting too much for my weary brain. Can you please tell me what is going on in my island? You being a British secret agent must know.'

'Hardly a secret agent, Xavi – just a representative of our Foreign Office. And as I told you before I am only here to find out what the Nazis are up to – and that puts us in the same boat.'

A puzzled look spread over Xavi's face, and with hands off the wheel, yet again, he shrugged his massive shoulders and held both hands openly upwards, 'Same boat? Si, Señor, we are on the same boat – the "Sea Dolphin".'

With a laugh Scott explained, 'Er, no Xavi. What it means is – we both want to know what's going on. Leave it with me. I will check out Punta Gaunché for you, but meanwhile how do I get around the Teno road block?'

'By sea. Climb the cliffs. Pepé will show you how. Him and Paco did it when they were youngsters. Since you are going to do the checkings for me – I tell you my big secret.'

'You've got more?'

'Oh Yes, Jordan Hill – plenty more. We "Free Canaries" never sleep. Eyes everywhere. A German merchantman was being off loaded three days ago when one of the crane's slings slipped leaving a long timber crate dangling by one end. The contents broke through one end of the crate but did not fall to the dockside. In doing this, it exposed....a gun barrel....a very massive gun barrel. There were many more massive and heavy crates off-loaded. There were also sections of steel structures that my men say looked like electric power pylons.'

This news brought a tingle of excitement to Scott's voice. 'Where are these items now?'

'The power pylons have been transported to Punta Gaunche and the big crates are in a dockside shed under guard by the *Civilies* – the Guardia Civil.'

Scott needed thinking time to analyse this valuable information; time that he did not have for they were entering the harbour walls of Los Gigantes. After docking Xavi excused himself to supervise the refuelling, victualing and cleaning of the "Sea Dolphin" for the following morning. Scott adjourned to the café forecourt for a beer and to analyse Xavi's vital information whilst enjoying the last of the day's sunshine. Xavi joined him later and declaring himself free invited Scott to join him, his wife Olivia and a niece recently arrived from Spain for dinner. Scott, anxious to further analyse the new scenario declined, offering up the excuse that he had another appointment. He did, however, offer Xavi a lift home which was accepted. They stopped two minutes later at a large bungalow style residence set into the cliffs with a panoramic view overlooking the Atlantic.

During the pillion journey home Xavi had given thought to his niece Nina. When he had left in the morning the poor girl was having one of her fits of depression. He had since her arrival been taking her aboard the "Sea Dolphin" to help with the catering in the hope that it would take her out of herself. It had worked until this morning when she refused to leave her bedroom. He was now thankful that Jordan Hill had declined his invite. As Xavi hopped off the pillion, Scott removed his helmet and goggles to wipe away perspiration from his forehead that had been running inside his goggles and nipping his eyes.

With this chore completed he was about to give Xavi a departing handshake when a young attractive female rushed from the house with arms wide in the air holding a parcel and wailing, 'Ramón. My Ramón. I knew you would come back to me my sweet love – I have your birthday present.' Xavi moved quickly to intercept her by putting his strong arms around her shoulders and holding her close to him.

Through the open front door of the bungalow a small dark haired woman rushed forward and in a voice full of concern trembled, 'Nina, that is not Ramón, my love. Do not torture yourself so. Please come inside and lie down.' She reached Xavi and took a reluctant Nina in her arms and comforted her back to the house. Nina kept looking back with tears rolling down her cheeks, a gift wrapped parcel dangling from her hand.

Xavi sighed heavily. 'Tragic case Jordan Hill. Poor Nina saw her papa, who is, er was – my brother, and her fiancée, Ramón die on the same day in Oviedo. An act of barbarism that the Nationalists will pay for.' He spat on the ground. Scott, who well remembered the terrible massacre of women and children in Oviedo, shook his head in sympathy and clapped Xavi on the shoulder. The silence lingered being finally broken by Xavi. 'I have seen the photographs of Ramón that Nina keeps in her bedroom – you are his twin, Jordan Hill. A remarkable likeness.'

As they were about to bid each other good night, Xavi suddenly remembered something. '!Perdón! Jordan Hill, there is something I forget to tell you. In Los Cristianos the Army have started building a gun emplacement. 'Adiós amigo.' With that he turned and with shoulders slumped turned towards his unhappy home.

***

After manoeuvring his way up the scenic but tortuous S bends from the coast to the main road above Los Gigantes Scott turned north west and was in Santiago del Teide within minutes. He turned off the main road down into the quaint old wine making village of Masca and through to the Guardia Civil road block at Buenavista. He was stopped and showed his papers to the Guardia officer. In broken Spanish he explained that he worked for Cantravel and had taken his motor bike for a spin to get to know the island. He was curtly informed that this area was a prohibited zone but was allowed to continue along the coast road to Puerto de la Cruz where he dined. When he finished he headed straight for his chalet. He opened the door to find an envelope lying on the floor. It was from Sandie advising him that she was on theatre duty tonight but if he sought company she would be in her chalet from midnight onwards. As tempting as the offer was he needed rest for a busy tomorrow. He then started his report for Sir James regarding today's findings from Xavi when it dawned on him that it would be better if he could reconnoitre the docks before reporting to Sir James. He headed for the bathroom to do his bedtime toiletries when suddenly the phone rang. He looked at his watch, gone midnight – Sandie. Suddenly, he didn't feel so tired. Lifting the phone and adopting a husky voice he whispered, 'Hello there, you gorgeous Texas….'

A Texas voice answered, but not Sandie's. 'I've told you before Jordy honey – we're still only at the shaking hands stage in our relation……'

'Marcus! What the bloody hell time is this to be phoning anybody?'

'Shucks. The way you answered it sounded to me like you were awaiting a call from – *an anybody*. I trust you ain't trying to deflower a fine Texas gal.'

Scott, caught out, laughed. 'What can I do for you, Marcus?'

'I just got back from Gibraltar five minutes ago…'

Realising this must be the despatch he awaited from Sir James, Scott replied abruptly, 'Good. I'll be right over.' Then 'bugger,' muttered under his breath as he was slamming the receiver back on its cradle; annoyed that his assignation with Sandie was doomed.

Marcus having caught Scott's whispered, under-breath, "bugger" before the receiver hit the cradle, hooted, 'Now then – temper, temper, Jordy. Don't shoot the messenger. She'll still be there when you get back.' Scott gnashed his teeth as he hung up.

Twenty minutes later he was sitting in Marcus' kitchen downing Kentucky Bourbon whiskey and listening to Marcus' tale of having picked up his coded signal from the BBC shipping forecast then taken to the air at 6-30am to arrive in Gibraltar where he had met Sir James (a swell guy) who handed him the despatch which had to be delivered to Scott the minute he arrived back in Tenerife. He had also met a cracking looking French gal, Yvonne, who he thought was obviously a bit retarded in that she had asked after him. Ignoring Marcus' inane ramblings Scott finished his decryption.

The despatch read: *Congrats Jordanhill. Excellent intel received from you. Do nothing. Repeat. Nothing but observe the situation until instructed otherwise. I do not want an International situation arising. I should not have to remind you that our mission does not have the backing of HMG. Further: Received info from well-placed German intelligence source via Churchill that Franco intends to build three gun emplacements along the south coast of Tenerife. One currently building at Los Cristianos. Please inform how far work on these has commenced. Further: Hitler has agreed funding fourth gun emplacement at Punta Gaunché. Assume this to protect covert works under. Re: this covert work. How is it accessed? Sea only or? Further: Admiralty ask – can you find out type of guns being used in emplacements. N.B Do not treat this as an instruction to start WW2. Suggest you try diplomacy. You will find it under D in the dictionary. Destroy when read. G.*

When he finished reading Scott struck a match, lit a cigarette took a long deep satisfying draw and then set fire to the corner of the despatch and placed it in a saucer to burn itself out. He leant back in his chair, exhaled, and gave a contented sigh. Things were beginning to click into place.

'By the look on your face I'd say you got good news, ole buddy,' said Marcus lifting the saucer to the sink and dowsing the still smouldering ashes before emptying them into the waste bin.

'Sure was, ole buddy,' drawled Scott in a passable Texan accent.

'All going well I'll possibly need you to deliver a despatch to Gibraltar day after tomorrow. Alright with you, ace?'

'Yeah buddy,' replied Marcus snapping a smart salute.

'Thanks pal. Have a nice day,' he drawled again as he returned Marcus' salute.

It flitted through Scott's mind that here was no reason for his accent to be anything other than passable Texan considering the company he kept – Marcus, Sandie, Hank and Lex – even Eugene.

With hands on the pillion, he straddle jumped into the drive seat and feeling exhilarated at his good news kick started the bike, twisted the accelerator and with rear wheel spin roared off into the early morning chill of a new day – a day he couldn't wait to get started.

Chapter 26

Scott's eagerly awaited new day did not start bright and early as anticipated. Due to his nocturnal visit to Marcus he found himself eating a late breakfast of toast, honey and green tea, as he gave thought to his encounter with the Guardia Civil at the Buenavista road block. Whilst stopped astride the Norton he had observed in the darkness bright lights in the distance and the dull rattle of pneumatic drills hanging heavy in the night air. Work was definitely under way on an unseen project. A project that he hoped with the help of Pepé to discover tonight. His deliberation over he jogged over to the gymnasium where he intended to spend time before lunch.

Whilst Scott had been piling up the miles on the fixed exercise bike to tone up his leg muscles he had been aware of a lone female doing bending and stretching exercises. With her back towards him she was currently in the stooped position touching her toes. The sight revealed firm buttocks graduating into well-muscled but shapely legs. Doing body twists to left and right with arms straight out to her side she began to rise and in doing so exposed a firm bust outline.

Having appreciated the view he dismounted the exercise bike and was towelling himself down when a husky German accented English voice smoothed, 'Nice body – I like men who keep themselves in shape.'

Scott looked closely at her; not as young as the figure had suggested. Perhaps mid-forties but still a very attractive natural blonde with just a hint of crow's feet round the eyes in an otherwise flawless complexion. 'You *too* look in excellent shape,' he replied, a smile twitching at the corners of his mouth as he looked her over.

'Why thank you kindly,' she purred, as she curtseyed at his compliment – showing the swelling of her well-endowed bosom popping above the low cut neckline of her sleeveless athletic top. Righting herself she extended her slim elegant fingers, 'My name is Marlene. And you are?'

'I'm Jordan Hill, head diving instructor,' he replied, pointing at his photograph amongst heads of departments hanging nearby.

'Doesn't do you justice. You really are the handsomest of men.' Scott immediately went on guard. A suspicious look must have passed over his face for she continued, 'Ah! The British problem of accepting compliments from foreigners. We foreigners are too forward, yes?'

'Never crossed my mind,' he lied.

'Very gallant of you, Jordan. But I have to apologise to you – for I have been a trifle frugal with the truth. My name is Lady Marlene Fitzgerald. I married Lord Charles when I retired from modelling for the Paris fashion houses. I am now a naturalised British subject – of course.'

'Not every day I get to meet a Lady, My Lady,' he said, bowing with a mocking touch of his forelock. 'Are you having a pleasant time in Tenerife?'

'Mostly. I enjoy the days. Beach parties, swimming, excursions, even the gymnasium,' she chortled, making chortling sound sexy. Scott was so preoccupied with the thought of her lovely figure traipsing the catwalks of Paris that he almost missed her parting remark. 'But the evenings are a bit of a bore. With Charles being several years older than me he retires to bed early. What would make it perfect would be good company.....yours.' She dragged a well-manicured red painted nail down his exposed forearm – sending a shiver down his spine – then with lips pouted kissed the finger and applied it to Scott's lips. With her firm bottom moving in time to her rhythmical practised cat walk she exited the gymnasium.

One for the diary thought Scott, as he made a mental note to check how long she had left of her holiday.

***

After a lunch of chicken and pasta Scott changed into his motor cycling gear, refuelled the Norton and set off for Los Cristianos to carry out the wishes of the Admiralty, all as per the latest despatch from Sir James. He took the scenic, narrow, twisting S-bend abounding road to Santiago del Teide, being alert this time for goats, then onward on the equally treacherous high coast road through Guia de Isora to Adeje at which point he started down towards the south coast. The landscape had changed dramatically from verdant valleys between the high mountain peaks to what appeared to be arid wasteland caused mainly by the considerably warmer southern climate. Riding through the village of Playa de las Americas (earmarked for future development by Cantravel) he shortly arrived at the newly rebuilt port of Los Cristianos where he found a café overlooking the harbour and Montana Guaza. The latter reminding him of a beached whale with its great lump head inland and tapering body forming a headland jutting into the Atlantic.

From a map of the area laid on the table before him, he found this headland with its lighthouse to be known as Punta de la Rasca. Except for the summit (the whale's head) rising inland and abutting the main road to Santa Cruz, the mountain did not appear particularly high nor steep-sided apart from a long cliff face where it jutted into the Atlantic to form one side of the bay – the harbour forming the other. Xavi had led him to believe that the gun emplacement was located on the beach at the foot of the cliff face near where it met the shoreline.

Using his binoculars Scott noticed a volcanic cinder-ash road running around the shallow bay past a small enclave of typical Canarian style cottages and further along single storey commercial buildings relating to the fish industry. These petered out as they approached the mountain to be replaced by a corrugated fence with a gatehouse and barrier across the road. After paying his bill Scott mounted the Norton and rode towards the gatehouse and was as he expected stopped and turned back by the Guardia Civil. Making a deliberate hardship of turning the heavy bike he was able to hear the noise of workings which he could not see. But he was able to determine that the fence carried on from the gatehouse until it struck the vertical face of the cliff. If he was to find out what was going on inside it would have to be from atop the mountain.

Once he had turned the bike he climbed his way back to the main Santa Cruz road, rode past the inland start of the mountain (the whale's head) and further on turned right into the village of Guaza. When he cleared the village he found himself on the opposite side of the mountain from Los Cristianos. Five hundred metres further on he found a sign post and the entrance to the banana plantation he was looking for – the Tenerife Banana Co-Operative. As per Xavi's instructions there was to the side of this main entrance a single track path leading in a zig-zag pattern upwards to the low hog backbone of the mountain. Scott took this rock strewn path and where possible rode but at times had to get off and push the heavy bike up the treacherous terrain. By the time he reached the top his legs and arms were aching. He shuddered to think what they would have been like had he not spent time in the gym over the last two days. However, once on top the going eased as he followed a well-worn path through gorse and bracken until Los Cristianos came into view far below. This was the path the locals used to communicate between Guaza and Los Cristianos. Fortunately there was no sign of life nor, importantly, the Guardia Civil. Before Scott hid the bike amongst the gorse and bracken he removed from the panniers a camouflaged over-cape and hat, binoculars and a roll of electrical tape. Donning the over-cape and hat he worked his way slowly along and down the stepped mountain face from one outcrop of rock or bush to another until he came to a flat projecting ledge surrounded by gorse which camouflaged him from the fenced-off building site below. He tore off strips of the black electric tape and applied them over the lens of the binoculars to prevent reflective glare from the sun giving away his position, then lying flat he trained them between the gorse bushes. Through the slits formed by the taped lens he observed that work had progressed to the stage that the heavily reinforced concrete walls of the gun blockhouse were being poured off an already cast concrete raft foundation by Spanish Army sappers dressed in fatigues. Of special interest to Scott was a large calibre gun of a Howitzer type being prepared for lifting into place by crane before the concrete roof was poured. He used his German manufactured Leica camera to take several zoom lens photographs of the gun and the various other workings for Admiralty recognition purposes. There were none of Xavi's alleged electric pylons in evidence and having established the operation was Spanish Army with no apparent German involvement, Scott decided to leave. He had what Sir James had requested on behalf of the Admiralty – photographs of the Howitzer gun and its location.

Surprised at the lack of security on the mountain Scott retreated without incident back through the village of Guaza onto the main road to Santa Cruz which he took for onward travel to the now familiar road between Santa Cruz and Puerto de la Cruz. A look at his watch confirmed he was in good time for an evening meal before his rendezvous with Pepe.

***

The Cantravel speedboat, trailer and van were parked every evening after work in Scott's driveway and were in position when he arrived from La Laguna where he had stopped off at a roadside tavern for his evening meal. They were being used for tonight's mission. With easy agility he hopped up onto the trailer and into the speedboat cabin to check the fuel gauge. Hank had carried out his instructions – the tank was full. After a shower he dressed in a black leather zipped jerkin and a black polo neck sweater under a black waterproof boiler suit. A pair of black robust climbing boots completed his attire. He then checked the action of his PPK before sliding it into his shoulder holster inside the jerkin. Ropes, grapnel hooks and torches he gathered from the garage and transferred to the van. Fifteen minutes later he was alongside the slipway at Puerto harbour awaiting Pepé. A further fifteen minutes and he and Pepé had the speedboat launched and twenty minutes later they were at the base of the steep towering cliffs some twenty metres from the underwater entrance to the Great Fissure at Punta Gaunché. Pepé acting as skipper brought the boat skilfully into a small sheltered inlet in the rocks and tied-up to a rock projection alongside a flat rock acting as a landing stage.

'You've done this before,' remarked Scott.

'Si Jordan, many times. This was me and Paco's secret pirate hideaway when we were youngsters. From here we plundered the Spanish gold being taken to Cadiz. Happy days,' he laughed, brandishing an imaginary cutlass.

With a finger to his lips Scott whispered, 'Sh! No more talk. Battle orders from now on.'

Pepé nodded acknowledgement as pointing upwards he whispered, 'The cliffs look a formidable obstacle viewed from the sea but actually remain as the island's original seabed eruption – full of jagged stepped ledges where the seabirds nest and leave guano.'

Scott whispered, 'So I head for the bird droppings and I'll find a ledge to use as a toe and finger hold. Yes?'

'Si. But you will need one of these.' He handed Scott a mountaineers' pick with a leather thong wrist attachment. 'If you miss a toe or finger hold use it. The climb should be easy but watch your feet – the ledges are slippery with the droppings. Tonight we are lucky, there is no wind and there are no birds nesting. I will lead and secure the rope and you climb making use of the rope. So if nothing has changed in the last ten years we will soon be at the top – follow me.' Pepé then picked up the stolen machine pistol, from the Perez and Schuster raid, and slung the strap over and across his shoulder to join the rope and grapnel hook already wound round his shoulder and waist.

The moon was full which would further assist their climb but would hinder them when they reached the summit. Extreme caution would then be needed. With this in mind Scott warned, 'Don't go over the top until I check all is clear.' And, looking upwards at Pepé's rear as he secured the rope around his waist, he growled, 'I don't like the thought of a machine pistol pointing downwards at my head – turn that bloody pistol pointing upwards.' One of the dangers of having a civilian in tow he reflected.

Pepé's answer was to turn and give him the thumbs-up, rectify the position of the errant machine-pistol, and continue his climb. Scott followed with a haversack on his back. After forty minutes of arduous climbing they reached the last ledge at three metres from the top only to encounter a further challenge – an overhang. Asked how he had overcome this problem previously, Pepé, responded with a shrugged gesture that he hadn't; the problem hadn't existed – for he had obviously now taken the wrong route up the face. As Pepé recalled there had been a bush growing on the precipice edge that Paco and he had used to haul themselves up and onto the top. Pepé suggested the use of the grapnel hook which Scott vetoed on account that he did not know how close to the edge the workings above were taking place – for the renewed increased noise level of machinery suggested very close.

Casting his eyes around their predicament Scott observed the ledge alongside to have no overhang and a mature gorse bush growing at the cliff edge. This obviously had been the ledge Pepé had been aiming for and missed. The problem now was the gap between their ledge and the other was too large to step and too dangerous to jump because of the guano. Scott was thinking there was no alternative but to descend and start again when Pepé, who had also noticed the opposite ledge and gorse bush, wound the grapnel hook up with a side-ways wrist action with his arm in space to gain extra rope momentum then let it go overarm. It arced gracefully through the air and on landing the hook buried itself into the bush. He gave it a good tug. It didn't budge. He gauged the rope length, re-gripped and swung out into space towards the ledge. Scott caught himself holding his breath as Pepé was in mid-air. The roots held and Pepé landed safely on the ledge. Pepé once again tugged on the grapnel hook entangled in the bush roots and finding them solid he flung the loose end of the rope back to Scott. Catching the rope Scott hauled on it – it held. He then checked the swing length and satisfied launched himself into space. Scott felt something give. Pepé to his horror saw one of the gorse bush roots holding the grapnel hook coming adrift from the soil. He instantly launched himself at the moving hook jamming it in place with both hands and forearms against the rock face whilst his legs took the strain. Scott, aware of the sudden shift in the arc's orbit as the ledge rushed towards him, gauged that his feet were not going to land on the ledge – he was coming in at knee high and even that was provided the grapnel hook held. His timing was going to be crucial, as was the arc orbit remaining constant. Pepé was aware of this. His leg muscles were screaming in agony as he pressed his full body weight against the now stationary grapnel hook. As Scott neared the jagged rock ledge at speed he twisted his body in an upward spiralling thrust. He let go of the rope just as his buttocks cleared the ledge with little more than a centimetre to spare and slid on the slippery guano surface towards the rock face. He came to rest with a jarring thump against the rock face – fortunately his haversack bore the brunt of the impact. Slightly concussed, Scott felt hands move him into a more comfortable position.

Through his blurred vision the face of Pepé asked anxiously, 'How are you, Jordan?'

'Fine thanks Pepé. Just passing – thought I would drop in to see you.'

A grimace crossed Pepé's face as he helped Scott to his feet. Scott who had seen Pepé's heroics with the grapnel hook out the corner of his eye asked, 'Are you in pain?'

'Si, Jordan. Your joke – it pains me.'

With no need to worry about their voices carrying due to noise from pneumatic hammers in the distance, they broke out into laughter which helped ease the tension they were both feeling after their ordeal. It was then that Scott noticed Pepé's real pain – blood dripping from his thorn torn hands. Scott removed from his haversack a first aid kit for such emergencies. Pepé waved the first aid kit away claiming the bleeding to be no more than from superficial scratches.

Irrespective of Pepé's protestations, Scott thrust the first aid kit into his bloody hands, clapped him on the shoulder and thanked him. 'Gracias amigo. That's one I owe you.'

An embarrassed Pepé replied, 'Thank you, Jordan. I know you would have done the same for me. After all, I have to save you for it is you that is helping us to get information about what is happening to our island.'

Scott felt decidedly uneasy at that comment knowing the truth to be the opposite. Advising Pepé to stay where he was until he checked out what lay above the overhang he fixed his balaclava in place and with the aid of the exposed gorse bush roots and rock face toe holds he hauled himself up to balance precariously on his stomach on the overhanging precipice edge and with legs dangling in mid-air he cautiously peered over the edge. Being all clear he, with a final look back before rolling over the precipice, saw Pepé wince as he applied iodine and bandages to his hands and arms. This brought a wry smile to Scott's face. He had seen enough wounds to know that superficial scratches don't bleed as profusely as Pepé's had. But he was aware that the letting of that blood had saved his life.

When he rolled over the top he was confronted by a large mound of excavation spoil rising two metres in height. To the side of this mound were bushes, bracken and outcrops of rock extending inland in the distance towards the main Teno road. This was the road that the Guardia Civil's road block at Buenavista Norte had stopped Scott from travelling along. He belly crawled through light bracken to the mound then clambered up and cautiously looked over. From this vantage point he viewed through his night binoculars the promontory of Punta Gaunché. It stood higher than the surrounding cliffs and was bathed in a battery of fluorescent lighting hung from lighting standards. This must have been the lighting glow he had seen in the distance when stopped at the Buenavista check point. He reckoned that the raised headland promontory of Punta Gaunché must command views to Los Cristianos in the south and Puerto de la Cruz to the north and beyond. Ideal location for a giant Howitzer gun on a turntable carriage. He trained his binoculars on the workers within the lighted area. They were stripped to the waist, bodies glistening with sweat, vibrating, pouring and levelling concrete over steel reinforcing bars to form a raft foundation at the extreme seaward point of the headland – the foundation for the gun. To the inland unfinished side of the foundation engineers were setting the levels for the continuation. Scott could tell from the set-out of the corner-profiles that this continuation conformed to the German plans from the war for the gun crew quarters, observation, arsenal and blockhouse for a Howitzer gun. He could see no sign of the gun being on site.

The Nazis by working twenty four hours were well under way with Hitler's gun emplacement bribe to Franco.

Scott crawled back to the gorse bush and signalled Pepé to join him. After clambering to the top of the mound and allowing Pepé to peep over he shouted in his ear, 'There's your missing seamen.'

Pepe nodded and shouted, 'Where's that damned drilling coming from?'

Through cupped hands close to Pepé's ear he shouted, 'Don't know but I intend to find out. You wait here and no shooting unless your life is threatened. This is a reccy mission. I don't want anybody knowing we've been here.'

A disappointed Pepé blurted out, 'I save you and still you don't trust me.'

'Of course I trust you. It's just from here on things can get dangerous. There are men out there trained to kill and they won't hesitate.'

'But I have my machine pistol…'

'All the more reason to be killed. What would I tell your uncle Xavi if I was responsible for your death?' This Scott hoped would pacify Pepé.

However, Pepé persisted, 'You would not be here if I had not led you.'

'Granted. But that is all I agreed with Xavi,' Scott said firmly, for he had no intention of allowing Pepe as an untrained civilian to accompany him further. He could endanger both their lives. However, he did not wish to offend Pepé being well aware that he had just saved his life. So he settled on a compromise. 'Look Pepé, it is imperative that I come out of this alive with my intelligence findings for Xavi so I do not intend confrontations. Should anything unforeseen happen I will run for my life and will need you to cover my back.' At this he saw Pepé, as he had intended, become alert on realising he had something important to accomplish. 'Can you see those generators under that arc light?' Pepé nodded. 'Well, I want you – should you hear shooting – to riddle the generators and put out the lights. This will cause confusion and give me a chance to escape. This is of *vital importance* to me. As soon as you shoot up the generators – head for the boat.'

'What about you?'

'Give me five minutes and then you clear off – and that's an order.' Pepé was about to argue. 'I repeat. That's an order. If I don't show I will have headed into the mountains. For Xavi's "Free Canaries" sake it is imperative we come out of this alive.'

Pepé, now appreciating the importance of his role for his uncle acknowledged acceptance of Scott's hectoring by throwing a two finger American salute over his right eyebrow. His mental game having worked on Pepé, Scott heaved a sigh of relief.

An unexpected solitary, large dark-cloud, flitting across the moon suddenly gave Scott extra protection. Taking advantage of this good fortune he rolled down the excavation spoil and crawled into the shadows then in a low crouch he headed towards the noise of the drilling. From his hidden position in the rocks he could make out from light given off by the gatehouse on the Teno road entry that the new entry road ran past him to the gun emplacement, meaning he had to cross it to get to the drilling activity. He crawled from the shadows of his concealment and belly crawled across the lit-up compacted volcanic ash road expecting at any minute to hear a warning followed by the sharp retort of a rifle from one of the Nazi gate guards. However, he crossed unnoticed and rolled safely into a hollow. Rising slowly to his knees he found himself to be at the beginning of a crescent-shaped bluff with trees running parallel to the new entry road and continuing up the crescent bluff. The trees made any activity behind them obscure from the Teno Road. The drilling was coming from behind these trees. Scott's eyes, now adjusted to the gloom picked out large square concrete pipes. Where had they come from he wondered. Xavi had made no mention of them being at the docks. To the side of the pipes was a path between the trees leading to the drilling cacophony. He worked his way down the path flitting from tree to tree for cover until he located the drilling. It was coming from a team of operators bathed in fluorescent light drilling a hole in the rock floor to finish the last of four concrete foundations, the other three having already been poured. In the middle of the foundations was a set-in concrete surveyors' marker pole. Scott was prepared to bet the surveyors' pole represented the coordinates for a shaft into the fissure below. Alongside this activity structural engineers busied themselves fitting together steel angle sections . He had found Xavi's alleged electric power pylons – a drilling rig waiting to be, when finally assembled by the engineers, erected onto the foundations by a mobile crane standing to the side of the work. Binocular scanning around the site he also found the reason for the increased importation of prefabricated timber buildings into the Santa Cruz docks – barracks for Xavi's missing seamen.

With all Xavi's information clicking into place Scott decided now was the time to move from his observation spot when he heard the chilling words in German, "Halt. Who goes there?" Scott immediately withdrew his PPK. Steadying it in both hands he levelled it at the direction of the challenge. Suddenly, a silhouetted figure with his back to him appeared from behind a rock projection three metres in front buttoning up his flies. He held his fire as the figure acknowledged the challenge, 'It's me Fritz. I had to attend to a call of nature.' As the silhouette entered the lit area Scott noticed the SS lightning-flash runes on the wing collar of his black jacket – the Waffen SS – Hitler's elite guard. This confirmed Sir James' despatch – the direct hand of Hitler *was* involved here.

He gave the lit areas a wide berth on the return to Pepé and thirty minutes later, having abseiled down the cliff face in stages they manoeuvred out into the Atlantic with a course set for Puerto. Pepé, full of curiosity asked questions. Scott was prepared. He told him about the important location of the gun emplacement but when asked about the drilling he said that it was related to the new access road into the site from the road to Teno. And when further questioned about the electric power pylons he answered – to carry the power provided by the generators. He said nothing of the shaft into the fissure. Pepé would find out when he told Xavi. Satisfied Pepé then concentrated on his seamanship for the Atlantic was beginning to cut up rough.

After returning safely to harbour and with the boat on its trailer and hitched to the van they were about to shake hands when Scott enquired if Pepé knew his way around the Santa Cruz docks. Unfortunately, Pepé regretted, he had little knowledge of the docks but his uncle Sergio was the port manager. Scott should get Xavi to arrange an introduction. Asking Scott why he wanted to know, Scott said it was only natural under the circumstances to be inquisitive about the docks.

Given that information about Pepé's uncle Sergio, Scott had no doubts that uncle Sergio was the source of Xavi's recent fund of intelligence on the dock movements and more than likely a leading member of the "Free Canaries Movement". Scott looked at his watch as he slid behind the wheel of the Diving Unit van.
It showed 2-10am.

Chapter 27

Scott felt as though his head had just touched the pillow when his alarm, set for 6-45am, awoke him. He needed to be in Los Gigantes for 8-00am to allow him a full hour with Xavi before the "Sea Dolphin" sailed for Puerto to pick up its Cantravel passengers. With a quick shower and a strong cup of coffee he had the Norton wend its way over the treacherous road to Santiago del Teide and down into Los Gigantes on the coast.

When he arrived in Los Gigantes harbour he found Xavi at the foot of the gangway supervising last minute loading. Noticing Scott he broke away from his chores to greet him with a warm pumping handshake and an embrace. 'You have for me good news, Jordan Hill?'

'Yes and no, Xavi. But can we discuss my news over breakfast somewhere please. My stomach thinks my mouth has healed up.'

'Ah! You English and your sayings. Come. Follow me.' Xavi led him to a nearby café where they sat outside in the early morning sunshine. Scott ordered scrambled eggs on toast and coffee. Xavi ordered a large beer. 'Now, Jordan Hill, what news have you?'

'First a question, if that's agreeable.'

Xavi nodded his head as he rolled the ever present cigar from corner to corner of his mouth. 'Si.' Before Scott started talking he looked around furtively only for Xavi to smile and say, 'No need to worry Jordan Hill – only friendly ears in this café. Please to start.'

Scott got straight to the point. 'What are the political leanings of your "Free Canaries Movement"?'

'We have none, other than to throw off the shackles of Madrid.'

Scott's reply was deliberately provocative, 'And become a dictatorship like….'

He didn't get finished as Xavi thumped the table with a fist. 'No! No. No.' A hush descended over the café. 'You no understand, Jordan Hill. We want no outside interference in our affairs. No British, French, German, Italian or Russian nosey peoples. And my views on Spain are well documented.' He sat down to applause from the early morning breakfast diners whom he acknowledged with a curt wave. Xavi's oft, but well-rehearsed spiel over, the diners returned to their interrupted breakfasts.

Scott having manipulated the discussion round to where he wanted it quickly cut in before Xavi could start his rhetoric again. 'I fully understand Xavi. *Now,* I can answer your question.' In a lowered voice he explained his previous evenings reconnoitre of Punta Gaunché with Pepé, including the sinking of the shaft into the fissure below. When Scott finished Xavi inquired what he made of the findings. Scott lit a cigarette and answered slowly but deliberately, 'You claimed you want no outside interference – but you already have it...'

With shrugged shoulders and an upward hand gesture, Xavi said, 'From who Jordan Hill?'

'Nazi Germany – the gun at Punta Gaunché.'

'Pah!' Xavi exclaimed disgustedly. 'That's just Hitler's bribe to Madrid to allow him passage into your Gibraltar.'

'*Or passage into your Tenerife*?' queried Scott.

'Never! Once the Nazis have finished the big *boom-boom* they will leave,' declared Xavi in a voice of thunder.

The remainder of the clientele, at Xavi's raised voice, elected to go about their business elsewhere. Scott then played his trump card. 'But they won't leave their U-Boat base below the big boom-boom.'

'What U-Boat base? Below where?' growled a shocked Xavi.

'Why do you think they are sinking the shaft I told you about at the horseshoe bluff....'

'You said to access the fissure below....' Xavi muttered with a scowl creased forehead. 'For....'

'For it to be used as a base to attack British shipping,' interrupted Scott. 'But....' he stopped for effect. 'But... also as a base to attack Tenerife from *within*. The ammo and arms, brought into Perez and Scuster's warehouse as "agricultural machinery" will be transferred to the fissure for use by Nazi troopers brought in by U – boat. Then it's up the shaft and.....' Scott could tell by the look on Xavi's face that without finishing he had convinced him of the Hitler's heinous intentions.

A growl emanated from deep within Xavi as he roared, 'The Nazi bastards. I will rid the island of the swine.'

Now well used to Xavi's outbursts, Scott answered calmly, 'Not the answer Xavi. That would cause Franco and the Generals to come down on you like a ton of bricks – and we don't want that, do we?'

'What then is the answer, Jordan Hill? Negotiations? I am sick of hearing about negotiations. We will soon be negotiating the negotiations....'

Scott hastily interrupted fearing another well-rehearsed tirade. 'There's a better solution. I have an idea but I cannot put it into operation until I obtain the professional opinion of an expert and importantly the go ahead from my chief. But to achieve these aims I need to be in London. So please Xavi, do nothing until I return – promise? Just sit on your hands.'

'I promise Jordan Hill, to sit on my hands,' he guffawed as he stood up then sat on his hands. 'You English and your sayings.' This eased the tension that had been building up between them.

'Thank you Xavi. I have a further favour to ask you but before I do, can you tell me about the large square concrete pipes at Punta Gaunché?'

A frown appeared on Xavi's weather beaten face and the cigar ceased its usual roller coaster ride around his mouth. 'Ah! If it's the ones I think, they were to be used for a new sewer in Santa Cruz / La Laguna area a few years ago but the then Nationalist government...' He spat on the ground. '...withdrew central funding and the much needed work never transpired. They were stored in a council yard somewhere near Tacaronte. Does that answer your question, amigo?' Scott nodded agreement. 'Now, your favour please.'

'I have a mission to complete tonight before I leave for London and I need access into the docks. I believe Pepé's uncle Sergio is the port manager – could you get him to help?' He told Xavi his requirements.

Xavi rose from the table and entered the café. He returned five minutes later. 'It is done Jordan Hill. You meet Sergio in the Café Olé on the dock road at one o'clock today. Nobody stops the port manager, he big jefe – boss – not even the Guardia Civil.' He finished his beer and lit a cigar.

Scott thanked him for his assistance and took money from his pocket to pay for his breakfast and Xavi's beer only for Xavi to push his hand aside informing him that he owned the café.

A whistle from Xavi's engineer aboard the "Sea Dolphin" brought about his departure. As they shook hands Xavi asked if Scott wanted a lift back to Puerto. He declined due to a previous arrangement in Los Rodeos.

As he waved farewell to Xavi from the quayside Scott heaved a sigh of relief. He had achieved what he had set out to achieve – the backing of Drago's (Xavi's) "Free Canaries Movement".

Scott then took the long coast road to Santa Cruz and from there to Los Rodeos and Marcus. On completion of his instructions and the usual entertaining and enlightening discussion with Marcus he retraced his steps to Santa Cruz and his lunch appointment with Sergio.

***

The Café Olé turned out to be an up market restaurant situated north of the port opposite Terrasitas beach. Scott parked the Norton on the beach side of the road past the restaurant. He crossed the road and wandered slowly back towards the restaurant giving him time to survey the clientele dining al fresco in the open forecourt. One glance was enough to convince him that he would look somewhat out of place in his black leather jerkin with its holstered PPK amongst the smart business suits on display. However, as he was about to enter the restaurant a tall, well-dressed gent, studying the outside menu lectern turned and took his elbow and directed him back the way he had come. Scott did not react; he recognised the person from Xavi's description – Sergio.

As they walked Sergio was talking in perfect English, 'Too many nosey Nationalists patrons in there – the food over-praised and over-priced.' By this time they were about to enter a paint-peeling, dingy looking bar, down a lane off the dock road. 'Whereas, in here is Republican owned, discreet, the food excellent, the wine palatable and reasonably priced.' He was extolling its virtues as they entered an interior belying the bar's exterior appearance. It was of exposed brick barrel vault arches, ceramic tiled floor, solid oak carver chairs with spotless red and white square chequered tablecloths. And busy.

As they took a reserved seat in a secluded and private alcove Sergio extended his hand. 'My name is Sergio Bello – yours I believe is Jordan Hill.' They shook hands.

'Pleased to meet you, Sergio. Nice place,' said Scott enjoying the cool ambience of the bar as opposed to the oppressive heat outside.

Over an excellent shared platter of locally caught sea food, Sergio, based on what Xavi had imparted to him about Scott's requirements informed Scott how far he had progressed. First, he could not furnish Scott with details of the gun because since the gun barrel incident the Guardia Civil security had been tightened around the storage warehouse. Scott enquired who did have access apart from the Guardia to be told: three German ordinance engineers and three others including a woman – possibly Gestapo. All with dock gate passes issued from Madrid. Regarding getting Scott into the docks he was to gain access as Antonio Bello, chief of security at the new Los Cristianos harbour – ostensibly to seek knowledge of the workings of a twenty four hour port. Sergio handed him his credentials. Scott had enquired as to what would happen if the gate guard checked on an Antonio Bello with Los Cristianos. Not a problem replied Sergio. He *is* chief of security at Los Cristianos and he *is* in Santa Cruz shopping with his wife as we speak – and he *is* my cousin. Sergio then relayed Xavi's and his plan to Scott – the rest was up to him. With regards to Scott's port departure – a van bearing the name Nevas Catering, purporting to be delivering emergency provisions to a liner, would be parked near the dockside crane which would have moved on its rails to be adjacent to the targeted warehouse. The nightshift crane driver, one of the "Movement", had been issued his instructions. Scott thanked Sergio for his excellent planning and asked where his bike could be parked.

'I will show you. Where are you parked now?' Scott pointed across the road to his Norton. 'Follow me,' Sergio said as he climbed behind the wheel of a Hispano Suiza luxury sedan.

Two minutes later, still in the dockside area, Sergio pulled up outside large double timber gates. He left Scott and disappeared through a door in the adjacent building; the building bore the name Nevas Catering. Shortly after, one of the gates opened and Sergio waved him enter. He parked between an unlettered van which he recognised – the one used in the raid on Perez and Schuster and a van bearing the name Nevas Catering. He was in "The Movement's" headquarters.

Returning to the docks Sergio's Hispano stopped at the barrier and a security guard raced from the gatehouse bidding Señor Bello a good afternoon – did he have a pleasant lunch. Sergio nodded and introduced his passenger. The guard saluted, lifted the barrier, and Scott was inside the docks. They stopped at the main office block in a reserved parking bay and entered Sergio's upper floor, plush carpeted, oak panelled office. Sergio ordered coffee from his secretary.

Sergio said as he sipped his coffee, 'I have a problem, Jordan. How do I introduce you if you don't speak Spanish?' This was spoken with a whimsical smile flitting across his lips.

Scott had expected this. It was time to come clean so he answered in Madrid accented Spanish, 'I do indeed speak Spanish.'

'I told Xavi you would when he raised the problem, for you cannot have an agent working successfully in a foreign land that does not speak the language.'

'I meant Xavi no harm. As you will appreciate it is to my advantage to let others think I don't speak or understand their tongue.'

'Xavi will not take offence. He is delighted that he can communicate with you in English. He tells me that he is now near to being fluent due to your teaching. Of this he is very proud,' he chortled.

'Let's just say we communicate. I certainly don't need to teach you English, you are grammatically perfect – where did you learn?'

'University of Madrid – international business studies – and you?'

'Cambridge University.'

'Ah! Where all the communist sympathisers come from.' He held a hand up. 'I joke, Jordan. I do not include you in my flippancy for there are just as many communists in Madrid. Come, I will show you around my domain. I just have time before my managers' meeting at 5-00pm.'

After being shown around the docks Sergio suggested Scott rough up his very polite Madrid accent to something more colloquial for dock usage as they entered the security office. Sergio then introduced him to the senior security officer whom, prior to meeting him, Scott had been advised was not a member of "The Movement" and a possible spy for the Guardia Civil. Sergio looked at his watch and excused himself to attend his managers' meeting. With the security officer having ties to the Guardia and with every possibility of being asked awkward questions about Los Cristianos port security Scott elected to excuse himself from the security office on the pretext of hunger. Coffee and doughnut finished in the dock canteen he passed the remaining time retracing his footsteps until he received the signal for the operation to commence. He started by watching cruise liners being provisioned and bunkered, others being manoeuvred by tugs into their allotted berths and merchant ships from all corners of the globe off-loading their cargoes. In return bananas being loaded for export. Bananas and tourists. It was this imbalance of trade and the cessation of subsidies from Madrid should Xavi's dream of an independent Canary Government become reality that made Scott doubt the viability of his "Free Canary Movement" – not unless tourism was made cheaper for the masses in the near future.

Scott, amazed at how quickly time had passed finished his tour with a survey of the guarded warehouse. He glanced at his watch 8-00pm. Darkness had descended. As he looked up from his watch he caught out the corner of his eye the ghostly silent movement of the jib on the giant dockside crane swing towards the targeted warehouse and stop with jib and hoist cradle over one half of the sloping corrugated iron roof of the warehouse. This was the signal. He was at go. With the sky dark and overcast he moved into the shadow of the long row of warehouses. From an overhead light fixed to the projecting eaves of the target warehouse he witnessed two Guardia Civil officers at the closed sliding doors. They were deep in conversation – the topic obviously football as one of the officers was showing off his nimble footwork on an imaginary ball. Scott took advantage of this diversion to slip surreptitiously across the quayside road to the crane. He waited at the foot of the access ladder to the operator's cabin. Nothing moved nor was there any sound other than the shrill whistle of a ship somewhere in the docks. He began his vertical twenty metre climb up a steel safety ladder to the cabin and with legs aching from the climb he lifted the floor hatch into the cabin. The operator smiling at Scott's obvious discomfort as he clambered through the hatch handed him a jemmy, a torch and a coil of rope and pointed towards a door leading to the jib. Scott wound the coiled rope diagonally over his shoulder, nodded his thanks and opened the door to encounter ahead thirty metres of jib swaying in the wind. The cradle and hook runner mechanism hanging under the jib had stopped twenty five metres along the jib over an opening roof-light in the sloping corrugated iron roof below. He began his journey along the swaying jib twenty plus metres above the quayside road. The jib construction of steel angles held together with riveted cross-latticed flat bars formed a metre square box girder. Unfortunately, the depth and the crossed latticed flat bars did not allow him entry inside the box and with the runner mechanism for cradle and hook hanging from the underside of the jib now located near a roof light half way up the slope of the roof he was left with no alternative but to crawl along the top of the jib on his hands and knees. As Sergio had pointed out – to have used the cradle to transport him to the roof-light would have meant movement noise from the cradle wheels that would have had the guards looking up to find Scott dangling from the hook. Due to the unpredictable swaying of the boom, coupled with nowhere secure to place his feet for balance, walking along the boom was out of the question so he had no alternative but to get down on hands and knees and crawl. The hand holds were relatively comfortable apart from the odd sharp edge of a rusted flat bar but his knees were feeling the effects of balancing on the narrow flat bars and were being continually scuffed on projecting rivet heads. Gritting his teeth he crawled on cursing each knee scuff until he reached the cradle. The transfer from top of jib to cradle and hook proved to be problematic. In the end he lay on his stomach, dropped his legs over the side and worked his way down the metre depth of the jib using the lattice flat bars until he ended up hanging from the bottom boom angle by his finger-tips. Swinging to and fro he ensnared the wire rope holding the hook with his ankles and set it in motion. He gauged his swing from the boom to coincide with the hook swinging towards him. He let go the boom and with an arm-wrenching jerk grabbed the hook and hung on. The operator who had been glued to his cabin window witnessing the trapeze act lowered the hook gently to the roof. Scott rolled off and lay on the roof breathless. Regaining his breath he massaged his knees then removed the coil of rope from his shoulders and attached one end to the hook. He then looked through the dirty window and seeing no signs of life in the darkened interior started to jemmy the roof light. Five minutes later he had it open and attached the rope to the hook and dropped the rope into the abyss then clutching it he slid down with ankle looped around fireman style until his feet contacted the concrete floor. Scott waited until his eyes became accustomed to the dark. From the light filtering through the roof-light he made out two large silhouettes: one suspended three metres above floor level. He withdrew the torch from inside his jerkin and from the torchlight discovered the silhouette to be a large diameter gun barrel waiting to be fitted to the second silhouette alongside which was a massive structure on wide crawler tracks. This Scott recognised as a converted tank and from the oxy-acetylene gas cylinders and cutting and welding torches lying around the ordinance engineers had been busy. Where the gun turret would have sat on the tank body there now was an enormous turntable with a solid steel cradle awaiting the gun barrel. Scott knew this solid steel cradle on the turntable as a Krupps forty-two calibre Gamma-Great howitzer (Big Bertha) as used in the war. Old – but from the look of it totally overhauled and with a range of eight miles – very effective. From memory of photographs he had seen of the war he recalled the cradle section as being fixed in concrete. But what he was now witnessing was a swivel action alternative – ideal for the Punta Gaunché promontory. Scott assumed that once it was fully assembled and found to be in battle order it would be dismantled otherwise it would be too wide for the roads. The transporting of this fearful weapon to Punta Gauché would be easy to track. He now realised that what he had for the Admiralty was in intelligence parlance, "pure gold". The sooner Sir James received this information the better.

    A good night's work Scott was thinking as he retraced his steps towards the dangling roof-light rope when suddenly the warehouse was bathed in light and a voice of recent acquaintance spoke in German accented English, 'Good evening, Mister Harley Davidson, good of you to *drop in* to answer a few questions – if you will excuse my feeble English pun.'

Scott turned to face the voice – it was who he thought – the German who had spoken to him at the pavement café in Santa Cruz only this time he *was* wearing his black leather Gestapo overcoat and a Schmeisser machine pistol held at his waist. To make any attempt to draw the PPK would be futile. Mister leather coat wasn't alone, only trouble was that Scott didn't know this until there was an explosion at the back of his head as a leather bound cosh struck him behind the ear. He folded to his knees. A hand relieved him of his PPK pistol then as he sagged to the floor he was dragged by his armpits with his shoe toecaps scraping the concrete floor towards the office. The bearers, one to each arm, used his head as a battering ram to open the door which, fortunately, was unlatched. He was then unceremoniously dumped into a metal framed chair. The chair had arm and leg clamps – the fact that he remembered these actions meant he was only concussed. He could only assume that most of the blow to the back of his head had been absorbed by the upturned collar of his heavy leather jerkin. He feigned full unconsciousness. The dark of the office was broken by a powerful lamp being switched on and directed at him. With his head dropped onto his chest and still keeping up the pretence he saw an electric cable clamped to the steel frame of the chair and running towards the source of the light.

The voice of leather coat shrilled from behind the light. 'Gunter, fix the clamps to the Englishman. This time he will talk to me,' he finished with a sinister cackle.

'Yes, Captain Kruger. May I give him a couple of slaps to make sure he is still unconscious while I clamp him to the chair?'

'Not too hard with the slaps. I want him fit to talk.'

That's a fatal mistake thought Scott as through slit eyes from his dangling head he saw Gunter standing in front of him with fist raised to strike. This position left Gunter wide open to abuse and Scott took it. He resisted the urge to kick him between the legs instead he waited until Gunter unleashed his punch then flung himself backwards in his chair. Suddenly, finding no resistance to his blow, Gunter, totally off balance lurched forward as Scott travelling backwards in his tipped chair brought his right foot up with all the strength he could muster to contact Gunter in the throat. Scott felt the toe of his shoe crumple the life out of Gunter. As he hit the floor he rolled sideways out of the line of fire he expected from behind the lamp light. Instead he heard a familiar *whurp-whurp* of displaced air as simultaneously the overhead office light came on. Scott looked towards the desk lamp light in time to witness a shocked Captain Kruger with Luger pistol still in hand being struck violently in his eye socket by a large adjustable wrench. Kruger dropped over his desk, his Luger falling onto the desk top to join Scott's PPK. Obviously slingshots don't just project bricks thought Scott as out the corner of his eye he noticed Sergio sitting slumped and unconscious with arms and legs tied to a chair – his face a mass of bruises with blood dripping onto his once pristine white shirt from a split lip. There was a roar of anger from behind Scott from the slingshot exponent as Xavi, also realising his brother-in-law's plight, rushed past Scott wielding a knife towards the stricken Kruger.

Scott, his head throbbing and too late to stop Xavi's dash towards Kruger scrambled to his feet screaming, 'Xavi. No knife – *please!*'

Xavi grabbed Kruger by the hair bringing a loud groan from the badly injured Nazi which was silenced by a vicious kick to his groin. He then dragged him, still by the hair, to position him on his knees in front of Sergio yelling, 'You did this – you son of a pig fucker. For this you die.'

Kruger's face contorted in pain pleaded, 'Please, please, it wasn't me. It was…..'

Xavi's large calloused hands encircle Kruger's throat and squeezed until Kruger's one good eye seemed to pop from its socket. 'You die – bastard Nazi.' He did, grotesquely gurgling with tongue projecting as Xavi choked the life from him. Deed done a still angry Xavi turned on Scott, 'Why you no let me slit the fucker's throat? It easier to do. Strangling peoples give you sore thumbs.'

'Because Xavi, I have an idea to get us out of here without anybody knowing otherwise. But first let's get Sergio out of here.'

They untied Sergio and cleaned him as best as they could and got him to drink a little water to which he responded. Between them they supported a now almost coherent Sergio to the rope dangling from the roof-light. Xavi wound the rope round Sergio, wrapped himself around him and fixed a foothold in the rope then he gave the torch three quick flashes through the roof light and the crane operator raised them gently to roof level. At roof level Xavi unwound Sergio who still shaken by his ordeal was muttering about his betrayal of Scott. Xavi enquired sympathetically of Sergio the nature of the alleged betrayal. Sergio explained that he had been grabbed by Kruger and Gunter when he had finished his managers' meeting. Why was he grabbed Xavi enquired? Because Kruger had seen him walking round the docks with Jordan and recognised him and wanted to know what he knew about Jordan. Who was he? What was he doing in the docks? Sergio told Kruger that Jordan was his brother. Kruger did not believe him and had Gunter torture him repeatedly. He had resisted until they threatened his wife and children. Kruger promised to let him live and do no harm to his family if he explained why Jordan was in the docks. Kruger said Jordan was English and no friend of Spain. Sergio knew this to be untrue. The beatings and electric shocks he could take but at the thought of harm to his family he had capitulated. He then broke down crying in Xavi's arms. Xavi calmed him and clapping him on the shoulder said he would have done the same himself – there was nothing to be ashamed of and that he would be back in ten minutes. He then grabbed the rope and started to slide down, cursing Kruger as he slid and muttering that he was going to kill the bastard over again.

Whilst this was going on Scott had been clearing the office of any signs of disturbance including cleaning up Sergio's spilt blood. He finished in time to meet Xavi at the foot of the rope. Sensing trouble he put a restraining hand on Xavi. 'No good killing the same guy twice – well not just yet. Now take it easy amigo and tell me what Sergio said to get you upset again.' Xavi explained Sergio's family dilemma. Scott nodded his understanding. 'Kruger would never have let him live. His Hispano would have been found at the bottom of a gorge on a dangerous bend as had similarly happened to Perez.'

Scott noted that Xavi had calmed sufficiently to allow him to outline his plan. There had been no shooting, not a lot of blood – and what had been spilled he had cleaned up – so he reckoned they could make the demise of Kruger and Gunter look like an accident. He explained his plan. This obviously appealed to Xavi for he took off promptly for the office and the next Scott was aware of was Xavi dragging Kruger by the hair and Gunter, who was bald, by the collar of his leather coat and place them directly under the suspended gun barrel. Gunter's leather hat he flung on top of them and crossed himself. Xavi then grasped the dangling controls of the overhead crane and pressed the release button. Near to two tonnes of steel dropped from a height onto a human body can make a mess – it did. The landing of the barrel made a resonating echo sound around the warehouse loud enough to alert the guards stationed outside. Scott and Xavi raced for the rope. Xavi gave three flash torch signals on the run and the rope lifted with both clinging on. They had just stepped on to the roof and closed the roof-light when the pass door in the warehouse sliding doors burst open and the two guards entered with drawn guns to discover the gruesome "accident". Xavi lifted a shaky Sergio to his feet and secured him to the rope then wrapped himself round as before. Scott caught the trailing rope and gave the signal to lift. The hook and rope rose as the jib swung clear of the roof and with no guards below to witness the move the cradle clanked in towards the crane allowing the hook to descend and place its passengers at the back doors of a familiar white van bearing the name Nevas Catering. They bundled Sergio into the back then Scott followed.

Sergio started to apologise to Scott. Scott told him to think nothing of it – he was the one that should be apologising for bringing pain and suffering to Sergio. Sergio's face showed his delight at being understood and forgiven. They shook hands and hugged continental style. Xavi drove through the gates unchallenged – it had been just another delivery from Nevas Catering.

On their approach to Nevas Catering the gates were opened and the white van swept into the yard alongside Scott's Norton. Sergio was immediately taken inside for attention leaving Xavi and Scott alone in the yard. This gave Scott the opportunity to thank Xavi for his timely intervention between him and Kruger and enquire as to how Xavi had arrived on the scene. Xavi said he had received a phone call at Nevis Catering where a meeting of the FCM was taking place from Sergio's wife asking if he knew where Sergio was since he hadn't shown up for his evening meal – a thing that never happened – he always ate with the children. Xavi knowing Jordan was at the port put two and two together and suspected trouble. That's when Nevas Catering decided to make an emergency delivery. A word with his man on the crane established that there had been a considerable time lapse since he had seen the man he had lowered down through the roof light. It was then that he realised there was obviously trouble below. The explanation finished they shook hands and departed.

First Pepé and now Xavi. The list of those saving his life was growing. To clear his indebtedness his overall plan had to work. Thirty minutes later Scott opened his bungalow door. He felt tired and exhausted and he still had his report to write for Sir James.

Chapter 28

London

Scott's alarm clock awoke him at 5-00am and by the time he had showered, shaved and gulped down a cup of coffee and toast and grabbed his pre-packed duffel bag it left him twenty minutes to keep his rendezvous with Marcus. With five minutes to spare he arrived at Los Rodeos and saluted the bronze effigy of Louis Bleriot as he entered the airport's confines and slid to a halt on the runway entrance to Bentyk Aviation. The Bleriot 290 was already on the tarmac with its propellers idling and Louis, Marcus' son, out giving the plane a final check. Dismounting the Norton he saw a welding flash from the hanger and popped his head in to investigate. Marcus was busy welding together a steel angle construction.

As he approached, Marcus prised his goggles onto the top of his head, withdrew a cigar from the bib pocket of his boiler suit and lit it from the flame of the welding torch. He took a satisfactory draw before extinguishing the flame. 'Whatcha think, buddy?'

Scott stood back from the contraption. 'You've been busy since I saw you yesterday morning. Looks good but will it work?'

'Well, if it don't I can always do what I did in the war. Throw 'em.'

'Glad you mentioned that Marcus. A young man called Pepé will deliver what you asked for in the next couple of days.'

Marcus slipped into his flying suit and they climbed aboard. Louis then withdrew the steps from the wing, the engines roared and they were airborne. Scott, with only five hours sleep in the last twenty four, instantly fell asleep only to be abruptly awoken four hours later by a shuddering jolt. Marcus was talking. 'Sorry Scotty, Atlantic's cutting up a bit rough. Waves are a bit higher than recommended.'

Scott, rubbing sleep from his eyes, sleepily mumbled, 'Waves? What waves? And anyway what's the recommended whatever to do with anything?'

'Three feet – and I'd say they're a bit higher...nearer four.'

Looking out the window and seeing nothing but spray and spume Scott exclaimed, 'A bit higher! If I'd known you were going to fly this thing underwater I would've brought my re-breather unit.'

'Typical Marine bullshit. At the first sign of trouble you crap yourself. All that's happening is the hull is having trouble slicing its way through the crest of the waves. And the wing floats aint helping any either. But don't worry I've done this dozens of times.... Holy shit....' Marcus broke off as he suddenly found himself fighting the control stick as they were lifted and shunted dramatically sideways towards a stonework harbour wall. As the cause of the shunt expended its energy by smashing against the wall and sending a rebounded mountainous band of water arcing over their heads Marcus calmly said, 'Sure glad that son-of-a-bitch didn't land on us or....' He didn't finish as he revved up the engine to make a bolt for the harbour opening which had suddenly come into view through the spray coming off the turbulent sea. Once inside the sanctity of the harbour he turned to Scott and said, 'Boy, that sure was fun – welcome to Casablanca.'

An up-tight Scott retorted, 'Might have been fun for you but why the hell didn't you use the landing strip like any *normal* human being?'

A satisfied smirk twitched across Marcus' mouth. 'Well you see Scotty, it's like this – I didn't actually feel like putting us down alongside the Nazis' Conder Legion troop-plane that was on the landing strip...Now let's get refuelled an' get the hell outa here before they come a nosing around.'

'Apologies Marcus. Sir James will be delighted with that intelligence.'

'There you go then, buddy. I get you valuable intel whilst *you* sleep and all I get is nasty insults.'

'I said sorry Marcus. How many times do I have to say.....'

Marcus wasn't listening. He had brought the plane alongside a jetty bearing a fuel pump and was collecting the thrown rope for tethering.

When they landed in Gibraltar on time at the estimated 2-30pm, Marcus with the Bleriot once again in sea-float mode had sat the sesquiplane smoothly down on the calmer waters of Gibraltar Bay and taxied into the inner harbour where he was tied up at a timber jetty by a naval ensign. On the opposite side of the jetty a Fleet Air Arm, Blackburn Perth, flying-boat with its propellers idling was being untied from its mooring. Scott grabbed his duffel bag from under his seat, clapped Marcus on the back, thanked him for a pleasant flight and asked to be picked up for the return journey three days hence. He then jumped onto a floating gangplank and crouching low, using the projecting staggered wings of both aircraft for cover from any onshore observers, used the opposite floating gangplank to clamber aboard the Blackburn which instantly revved up its two mighty engines set on the top wing of the bi-plane and manoeuvred into the Bay. It then took-off leaving a gentle wake lapping against the stone harbour walls. This final action completed a smoothly executed security transfer between the aircraft from any prying eyes, a fact he assumed to be the reason why Yvonne had not been in evidence to greet him.

***

The Blackburn landed on the Solent at midnight. When Scott disembarked he found the weather to be cold, damp and miserable. A shiver ran down his spine to welcome him home. Looking around he saw the familiar Foreign Office pennants blowing in the chill wind from a discreetly parked Daimler in the car park. As he approached the car a liveried chauffeur opened the rear door and relieved him of his duffel bag. He settled comfortably into the warm welcoming interior. Sinking into the luxurious soft leather seat he fell asleep only to wake up ninety minutes later as the Daimler drew up outside his lodgings. The front door opened and Jean his elderly but attractive landlady rushed down the steps to greet him like her own son. Against Scott's protests she took the duffel bag from the chauffeur and led her travel weary lodger by the arm into the kitchen. Minutes later he was tucking into one of her gourmet stews whilst she gazed lovingly at him – so happy he was home but frightened to ask for how long – for being ex SIS herself she knew he wouldn't say. Enjoy the moment she told herself for she worried when he was operational. One man missing from her life – her dear Alf had been killed in the war – was enough to bear without the thought of anything happening to Scott. (Even if that was his name, for with agents you never knew). She loved him dearly wishing she was thirty years younger just like that very good-looking young lady Elizabeth had sent for lodgings two days ago. Meanwhile, Scott had finished his meal and yawning he bid Jean goodnight and on kissing her affectionately on the cheek he then received the news he knew Jean had been keeping until he had eaten – Sir James wanted him in the office for 9-00am. She had ordered him a taxi for 8-30am. Now that she was up at this hour she might just as well set the places for breakfast. Such now was her lot in life – damn the war – she was lonely. How she missed Alf.

***

Being used to the comings and goings of agents, Ernest, the duty FO security door porter said to Scott as if he had last seen him yesterday, 'Good morning sir, and a better one it is too – I'm happy to say.'

'Good morning to you, Ernest, I assume Sir James has arrived.'

'Been in since 7-30am and the new girl too.'

Now anxious to see who Ernest meant by the "new girl", Scott scurried off thinking despondently that in his absence Elizabeth had left "The Service". To expedite his anxiety, even though Liz had advised against it, he took the short cut through the general office. As he entered the clickety-clack of the typewriter keys came to a slowly orchestrated stop as in turn each typist realised Scott was in the office. He flashed his even white toothed smile and with a sweeping hand action, took a bow. Many a heart was beating rapidly in the bosom of the typing pool as he knocked and entered the ante-room office to discover to his delight Elizabeth thumping away on the typewriter with earplugs attached to a Dictaphone.

She immediately leapt from behind her desk and took both his hands in hers and twirled him around. 'Well, well, well, look at my sun-tanned Adonis. I've missed you terribly but I do know you've been living dangerously, against Sir James wishes – you naughty boy.'

'Am I in trouble?'

'You're always in trouble Scott – but never with me.'

Scott with a thumb motion over his shoulder towards Sir James' office asked, 'How's your romance going?'

'I'm pleased to tell you that I took your advice and invited him to dinner at my place instead of Ferraris and things are blossoming. How are you getting on with Yvonne? She's just your type.'

'Now then, Liz, stop your match making. We're just ships that pass in the night. She's in Gibraltar now as you must know…'

'Au contraire, Scott. I happen to know she's in London. She left Sir James about ten minutes ago for the Ministry of Defence to check on civilian contractors being used for works in Gibraltar.'

'Are we still having problems there?'

'Sir James has just returned from Gib with Yvonne. The threat of sabotage looms large. I wouldn't be surprised if that is your next assignment.'

'When is Yvonne returning to Gib?'

'Tomorrow I understand, depending on what happens at the MOD.'

The intercom buzzed. She opened the line. A familiar Glaswegian growl came over the line, 'Don't you think it's time you sent Romeo in. He's five minutes late already.'

'Yes, Sir James,' she giggled.

Scott knocked on Sir James' door and entered. Sir James bade him sit. No niceties. He got straight to the point as was his usual. 'Gibraltar phoned yesterday to say you were on your way. I don't recall inviting you – so, to what do I owe the honour of a personal appearance, Rutherford?'

Scott withdrew his report from the inside pocket of his Saville Row tailored jacket. Sir James, receiving the report laid it on his desk as usual and growled, 'Tell me about it – I'll read it later.'

Scott recapped all, culminating in the gun for Punta Gaunché. Sir James had listened intently and taken notes without interruption. 'My congratulations to you, Rutherford. Your intelligence regarding the guns will be of immense interest to the Admiralty. In fact I would go so far as to say the Admiralty will consider your findings more than adequate payment for their funding of the operation so far. Would have cost them twice as much had they used their own intelligence section. And no doubt they would have buggered things up. Damned good mind to ask them for more funding,' he chuckled, as he referred to his notes. 'Now tell me, this Xavi or Drago person being as you say, anti – British, German, French et al… '

'And anti – Spanish, sir.'

'And Spanish. How did you manage to convince him to support us?

'To start with, I told him we had heard the Germans were active on the island and that I had been sent to find out what they were up to. I, of course, didn't tell him we were looking for suitable submarine bases nor that the Nazis had beaten us to it.' That reminder received a grunt from Sir James. 'Then knowing Xavi's strong feelings about independence from Spain I managed to convince him that what he thought was a bribe from Hitler – the gun emplacement at Punta Gaunché – was in fact Hitler's first move to get a conquering toe hold in his beloved Tenerife. And that's when I offered him the assistance of HMG to rid him of the threat of Nazi occupation,' he hurriedly finished, expecting a "You did bloody what?" blast from Sir James.

Instead, to his surprise, he received a quiet handclap. 'Excellent strategy, Rutherford, provided of course you haven't agreed with him to go to war with Germany and Spain.'

'Nothing quite so drastic, Sir James. And I have told him it depends on your approval….'

'That's damned decent of you, Rutherford. Do continue…'

'….your approval *and* depending on the outcome of a phone call to America.'

'Ah! No doubt to your friend President Roosevelt….'

Ignoring the sarcasm Scott pressed on, 'Not quite. A Professor Charley Rogers, head of geo-physics at Harvard University.'

'Where did you meet him?'

'*She* was one of the deported NGM scientists from Tenerife.'

'A *she?* Mind you, from what I've heard from sources, I don't suppose I should be that surprised. Give me her details and I'll get the switchboard to put you through. It might take some time. This Xavi fellow was born in Oviedo you know. So why does he hate the Spanish? I don't recall Madrid being particularly tyrannical towards the Canaries. Any ideas?'

'I think I met the reason. She's a young lady from Oviedo…..'

'*Good god, Rutherford – not her as well*!'

298

'Certainly not,' Scott denied adamantly. 'She's Xavi's niece – lost her father *and* fiancée in one fateful day when the Nationalists carried out that barbaric bombing atrocity in Oviedo. And of course he is a staunch Republican and the way things are going in Spain between them and the Nationalists......'

'Quite so, Rutherford. The one thing that intrigues me is that Xavi must obviously now realise that the drilling rig is there to break through to the fissure – so how did you explain that to him?'

'To allow Nazi troopers brought in by U-Boat land entry access to arms and ammunition for a future invasion of island. The arms and ammo being stored initially in Perez and Schuster's warehouse as "agricultural machinery" then relabelled as "spare parts" before being stored in the cave. Don't forget Xavi has actually robbed arms from Perez and Schuster so he knows the arms part of my story to be true.'

'I have to admit you have a vivid imagination, Rutherford. But why *did you* mention U-Boats to him?'

'To focus his attention I had to tell him that the cave would be eventually used by U-Boats to bring in storm troopers when Hitler thought the time right to invade Tenerife otherwise he would not have agreed to help blow up Magec's cave. He thinks that we are blowing up the cave to save it from being used as a weapons store by the Nazis against him and his beloved Tenerife.'

The phone rang. Sir James enquired who and handed the phone to Scott. This could be awkward Scott thought as Sir James, who had just poured himself a large Glenmorangie, showed no sign of leaving the room.

Accepting the phone from Sir James, Scott answered in a business like voice, 'Good morning Professor Rogers – Jordan Hill speaking.'

'It certainly is a good morning hearing from you again, Jordan, even though it's four in the morning over here. Anyhow what's with the professor bit? That person who answered the phone, he still in the room?'

'Yes.... And it's nice to hear from you, too.'

'OK I get it – fire away. But once you're free I want a proper call, understand?'

'Yes....It was indeed *most* unfortunate your leaving Tenerife the way you did.'

'You remembered. Well at least that's a start.'

'How could I forget, professor. Shocking treatment. Now, if you don't mind my asking what I need is information about that area you were working on ....'

'Only if you promise to phone – promise?'

'Yes.... That's the one – the area near the Chinyero cinder cone. Regards the seismic disruptions could you....' Scott explained his requirements. Charley obliged but only on his solemn oath that he would phone. She was missing him dreadfully. He promised.

When he put the phone down Sir James, with a knowing smile twitching around his mouth, said amiably, 'That appeared to go well, Rutherford. Usually when I have dealings with academe they won't part with information unless it's a deal of some sort.' But then again I don't go round sleeping with them he mused enviously but said nothing.

'Er, indeed, Sir James. Fortunately I didn't have any problem with Charl..er..Professor Rogers,' he finished lamely as he noticed the satisfied smirk on Sir James' face.

'Now tell me your intended plan of action, Rutherford.'

Scott obliged in full, finishing, 'But I could be doing with advice from Ordnance regarding the explosives.'

'Got the very man for you.' Sir James lifted the phone and asked for a Captain Harper, bomb disposal, Aldershot barracks. The call completed he turned to Scott, 'See a Captain Harper, Aldershot, 3-00pm today. Need transport?'

'No thank you, sir. Chance to take the Lagonda out for a spin and check it over for winter.'

'When you arrive back in Tenerife how long do you need to set up your side of things?'

'Ten days – depending on the weather.'

'Good. Now having listened to your plan you are no doubt waiting for my approval...'

'I would never be that presumptuous, sir.'

Sir James waved away his interruption. 'Having listened to your proposal I find it intriguing – acceptable to a degree – but fraught with danger. Not only personal danger or danger to the department but international danger. If it should go awry we will not only have diplomatic relations with Spain severed but a full escalation of war with Germany.' That's it he's not going to accept my plan reasoned Scott and I can't say that I blame him – the idea is crazy. However, much to his surprise Sir James shocked him. 'So, Rutherford, in granting you permission I would ask you not to upset HMG, for Mr Baldwin would have the deuce of a job convincing the League of Nations that he knew nothing of the event – which of course being covert he wouldn't. Awkward situation but if there's one person I know can handle it – it's you. Best of luck Rutherford. He rose and shook hands with Scott. 'I only wish I was coming with you.' Scott stared at him dumbfounded. 'Well, what's up man. The cat got your tongue?'

When Scott departed Sir James stretched into his bottom drawer and brought out the Glenmorangie, his leg was playing up something awful. Always did in times of stress and this was one of the most stressful decisions he had ever made, not lessened any when Rutherford had declined assistance saying that for security reasons he was convinced that a pleasure boat skipper named Xavi and his motley gang of "Free Canarians", along with some maverick Yank called Marcus, could handle the job. He mopped the perspiration from his forehead with a silk handkerchief and lifted the phone to contact Churchill of his decision. It was the same type of daredevil mission he and Winston had undertaken during the war but then again that was war...this could be the cause of another war if Rutherford failed. It had not been intended that Operation TENALT should have this outcome.

Elizabeth heard footsteps on the other side of Sir James' office door on the solid oak flooring. That would be Scott. She could usually tell from the footsteps the outcome of the meeting. The door opened and a non-exuberant Scott turned to close it behind him. She felt her shoulders sag in disappointment for him. Suddenly, he sprang into life with a jig and rushed to her, got her onto her feet and danced her around the desk. Returning her to her chair he kissed her on both cheeks and chirruped, 'He accepted my plan – Liz. Can you believe that? Waheeey.'

She gave him her best wishes, secretly praying that he would come back safely – for she knew from Sir James that the operation was already fraught with danger and that was before she was to hear of Scott's outrageous plan of action.

Scott then took himself off to the basement car park where Percy the FO fleet manager looked after the Lagonda in his absence.

***

Yvonne knew of Scott's meeting with Sir James and had made up her mind that on her return from the MOD she would confront Scott and apologise for her earlier boorish behaviour in Tenerife. After all he was a single man and if he wished to waste his time with that Texas trollop Sandie that was up to him. She was going to do this for the harmony of the team and hoped her gesture of humility would knock some of the arrogance out of him. She arrived back at the office by taxi in time to see a dark green Lagonda move towards Westminster Bridge.

***

Scott cared lovingly for his sleek, ten year old, two seat, Lagonda sports coupe and it showed in the condition of the gleaming coachwork. Having just completed an inspection it showed there to be only one blemish, the waxed canvas up and over hood was showing signs of wear and tear at the folds. He would get Percy to attend to this matter during his absence. The day being dry, bright and fresh, he drove with the hood down to admiring glances from pedestrians and fellow motorists alike as he threaded his way through busy London traffic heading for the A3 trunk road to Aldershot. Once on the A3 he hit the accelerator and thrilled again as the mighty six cylinder, four and a half litre engine, transferred its power through wire spoke wheels to reach speeds of one hundred miles per hour on the straights.

He turned off just past Guildford into Aldershot. Captain Harper, head of bomb disposal, listened to Scott's problem and arranged for a mock-up to show him the correct detonation procedures to follow. It was slow and tedious and by the time Scott had mastered the technique it was near to dinner and he had promised Jean he would be back for her home made steak and onion pie and bread and butter pudding.

He floored the accelerator and screeched to a halt outside his lodgings with ten minutes to spare of Jean's strict 6-00pm deadline. He dashed into the downstairs cloakroom and spruced himself up. As he ventured towards the dining room he met Jean on the way out having just delivered the main course to her only other "guest" dining tonight. The other two "guests" were out on business. The other "guest" turned out to be a female. She was sitting with her back to him looking out the window. She looked very attractive. Her lustrous brunette hair sat on a slender neck. She was poised to take a mouthful of pie when she froze as she looked at his reflection in the window. She put her cutlery down and stood up with her shoulder length hair swinging gently as she turned to face Scott who, unable to help himself, blurted, 'What the hell are you doing here?'

'As I'm fed up telling you Scott – a *"nice to see you again, Yvonne"* wouldn't go amiss.'

They glowered at each other. Then she remembered her promise to herself about team harmony and was about to apologise when Scott leant towards her and kissed her. 'Nice to see you again, Yvonne.' They laughed. He moved the cutlery from his table to join her.

Jean witnessed this through the part open door. This should be of interest to Elizabeth whom she had promised to keep notified of any developments between her two "guests".

After dinner Scott and Yvonne went for a run in the Lagonda. The weather had turned cold and overcast, not that they noticed it playing darts, drinking beer and huddling together in front of an open fire in a Sussex country pub. As they slipped into the Lagonda in the car park, Scott regretted that it was a cramped two seater. However, the effort had to be made. It was then that the torrential rain started. Bugger that damaged hood.

The soaked to the skin pair garaged the Lagonda in the FO basement car park and took a taxi to their lodgings.

The following morning Scott and Yvonne departed for the Fleet Air Arm base at Lee-On-Solent. Jean felt pangs of jealousy as they departed. How she missed her Alf.

***

The Saro A27 flying-boat, on its final test before being

commissioned by the Fleet Air Arm, took a buffeting over the English Channel and Bay of Biscay on route for Biarritz near to France's border with Spain. It required refuelling because its range of one thousand three hundred miles was some seven hundred miles short of reaching Gibraltar. The buffeting gave Yvonne the excuse to clutch Scott's arm and hold on longer than was necessary for she knew that when they arrived in Gibraltar Scott would immediately transfer to Marcus' plane and be off under cover of the sheltering wings of the two strategically staggered planes. She found every moment spent with him to be precious, irrespective of last evening's disastrous attempts at seduction in the confines of the Lagonda. She felt they were cursed by circumstances – this time a rent in the canvas hood had been responsible for them being soaked through to their underwear. However, she was happy that at least team harmony had been resumed.

Flying low off the Atlantic coast of Spain, Scott looked out his port window at the Rock of Gibraltar as the pilot slid the flying boat in a gentle descending glide towards Gibraltar Bay and the sanctuary of the inner harbour. It was only on looking out the starboard window that he truly realised the strategic importance of Gibraltar in relation to the Straits of Gibraltar – the gateway to the Mediterranean – when he saw Morocco within touching distance.

Safely down the pilot taxied to the inner harbour jetty. Scott, now back to SIS operational duty, gave Yvonne a quick handshake and a peck on her cheek before grabbing his duffel bag and in a low crouch hidden by the wings of the two planes once again, ran gingerly across the bobbing and floating gangway to join Marcus' idling Bleriot. Marcus, manoeuvring into the Bay, wasted no time bringing the Rolls Royce engines up to full power to get them airborne.

Yvonne grimaced. Not even a "See you soon, Yvonne".

***

During the flight Scott informed Marcus that he had been given the green light for Operation TENALT – zero hour to start ten days from tomorrow, weather permitting. He asked Marcus if he was ready for action and was informed that he couldn't wait. This was proved by the fact that Marcus had already carried out a test run at night over the target and found that when flying inland the peaks of the mountains were too close for safe low night-flying. However, he had found a passage between the peaks that would allow the target to be approached at night low from the sea by entering from the north over Garachico and exiting south over Los Gigantes. Marcus added that further, on the plus side, was the fact that the target glowed at night and the contraption was working. Also the bundles had been delivered by Pepé. Scott was relieved to discover that Marcus had handled his task professionally. On reflection he wouldn't have expected anything else other than perfection from the decorated air ace.

It was close to midnight that a travel weary Scott mounted the Norton at Los Rodeos and shook hands with Marcus, informing him he would keep in touch regarding zero hour. The hour would be 3-00am when all were asleep.

Chapter 29

Ten days to zero hour

As Scott parked the Norton in the driveway he noticed the bedroom light was on – Sandie! He was going to have to tell her once and for all that she couldn't just come and go as she pleased especially now that he was "active in the field" – but he would let her down gently. He opened the front door, dropped his holdall on the floor, and tip-toed stealthily to the bedroom door and with forefinger raised to emphasize his point he entered.

She lay on the bed in a provocative pose in her black lace bra, panties and suspender belt with one black seamed silk stocking leg bent at the knee under her – the other pointing straight towards him. With her high heel shoes neatly together on the floor she was leaning on her elbow reading a magazine. Feeling foolish Scott dropped his hectoring finger and gaining control of his eyes enquired, 'Well hello. What brings you here?' Not that it mattered he thought going back to studying her sexy pose.

She replied in husky German accented but perfect English, 'Since you didn't come to me – I brought myself to you. 'Do you like what you see?' asked Lady Marlene Fitzgerald as she wafted an elegant hand over her body. What he thought was – that there was a familiar feeling beginning in his genitals. His other feeling of weariness had suddenly evaporated and thinking it would be rude to ignore such hospitality he started to hastily strip off his clothes. Discarding them in a heap on the floor he leapt enthusiastically onto the bed to straddle her only to find that on landing off balance on one knee she rolled him onto his back then straddled him lowering herself full length on top and with one arm round his neck started to nibble his ear whilst the other felt under the pillow.

Meanwhile, a now solidly erect Scott, was happily trying to ease off her panties when he suddenly recognised the feel of cold steel against his temple and the cool voice, 'One false move and you die, Mister Hill.' This spoken as she kneed him in the scrotum and leapt off the bed. She stood in front of him with a triumphant grin on her face, the Luger steady and unwavering as she slipped in to her shoes.

Naked and annoyed at himself for being duped Scott sat up in bed massaging his agonising injury. 'Not very lady-like, my Lady,' he said, through gritted teeth.

'You English and your stupid jokes. We will see who has the last joke.'

'Last laugh,' he corrected. 'If you'll pardon my saying so Marlene, it seems to me a slightly excessive way of doing things just because I didn't make arrangements to meet you in the cocktail bar. If all you were looking for was a bit of extramarital sex all you had to do was ask and I would have willingly obliged,' he rambled, knowing that in this situation he had to play for time. So trivial banter it would have to be until the pain in his now limp manhood subsided and the opportunity presented itself to correct his predicament arose.

'Enough of this rubbish. The thought of relations with you makes me sick….'

'Ah! You must be lesbian then,' he goaded.

She ignored the taunt. But more time had been gained. Every second counted. 'You will answer my questions – no more time wasting tactics or you die.'

With her knowledge of his "time wasting" answers, Scott realised he was dealing with a similar like professional and had no illusions that the outcome would be the death of one of them and right now the odds were heavily stacked against his survival. However, it was imperative that he survived for his death would herald the end of "Operation TENALT". And Sir James would not like that. So in answer to her question he replied, 'Fire away.' He immediately regretted his choice of words as he looked down the barrel of the Luger. 'Er, sorry Marlene – wrong terminology in the circumstances. You know the gun…'

'Shut up! I won't warn you again. Only answers from now on Jordan Hill.' He nodded acknowledgement thus allowing her to continue for he had to keep her talking to find out what she knew before he killed her – for kill her he must. 'Three days ago, in the docks, two of my men met with an alleged accidental death according to the local idiot police chief but I know it was murder.

And you the murderer. Am I right?'

'Two of your men? Would that be your chauffer and the gardener, your Ladyship?'

Temper flaring she raised the Luger to pistol whip him, then taking a step backwards sensibly thought better of it. More time wasted. 'I asked you if I was right, Mister Hill.'

Managing to take his eyes off the low cut of her panties around her crotch he replied, 'You've obviously mixed me up with somebody else, Marlene. Come back to bed,' he said patting the sheets. 'I mean why would I be in the docks?'

'I don't know – *as yet*. But I do have a good idea and I do know you were there. Captain Kruger saw you walking around with the port manager in the vicinity of the warehouse. The warehouse where you eventually murdered him. '

'Captain Kruger?'

'One of the dead men. He spoke to you about your Harley Davidson at a café in Santa Cruz.'

'Yeah. I remember now, the German guy – he liked the Harley.'

'You tried to convince him you were Spanish.'

'Well, I get fed up having to constantly answer questions about the bike so I just pretend to be some other nationality.'

'Good try. But he also saw the bike in the vicinity on the night of the raid at the Perez and Schuster warehouse where four Kreigsmarine Kommandos were badly injured. You are a very dangerous man Mister Hill.'

The mysterious shadow at the Perez and Schuster warehouse was finally solved. Still playing for time Scott made the statement, 'There's more than one Harley on the island.'

'No there's not. I checked.'

Scott shrugged his shoulders. 'Just because this Kruger geezer saw a Harley near a warehouse and allegedly saw me in the docks you try to pin his death on me – not much to go on, is it?' And now resorting to angering her, he said wilfully, 'Sounds to me like he was resorting to lies to get in to your panties.'

He was successful, her nostrils flared as she spat back, 'He did not lie he was a good officer – a credit to the Third Reich…..'

Scott noted there was no denial regarding Kruger being her lover and knowing he had her rattled and that she still didn't have what she wanted he risked a further taunt, so he interrupted her. 'And I'll bet he communicated direct with Berlin about me and not through you.'

'Ah! So you admit after all your time wasting that it *was you*. Well, I can tell you, Englishman, Kruger did not deal with Berlin. I was his control. I am Colonel Maria von Reus of the Waffen SS – answerable only to the Führer – Kruger was my top agent and he would not have dared to go direct to the Führer without my consent.'

'Could of course be that Adolf had Kruger watching you.' Another time wasting statement.

'Shut up! I know what you're up to. Trying to cling futilely to your miserable life. When I find out what you know I will make my report to the Führer. So now to save further bother please tell me all you know. Then I promise to make your death quick. A bullet between the eyes would be better than being crushed by a gun barrel – yes?'

'Without Kruger and his stooge you haven't got the guts to do your own dirty work, Marlene. I doubt if you even know how to fire that. I wouldn't be surprised if you've still got the safety catch on – so you'll get nothing out of me.'

'I believe you. And since, as you point out, I no longer have any help to gain this information due to your psychopathic ways, I regret – as you English say – you will have to prepare to meet your Waterloo. Because the one thing I do know, is how to use my Luger. So good bye Mister Hill.'

Her Luger, with the silencer fitted, had become heavy with Scott's continuous prevarications and procrastinations and had drooped slightly. She took time to corrected this with both hands and was taking aim and about to squeeze the trigger.

Scott knew he had ran out of time and decided to lunge himself at her rather than allow his execution when suddenly there was a noise from the lounge. The noise of a key trying to find the lock. The door opened and a Texas drawl hollered, 'Hiya, Jordy baby. It's me Sandie. I'll just make us some coffee before we hit the sack.'

Scott noticed Marlene's hesitant half turn towards Sandie's voice and being already poised to attack he took advantage of her momentary lapse in concentration and leapt from the bed bringing the edge of his hand viciously down in a killer neck chop. She died instantly with her head turned towards him showing amazement as she gurgled her death sonnet. Scott quickly dumped her on the bed and kicked the Luger under as she landed like a rag doll. The door opened and in bounced Sandie to survey the scene before her: Scott now in his underpants hopping on one leg trying to get into his slacks and an unknown scantily dressed female in her sexy black underwear lying on the bed sound asleep.

Pointing at the lifeless form of Marlene she wailed, 'You bastard, two faced skunk Jordy, how could you do this to me? I never want to speak to you again – ever!' She burst into tears as she stormed out to the customary slamming of the door as the situation demanded.

Scott exhaled loudly. He felt as low as he ever had – Sandie had just saved his life and had been subjected to unjust humiliation. Well so much for his letting her down lightly. She had not deserved to be humiliated but there was little he could do to remedy the situation with a dead woman lying on the bed. And there was no way he wanted to get Sandie involved. He would think of some way of pacifying her eventually but in the meantime he required help to remove the body.

He phoned Pepé. Whilst he was waiting for Pepé's help it gave him time to reflect on the outcome of his fatal tête-à-tête with Marlene. He had just killed an officer in Hitler's elite guard but with it being a covert action by Hitler he doubted if a full scale manhunt would ensue. Nor – should Hitler decide otherwise – would his thugs know who to look for because he had tricked Marlene into letting it slip that Berlin had not been notified of his actions – she had been acting on her own volition and had not as yet sent a report to Hitler. And between them, he and Xavi had wiped out Marlene's cell – Kruger, Gunter and herself.

Half an hour later Pepé arrived in a Nevas Catering van. Marlene was rolled up in a red threadbare carpet. Scott felt it only appropriate that "Her Ladyship", in death, should be given the red carpet treatment.

He retired to bed.

Chapter 30

A high speed dash on the Norton down the coast road and he was in the harbour waiting for the "Sea Dolphin" to dock before the Cantravel tourists arrived. Xavi noticing Scott sitting on a quayside capstan bid him come aboard and seated him on the bridge with a bottle of beer in hand whilst he was as usual up and down shouting orders and abuse at his crew. When things were to Xavi's liking he sat down and asked Scott to proceed. Scott, preying on Xavi's patriotism, informed him he had permission from his chief to commence the operation to free Tenerife from Hitler's toe-hold at Punta Gaunché. At this news Xavi hugged him, thumped him on the back, god blessed Churchill, the King, the Tower of London, Arsenal football club and pumped his hand until his arm ached.

Scott then carefully outlined his modus operandi. Xavi was shocked at the audaciousness of the plan but agreed. He enquired as to when Scott intended to implement the plan. Scott replied that he had checked with the Met Office before he had departed London and had been advised that the next suitable weather conditions would be in twelve days. This was a necessary lie for his plan to succeed and was contrary to his intended ten day deadline which he still intended to keep. Scott then disclosed to Xavi his requirements for the operation. Xavi, in appreciating that time was of the essence, departed the bridge with Scott to make the necessary arrangements by telephone from the harbour café. As Scott sat outside with a coffee and brandy he witnessed the arrival of the Cantravel buses in the harbour car park and was relieved to see Sandie looking none the worse for her ordeal. Xavi arrived ten minutes later to confirm that everybody had been contacted and understood their parts which would be acted upon immediately. The whistle sounded aboard the "Sea Dolphin" causing Xavi to leave post haste. Scott finished his coffee and rose from the table leaving enough pesetas to cover the drinks and a tip. He mounted the Norton and moved on to his next port of call. Operation TENALT was finally coming to fruition.

***

Scott caught up with Hank on one of Pepé's diving sites with the intention of recruiting him unknowingly to Operation TENALT. He informed Hank that the explosives they were about to use were to reshape a cave into an underwater theme park that he had been commissioned to find for Mr Crozier. On the instructions of Mr Crozier the work was to be carried out at night because he did not want his competitors to know that Scott had found the Holy Grail of underwater caves – the Great Fissure. Hank, being a long and loyal employee of Mr Crozier agreed without hesitation. On a vow of secrecy he told Pepé the real truth about the intended operation and passed on Xavi's instructions to him regarding the explosives.

***

Scott's next stop took him to Los Cristianos, to one of the phone calls Xavi had made from the café, where he renewed his acquaintance with Paco's uncle Tony the owner of Los Cristianos Sea Salvage. Tony showed him an insurance write off – a yacht that had been badly damaged on the rocks off the island of Gomera and had been towed into harbour late last night. They agreed it would be suitable for Scott's requirements and the breaking into two sections of the yacht began. Tony intended to set sail under the cover of darkness for the rendezvous point they had agreed upon. They adjourned to a quayside café for refreshments. On the bar lay a copy of El Día. As he was waiting to order he scanned the pages. A small article headline caught his eye. It reported an unnamed woman had been washed ashore on Teresitas beach in swimwear. According to a police statement she had been diving north of Teresitas and struck an underwater rock resulting in a broken neck. The police were trying to identify the tourist. The article went on to warn of the dangers of underwater rocks. A tragic accident, one that all tourists should be made aware of.

'RIP Marlene,' muttered Scott, setting the paper back on the counter.

***

Later that evening a salvage boat converted from a large high prow Canarian style fishing boat was anchored close to the treacherous rocks known locally as the Maquinilla de Rocas (Razor

Rocks) just slightly north of the Teno lighthouse. The sea was rough, the wind howling and the rain driving in horizontally as the vessel's arc lights were trained on the foredeck crane as it lifted one section of a yacht towards the Razor Rocks under the command of the grizzled, weather beaten, veteran captain. The crane gave a violent shudder as a wave hit the bows causing the load to swing dangerously over the rocks in the now gale force wind. The captain gave the order and the slings holding the load were released and the partial section of a yacht smashed downward into the raging maelstrom of the Atlantic waters and the Maquinilla de Rocas. The sudden release of the load caused the foredeck to lift but the wily captain had foreseen this and given the order to tightened the winches holding the bow anchor in place. The process was repeated with the aft crane and the other section of yacht.

With the arc lights now trained on the rocks the grizzled captain with a damp, chewed cigar in mouth and lashing rain streaming off his Sou'wester, growled, 'What you think, Paco, good job, yes?'

'Yes, Uncle Tony. But what about the lighthouse keeper?'

The cigar now a sodden stump was spat overboard before Uncle Tony roared with laughter, 'Old Roberto – he no see past the end of his nose in good weather never mind this shit. Come we go inside and have a hot Ron Miel to take the chill out of the bones.' Taking over the wheel from the mate he said in a matter-of-fact tone, 'I'll be glad when that friend of Xavi – Jordan Hill – picks the dynamite up.'

Paco, in a voice near to panic, shrilled, '*What dynamite*?'

'It's in the hold. Pepé delivered it before you came aboard.'

The explosives Pepé had delivered to Tony were part of the raid on the Perez and Schuster warehouse. On Xavi's orders passed on by Scott he had removed the explosives from their hiding place in one of the many caves in the mountains.

Paco had a sleepless night.

Nine days to zero hour

Scott spent most of the day checking and rechecking Captain Harper's explosive chart and trying to rest and sleep, as did his companions Pepé and Hank, for their upcoming night shift in Magec's cave.

The Cantravel diving classes were to be left in control of Lex who, when his working day was over, had been instructed to make sure the speed-boat and van were fuelled and returned to Scott's driveway for a night time operation. Lex had been naturally curious regarding Scott and Hank's impending nocturnal absence and had been told in strictest confidence that they were trying to find an ancient shipwreck that Pepé knew existed. The reason for night work was that it was Spanish gold bounty dating from the sixteenth century and they didn't want others to know of their interest. They would share any bounty with him if they found the wreck. This seemed to satisfy Lex and saved the cancellation of the Cantravel daytime diving and swimming classes which Scott was delighted about for he did not want to further inconvenience the generous Eugene's business interests.

Using the van Scott collected Hank from his chalet at 9-00pm then drove to Puerto harbour to meet Pepé where they launched the boat and headed for their rendezvous. The gale force wind and lashing rain of yesterday had receded and been replaced by a gentle swell. Pepé, who was familiar with the water, was at the helm navigating his way through the hazardous rocks. Their rendezvous heaved into sight as they came out of a deep swell. It was showing warning lights, aloft, amid-ships, fore and aft as it bobbed at anchor on the Atlantic swell. The amid-ships arc light guided Pepé to a fixed metal ladder hung from the gunwale. Pepé made fast the boat to the ladder and they scrambled up into the salvage vessel to be met by skipper Tony who invited them into the wheelhouse for a hot Ron Miel to take "the chill out the bones" which seemed to be the gnarled old sea-dogs remedy for all ills.

They clinked mugs to the success of the mission. Tony had agreed with Scott that he would act as supply vessel for the dynamite whilst appearing to passing shipping to be salvaging the wrecked yacht off the Razor Rocks.

The crane was already loading the speed-boat with the dynamite which Scott had asked to be repacked in ten kilo waterproof bags for ease of handling underwater. The loading complete, Paco joined Scott and Hank on board and with Pepé at the wheel they cut through the swell and ten minutes later found themselves standing-to off Punta Gaunché – Magec's Cave.

Scott had worked out a handling system for the dynamite between the boat and the cave based on two men active underwater and two in the boat. Of the two in the boat: one would rest whilst the other lowered the waterproof bundles of dynamite by rope to the to the cave entrance where the third member would take the bagged parcel and swim with it through the tunnel into the cave and surface inside to hand the parcel to the fourth member on the wide ledge that he knew to be there from Pepé's reconnoitre and his prior knowledge of the Nazi's cave drawing. The fourth person would take the dynamite and store it ready for further action later. They would rotate positions every thirty minutes. The idea sounded simple except for a human frailty – exhaustion. Scott had based his calculation on an eight hour shift (9-00pm – 5am) of which he hoped to achieve six hours actually working. His main limitations were the fact that the filters in the re-breathers were only good for three hours and a work load of ten kilos per journey for the dynamite was going to make his deadline of ten days marginal. This was the reason he had invited Paco along as an extra hand. At the end of day one Paco was beginning to regret having accepted the invite. His muscles were aching due to the swim through the tunnel with the package. As indeed were the muscles of the others. The first dive worked well but was slow, time consuming and back breaking. They managed another three dives before Scott during his rest period on board the boat realised it was only a half hour to the end of the shift and called a halt. This was two fewer dives per day than that allowed for in his estimated ten day operation. On the way back to Puerto they discussed ways of speeding up the operation for all agreed that time and energy were lost in the stretch from the entrance of the underwater tunnel to inside the cave. They had all struggled with the awkward ten kilo load. They did not come up with a suitable solution until they were back in harbour and winching the boat onto the trailer when Scott had his Eureka moment – a hand operated winch similar to that they were using on the trailer be set up inside the cave. Scott sketched out a feasible design based on pulleys and ropes on his cigarette packet.

Tony, with a few modifications to the pulleys, would have all the necessary chandlery items at his dockyard in Los Cristianos.

***

Eight days to zero hour

As darkness descended, Scott, Hank, Pepé and Paco left Puerto earlier than usual to collect the chandlery from the salvage vessel and put in place Scott's design which, he hoped, would ease the fatigue problem they had experienced. It basically consisted of the waterproof-bagged dynamite hooked to a continuous rope wound around pulleys plying between the cave entrance and its inner cavern. This installation took the whole of the working period. The following day they tested the system. The dynamite was lowered from the boat as previous by the first diver. This waterproof-load when lowered from the boat to the cave entrance was then transferred via S hooks by the second diver onto the continuous rope which was wound round a pulley wheel welded to a grapnel hook and jammed between rocks at the cave entrance. After alerting the third diver with a tug on the rope, the second diver then swam through the tunnel escorting the load which was being winched-in by the third diver from inside the cave using a hand winch which had its pulley/grapnel hook also jammed between rocks. The escorting diver then helped to load the dynamite onto the cave's ledge for later use. Loading task completed the escorting diver took up winch duty whilst the other returned to the boat for his rest period. Thus began the rotation of personnel. A rotation that proved to be successful in that it caught up the lost diving time on day one and the installation time setting up the rope conveyor system on day two. It was a success and allowed them to finish on schedule. At this juncture, with the final departure of his dynamite packages from the hold, a relieved Captain Tony who had been pacing his re-salvage work to coincide with the reduction of his dangerous cargo upped anchor and returned to Los Cristianos.

After studying Captain Harper's circuit diagrams the next two days were spent strategically placing explosives in hidden crevices around the jagged cave face at a minimum height of two point four metres above the ledge in an interlinked continuous loop to be detonated on a timer from outside the cave. When the installation was completed a delighted Scott declared everything to his satisfaction. It had taken seven days in total leaving three days to Scott's actual zero hour.

***

Three days to zero hour

The following morning Xavi received word from a local goat herder he had charged with keeping an eye on the drilling of the shaft at Punta Gaunché that the Germans had broken through and were celebrating. He was aware that Jordan Hill would require this information urgently so on arrival in Puerto he phoned Scott's direct line from the harbour café. Scott who was in a sound sleep from his earlier nocturnal activities soon became wide awake at this bad news. He had expected to complete Operation TENALT before the breakthrough took place. There now existed the possibility that damage had been done to the explosive's wiring. Whilst the camouflaged dynamite packs had been concealed in recesses the black electrical link-wiring hung exposed between each pack and could result in damage from wayward splinters of rock caused by the breakthrough. With the system being continuous loop any break would render the installation useless. This concerned Scott and would have to be investigated.

Thinking it best not to involve Hank who did not know the real reason for the placing of the cave explosives, Scott phoned Pepé and explained about the shaft breakthrough and the need to check the wiring. Pepé agreed to take him in his boat to Punta Gaunché. They would depart the harbour at midnight.

Scott in his wet suit and re-breather unit entered the cave shortly after midnight whilst Pepé attended the safety line. Breaking water inside the cave he slipped his goggles round his neck to allow his eyes to accustom to the dark. Instead of darkness he encountered a dim illumination throwing up a massive silhouette presence in the water. His now accustomed eyes could not believe what they saw. Towering above him was the bulk of a German U-Boat. Up to now it had been pure supposition and speculation on his part because the "Treaty of Versailles" forbade Germany to possess a submarine fleet. But the proof was now sitting on the calm water which lapped gently against its grey hull. Hitler had abrogated the Treaty.

Outside the temporary illumination zone that ran off the U-Boat's generators Scott manoeuvred his way along the considerable length of the U-Boat and raised himself onto the wide ledge above water level. From his position in the shadows he could see from the illumination where the shaft had penetrated into the fissure by the amount of rubble that lay strewn directly below on the ledge. He had to give credit to the engineers above, for the shaft had broken through exactly mid-width of the ledge. Should Hitler achieve his ultimate aim Scott could imagine the U-Boat being armed, fuelled and provisioned from above, allowing it to ply its lethal trade in the Atlantic against the Royal Navy and merchant fleets. This passing thought brought him back to the present and set him thinking as to where were the crew? With none in evidence he crept around the walls local to the breakthrough. There was no damage to any of the link wiring. But as he was preparing to re-enter the water he heard rattling and banging from inside the shaft and seconds later an open steel mesh cage suspended from a steel hawser emerged with two officers. They clambered over the fallen rubble and walked towards the U – boat.

As Scott sank back further into the shadow he heard them talking. 'The sooner our engineers get this bloody hole lined with those concrete pipes and a proper hoist working the better I'll feel. This is a death trap.'

'Couldn't agree more, Commander. But our crew and engineers seem to have been well-catered-for in the barracks above,' answered the other, a tall thin hooked nosed officer dressed in the black uniform of the SS complete with the Totenkopf (skull and crossbones) badge on his cap.

'Indeed they are. But it's not for me Fritz. I'm bunking here, as you are, until the shaft is finished or until such times as I receive further orders from Kruger. I can't believe Kruger forgot we were due in today. I hope he has a fucking good reason for his failure to show,' he growled as they boarded the U-Boat via a ladder propped against the hull.

'Herr Hitler, will also require an answer from Kruger,' added Fritz.

"Hitler better get himself a medium if he wants an answer from

Kruger," Scott muttered as he slipped silently into the water noting as he did the U4 designation and Swastika on the U-Boat's conning tower. However, what he didn't notice was a pair of concerned eyes watching from the tower and observing the merest of ripples reflecting off the water's surface as he disappeared below.

During the voyage back to Puerto he confirmed to Pepe that the wiring was intact – but made no mention of the U-Boat. That would remain his secret for he had only hinted to Xavi about the future possibility of U – Boat activity.

***

Penultimate day to zero.

Scott collapsed into bed exhausted. A final look at his bedside clock showed 3-00am – twenty four hours to zero. When he awoke it was almost lunch time. He made himself a chicken sandwich and sat down with a large Glenfiddich malt to scrutinise his planning to make sure he had missed nothing. Satisfied, he realised the success of Operation TENALT now depended entirely on himself and Marcus.

Having not been in contact with Marcus since he disclosed the date for zero hour he decided to phone him. The phone answered in the usual Texas drawl, 'Howdy, pardner. You're through to…'

'Marcus! Are you OK for tonight?' Scott cut in sharply, trying to convey a sense of urgency by interrupting Marcus' usual friendly claptrap.

'Why Scotty? What's happening tonight?'

'What do you mean what's happening *tonight*?' replied Scott, in panic. '3-00am. Zero hour! That's what's happening tonight.'

'Yeah, well, I'm good an' ready for that alright.'

'Well what's the point in asking what's happening tonight.'

'Because the happening that's happening tonight is not happening tonight it's happening tomorrow morning. 3-00am is morning, not night – right?'

'Marcus!'

There was deep throated guffawing from the phone. 'Listen to me, ole buddy – as sure as all the shit that comes out the White House – I'll be there. Do you think I'd miss the opportunity to stick one up the Krauts? I still owe them one for my leg. So, set your watch by me – 3-00am GMT it is. See you back in the ranch later. Gotta go. Got a little bit of fine tuning to do on the Sopwith.'

'The Sopwith?' queried Scott, in amazement at the choice of the twenty year old plane.

'Always was going to be, Scotty. It can turn on a nickel. An' that's what I need when I'm working my butt of between those nasty son of a bitch tear-the-ass-out-of-your-breeks-peaks in the dark believe me.'

'I believe you Marcus,' sighed Scott, with a shake of the head and a loud lip reverberation with fingers crossed.

***

Scott, with head low over the handlebars and open jerkin flapping wildly in the wind, hammered the Norton at speeds reaching 100mph down the coast road to Puerto harbour to meet Pepé and Hank finishing their Cantravel afternoon diving session. He took Hank aside and told him that after studying the wiring diagrams he might have wired the timer/detonator wrongly and he needed the boat tonight to check on this possible error. Hank accepted this and offered his help. Scott thanked him for his offer of help but said he could, with the detonator being concealed externally above high tide level, handle this alone. Hank drove the Cantravel diving unit back to base leaving the trailer in the usual spare ground. Scott then had the speedboat refuelled and arranged with the harbour master to leave the boat moored in the harbour.

From his mooring tied alongside the harbour wall in Puerto, Scott recognised the Spanish growl that was asking permission to come aboard. Permission given, Xavi clambered aboard looking extremely flustered and perplexed. He said he had seen Scott arrive at the harbour and moor the speedboat. Scott explained to him his doubts over the wiring of the timer and the need to confirm all was well. Xavi nodded his understanding and said he trusted Scott wouldn't mind his unannounced arrival but he was the bearer of bad news – Nina had gone missing. She had been on board the "Sea Dolphin" serving meals and drinks but when it had come time to depart home for Los Gigantes she could not be found. Xavi explained she had been quite normal during the cruise and gave no indication of her intent otherwise. His crew were out searching the local vicinity but so far had been unsuccessful. He wondered if she may have seen him and mistaken him for Ramôn again. Scott suspecting that Xavi might be thinking Nina was on board instigated a search of the boat which revealed nothing. Xavi apologised and left for Los Gigantes a worried man. A disturbing episode but one that Scott could not allow himself to get involved in due to his main objective Operation – TENALT.

Scott chose a restaurant perched on the foreshore rocks of Puerto's San Telmo promenade for his evening meal. The angry sea crashed off the rocks below the dining room window – a bad omen weather wise for what lay ahead. His meal finished, he retired to the boat to rest for the long night ahead. He intended to sail for his quarry at 2-00am, fix the timer to detonate at 3-01am and be back in Puerto for 3-30am, so he set his bedside alarm for 1-30am. He looked at his watch 8-00pm. He woke ten minutes before the alarm, splashed water on his face and refreshed himself with a coffee from his flask then slipped into his wet suit. He laid his Walther PPK pistol which he felt naked without on the steering console and departed Puerto at 2-00am. He was heading for Pepé's secret boyhood harbour just short of Magec's cave. With the sea still rough and turbulent he was now wishing Pepé was skippering the boat to enable him an easier passage than he was experiencing through the hazardous and time consuming entry into the small lagoon. However, with the use of the searchlight which he would have preferred not to have used he found the flat rock landing stage Pepe had utilised previously and tied up to the same projecting rock outcrop. A quick look at his watch showed 2-25am. He had lost time negotiating the rocks into the lagoon but still had plenty of time to set the timer and reach the safety of open waters and head back to Puerto.

He was just about to slip over the gunwale onto the makeshift jetty when he was caught in the glare of powerful torchlight and a German voice demanded he stop and raise his hands.

Scott replied in Spanish, 'Who's there?'

The unseen voice, to Scott's surprise, snarled in German accented Spanish, 'Shut the fuck up Spic and get your hands high.'

'*A bloody sentry. Bugger having had to use the searchlight. He must have seen me coming a mile off,*' Scott muttered under his breath.

Scott was not to know that the result of a sentry being posted had little to do with the searchlight but more that of the keen eye of the U-Boat Commander who having spotted from his conning tower the ripple wake of Scott slipping below the water in the cave and recognising the ripple as that of a possible diver, felt it needed investigating.

Scott slowly turned to face the voice and put his hands in the air. By a shaft of moonlight he glimpsed the silhouetted figure belonging to the voice – he was wearing a wet suit and a re-breather unit and held a machine pistol at his hip. 'My commander will want a word with you,' he finished motioning the machine pistol to indicate to Scott to get out of the boat. A quick glimpse at his watch showed 2-30am.

Scott had pulled back from stepping over the gunwale and was now standing at the steering wheel fumbling one handed in the dark for the PPK that he had deposited on the steering console when he had sailed from Puerto but could not now find as he groped in the dark. Bugger. With the rough sea it must have fallen onto the deck. Unable to locate the PPK he innocently replied to the sentry's question, 'Why?'

'None of your business, Spic. Out – Out now!' was the repeated snarled reply with a savage sideway motion of the machine pistol.

Scott put one foot up on the gunwale to prise himself up when he heard the clatter of tumbling rubble from above as another German arrived. 'Everything under control, Jorg?'

'Yes, Lieutenant.' The silhouette of the new arrival, also in re-breather gear, stood alongside Jorg with a raised Luger pistol.

Scott formulated a new plan of action. With his foot already on the gunwale he prepared to launch himself forward between both and secure at least one of their guns. He knew they would not cross fire for fear of hitting one another. As he flexed his standing leg for thrust he heard the instantly recognisable "plop" sound of a silencer from behind him. Jorg clutched his throat as rubber and neck parts exploded in a cloud of red flesh and gore. The Lieutenant in panic raised his pistol to fire – the last action he ever took as a second "plop" ripped through his wet suit and heart. The shock convulsed his trigger finger allowing a shot to be fired in Scott's direction. Scott then turned slowly to face the killer – it was the missing Nina. She was clutching at her heart, blood seeping through her fingers – the Lieutenant's wayward shot had unfortunately found her. Scott's silenced PPK lay at her feet. He rushed to her before she collapsed and laid her gently on the inside bench seat. A quick glanced at his watch showed 2-35am. No time to tend his saviour. As he jumped from the boat to retrieve the fallen weapons and throw them into the boat he noticed the SS flash runes on their wet suits before he savagely kicked both into the water. He found the hidden timer. His underwater Rotary watch showed 2-40am. He set the timer for 3-01am GMT. Zero hour – allowing him twenty minutes to clear the lagoon and head for open water and safety. It would be tight.

He clambered aboard the speed-boat and unhitched the rope. Nina was delirious. He had to get her medical attention immediately but first he had to exit the hazardous lagoon. The explosives had been designed by Captain Harper to implode but there was always the possibility that Scott had wired them wrongly and they would explode. If that happened he was staring death in the face for if flying debris didn't get him then the resultant tsunami would. Another glance at the watch showed 2-50am – ten minutes to clear the area. Had Scott been alone he would have thrown caution to the wind and propelled the boat at speed but care had to be taken because of Nina's condition. He reckoned he could have her in safe hands in Los Gigantes in twenty minutes so with searchlight full on he set about threading the boat cautiously through the needle rocks and trusted he had wired the explosives correctly to implode.

He was suddenly aware of Nina at his elbow mumbling in staccato bursts of her mistaken love for him, thinking him to be Ramôn. He put his arm around her shoulder and held her close and soothingly comforted her by telling her that he loved her too. She sighed deeply, face contorted in pain, contentedly enjoying his words as she lay back down on the bench seat. Another glance at his watch confirmed 2-58am, followed one minute later by the drone of a labouring aeroplane engine then a further minute later at 3-00am – zero hour – there was an enormous explosion and a pyrotechnic eruption of red hot lava embers shooting skywards accompanied by several further explosions coming from the Chinyero Cone area of the Santiago rift.

Marcus, the cause of the mayhem had taken off from Los Rodeos trailing plumes of white exhaust as the Sopwith Camel struggled to carry the additional load of his homemade "contraption" and its contents. When he reached the target at exactly 3-00am he had pulled a lever on the outside of the Sopwith to release from the "contraption" a barrage of dynamite bombs he had made from the sticks supplied by Pepé. This light metal frame cradle was hung under the timber and waxed fuselage and made the handling of the Sopwith dangerously sluggish. However, his aim had been perfect – straight into the glowing and festering fissure that Charley and her colleagues at the NGM had been researching at Chinyero. He was now desperately trying to avoid the geyser like inferno of red hot ash that had shot unexpectedly out of the fissure, fully aware that one red hot ember could set the wax coated canvas skin of his Sopwith on fire. However, with the heavy load of the bombs released he managed an extra engine surge to clear the dangerous pyrotechnic spectacular and head for safety over the coast.

Meanwhile below, Scott let out a whoop of delight as his timer set for 3-01am caused Punta Gaunché to implode. By the moonlight he watched in open-eyed amazement as the cliff face crumpled and slid into the Atlantic bringing with it the heavy Howitzer concrete foundation structure which shattered on the rocks below and then sank below the turbulent waters. His only regret being that the Howitzer gun itself had not been in place. However, he was faced with a new problem as he felt the boat rise under him. A quick glance behind him confirmed his worse fears as he witnessed the start of a tidal surge of water squeezing between the narrow inlet in the rocks that he had just vacated and was heading directly towards him as an enormous boat swamping wave. He opened the throttle wide and with all thought of caution a luxury he swung the wheel hard to port just missing a needle projecting rock formation and headed for the safe water of the Atlantic. Glancing over his shoulder again he saw the enormous seething swell of the frothing, angry water, raging through the narrow opening where he had been seconds before. In relief he let out a further whoop of exuberance which he immediately regretted as he returned his attention to the stricken Nina.

As she saw Scott turning towards her she said in a voice barely above a whisper, 'Ramôn, my love, I did good for you, didn't I? Those men meant to kill you as they did papa....' Her head drooped allowing blood to gurgle from the corner of her mouth. Scott realising that her life was ebbing away set the boat on a clear course and took his hands off the steering wheel. With one hand he cupped her chin in his hand whilst with the other he stroked her hair and said sweetly, 'Thank you my darling Nina for saving my life. You were right – those *were* the evil men that killed your papa.'

A look of serene contentment crossed her ravaged face at the realisation she had now avenged her papa and saved her beloved Ramôn. She then fumbled at her throat and with effort pulled the gold chain around her neck out of her blood soaked sweater to expose an attached ring – her Ramôn's. With a further weary effort she made Scott aware that she wanted him to take the ring off the chain. He unclasped the ring and on her frail indication of tapping her engagement ring he slipped it onto his wedding ring finger. She smiled lovingly and whispered, 'Have no fear my lovely Ramôn, for I will be with you for ever.'

Holding both her hands, Scott bent over and kissed her lovingly on the forehead, and told her tenderly, 'And I look forward to being with you for ever, my lovely Nina.'

Her trembling hand caressed his face. 'I will be waiting Ramôn.' Her eyes closed. Scott released a string of blasphemies as he closed Nina's lifeless eyes and returned the ring to her gold chain.

***

Due to the extraordinary pyrotechnics on Mount Teide the Los Gigantes harbour area was packed with panicking villagers watching the hot volcanic embers still shooting skywards – all anxious to know which way the lava was flowing. With Los Gigantes lying below the Santiago rift this was a natural concern. What they didn't know as yet was that there was no lava – nor would there be – *if* all had gone to plan.

Scott steered the boat into Los Gigantes harbour and tied up outside Xavi's café where Xavi, recognising the boat, was waiting to meet him. Climbing out of the boat Scott did not know what best to say so he just pointed to the prone body of Nina, and said, 'I found her, Xavi.'

With his eyes bulging in disbelief Xavi looked at Scott and in a quavering voice queried, 'Dead?' Scott nodded. Xavi crossed himself and let out at the top of his voice a long agonising wail, 'What bastard is responsible for this. My poor Nina…' This disturbance brought his wife rushing from the café to be joined by others who realising the gravity formed a tearful, mournful chain to lift the lifeless body of Nina to the ancient village church. With a supreme effort of self-control Xavi pulled himself together and suggested they adjourn to the café. Inside the empty café he went behind the bar and poured two large brandies. Once seated he asked Scott to tell him why, how, and who had killed Nina.

Scott recapped the story. He started with a repeat telling of his intention to check the detonator wiring for a fault due to the breakthrough of the shaft possibly causing damage to the wiring. Then of Nina's shooting of the Nazis and the wayward shot that killed her. It was at this point that he embellished the truth by telling Xavi that with Nina badly wounded he had decided to abandon checking the wiring and try to save her. It was just as they were clearing Punta Gaunché waters the Chinyero eruption took place followed by their cave explosives detonating. He further led Xavi to believe that the detonation of the cave explosives was the result of the Chinyero eruption.

When he finished Xavi looked at him with a puzzled look. 'Quite a coincidence that this should happen two days before our intended detonation, Jordan Hill. How do you think it was possible that the eruption caused the detonation of the explosives?'

Scott shrugged his shoulders and smoothly told his great lie. 'I don't really know, Xavi. I can only assume that the possible eruption, as predicted by the NGM scientists, actually happened and the superheated gases found their way to the cave through the labyrinth of lava tunnels that are known to lie within the mountain and then on reaching the cave set-off our explosives.'

'You were very fortunate in abandoning your check on the detonator wiring Jordan Hill, or you might not be standing here talking to me,' Xavi replied, with what Scott guiltily thought to be a tinge of suspicion, before adding, 'I suppose mother nature by acting two days early saved *us* from the guilt of being responsible for such a barbarous act of vandalism against Magec. Eh! Jordan Hill?' Scott, in relief, nodded agreement as Xavi continued, 'I should be happy but... with the death of Nina in my care... and my failure to find her.... I did try very hard to..,' he said more to himself than Scott. Then he took a deep breath, 'I assume Nina must have seen you go aboard your boat when we docked and because you look like her Ramón hid out somewhere until we called things off then stowed away in your boat when you were eating your evening meal in town.'

'That's the conclusion I had come to as well, Xavi. I only wish I could have saved her.' This was said with truthful conviction – no lies this time.

'Knowing you, Jordan Hill, I am in no doubt you did your best for her. Further, I would also like to thank you on behalf of my fellow "Free Canaries" for ridding us of the threat of a surprise attack from the fascists.'

Feeling guilty that he had, throughout the mission, taken advantage of Xavi, Scott cringed at these congratulations and helpfully warned, 'Please do not become complacent Xavi. You have not heard the last of the Nazis because your beautiful islands are of strategic importance. Be on your guard, my friend.'

'Complacent?'

'Contented with.'

'Si. I understand. Thanks to you and your Mr Churchill I will be alerts to any further *shenanigans*. See I use the new words you teach me, Jordan Hill,' he said proudly, adding, 'Howevers, you may also remind Mr Churchill that what happened to his Admiral Horatio Nelson in 1797 at the Battle of Santa Cruz can happen again. We also a hardy island nation. You tell Mr Churchill this no a threat – but advice.' Scott grinned and nodded his acknowledgement of the caustic comment as Xavi stopped and, with forefinger and thumb caressing his chin, he continued thoughtfully, 'You know, Jordan Hill that this could be Magec's revenge for the desecration of his cave.'

Scott expected the usual loud guffaw to follow but with nothing forthcoming he jokingly replied, 'I thought you only kept that sort of Gaunché folklore rubbish for your gullible tourists?'

It was then that Xavi guffawed. 'That's a good idea Jordan Hill. I now tell them the real truth about Magec's revenge. Because of the desecration to his cave he move to Mount Teide and become the fire god of revenge. He speak through the mountain. Is good. I like you, Jordan Hill, or whatever your *real name* is. I hope our paths will cross again, amigo. Oh! By the way, Jordan Hill – good news I don't have to pay Señor Alonso any back-hander money for my licence anymore. He apparently missed a bend and drove into the Atlantic.'

Scott nodded his head in understanding for he knew the moment he had revealed Señor Alonso's name to Xavi that the Minister of Tourism's fate had been sealed.

They shook hands warmly. Scott had elected not to disclose what he knew about the presence of the U-Boat for he knew Xavi would feel that his beloved island had been violated.

As Scott walked to the boat he knew he should be elated at his success but he could not actually shake off a feeling of despondency – the death of Nina weighed heavy on his conscious. She had surrendered her life saving him. Should he have aborted the mission? Could the time he had taken to set the timer been used to help save her life? If he had aborted the mission and rushed Nina back to Los Gigantes for medical assistance then he would have put Marcus' life in danger for nothing – albeit he had survived. And again, if he had aborted the mission then he would have let down Sir James' and Mr Churchill's months of planning and Eugene's generosity. The answer to these conundrums he would never know. He would have to content himself with the consolation that Nina had died happy in the knowledge that she had avenged her papa and Ramón and that he had thwarted Hitler from gaining his all-important toe-hold in Tenerife.

His jesting words in Berlin to Sir Eric, *"It's not all fun being a secret service agent"* had come home to roost – Bugger.

Chapter 31

Chartwell Two days after the eruption.

Winston Churchill and Sir James McKay were enjoying a pre-prandial drink in the library whilst awaiting the dinner gong. Sir James had just accepted an offer of a large Havana cigar. Between them on the coffee table lay a copy of The Times. Churchill swivelled the copy around for Sir James to read:

MOUNT TEIDE ERUPTS.

This natural disaster could have been averted claimed spokeswoman Professor Charlene Rogers of Harvard University. Professor Rogers speaking on behalf of her colleagues of the National Geographic Magazine(NGM), who had recently been deported from the Canary Island of Tenerife, gave the reason for the eruption affecting the collapse of the cliff face at Punta Gaunché as that of super-heated gas expansion through conduction by lava tubes. The eruption which the NGM had warned was possible before their deportation caused the walls of the fissure vent to implode cutting of any lava overflow. The pressure build up caused by the blockage sought another exit and found a lava tube leading into a giant fissure at Punta Gaunche. This fissure was known about through a scientific article by Professor Edwin von Nida……Lava tubes are old tunnels formed by underground eruptions…...Professor Rogers has been asked once again to investigate the disaster after the NGM's wrongful deportation by a corrupt member of the local government who had feared that their findings if published would be detrimental to island tourism. Mr Alonso, the member in question, has disappeared. The Guardia Civil suspect he may have fled to South America.

Churchill pointing at the headline commented, 'See you've even got The Times believing your shenanigans.'

'No comment,' replied Sir James with a smile lurking at the corner of his mouth.

'Considering Hitler beat us to the punch I must still congratulate you on an excellent result for Operation TENALT – albeit it was not quite the way we intended. That said, The Admiralty are over the moon at the destruction of the U-Boat base and seem to have forgotten that the prime purpose of the mission was to locate suitable sites for their bases. So it was just as well your man Rutherford was on the ball. Did you give him the idea?'

'No Winston. He did it entirely of his own volition with just a little help from your unnamed source in the Abwher regarding Hitler's deal with Franco for a gun emplacement at Punt Gauché. That gave him the idea to use this chap Xavi's fervent freedom from Spain movement, the FCM, to advance his plan.'

'And you tell me he pulled this off with this Xavi's rag-tag volunteers and a geriatric Texas pilot?'

'Indeed he did,' answered Sir James proudly. 'And Marcus, the geriatric pilot as you refer to him flew with your cousin during the war.'

'Second cousin,' corrected Churchill. 'Knew Crozier was a pilot in the Texas something or other,' he said as he waved away a blue fug hanging over the coffee table. 'However, it was a dangerous decision you made, Jimmy – allowing this Marcus chappie to drop bombs down a vent that was possibly about to erupt at any moment. It could have resulted in a *real* major disaster – taken the side out of Teide causing a tsunami to break across the Atlantic causing mayhem on the east coast seaboard of America. Then what would the arch appeaser, Baldwin, have said?'

Sir James lounged back in his chair, nonchalantly replying as he took a pull on his cigar, 'Said to whom, Winston? We can't be expected to apologise for a natural disaster when it was none of our doing.'

Churchill contemplated this as he exhaled a lingering cloud of smoke to join the tail end of the already dispersing fug before replying, 'But it all didn't really matter because you knew a disaster wasn't going to happen. Didn't you, Jimmy?'

'Er, yes, Winston. But it was by no means certain. Rutherford has a friend at Harvard, a geologist who was one of the scientists deported from Tenerife…'

'The real reason for their deportation, please.'

'Hitler. They were in his way. And as the Times reported – a corrupt official in Cabildo. Corrupt official now fishmeal. Need I say more?'

'No. Your man Rutherford?'

'Indirectly. He put the notion in Xavi's head.'

'Mm. Plays mind games as well, does your man. I take it this spokeswoman quoted in The Times article – this Professor Charlene Rogers – is a *close* associate of Rutherford?'

Sir James noted Churchill's keen observation regarding the professor's link to Rutherford. 'Er, yes. Rutherford claims that at great – *personal sacrifice* – for the nation…' he looked at Churchill who nodded his understanding of Rutherford's interpretation of personal sacrifice, '…he discovered from the professor that there had been a contingency plan to bomb the fissure should it show signs of eruption.'

'Good for him. Boy seems to have a way with the ladies.'

'Mmm. You could say that. He's like fly paper to the female sex. Let's say I would trust him with my life but not my grandmother. However, this contingency bombing was what Rutherford had intended but was afraid to implement in case, what you mentioned previously happened, he blew the side out of Teide and a tsunami developed. That was until an expert gave him the right strength of dynamite to use on the Chinyero vent. And that was all Rutherford needed. He already had, or I should say Xavi, already had the dynamite. The pyrotechnics are show – they will settle down in a couple of days.'

'And this remedial bombing was a certainty to succeed?'

Sir James hesitated. 'Er, not exactly, Winston. Never been tried before. Just theory. Rutherford carried out the practical.'

'I thought you said there was an expert advising Rutherford on the strength of explosives – this chap Harper of bomb disposal in Aldershot.'

'Er, not quite, Winston. That was for the demolition of the Great Fissure. For the Chinyero vent it was actually the chief engineer at Texoil…'

'The petrol company?………. What the Dickens has he to do with explosives?'

'Er, he has used them to put out oil-well fires.'

'You mean – you… you……' Churchill was lost for words.

Something many of his opponents on numerous occasions had prayed would happen during their disagreements with him. Sir James, expecting a rebuke, could only shrug his shoulders. Instead Churchill continued, 'Good man. No time for fence-sitters – excellent decision. However, with us not being at war there is one thing worrying me – the death toll. It must be considerable.'

'Not really, Winston. Rutherford reckons at that time in the morning it was just the Nazi U-Boat Commander and a SS lieutenant quartered in the U-Boat and a few Nazi SS guards around the shaft and generators. The rest of the crew were barracked well away from the promontory collapse and the sappers had stopped working twenty four hours a day on the gun emplacement. In fact an evacuation of their crew and workforce is taking place as we speak. And since there was no lava excretion from the Chinyero vent there were no civilian casualties in the Santiago area except for maybe a few goats grazing in the newly formed valley.'

'It's a pity the cave had to be destroyed. It would have been damned handy for the Navy. I don't suppose there was any other way?'

'Hardly Winston. The whole point in Hitler having the base was its secrecy. If we had shown our hand it then no longer remained a secret. Franco, oblivious to Hitler's chicanery as we know, would have been livid with him on finding out but without Hitler's aid come the inevitable civil war there was little he could do. Not to mention the small fact that had we acted aggressively it might well have precipitated another war. This way, believe me Winston, was for the best. Need I say more?'

'Thank you Jimmy. Well explained. However, I should imagine that Adolph must be slightly miffed at the loss of one of his new U-Boats.'

'I'll drink to that,' said an ebullient Sir James, raising his large cut crystal glass of Glenmorangie towards Churchill.

Churchill acknowledged the toast by clinking glasses with Sir James. 'What if this Professor Rogers finds out the real reason for the eruption?'

'I suppose Rutherford will just have to do his patriotic duty for Britannia again. If he is not already making arrangements to meet the good prof.'

'What can I say, Jimmy, other than the end has in this case truly justified the means. However, I must meet this man of yours – Rutherford.'

'I can arrange that Winston. He's on his way home as we speak. Bit of leave due to him before he heads for Gibraltar.'

'Still having trouble with saboteurs?'

Sir James nodded his head and sighed, 'Afraid so Winston. We have apprehended – not as you would expect – Nazis – but Gibraltarians and mainland Spaniards still disputing our right to the occupation of Gib...'

'But that was resolved by treaty back in 1713 or thereabouts....'

'Correct. But alas, not from their point of view. However, I can't help but feel that the Spanish fascist party, the Falangists, are the true force behind the unrest....'

'No doubt at Adolph's bidding...'

'I would imagine so.'

'And your man Rutherford is the chosen one to, er....'

'Indeed – Winston.'

***

Scott, after departing the grieving Xavi and friends and then making his way via Puerto harbour to pick up his Norton, had the following day headed to Los Rodeos for onward passage to London via Gibraltar. He found Marcus with an unlit cigar in his mouth cutting away his "contraption" from the underbelly of the vintage Sopwith Camel with an oxy-acetylene torch.

Noticing Scott approach, Marcus withdrew a stick of dynamite from his flying suit bib pocket and held it aloft. 'Lookee here, Scotty. One of these sons of a bitch didn't eject properly from the bomb disposal unit which ah damaged on landing. Lucky it didn't blow for there were sure as hell enough sparks a flying off the tarmac to ignite it,' he cheerfully chirped as he dropped his hand, still clutching the stick of explosive, to rest on his chest as he brought the flame of the torch up to light his cigar. There was only the merest of a fraction of an inch between the flame and the fuse of the dynamite.

'Bloody Hell.. Marcus,' wailed Scott, as he slid the Norton on an about-turn on the runway and rapidly departed the scene with

Marcus' manic laughter ringing in his ears.

***

Before leaving Los Rodeos for Gibraltar, Scott had purloined Marcus' copy of El Día. The front page sported a dramatic photograph of the Chinyero fissure still spouting its sulphuric gases and embers into the atmosphere above a photograph of the newly formed valley at Punta Gaunché. Inside, a small paragraph caught his eye forcing a knowing smile to cross his lips. Apparently, a sea salvage company based in Los Cristianos, Tenerife, were laying claim for the salvage rights to a German U-Boat (U4) conning tower found floating off the south coast of Tenerife. The article suggested that the U-Boat might have been destroyed in the underwater eruption from the disaster. This brought the writer to question as to why a German U-Boat, in violation of the Treaty of Versailles, should be patrolling off the shores of Tenerife. It brought the British government to the same conclusion.

Scott trusted that Hitler when confronted by the League of Nations with the damning Swastika on the conning tower and his obvious abrogation of the "Treaty of Versailles" would call a halt to his megalomaniac aspirations. Unfortunately, he had a hunch that this incident would only but dent Hitler's insane hegemony.

However, on a happier note he was due leave and a visit to New York to renew his acquaintance with Charley seemed in order.

Later in the day he touched down at Lee-on-Solent. Sir James and Elizabeth were awaiting his arrival.

Author's note

Punta Gaunché does not exist nor does the Great Fissure and with the fissure being a figment of my imagination then Albert Speer (Hitler's architect) was not responsible for the design drawing of the cave as the story would have you believe. The British Embassy in Willhelmstrasse Berlin was indeed the former Palais Strausberg but has been reconfigured to suit. The Chinyero cone eruption on Mount Teide, Tenerife, did take place in 1909 but has shown no signs of further activity as portrayed. For, dear reader, in the world of fiction liberties abound. However, much *is* fact notably the 1934 uprising of the workers in Oviedo, a mixture of socialist, communist, and anarchist factions who did capture the Nationalist Government of Spain's arms and ammunition factory. A rebellion that was eventually supressed by General Franco and his African Army leaving many thousands dead, including women and children. The lava caves in Mount Teide do exist – some as tourist attractions others as in the story carrying toxic gases which are closed to the public. Also Churchill did have an alternative plan involving Tenerife should Gibraltar be invaded by Nazi Germany.

However, I have taken the liberty to tweak time scales and locations to suit the story and have written about what *could* happen and what *could* have been said. The latter applies especially in my imaginary conversations between Churchill and Eden and Sir James. Also Hitler and Canaris. This is a basic prerogative of fiction. I trust this in no way detracts from my yarn.